SELF-CONCLUSION

LORAILLVON SERIES

T.K. Johnson (signature)

T.K. JOHNSON

Cover design by: Aaron Satterfield / Shutterstock Imagery
Library of Congress Control Number: 2018675309
Printed in the United States of America

BOOKS BY T.K. JOHNSON

THE LORAILLVON SERIES

These Favored Shadows
Self-Conclusion
Alter
Prophecy

TABLE OF CONTENTS

Table of Contents	4
Author's Note	7
Prologue	8
Chapter 1	10
Chapter 2	18
Chapter 3	28
Chapter 4	41
Chapter 5	57
Chapter 6	72
Chapter 7	85
Chapter 8	101
Chapter 9	112
Chapter 10	123
Chapter 11	137
Chapter 12	153
Chapter 13	162
Chapter 14	174
Chapter 15	189

Chapter 16	201
Chapter 17	214
Chapter 18	228
Chapter 19	238
Chapter 20	253
Chapter 21	269
Chapter 22	279
Chapter 23	289
Chapter 24	300
Chapter 25	315
Chapter 26	327
Chapter 27	339
Chapter 28	343
Chapter 29	351
Acknowledgments	362
About the Author	363
Alter	364

To Samuel. Your sacrifice, patience, and drive made this story a reality.

AUTHOR'S NOTE

Suicide rates have been rising steadily over the past decade. New research shows that trauma can be genetically transferred from one generation to another. Studies surrounding children/teens and screen time have proven that devices negatively effect the development of the brain (specifically the frontal lobe), resulting in impairment of self-control, empathy, and other social skills.

We are seeing generations that experience far more anxiety, depression, and suicidal ideation. Mental health is as serious as one's physical health. It is time to break the stigma. Many mental health conditions are treatable but not without taking the first step.

The title Self-Conclusion is not based around suicide or suicidal ideation, but describes the transformation that the main character, Kaylin, is able to achieve by overcoming her anxiety and fears with the help of those around her. She is able to end her unhealthy cycle of fear and loneliness. This allows her to conclude her old way of living and thinking in order to live a new and healthier life.

If you have a secret struggle and need someone to talk to, please know that you are not alone. Visit https://www.remedylive.com/ or text the number 494949 to talk to someone anonymously right now. Trained listeners are available 24/7 to help you through your current situation. Help break the stigma. Share your secret struggle. You are not alone.

If you feel that you may be a danger to yourself or others, please reach out to your local authorities right away. If you are struggling with thoughts of depression or suicide, please also call the Suicide National Hotline at 1-800-273-8255.

PROLOGUE

For the first time in her life, Sorrell was afraid.

Her feet tore through the forest beneath her. Moonlight beamed down through the trees to guide her way. The girl's arms pumped furiously at her side, willing her body to move even faster. She prayed no one was following her. Frantic thoughts flashed through her mind as she glanced back in fear.

If I don't get there first..., she shook the idea from her head, not wanting to think of the unsavory ending that would happen to her if this plan failed.

A breeze blew against her face. She heard the beating of wings ahead. That was her destination. She wasn't far now. Adrenaline pumped through Sorrell's veins giving her the extra edge she needed to go faster. She was almost there!

Splashing through a small brook she finally saw it: a large rock that shimmered in the light of the stars. A short way from the giant piece of granite lie a still figure. Sorrell slowed to a halt, hardly able to believe what her eyes beheld. The figure on the ground was a young girl. If a stranger were to walk by, they would mistake the unconscious figure to be Sorrell herself. They were identical in so many ways and yet Sorrell had no sister or family.

She walked slowly to the girl's side and studied her. The girl was barely breathing. She wore strange clothes and had marks on her skin that were foreign to Sorrell. With a cautious hand, she touched the skin of her reflection self. The girl's eyelids began to flutter.

I did it! she thought to herself. *The dragon was right. The prophecy has begun!*

Sorrell smiled at her accomplishment. How odd it was to gaze at a face designed like hers, as if looking into a reflection slightly altered.

So flurried by her achievement, Sorrell had neglected all the training that she spent a lifetime perfecting. Little did she know that someone was watching from above. Someone who had beaten her to the prize. Someone who had stumbled upon her secret.

CHAPTER 1

"Tell me about yourself," the woman said kindly.

Kaylin sat on her trembling hands, "I've never been to a therapist before. I'm not really sure what to talk about Miss....? I'm sorry, I forgot your name already."

"You may call me Dr. Donna," the woman plastered on a smile. "Describe yourself for me. What are things that you enjoy? How is school going for you this year?"

Kaylin licked her lips, "I'm a senior in high school. Everyone likes their senior year, right? My older sister graduated last year. I think you've met Justine."

Dr. Donna nodded. Justine was well known throughout their small town. She was a rebellious youth that had only grown in her antics since graduating high school. Though the Coleridge family had tried to hide their daughter's brash attitude, it was no secret that this particular household had logged more hours at the therapists' office than any others in their area code.

Dr. Donna knew the stories. She had been present for Justine's final therapy session a year ago. It resulted in the patient verbally attacking her doctor and throwing a desk monitor through a window. The Coleridge family had been especially unhappy when they received the bill.

To her relief, Dr. Donna could tell her new patient was quite different from that of the sister. Kaylin didn't seem the sort of girl to start shouting a string of profanities.

"Can you tell me about your family?" the doctor glanced quickly at her watch.

"Nice, white, and suburban."

Dr. Donna tapped her pen against the notepad.

"My mom wanted me to be... involved. With school stuff," Kaylin replied. "I've been in show choir for almost two years now. It's the geeky club that has kids singing and dancing to popular broadway tunes."

"Yes, I know what show choir is. Why did you choose that?"

"I can't read music that well so band didn't work out. My mom wanted me to be in a sport, but I'm not athletic either. When she heard they had practices after school hours, she said it would be good enough."

"What about your father and your sister?"

Kaylin shrugged.

"Do you know why your mother asked you to come in today?"

"To see if my family can set a record for broken windows?"

"That is very funny," but Dr. Donna wasn't laughing. "Why do you think you're here?"

Kaylin sighed, "Mom thinks I'm strange because I prefer to keep to myself. I don't have many friends. Socializing makes me feel uncomfortable. People make it clear that I don't belong."

"We call that introversion. People who get tired with a lot of social contact are known as introverts. These kind of people prefer to be alone to reenergize and tend to be more philosophical thinkers."

"In that case, I'm the next Aristotle. My family will be so proud," Kaylin grumbled. "My mom thinks I have a mental condition because I don't like talking to other people, but all anyone talks about is school and jobs. No one brings up the stuff that matters."

Dr. Donna scribbled on the yellow notepad.

"What do you consider to be 'stuff' that matters?"

Kaylin shifted in her seat. She had never been given the spotlight to talk about herself and it felt strange. The immaculate office made it that much more uncomfortable. Everything in the room had a designated place. Anything unsightly was hidden in a drawer. Dr. Donna clearly liked to give the right impression, much like Kaylin's mother did. This made the young girl feel like a shriveled plant in the lavish room.

"People struggle everyday with issues but they still seem to belong," Kaylin mumbled. "I'm here because I don't belong. People don't ignore my issues for some reason."

Dr. Donna glanced at her watch, "Your mom said she finds you sitting in front of your mirror a lot. Can you tell me about that?"

"Justine, my sister, used to see a therapist at this office. She said that they twisted her words and gave her a ridiculous diagnosis in order to please our parents. If I say something strange too, will you dose me up on medication and make money off my parents?"

Dr. Donna's plastered smile did not waver, "I'm here to help you. That is all I care about." She reached to her desk and picked up an oval mirror. "Describe the person that you see for me please, and would you do it in the third person? As if the reflection was someone else?"

Kaylin stared at the mirror, "I see a seventeen year old girl. She has boring, straight hair. It's a dirty color, not that pretty. She has too much acne and spots that are embarrassing."

"That's good," the doctor systematically cooed. "How does this girl feel?"

Kaylin rolled her eyes, "She feels stupid for talking about herself in the third person."

"I know it seems silly," Dr. Donna continued, "but keep going. Maybe we will hear something interesting."

"She's tired," Kaylin thought as she stared at herself. "She doesn't belong here. No one understands her so she looks in the mirror to figure out what she's doing wrong. Something about her must be different from everyone else or it wouldn't be so hard."

"What does the mirror show her?"

Kaylin stared at the face in the mirror, it was exactly as she described it to Dr. Donna.

"Sometimes…," she faltered, not sure if her secret should be told to this woman.

"It's okay, I'm trying to help. Tell me what the mirror shows you."

"It's not always me that is looking back. Have you ever looked at yourself long enough that it doesn't seem like you anymore? The world in the mirror seems somehow different? You wonder if your reflection might have moved. Even though you didn't."

"I'm not sure if I've ever experienced that."

"You would know if you had," she sighed. "Adults never take time to sit and pay attention anymore. Sometimes, when things are really bad at home, my reflection changes. It turns into someone else. Someone better. She's perfect. The girl that looks back at me is perfect in every way. Her skin, hair, body… all of it. Even the scars that I have are gone on her face. I can't really explain it."

Donna's notebook shut with a loud *snap*!

"Well that's all the time we have for today. I think we made some good progress for our first session."

The woman hurried to open the office door only to find Kaylin's mother hovering outside.

"Oh, Dr. Donna!" the woman exclaimed. "How wonderful. You are done right on time. Quite punctual, aren't you?"

"Beverly," the doctor cringed. "I do my best; don't like to keep parents waiting."

Beverly's eyes drifted past the therapist and immediately caught sight of the yellow notebook.

"She's been having trouble at school, did she mention? I told her to be sure to bring it up. It's simply not worth coming here if the girl doesn't talk about the real issues going on. Did she tell you about her diet? We are worried sick. All sugar and gluten. Her eating habits are simply atrocious!"

Mrs. Beverly Coleridge loved to use new words (she thought it made her sound more sophisticated). Her vocabulary was not vast so if she heard an acquaintance use language unfamiliar to her then she immediately felt out of style. In order to keep up her status with the other women of their community, she would try out a new word for exactly one week until moving on to another. This week the word was 'atrocious.' Last week everything was 'simply cumbersome.'

"I'm sure she has weather depression," Beverly continued. "The internet couldn't have spelled it out more clearly. When she's not staring into space in her bedroom, she's gazing out the window at the snow. Did she…," Beverly paused for the first time since opening her mouth. "Did she mention her father or… sister?"

Donna raised an eyebrow, "No, she didn't speak much about Justine or her father. Is it something we should discuss next time?"

Beverly waved a flippant hand, "Oh no, not at all. It seems you've already hit the main problems that she has. Quite intuitive of you, Doctor! Well if you will excuse us, time's up! We need to get going. See you next week," Beverly pushed Kaylin towards the exit.

Kill me now, Kaylin thought to herself.

The cold winter air bit her face as she navigated the frozen slush. Once in the car, there was five minutes of silence before Beverly burst with questions.

14

"How did it go? Do you feel any better? They're going to email me with your diagnosis."

Kaylin stared out the window, watching the bare trees pass by.

"You can choose to be happy if you want to. You just need to... smile more. Your attitude is a choice, and you are simply choosing not to be happy. If you fake a smile, it becomes real. I read it in a magazine the other day. That's what celebrities do, you know? Maybe that's the problem: your smile. The friends you have must not smile enough."

"Mom, I don't have any friends...let alone ones that smile."

"Don't be ridiculous," Beverly laughed at her daughter. "You have plenty of friends! How do you think they would feel if they heard you say that? Personally, I would be hurt. That is rude of you to even say."

"Name three of my friends," Kaylin argued.

"Ok well...," she paused. "There's the girl that lives right down the street from us. You two have been close for a long time."

"She sold us Girl Scout cookies three years ago. I don't even know her name."

"What about those two girls from your choir class? The one with the um... and there's that short one...? You know who I mean."

Kaylin shook her head, "Mom, one of them transferred schools our freshman year and the short one moved to California when I was seven. That's why she was short. We were seven."

"Don't be so dramatic! You talk to ... well you talk to girls in school everyday. Glee club kids are close! You all call yourselves thebians, or gleeks, or something silly like that."

"Thespians? That's theatre. The only reason choir kids look so happy together is because we have to smile on stage. If we don't, the judges dock us points and the choir teacher fails us."

"Then join the theatre! Make friends. I don't know what to tell you, Kaylin."

She slunk in her seat, "Fine, I'll join theatre."

"Oh I was kidding! Can you imagine how embarrassing that would be for me?" Beverly laughed.

Kaylin made a mental note to find out when the Spring musical started up.

"You see, this is why you need a therapist," Beverly sighed. "I can't understand you. You have everything you could possibly want, but all I hear is 'whine whine whine' from you. I'm quite excited to see how quickly these sessions will fix you. Kids these days feel so entitled."

"I don't see why I need to go back."

"Honey, this place costs money. The sooner we can figure out what's wrong with you the sooner your father will be off my back about the expense."

They drove in silence. The snow covered fields looked as bland as the grey sky. Kaylin longed to see green again. A tree blooming, grass, even a weed would suffice. She forgot what it felt like to be able to walk outside without spending ten minutes putting on layers of sweaters and coats. When they pulled into their driveway, her mom hurried her out of the car.

"I need to do some shopping," she said. "Get your homework done then work on your chores. No TV or other books tonight until your work is done. Oh, be a dear and clean the bathroom downstairs. It's atrocious! I've just been so busy. Actually… add that to your list of weekly chores. Since I'm swamped with errands lately, I really need you to step up and help around the house. Your dad will be home in an hour. Tell him I'll bring dinner. He can have some crackers before then if he gets hungry…"

"Mom, he's an adult. He can make his own dinner."

"Watch your attitude," Beverly scolded. "He works hard and likes to come home to a meal on the table. You'll understand when you're married one day."

"It isn't the 1960's," Kaylin grumbled.

The Coleridge household didn't carry jobs of enormous importance in their community, but Hank and Beverly Coleridge were adamant that their careers improved their social standing. Unlike the stereotypical white collar worker, Hank was a large man who had retained his muscle from his sporting days. His expectation each day after work was to eat a prepared meal, watch uninterrupted television, then sleep. Being the dutiful wife, Beverly submitted to this standard. She used her own free time to find distractions away from the house.

As Kaylin entered their living room, she was surprised to see her dad was already home. He was in his usual corner seat with a bag of chips in hand. The television was blaring an action scene from a murder mystery show.

"Hi, Dad," Kaylin muttered.

His eyes stared blankly at the flat screen on the wall.

"Mom had to pick up a few things," she tried again. "She'll be home soon with dinner."

Hank grunted, but whether it was in response to her or the TV show, she didn't know.

CHAPTER 2

"Did your sister bring you to school today?" one of the girls in class whispered to Kaylin.

"Why do you even hang out with her? She graduated," Kaylin said.

"We're all going out after practice so you'll need to find another way home," the girl replied.

"I'll call my mom. Thanks for letting me know."

The clique of girls turned at her in unison. Their leader scoffed, "Your mom can't know that Justine's out. Are you that stupid? We know that your dad locks her in her bedroom and has bars on the window. You're not going to rat her out."

"Justine made that up!" but her words fell on deaf ears.

Kaylin quickly blinked away tears. If these rumors were spreading through the school it meant more drama at home. Justine was constantly causing trouble, but never came home long enough to be dealt with.

Kaylin continued through classes wondering how she would get home after the final bell. At glee club practice, she did her best to sing the right notes and nail the choreography. She was slow to it pick up. Their instructor called her out on every mistake, though she never got Kaylin's name right. When practice finished, she slowly made her way to the front steps of the school.

"Now what," she mumbled to herself.

The parking lot was mostly empty. No one was on their way to get her. Kaylin imaged how much friendlier the situation would be if the wind wasn't hurting her face.

"Hey," a voice said behind her. She turned to see one of Justine's close friends.

"Hi," Kaylin replied in confusion. "Sorry, did I forget something?"

The girl looked Kaylin up and down with a judgmental eye. In hand-me-down Sofie shorts and an old t-shirt, Kaylin was not a stylish girl in the slightest. Her hair was falling out of its ponytail, and she was a sweaty mess from the choreography. Her makeup had worn off from the day. She was sure her acne was standing out.

In contrast, the tall girl across from her had an athletic body, dyed maroon hair, thick makeup, and name-brand workout apparel.

"I was working on my solo and didn't realize everyone left. What are you doing here?" she flipped her hair to the side as if posing for a picture.

Kaylin dropped her gaze, "My ride didn't work out so I'm... I don't know. Probably going to walk home now."

The girl looked out to her car, a brand new Mercedes that sparkled against the muddy snow. "I forgot clothes at my place and have to change before meeting up with everyone." She glanced wearily at Kaylin, "...everyone *else*, that is. I'll give you a lift to your house if you want."

Kaylin mumbled a quick thanks. Following her to the car, she was careful to knock the snow off her boots before getting in.

"It's new," the girl smiled. "My mom knew it was my *dream* to get a pink charger for Christmas but when they didn't have it... I decided not to wait. I picked this one out and they redid the interior for me."

"It's really nice," Kaylin attempted to sound sociable. "It smells new."

"Don't. Touch. Anything. You'll make it gross."

It was a fairly silent ride with only an occasional profanity that the girl quipped at other drivers. When they finally reached their small county road, she stopped the car after turning onto the street.

"Get out," she said.

"My house is half a mile that way," Kaylin pointed.

"I know."

"But I didn't touch anything!"

"I'm late to meet up with everyone. I don't have time to drive you all the way over there. So get out! I'm in a hurry."

Kaylin stumbled into the snow.

"By the way," her driver rolled down the passenger window. "You should seriously look into transferring schools. Everyone here knows how weird you are."

The shiny Mercedes sped away. Kaylin wiped a tear away before it froze to her cheek.

By the time she arrived at her house, she was a sobbing mess. Despite the fact that Beverly wouldn't notice the tears on her daughter's face, Kaylin tip toed her way through the hall to avoid her mother. The smell of oil diffusers filled Kaylin's nose.

"Hey girls, how was your day?" her mom shouted from the kitchen.

Kaylin hurried upstairs to her bedroom. The Coleridge sisters shared the larger of the two bedrooms while the other had been converted into a yoga studio for Beverly. It was the parents' way of trying to push Justine out of the house after graduating. So far, it hadn't worked.

Kaylin plopped herself on the floor in front of their tall, full-size mirror. They lived in an old house with dated architecture. The large mirror had come with the home. Old and cracked in a few places, it had more than a few smudges of mascara across its surface. Nail polish was splattered across the base, and the carpet beneath it was slightly brown from the years of spilled makeup.

Kaylin always found herself in that exact spot after a bad day. She looked at herself with disgust and confusion. It was the same face that stared back from the mirror. She looked harder, trying to figure out what was so wrong with her that everyone seemed to notice. She looked herself up and down the same way the girls at school did.

Ugly, pale, acne covered skin. My hair is boring and colorless, she thought to herself.

She hated her reflection.

Despite this, Kaylin spent hours in the mirror each morning to hide her face under makeup and try to fashion her hair in a cute style. She was addicted to keeping her skin clear but to no avail. The more she tried to make herself better, the more noticeable her flaws became.

Shifting her gaze, Kaylin looked into her own eyes. She leaned closer to the mirror until her nose touched the glass. Her eyes were blue, not bright or deep, just plain blue. She stared at them, focusing everything she had on each line, each fleck, each shade that might be incorporated with the blueness.

Stupid, boring, meaningless, weird, gross.

The words ran like a track through her head. They were the words people used to describe her. She had come to feel that they were the words that explained her best. Everything grew silent. She noticed that no floors were creaking from Beverly moving about. She couldn't hear the wind blowing outside her window. Even the sound of her own heart beat was gone.

Then Kaylin saw what she had been waiting for. The blue of her eyes shifted, as if a tremor ran through them. Her reflection's eyes were becoming lighter, more dazzling. There was a flash, almost like lightening, that spread across each eye. Ever so slowly, as if not moving at all, Kaylin slid her gaze to her forehead. The pigment of skin was slightly darker, more tan. It reminded her of when she was able to be outside during summer vacation. The skin of her reflection was smoother, as if the stress had melted away. The zit above her left eyebrow was gone. The red, swollen mark had completely disappeared from her temple. A little further up, her scar from chicken pox had vanished as well.

The reflection had changed enough that it was no longer Kaylin Coleridge gazing at herself in the mirror.

They'll say it is only my imagination, she thought, but Kaylin knew that wasn't true.

She blinked. Her reflection blinked half a second slower. It was not the first time she had seen this other girl, and she knew it was something special. A piece of hair fell into her face. She reached out to tuck it behind her ear. As she moved, her reflection remained still, watching her fix her hair. Kaylin studied the girl sitting across from her and noticed she didn't share any of Kaylin's birthmarks. Her bone structure was also slightly different than her own. Despite these things, they still looked almost identical.

Slowly reaching up, Kaylin twirled a piece of hair around her finger. The girl in the reflection watched then mimicked her. She made a silly face and watched as her reflection tried to mimic it as well. They laughed at one another, but no sound emitted. For all the times they'd been together, neither had tried to speak. Kaylin decided today was the day to take the next step.

She took a deep breath and laid her hands open in her lap. Her reflection cocked her head to the side, as if to question what the gesture meant. Kaylin sent up a silent prayer that her next action wouldn't break their connection.

Getting the sound to come out was difficult. The moment the word entered the air, she felt exhausted and tired, but it came out. It was the first word spoken between them. A simple 'hello.' Kaylin was so shocked by the effort that it took, she hardly noticed her reflection for a moment. When she looked back at her, the girl in the mirror was frozen in a crouched position. She had one foot under her, as if to stand.

The reflection brought her index finger up to the glass. She pressed her finger against the mirror but Kaylin saw no lines on her finger tips, as if no prints existed at all. She nodded to Kaylin and looked at her finger. Kaylin raised her finger to the same level and moved it towards the glass. The reflection nodded quickly, encouraging her to continue. Kaylin pressed her finger against the glass, matching it to that of her reflection.

Just as the contact was made, Kaylin heard a high pitched shriek. It was so deafening she thought her ears would bleed. The unexpectedness caused her to muffle the piercing volume with her hands. Her knees jumped to her chest as she balled herself protectively. As quickly as it came, the noise disappeared. Kaylin opened her eyes and slowly drew her hands away from her head. Her reflection was gone. Kaylin's own pale face stared back at her.

"Kaylin!" Beverly yelled from down the hall.

"What?" she croaked, tears stinging her eyes.

"I've been shouting your name for ages! What are you doing? Where is Justine?"

"I heard you," Kaylin whispered.

A small trickle of blood ran down her finger tip where she had touched the mirror. The sight of it made her heart quicken. Tomorrow she would try again. She had to see this other world. She had to meet the girl in the mirror.

She hurried to the living room to find Beverly and Hank waiting for her. Her heart skipped a beat when she saw the anger in her father's face. A vein pulsed on the side of his neck.

"Where is your sister, Kaylin?"

"I'm not sure." She shook her head, "Justine didn't pick me up, so I got a ride home."

Hank sighed. Beverly threw up her hands in defeat.

"Tell us," Hank grunted.

Tears filled Kaylin's eyes. As hard as she may try, she would always cry when she grew nervous around him. She was embarrassed by her tears but the fear inside blocked out the embarrassment. No matter what Justine did, it was Kaylin who felt guilty when their parents came to her for answers.

"I don't where she is. I almost had to walk home from school because she wasn't there to pick me up."

"We will not put up with this again, Kaylin." Beverly turned on her, "Tell your dad where she is!"

"I don't know!" she cried. "I've already told you. I got a ride home with someone else after practice. Justine never told me she wasn't coming home."

Her father's hand came out of no where, slapping her across the face. "Don't lie to your mother!" he shouted.

The force of the hit made her stumble back. She struggled not to fall to the floor. She immediately began to cry as she looked to her mother, pleading for her help.

"How many times do I have to tell you not to mumble?" Beverly clucked. "I can't hear you when you are mumbling. Look up at me and speak clearly! This is ridiculous, you are in high school."

"She knows where her sister is or she wouldn't be so worked up right now." Hank turned back to Kaylin as she flinched, "Tell us where your sister is, now!"

Kaylin sobbed harder, not able to contain her fear. Her face stung but she didn't dare touch it. She fought the desire to step further away from her father.

"Stop crying!" he yelled.

"I...I...," but she couldn't stop. She recognized the familiar catch of breath as she hyperventilated. The tears flowed despite her best efforts to stop them. Her mind raced for an escape plan.

Hank's hand flashed out again, slapping her hard enough that she fell into the chair behind her.

"I said to stop crying!" he boomed.

"Hank, that is enough," Beverly spoke calmly.

They stood in silence listening to Kaylin struggle to breathe through her tears. Her mom sat on the couch, smoothing out her blouse. Her dad stood over her impatiently. All eyes turned as the front door squealed open. Justine walked carelessly past the scene before her.

"What did Kaylin do this time?" she smiled sarcastically.

Hank advanced on her. Justine's eyes grew wide though she firmly stood her ground.

"Justine!" their mom shouted. "You deliberately disobeyed me by going out and not telling me anything about it. Even worse, you made Kaylin lie for you. I want to know where you are and why at all times."

"Not likely," Justine laughed.

"Apologize to your mother," their dad said, the anger growing in his voice.

"Uh, no. I didn't do anything wrong. I'm nineteen years old and have the right to do whatever I want."

"Not if you're living in my house!" Hank's body tensed.

"Whatever you say," she mocked. "I hate to break it to you, *Dad*, but you can't control me. You think as long as you hurt us you have authority but guess what? I can come and go as I please. Try and stop me."

Hank's eyes narrowed and quick as a flash, he reached out and grabbed her arm, yanking her toward him and smacking her across the face. Immediately a red blotch appeared on her cheek and began to swell. When it came to their father, Kaylin always knew he would get angry. In her mind, he was like one of those cartoon boxing fists. It wasn't the punch that she was afraid of so much as how tight the spring was being coiled up. The spring told her how hard the fist would hit. Her dad was a large man, and he still had muscle from his college football days. If he slapped them, it was going to hurt, but his level of anger determined the force behind the blow.

Justine, on the other hand, seemed to welcome any aggression that came her way. It fueled her fire. Kaylin always admired her sister's bravery when it came to standing up to their parents. Justine truly believed she could do whatever she wanted. It didn't matter that she slept on friends' couches or worked two jobs without anyone knowing. Her plan had been to move out the moment she turned eighteen. The only thing that had stopped her was lack of money and a consistent place to stay.

"How dare you," Justine whispered, pulling her arm out of his grasp. "Do NOT touch me!" She lunged at Hank.

That was Kaylin's cue. She quickly ducked for the door and hurried away as the screaming elevated behind her. At this point, she knew she would be in her room the rest of the night. She pulled out her homework and tried to focus. Tears continued to stream down her face and her cheek throbbed. The yelling carried into her room. She slammed her text book shut and pulled out her headphones. Sitting on the floor in front of their mirror, she cranked the volume and sobbed. To her disappointment, their voices traveled over the music. They would be at it for hours.

Kaylin stared at her reflection, waiting for the girl to appear. It took an hour until she saw the small flash run through her eye. Her reflection-self turned her head in curiosity, noticing Kaylin's tears. The girl brought a finger up to her cheek, the same cheek that was red from being slapped. Not knowing what to do, and too tired to try speaking, Kaylin continued to cry. A few times her reflection made silly faces, trying to cheer her up, but all Kaylin could manage was a weak smile.

Her body was raked with fear. She wondered if the fight would make its way to her room. For the next few hours, she and her reflection simply watched one another. When Kaylin finally started nodding off from exhaustion, she climbed into bed, listening to her music and wondering if Justine would be sleeping in their house tonight.

CHAPTER 3

The bell rang as Kaylin headed to her locker. She was swapping out notes when suddenly her locker door slammed shut. Jumping back with a gasp, she narrowly dodged a crushed hand.

"I'm not coming home tonight." Justine leaned against her locker. "You can ride the bus home since your rehearsal was cancelled."

Her voice was tired. A small, swollen scar on her left temple looked as if it was finally starting to heal. Kaylin knew it wasn't from their father, but a boyfriend that she dumped almost two weeks ago.

"Justine, why are you here? And how do you know my rehearsal was cancelled?"

"Someone said your director is out sick. Strep throat or something."

"Are you kidding me?" Kaylin grumbled. "Justine, I'm the last one to get dropped off. It is an hour's ride and I'm supposed to see the counselor again when I get home."

"You like to stare at stuff right? Do that."

Kaylin lowered her voice, "Do you really want to do this again? The fights every night... Why do you antagonize them?"

Justine's eyes narrowed in the same way Beverly's would when she was angry. Her lips became thin lines as she lowered her voice in return. "It's not my fault they don't believe me. I'm not out

28

sleeping with guys and doing drugs, okay? They just can't stand losing control or looking bad in front of their friends. Well guess what, they are never in control. They need to get that through their heads."

She stormed past her sister. Kaylin started putting in her locker combination to get the rest of her books. With one last class for the day, she hoped she could get to it before the bell rang.

An hour after being on the bus, she stumbled off with a headache throbbing through her temples. Being a senior in high school, it was embarrassing enough to ride the bus. The middle school kids making fun of her hadn't improved the situation. She quickly walked off as the underclassmen shouted names at her.

She hurried up the driveway and to the door. Walking in, she hoped to get to her room without her mom spotting her. Unfortunately, Beverly was waiting.

"Keep your coat on, young lady," she said. "We're late for your appointment. Get in the car."

Kaylin turned on her heels. She tossed her backpack to the backseat and immediately pulled her headphones from her pocket.

"Didn't you put any makeup on this morning?" Beverly asked. "You look awful! People tell a lot about you by how you take care of yourself, you know? It's called giving a good impression. You should really try harder to look presentable when you're in public. It's embarrassing for the rest of us."

"I did put on makeup," Kaylin murmured.

"Why were you on the bus? I said this morning that Justine would pick you up when her shift was done. Why didn't Justine bring you home? Where is she?"

Kaylin wanted to scream. "I don't know. I was told I had to ride the bus."

"Stop lying to me. You are sisters, which mean you tell each other everything. You share a room for goodness sake. Of course you know what she's up to. Besides, if she's at some new club then

29

I need to know about it. The ladies in my tennis group are looking for a great party venue for...," Beverly glanced at her daughter. "Well it's not like you care what I do everyday. As parents we are only supposed to ask how school was, right? What do you care about my social calendar."

"Mom, I don't know where Justine is."

"Fine. I'll let some other mom get the juicy gossip. I only hope they don't kick me out of the planning committee because I didn't bring anything to the table. How would you feel then?"

Kaylin turned up the volume to her headphones. When they arrived at the counselor's, Dr. Donna was waiting for them. She ushered Kaylin into her private office. Beverly watched anxiously from the lobby, waiting to ask the secretary everything she wanted to know about their sessions. The appointments had become quite a routine.

Kaylin sat in the dark grey armchair that was always her spot. As she waited for Dr. Donna, she stared at the new white orchids on the desk. Kaylin mused on how nice it was to see a real plant again. It was in full bloom despite the winter tundra outside.

"It's fake," Dr. Donna commented.

"Sorry, what?"

"The plant," she nodded to the orchid. "It's a fake flower that I picked up from the store a few days back. I thought it made things more cozy."

"I suppose so...," Kaylin sighed.

"Thank you for coming again," Dr. Donna sat across from her.

"Have you met my mom? I don't really have a choice."

At this point in her therapy, Kaylin had been given different medications to try. She lied about taking them but no one seemed to notice. Beverly would set them on the kitchen table each morning and Kaylin would throw them in the trash on her way into school.

Dr. Donna glanced at her watch. "I guess we should get started! Can you tell me what the past week has been like for you?"

Kaylin shifted in her seat, "There's been a lot of fighting at home. Justine said she's probably... staying out tonight." Kaylin searched for the right words, "My parents will probably end up blowing a lid when they find out."

"It seems that the way your family acts has a very deep connection with your low self-esteem. What can you tell me about them?"

"My family and I don't have much in common, but my stuffed bear is pretty cool. We talk sometimes."

"No sarcasm," Donna sighed.

"Sorry, he has a big personality for a stuffed animal. I didn't want to leave him out."

"Please focus. I can't help if you act like it's all a joke."

She slouched in her chair, "When I'm home, I try to stay out of everyone's way. They have a lot going on. I don't want to mess things up or get blamed."

"Do you believe you are the victim in your home? Does that statement resonate with you?" Donna glanced at her watch, trying to be discreet.

Kaylin shook her head, "I'm not always the victim, I'm usually the bystander. No one realizes how painful that can be though."

Dr. Donna wrote something in her notepad. Kaylin wondered if she was listening or making a shopping list. After the past few sessions, she had heard Dr. Donna mention things like depression and schizophrenia to Beverly. She wasn't surprised about being diagnosed with depression but the rest of it was nonsense, which is why she only pretended to take the medication.

"I know this may seem childish, but take this piece of paper and draw a heart." Dr. Donna handed a piece of blank paper and a pencil to Kaylin. "Now take these markers and color in the heart, except use the colors that you feel right now. For example, if you are happy then use yellow and if you are angry use red."

Kaylin picked up the gray marker. She filled in almost the entire heart except for a small sliver. She picked up the green marker and filled in the small bit of white space left. Donna studied the drawing.

"Why grey? What does that mean to you?"

"It's dull and slow. It makes the heart look less happy than white but still boring and plain. Grey feels like a rainy day that never ends... or like the sky outside. It's not sad. It's just... nothing. A minor key that clashes with the other chords."

Dr. Donna raised an eyebrow, "That's quite a description! You see emotions differently than other people. What about the green? What does the green represent for you?"

Kaylin's hands began to shake.

"Green is hope."

"Judging by this heart, you don't seem very happy in life. What is it that gives you hope? Is it that you'll be graduating soon and there will be lots of change?"

Kaylin shook her head, "My mirror... gives me hope."

Donna sat back with a confused expression.

"The girl that I see in the mirror," Kaylin clarified. "She gives me hope that there is a better world out there somewhere."

"But the girl that you see in the mirror... that's you, Kaylin. You are giving yourself hope and that's a great step! It sounds like we've come a long way."

"No," Kaylin interrupted. "It's not me. I tried explaining it to you last time, but my reflection... changes. Someone else is in there. Someone else lives in a different world inside my mirror. I've talked to her."

Dr. Donna glanced at her watch. On her yellow notepad, she scribbled the name of a new prescription to try on her patient.

When Kaylin and Beverly got home from the appointment, they heard shouting coming from inside the house. It was already dark and Kaylin had every intention to hide in her room for the rest of the night. Beverly immediately hurried into the house, curious as usual.

Kaylin went straight to her mirror. She felt exhausted from the tension and could hear her mom screaming at someone from down the hall. She knew her dad was mad about the cost of Kaylin's appointments and prescriptions. Her parents had been in numerous fights about it in the last few weeks. She felt guilty for causing more pain and anger among them.

Kaylin looked up to her reflection and her breath caught in her lungs. There she was, her reflection-self! It had never happened so quickly before. She gave a small smile and Kaylin smiled back, her eyes slightly squinting as she did. Kaylin noticed the girl's tan skin and perfect complexion. She couldn't help but feel a pang of jealousy. The girl's eyes were more even than her own as well. Another piece of perfection that Kaylin didn't have. They were big and bright blue around her perfect nose.

If only I could be so beautiful, she thought to herself.

There was a noise like tinkling bells and she saw that the girl was moving into a crouching position. She extended a long, thin finger towards the mirror, pressing it against the glass. Kaylin was amazed, once again, to see that she had no lines on her skin, no finger print. She struggled to take a breath then form a word. Trying to speak to her reflection was like having a tongue coated in peanut butter. It was heavy and hard to shape out a sound. Finally she managed to say her name, 'Kaylin.' When the final syllable came out, her body was tired and shaking. It was as if saying that one word drained all of the energy from her. The girl in the reflection nodded and looked to her finger. Kaylin nodded back. She was supposed to try again. She was supposed to go into the other world.

Kaylin slowly extended a finger towards her. She pressed it to the glass. She was careful not to take her gaze away from the mirror. The moment she looked away, it would all be over. Her finger felt like it had been dipped into wax and the wax was molding around it, hardening. The reflection girl smiled even wider and made a motion with her hand like she was pushing something away from her. Kaylin understood immediately. She pressed her finger harder into the glass, as if to go through it. The glass around her hand began to vibrate but she didn't take her eyes from the girl in the mirror. She was nodding excitedly and looked as if she may even be laughing. Kaylin kept pushing into the glass until her hand sank into it.

She couldn't believe her eyes, but she knew it was real. Kaylin's body ached from the effort of speaking, but she pushed her hand into the glass with everything she had. Suddenly, she felt it slide through. The thick, waxlike feeling grew around her hand. Her wrist went into the glass and she felt white hot lines shoot through her arm, as if someone was slicing into it. Doing her best to ignore the pain, Kaylin pushed until her elbow was in. She pressed her other hand against the mirror and it sunk in as well. Both arms seared with pain. She tried to ask what was happening but no sound came out of her mouth.

She felt something warm trickle down her arms. Suddenly there was that loud noise. Her reflection's eyes looked disappointed. The noise whistled through Kaylin's ears and instinctively she reached to cover them. The sound resounded through her head until she felt someone grab her shoulder.

"Kaylin!" Justine yelled.

She pulled her hands away from her ears and looked up at her sister. The room was silent, still, and the same as when she had first sat down.

"Kaylin, what the hell? You are such a freak! What is wrong with you?" Justine pulled her back, away from the mirror. She was both furious and concerned for her sister.

"What are you doing here?" is all Kaylin could manage to reply.

"Are you kidding me? You are such an idiot! Clean this crap up before Mom gets in here," she glanced down at Kaylin's arms.

She followed Justine's gaze and gave a shout of surprise. There were vertical cuts down her arms, following the patterns of her veins. From the inside of her elbows to her wrists, blood was sliding down and pooling up at her finger tips. Red spots had already appeared on the carpet beneath her.

"It was like a horror movie walking in here. Seriously, if you want attention you are going about it all wrong. If you start cutting then Mom will take you to see another therapist to pump you with new pills. She'll only see you as another problem to fix."

Justine tossed a towel at Kaylin then went to her side of the room. Kaylin heard her pull out a bag and start stuffing things into it. Fussing with the towel, Kaylin tenderly wiped the blood from her arms.

"I wasn't cutting, Justine. You know I don't do that."

"I don't know anything about you," she replied through their fabric room divider. "All I know is that I walk up here seeing you covered in blood, I was yelling your name, and you didn't flinch. Find a new hobby until we don't share a room anymore, okay? I don't want to be the one having to call an ambulance next time."

They heard footsteps coming down the hall. Kaylin quickly tried wiping the blood from the carpet. She caught a glimpse of herself in the mirror as she scrubbed. The girl was gone.

Simple, boring, meaningless, gross... me.

The footsteps grew closer. Kaylin wiped away the last of the blood, tossing the towel under her bed. Her arms stung with pain as she moved. She did her best not to start crying. Pain tolerance was always Justine's inherited gift, not Kaylin's. Their mother swung the door open and looked about the room.

"In the kitchen. Now!" she commanded.

Her lips were pressed into a thin line. Her face was red.

Justine rolled her eyes and left the room. Kaylin sat on the bed, knowing she was about to hear another fight being broadcast up to her.

"You too, Kaylin."

"Me?" she asked in surprise.

Beverly walked out of the room, leaving the door open behind her. Kaylin could hardly believe it. What had happened? She was the bystander. Why did they need her to be in the room to watch another fight take place?

They want witnesses! Her mind spun with absurd scenarios.

She stood from her bed like a zombie and followed her mother through the hall. Her feet moved without her knowing it. The smell of diffusing oils filled her nose the moment she got to the kitchen. The little puffs of smoke from the diffuser caught her attention as she passed. It reminded her of the grey heart she had drawn in therapy.

They entered the kitchen. Their father stood against the counter. Justine was sitting at the table, sucking on a lollipop nonchalantly.

"Now," her mother said, sitting at the table as well. "We are going to figure out what is going on. No lies, no secrets, no covering for one another. Family meeting!"

Kaylin was confused, *What is going on? We don't have family meetings.*

She shot a look to Justine who was staring back at her. She glanced down at Kaylin's arms. Kaylin followed her gaze to see that her arms were still bleeding. She painfully folded them across her body to hide it before their parents saw.

"We had a call from the school today, asking if there had been any issues here at home. They heard rumors that….," Beverly's voice faltered. "They told us that there were rumors going around that our daughters were being seriously abused."

Kaylin's hands started to shake with fear. She remembered seeing girls at school whispering as she walked by. She remembered hearing the comments that Justine's friends had made during class when the teacher wasn't listening.

"We need to clear things up right away before the police get involved," Hank said. "These rumors are saying terrible things about us as your parents and about us as a family. The school told us that they've heard that we make you kids inhale chemicals, lock you in the basement, break your arms…"

Justine audibly scoffed and rolled her eyes.

"Young lady," their mother said. "Have you been telling people things that aren't true about what goes on in this house? With your attitude…"

"I don't tell people anything," she defended. "It's not anyone's business. That's something you two still need to figure out."

Hank's face grew red with anger but he took a deep breath, turning to Kaylin.

"Sweetheart. We know you've been going through a hard time," he said. "Did you tell your friends things that weren't true? Your mother and I are very concerned about you."

Kaylin shook her head, eyes growing wide with fear. "I haven't said anything! I told the counselor that you guys fight sometimes, but I only mentioned yelling. Nothing about you hurting us."

Justine casually stood from the table, popping the sucker out of her mouth with a loud smacking noise. She tossed the half-eaten lollipop into the sink with a clang.

"Throw that in the trash," Hank said calmly.

Kaylin could see the spring begin to coil.

"You throw it away," Justine snorted.

He grabbed the lollipop and threw it at her. Justine ducked in time to miss the sucker as it shattered against the fridge behind her. Kaylin jumped in her seat. She immediately stared at the floor in fear, afraid of what would have happened if he had thrown anything but a sucker. Justine glanced back and narrowed her eyes at the small dent in the refrigerator door.

"We need to get to the bottom of this and without playing the blame game," their mother piped up before Justine could start anything. "Girls, you need to stop covering for each other and tell us the truth."

They all stood in silence. Kaylin kept her eyes on the ground. Justine finally spoke up with an annoyed sigh.

"Fine, I'll tell you. I'm moving to Miami at the end of the month. I told some friends about it and they thought it was because my parents were kicking me out. They've seen how mom avoids coming home after work everyday and her obsessive attitude. I guess they assumed you were starving me so I finally had to leave."

Kaylin watched in horror as Hank's muscles tensed. In one smooth motion, he grabbed Justine around the throat and slammed her against the fridge. His whole body shook with rage.

"Do you know what you've done? What you've made people think about us? How dare you!" he screamed in her face.

Justine's eyes were instantly filled with fear. She cried out, grasping at his arm, trying to pull free. Kaylin watched in terror. Her arms trembled uncontrollably at her side.

"Dad, please... let go!" Justine gasped.

Hank smacked her across the face and Justine fell back into the fridge from the force of his arm.

"Don't you say another word."

Their mom turned to Kaylin, not noticing the blood that had soaked through her shirt. The blood that was now dripping down her arms. "Kaylin, what have you heard at school? Did any of Justine's friends say anything to you?"

She shook her head out of fear. Her mind raced, trying to think of what to say to keep herself from getting hurt too. "Someone mentioned something about it but...," she hesitated and glanced towards Justine. "They said that Justine told them she had a broken arm...," she whispered.

Kaylin watched as Hank pulled Justine away from the wall. He raised his arm and Kaylin could see the coil tightening in her mind. That cartoon spring that pulled tightly together to determine the force of the hit on those silly puppets. The coil on her father's arm was tighter than she'd seen it in a long time. His arm came down. Once, twice, three times.

Kaylin shouted for him to stop but no one heard her. Beverly was yelling. Justine was crying. Hank was growling in fury. Tears were streaming down her face and blood was still dripping from the slits on her arms and wrists. No one noticed.

She ran. Kaylin sprinted up the stairs and into her bedroom, slamming the door shut. She moved without thinking, pulling her shoes out of the closet and a sweater from the drawer. She threw them on and began filling a bag with clothes, makeup, odds and ends around her room.

Run away, she thought. *That's what Justine is always saying. That's what she does to escape from danger. Run away.* She moved frantically, her heart racing and adrenaline pumping through her system. Her arms didn't hurt anymore. Nothing hurt anymore.

I don't belong here. It's not safe. Run away. Fast! Run away.

With her bag full, she froze and looked about the room. How would she get away? If she tried walking out, they might see her. Could she climb out the window?

Run, Kaylin!

She saw something move next to her. The world around her became still. Her heart seemed to beat in slow motion. She could hear the gentle *thump... thump*. She dropped her bag. There, in the mirror, was her perfect reflection-self. Kaylin ignored the worried look on the other girl's face and pressed her bloody hand against the mirror. Her reflection nodded, pressing her printless palm against the glass as well.

Immediately, Kaylin's arm slipped into the mirror. The searing pain ripped through her but she didn't care. She pressed her other arm through the glass and took a deep breath.

Run away, she thought. *Run where they can't find you. You don't belong here. Stupid, gross, immature, ugly, weird. They don't want you. Run away and don't come back.*

She looked at her reflection. The girl smiled. Without a second thought, Kaylin stepped into the mirror.

CHAPTER 4

She was cold. The blood in her veins ran like ice and she couldn't breathe. A breeze rustled her hair. There were crickets chirping. She heard the sound of water trickling nearby. Her limbs felt like boulders when she tried to move. Pain shot through them like knives stabbing into her bone. It reminded her of when her arm would fall asleep and it was too painful to even twitch a finger.

Ever so slowly, she forced her eyes open. The landscape about her was blurry. Moonlight poured through the leaves above, bathing the forest in the brightest night she had ever seen. Small balls of light floated through her field of vision but she couldn't make them out.

Kaylin tried to speak but realized she could not draw breath. She let her head fall to the side, looking for help. A short distance away, she could make out a hazy outline. She blinked again, trying to clear the blurriness. Someone sat on a large rock only a few yards from her. A large mass moved behind the person as they turned in her direction. She tried crying out for help but her lips remained motionless.

Panic flooded her thoughts as she struggled to inhale. She attempted to move, but her body protested with pain. The trees above her spun. Kaylin's eyes closed as her surroundings faded from conscious thought. Pain seared through her body. It was as if she was being ripped apart then put back together. Her limbs burned with a white-hot pain. She didn't know if she was freezing or burning from the inside out.

After what seemed to be hours, there was immediate relief. The torture ceased and she could feel the ground beneath her. Her arms and legs tingled. She gasped for breath. The air was almost too overwhelming as it flowed into her lungs. As her body readjusted to the oxygen, she focused on calming herself out of her panic.

Kaylin struggled to open her eyes again. The world around her was slow to come into focus. When it did she saw her own face gazing back at her. The face above her moved independently despite its resemblance to Kaylin herself. Suddenly, she remembered the fight in the kitchen. She recalled her bag had been packed and she was going to run away, the way Justine was always doing.

But then the mirror moved…

She bolted upright but screamed in agony. Her bones ached as if they belonged in the grave. Despite the throbbing, Kaylin couldn't see any blood or broken bones. She didn't appear to be injured.

"Agh…," the words stuck in Kaylin's throat. It felt raw when she tried to speak.

"Are you injured?" the other girl asked. "Can you speak? I never believed you would come. I didn't think it possible." She had a gentle smile.

Kaylin moved her gaze to the odd surroundings about them. She was in a forest lying on a mixture of fall leaves, dirt, and spring blossoms. The forest was bathed in pale moonlight. She could see quite well despite the hour. Small balls of light with shimmering tails floated aimlessly through the air.

What are they? Kaylin wondered.

The girl followed Kaylin's gaze.

"It's only bits of magic. Scraps that float across the land. They are nothing to fear. You won't even notice if they touch you."

Kaylin lifted her hand to a small ball of light. It moved towards her as if curious. Before she could touch it, the light drifted away on cool breeze. The leaves above them rustled gently. Kaylin noticed that the air tasted sweet on her tongue. The sounds, warm air, and cool earth beneath her was like a dream.

"Am I...," she cleared her throat, "Am I in Narnia?"

The girl beside her raised a brow.

"Middle Earth?" she took a gander.

"This is Loraillvon. I am Sorrell," the girl said. "We found one another through our reflections. You were in such pain. I thought if you could escape, you might be safe. This has never been done before. You are very special."

"My name is Kaylin."

"Is that what they call you?" Sorrell asked.

Different words flashed through Kaylin's mind: *ugly, weird, immature, freak, gross, stupid.* She shook her head and for a minute the memories seemed more painful than her current physical state.

"It's one of the things they call me," she mumbled.

Sorrell's smile disappeared. Her eyes shot up, looking deeper into the forest. Kaylin noticed that her ears had a slight point to them.

What's wrong with her? Are we in danger? Kaylin thought frantically.

"I hope not," Sorrell whispered.

Did I say that out loud? she thought again.

"No," Sorrell replied, "It was only in your mind. If you are able to stand, Kaylin, do so now."

Sorrell's voice had a slight tremor at her words. Kaylin muffled a cry of pain as she hurried to stand.

"We don't have much time," Sorrell whispered. "I'm sorry for these circumstances. As I said, this has never been done before. I was hoping to bring you here sooner, but I'm glad you arrived in Loraillvon tonight of all nights. To be able to see the Ceremony in your first hours here!"

"What ceremony?"

Sorrell ignored her question, "If anyone speaks to you, tell them you are from the deep mountains. I'll introduce you when the time is right. Whatever happens, stay by my side. I've seen your world, Kaylin, and it is vastly different from mine. Our magic might effect you in ways that I cannot predict. I have planned for your arrival, but you must stay with me. No matter what."

With that, Sorrell gracefully positioned her feet like a ballerina and bent a knee.

"What are you doing?" Kaylin asked, worried that the girl, Sorrell, might be sick.

A man's voice spoke out, "Sorrell is showing respect, as is our custom."

A tall man emerged from the trees. Garbed in a white tunic with a gold embroidered dragon, he looked like a gallant knight from one of Kaylin's fairytales. He had a glittering sword on his hip, a bow strung across his chest, and boots with large flaps. His build was solid with muscles that made his tunic seem too tight. Like Sorrell, the man was perfect. From his shiny blonde hair to his porcelain skin. This man was the type that would walk by Kaylin at school without noticing she was even there.

"Prince, I was on my way to the Choosing Ceremony."

"I know it's a formal occasion, but you don't have to bow Sorrell. It's not like the council is here. But why are you so far out? The celebration wasn't too much for you I hope?"

Sorrell stood from her pose, "This is an old friend from the mountains. She is here to make the Choice. We wanted to catch up before the night wore on. I suppose I lost track of time. My apologies for tarrying."

The prince smiled kindly, "It is no one's fault. I saw you slip away before the feast and wanted to make sure you hadn't wandered too far. I know how you lose yourself at times." He moved his gaze to Kaylin, "I apologize if I surprised you. It must be your first time meeting royalty. I am, obviously, your Prince. We are pleased to have you arrive for the Choosing. Please, return with me and we shall not miss your name being called."

Sorrell gave a sigh of relief and grabbed Kaylin's wrist, pulling her after the Prince.

"He didn't notice you were different," Sorrell whispered to Kaylin.

Most people don't notice me at all, Kaylin thought in reply.

There was no trail to follow, but somehow the Prince knew where to lead them. The trees slowly started to grow thicker. The light from the moon never had trouble getting through the branches. Kaylin did her best not to stumble over her own feet. Her new companions seemed to have no trouble navigating the large roots and stones.

The little balls of light floated in lazy patterns around them. Kaylin's heart skipped a beat when one seemed to pass through her. When she looked back, the ball of light had grown brighter before disappearing from view.

Somewhere ahead of them, a bell was struck. Then another. A sweet, light sound rang throughout the forest. As they continued more bells rang, joining the others to create a brass chorus. Reed pipes and stringed instruments entered the melody. Below her feet, Kaylin saw a well worn trail forming. Firelight peeked through the trees ahead as the Prince glided towards the music.

The magic balls of light bounced and danced through the trees as if inviting them in. Kaylin could hear cheering and laughter in the direction of the firelight. Her mind grew hazy and the aching that had been in her bones morphed into a numbing sensation. With each ting of a bell and she felt happier. She smiled to herself, although she didn't know why.

"Did you enjoy your training?" the Prince asked her.

Kaylin gave him a goofy smile, unable to focus.

"She told me earlier that the plains were her favorite," Sorrell said quickly, drawing the Prince's attention away from Kaylin. "She hopes to be placed there during the Choosing."

"I hope all goes as you wish. Sorrell is a cautionary tale for all of us," he winked.

"What does that mean?" Kaylin squeaked happily.

Sorrell's composure faded for a brief moment, "This ceremony is held in order for each new adult to take their place among the people. It is not a formality but a necessity. They choose which region they wish to live and what their trade will be. While I wished to be in the House of the Guard, I was instead placed in the Queen's House. The heart and the mind do not always want the same thing. I, myself, did not fully get to make my Choice."

"Don't be so glum, Sorrell. The years since have been an adventure. It is clear that the Queen's House is truly what you desired, even if you didn't know it at the time. We all know how you love to stuff your nose in those dusty old scrolls."

The music grew louder and more frivolous. Kaylin bounced with each step. They soon approached a path lined with torches. It led them into the swell of laughter and light. Despite the music's effect, Kaylin saw every detail of her new surroundings. The trees had girths as large as houses. Ladders were placed against their trucks and climbed to the thick branches high above. Balconies were built among the branches like luxurious tree houses.

They walked past trees that had stairs carved into their trunks and spiraled into the canopies. Huts and strange houses made of rock were scattered throughout the forest. There was singing, flute playing, and shouts of excitement awaiting them.

Kaylin rounded a large hut to see hundreds of people gathered in a massive clearing amongst the trees. It was a perfect circle with trees so tall that she could not see where they ended. Children sprinted around the adults, shouting to one another and giggling. Men and women stood in groups talking or gathered around tables eating and drinking merrily.

"Welcome to the Choosing Ceremony!" Sorrell whispered excitedly in her ear.

Banners and flowers were strung high above the clearing and looped from tree to tree. People were dancing with a joy and grace that Kaylin had never seen before. Men and women stood in groups wearing green, cotton tunics and large leaves that had been sewn together. Others were dancing with blue dresses made of silk that ruffled around their bodies as they moved. At a particularly large table, there were men with grey leather trousers eating merrily and laughing with mugs in their hands. The tables around the clearing were full of fruits and vegetables and other morsels that Kaylin had never beheld. The air smelled of pine and incense.

At the opposite end of the clearing, two of the largest trees were merged and grown together. Where the trunks met, a ledge like a terrace faced the clearing. Silk banners hung from the platform along with garlands of flowers and ivy. The centermost banner was white with a golden dragon embroidered on it, matching the prince's tunic exactly. Behind the terrace was an archway that lead to a room within the tree.

Sorrell giggled at Kaylin's dazed expression, "It's the largest ceremony of the year. Everyone that is able to comes. Hurry now, the prince is going to begin the Choosing. We need a good spot!"

She pulled Kaylin behind her as they moved among the crowds toward the center of the clearing where the dancing was. When they had a clear view, Sorrell pointed to the balcony adorned with banners.

"The queen is coming!"

Kaylin, still dazed, looked up. Men and women in white and gold filed onto the balcony. A woman like an angel seemed to float to the center of the platform. Everyone around Kaylin began shouting and cheering. Even Sorrell yelled something behind her while the musicians played a fanfare.

The queen's strawberry-blonde hair was so long it hung behind her knees. She wore a floor length dress of white and gold silk that moved like ripples of water. Like everyone else that Kaylin had seen in the clearing, this woman was absolutely perfect. She had flawless skin and her body was poised and postured. Between the woman's shoulders protruded two wings. They were pure white and hung on the queen's back like a giant beast, instilling awe and fear to all who gazed upon her. The moon and firelight created an ominous glow around them.

"Are they real?" Kaylin whispered.

"Is what real?" Sorrell replied, still applauding with the crowd.

The queen held up a hand and all fell silent, "Today we welcome our children to make their Choice..." Cheers and thunderous applause erupted through the crowd once again. The queen's voice was like musical wind chimes as she spoke. "Every year, our young ones go into their year of training with the seven Houses. In the final season, we gather for those who have come of age to Choose. We celebrate their decisions as they enter Community as men and women, starting a life of their own."

"What does she mean?" Kaylin asked Sorrell.

"We have seven Houses where we learn specific talents and skills. At age, each child leaves their home and spends time learning these crafts in their origin place. After they've been to each House, they come here, to the Choosing Ceremony. They pick which House they want to belong to. It becomes their permanent vocation."

"Do they have to leave their families?" Kaylin asked.

"They can either return home or move to a new region. They can appropriately apprentice and master their House craft anywhere they choose to live."

"Well that's the easiest choice ever," Kaylin mumbled to herself.

"If the House Masters will bring forth their talismans, we will begin."

Men and women began to emerge from the crowd, each holding an object to represent their House. Seven individuals stood in a wide circle with their backs to one another.

The queen glided back a few paces and a thin, white haired man took her place.

He opened a scroll and read out a name, "Yuton, Son of the Forest."

"We are sons and daughters of our original home," Sorrell said to Kaylin when she saw her quizzical expression. "He will always be a Son of the Forest no matter where he chooses to go next. We can never leave home behind," she said with a smile.

A boy of sixteen years stepped to the middle of the circle. He was largely built with a strong torso and thick arms. He extended an open palm to one of the House Masters in the circle. The animals and crickets of the forest grew as quiet as the crowd, watching from the trees above. Keeping his hand extended, the boy slowly walked to each member in the circle, letting his hand hover in front of the talismans they held.

When he reached the fifth Master, his hand began to tremble. The talisman that this House Master held was a long piece of wood and steel that had been twisted and melded together. The talisman floated from the Master's hands to the boy's. He grasped it firmly then turned to the queen. Holding it up for all to see, the crowd erupted in cheer.

"House of the Builders!" the white haired man declared. The boy beamed as he brandished the talisman even higher. Kaylin guessed that he got his Choice. "What shall be your place and name young one?"

The boy shouted for all to hear, "I will be Tyre, and I wish to remain in the forest."

The old man smiled down at him, "You have made your Choice."

The crowd cried out in praise yet again. Tyre returned the talisman to its Master then reentered the throng of people. He was clapped on the back and congratulated. A group of other men and women garbed in tunics and leather aprons in their hands approached him with enthusiasm. They had blackened arms from working too close to the fires. When he approached, they put a leather apron over his head and all hurried to shake his hand.

Sorrell leaned over to Kaylin, "He is now a man among all people. He must prove himself worthy of his new name by using his craft." She looked back at Tyre, "I think he will become one of the greatest Builders we've seen for some time!"

"How did it float like that?" Kaylin said in awe. "Was that magic?"

"Whittle, Daughter of the Plains," the man shouted over the crowd.

Everyone grew silent once again as a petite girl stepped from behind the line of people. Though she was small, she walked forward with a confident air that border-lined arrogance. She seemed to dance as she moved and extended her hand with a large flourish. Kaylin couldn't help but remember the throng of popular girls from her high school.

Whittle glided past the first two Masters with a smirk on her face, watching the crowd as if it were all a performance. She stopped before the third Master and waited. Her smirk melted away. Her eyes frantically looked to the Master but nothing happened. Someone from the crowd motioned for her to move on. Her eyes filled with tears and she took a step forward. The talisman of the fourth Master immediately flew into her hand. It was a small, lace doily. She held it up for all to see.

"House of Healers!" the white haired man trumpeted. "What shall be your place?"

"If you please sir," she said in almost a whisper, "I wish to move to the Ocean and be known as Maresa."

A small mumble went through the crowd.

"You have made your Choice," the man said with a gentle smile.

He motioned towards a group of slender figures a short ways from her. They were dressed in blue garb that resembled the colors of the sea. She made her way to the group as they cheered.

"It is not uncommon for people to move but she had lingered over the bowl for the Queen's House. Most people that join the queen must work in Kien Illae which lies on the boarder of the mountains and plains. It is a grander lifestyle from that of the Ocean. She has made a drastic change and did not get her first choice. The other Healers will be especially attentive in helping her make the transition," Sorrell explained.

The man on the balcony continued to call out names and the night wore on. People went to the Master's circle one by one and made their choice. It was an even mix of those who moved and those who stayed. The talismans floated up to their hands one by one as each young person learned their place among the people. To Kaylin's amazement, no one ever drifted away from the watching crowd. People did not grow bored watching the newcomers walk around the circle. With each new Choice, people cheered with the greatest enthusiasm. When the last name was called, the queen approached once again.

Her voice rang out through the forest, "Our children have Chosen. Now join us to provide for our great nation of Loraillvon. Our prayers and dreams go with them as…"

"Wait!" someone shouted from below.

Kaylin turned to see Sorrell standing with her hand in the air. What is she doing? Kaylin thought.

"Apologies, my Queen, but we have missed a name," Sorrell stepped out from the throng of people.

"I'm sorry, Sorrell. I did not realize. Who have we missed to call, and how was the error made?" the queen asked with sincerity.

Sorrell took Kaylin by the hand. "This is a daughter of the Mountain, Kaylin. Her day of birth falls only a few days after the Choosing Ceremony so she is later than most."

Kaylin tried to pull away, but Sorrell held her tightly. The queen's eyes moved to Kaylin. It felt as though the queen read her like a book. Her body began to shake as the winged woman sized her up. For a moment, Kaylin thought she saw the queen notice the blemish on her left temple and the scar above her eyebrow. Her eyes flashed with anger, but the next instant her smile was sweet and compassionate once again, as if nothing had changed.

"Let her make the Choice," she said.

The crowd cheered with the excitement of one final display. The white haired man took his place next to the queen, ready to do his part. All eyes turned to Kaylin. Adrenaline flooded her veins and made her trembling all the worse.

It's only stage fright, she thought. *What was Sorrell thinking?*

Kaylin quickly looked for her reflection-self but Sorrell seemed to have disappeared back into the crowd. They watched intently as she moved towards the House Masters. Some of the faces that she saw looked happy while others nodded compassionately, as if to encourage her that it would all be okay.

Her heart pounded wildly. The first Master looked at her kindly as she approached. She started to lift her hand, but a stern face caught her attention. There was a man standing across from her that watched her most curiously. He was tall and thin with dark hair. His eyes were green, so wildly green that it surprised Kaylin. He looked at her so intently that she blushed upon noticing.

"Please, lift your hand to the talisman," the queen said.

Kaylin quickly looked away from the man. She lifted her palm and waited. She was thankful for watching so many others. She knew what to do despite her nerves. The Master that she had approached was for the Healers. The small doily remained motionless. Kaylin started walking around the circle, passing the talisman shield of the Guard, the small whale figurine for House of Beasts, the wood and steel for Builders, and the large seed for Farmers. As she moved, nothing else did. She grew more nervous with each step. Her hands trembled as she knew all eyes were on her.

The girl that was forgotten, she thought.

She approached the Master for House of Mages and slowed her steps. Surely the small bottle that this Master held would magically rise for her. When nothing happened Kaylin stepped forward to the final Master. The House of the queen talisman was a large, white feather. Kaylin wondered if it was from the queen's own wings. She held her palm out and her heart jumped with realization. If a feather floated up to her, she would be with Sorrell. That was her House. Of course she would be assigned to the same place as her reflection-self.

She waited. The forest was silent. Kaylin wondered if even the stream had ceased flowing for this event. Nothing happened. Kaylin's arm began trembling harder from holding it up for so long. She was scared to look up at the crowd. Would they think she was a failure? Would they force her to leave seeing that she had no place among them? She looked hard at the feather and willed it to float to her hand.

Out of fear, she glanced to the crowd before her. The dark haired man stood at the center of her gaze. His green eyes bore into her. He seemed not to notice the talismans had rejected her.

Kaylin saw that he wore brown trousers and a tunic similar to the Prince's. He had no bow slung over his chest but had a sword on his hip. His skin was tan and his dark hair looked ruffled as if a strong breeze had blown it out of place. So caught up by his gaze, Kaylin didn't realize that she had lowered her hand without a talisman.

"Place yourself in the center," she heard.

Kaylin jumped, forgetting the crowd around her. She couldn't clear her head of the man's face, knowing he was still watching.

"My dear," the queen said from the terrace above, "Go to the center of the circle. Open your palms."

The House Masters rejoined the crowd. Kaylin took their place in the middle of circle, making sure to stand so that she was facing the queen. She saw Sorrell standing beneath the balcony. The people stood bewildered. Sorrell, on the other hand, was giddy with excitement. Kaylin shot her a glare and extended her hands out to her sides. She turned her palms face up and waited.

The talismans around her shook as a small tremor ran through the ground. Kaylin quickly tried to put her hands back down but they wouldn't move. She tried again but it was as if invisible ropes were holding her arms in their exact position. The talismans lifted from their Masters' hands in the crowd.

To her dismay, the feather from the House of the Queen began to float around her. The doily of the Healers followed as did the other talismans. They floated about her, circling faster and faster. A strong wind blew through the clearing, cycling around her. Kaylin closed her eyes as leaves and earth blew into the fold. She heard people cry out. For a moment, she thought her feet lifted off the ground. Without warning, the torrent of wind ceased its rotation and blew in all directions, billowing through the watching crowd and knocking them off their feet.

The talismans dropped to the ground as Kaylin gasped for air. She fell to her knees. Sorrell ran to her side. People in white and green tunics drew swords and bows and rushed to surround the two girls.

"No!" Kaylin screamed in fear. "Please don't hurt me! Please… I'm not from here… The mountains! She told me to say the mountains! Don't hurt me!" She threw her hands up in surrender.

Sorrell paid no attention to the weapons. Instead, she looked to the queen in challenge. The crowd watched with fear. Only two people remained where they were - the man with the green eyes and the Prince.

"What is your new name, young one?" the white haired man asked from the queen's side.

Kaylin's thoughts were frantic.

"You must choose a name or you cannot leave the circle. It is law."

She tried to think of a name, any name. But only one word echoed through her mind.

"Eloria."

Gasps ran through the forest. People whispered to one another in excitement. Sorrell remained motionless despite the wave of surprise around them.

"What did you say?" the queen asked, bewildered.

Kaylin's voice trembled, "Uh… I said Eloria?"

The man with green eyes approached them slowly. She noticed his hand upon his sword hilt. His knuckles were white. A silver ring on his finger glinted in the torchlight. Sorrell watched him closely as he moved. His gaze looked to Sorrell then Kaylin, studying them both.

"Eloria?" he whispered.

She felt a tingle run down her spine. She shivered despite the warm night.

The Prince stepped forward, almost cautiously, and pulled the green eyed man away. He looked at the man then back at Kaylin. After a moment he squared his shoulders, standing tall over the two girls.

"You have made your Choice," he stated.

He put a hand on the other man's shoulder, half guiding and half pushing him back into the crowd.

"Bring her to me," the queen commanded from her perch.

CHAPTER 5

An armed man in a leather tunic grabbed Kaylin from behind. She dared not struggle against him as she was marched towards the queen's tree.

"This has been a new and exciting Celebration of Choosing," she heard the queen say to the people below. "Let us all be grateful for what has been provided us and how we provide for others. Enjoy the feast and may all your Houses become Home."

Music began to play once more and Kaylin felt her mind go fuzzy. They were prodded to the back side of the tree where there was a large doorway carved from the base. Inside the tree, they stood in a room twenty feet high with a wood carved stairway that spiraled up the tree's inner wall.

"Move, Sorrell!" a Guard commanded.

Kaylin hurried up the stairs alongside her companion, trying to keep up before getting a blade in her back. They entered an even larger room with two thrones made of wood that seemed to be carved from the tree itself. The queen stood by the smaller throne along with dozens of others. To her right, Kaylin could see the archway that led to the terrace. The music and laughter drifted in from where the people had gone back to their celebration.

The queen turned to the small company entering the room. Her dress rippled around her like a crashing wave. Her wings were more beautiful and terrifying up close. Kaylin could see they were as much a part of the queen as gills were to a fish. The queen looked at each of them but her expression changed slightly when she saw the man behind them. Kaylin looked back as well to see dark hair and bright green eyes staring at her.

"My queen," Sorrell spoke up, "I cannot explain it, but she has made her Choice. It cannot be undone."

"Lower your weapons," the queen told the Guards. She turned her gaze to Sorrell and her eyes flared with anger, "You did not happen upon her by accident. What have you done?"

Sorrell was silent.

"It's not her fault," Kaylin piped in. "I was in my room, you see, and I just sort of… saw her. I pushed on the mirror and woke up here."

"She is Eloria. That is the name she has Chosen," Sorrell said boldly.

"You will choose a new name," said the Prince, moving to stand beside his mother. "Be hasty now. Pick a name."

Kaylin was exhausted and didn't know what to do, "I choose Kaylin."

"That is your old name, you must choose a new name."

"Alright…" But her mind was blank. It was as if she saw on old acquaintance but their name had completely left her mind. The difference was she couldn't think of any name. Only Eloria echoed through her mind. "Call me the Doctor," she joked.

"Doctor who?" he asked.

"That is not a name," the queen said.

Kaylin felt confused and jumbled. Every time a name came to mind it disappeared almost as quickly. She looked desperately to Sorrell for help.

Sorrell understood.

"She has no other name. If you feel that Eloria is an unfit name, let her earn it like everyone else. She will prove worthy, I am sure of it."

"Sorrell," Kaylin whispered. "No talisman rose from its bowl for me. How am I supposed to 'earn the name' if I have no skill or place here?"

"You are mistaken. Every talisman rose from its bowl for you."

The queen turned away from them, her wings neatly folded and the tips raised slightly above the floor.

"We have no way of proving that you are not a danger to our people. If you are the Eloria we have been waiting for then you are as dangerous to us as the Evil Ones."

The man with the green eyes scoffed loudly behind them.

"Let us summon a dragon," the Prince's eyes lit up. "They will look into her mind and tell us her intentions."

"The closest dragon is leagues from here, and it would never heed a royal summons. It would find it disrespectful as well as inconvenient to make the journey."

"She wasn't safe in her world. I brought her through because she was in danger. Please, don't punish her for my mistake," Sorrell begged.

"This girl is hardly a danger to us," the man with the green eyes spoke up. "And a name is nothing to fear. Even if it is *that* name."

The Prince and Sorrell both looked to the queen for a rebuttal.

"Very well," she sighed. "You shall be called Eloria. Everyone attending the Celebration is now aware of that fact. Word will spread quickly throughout Loraillvon of your arrival."

"I don't understand," Kaylin said. "What's wrong with that name?"

The queen paid no attention to her question. "Our people are kind and will treat you with respect as a guest. Please do the same. It seems only fair that we give you a chance to earn your name. To do this, you must learn the ways of our people. If you refuse or fail, we will detain you until we can find a way to return you home. If you are to be Eloria, then you must call yourself and think of yourself as such. We will do the same. Is this understood?"

Kaylin nodded but kept her eyes on the floor in front of her, "I don't want to go back to my home."

The Prince placed a large hand on her shoulder, "Do not be afraid. We are pleased you are here. It's just that you arrived in an... unexpected way. Please forgive us if we've frightened you. We are a people that help and care for one another. We hold hospitality in high regard. We would like to do the same for you."

"Thank you," she smiled to him.

"Thank you," Sorrell repeated.

The Prince seemed more pleased when Sorrell said it.

The queen looked to Sorrell and the Prince, "I'm glad you all accept my decision. Therefore, the three of you shall teach her our ways. Look after her, teach her our history, culture, and help her apprentice for each House. When I feel it is time, I shall request you come to Kien Illae. We will evaluate if she has understood."

The man with the green eyes quickly stepped forward, "Pardon, my queen. Perhaps I misunderstood. Did you say 'three'?"

His voice was rich and musical. Kaylin felt pure pleasure in the way he formed words even though he had an accent. Behind the beauty of his voice she thought she heard a faint hint of pain and mourning, as if there were some deep scar to his past.

You can't hear that from someone's voice Kaylin, you idiot, she thought to herself.

"It is Eloria now," Sorrell said to her. "You must call yourself Eloria. It is very important."

"Of course," the queen gasped. "You drew her here, didn't you Sorrell? But you are able hear each others thoughts?"

Sorrell nodded but said nothing. The queen laughed, like the sound of small wind chimes, and folded her hands in front of her.

"We always wondered at your purpose for the Queen's House, dear one. Perhaps you have found it all on your own. We knew you wished for another House at your own Choosing but look at what you have accomplished! I wonder if you would not share this secret that you have…," the queen waited but Sorrell said nothing. "Very well. Be careful what knowledge you have gained while in the library's books and stories," the queen warned. "Knowledge can be a sword for good or evil; all dependent on your application of wisdom. You seem to have something larger planned but I shall wait patiently to see it unravel." She shook her head, still smiling. "As for your question, Killian, I did say three."

The man with the green eyes, Killian, looked disgusted.

"If the Prince is to help this girl learn of our kingdom, he needs his most loyal Guard. Think of it as your consequence for earlier this evening," the queen said with a twinge of humor in her tone.

Scolded by the queen. Ouch, Kaylin thought. Sorrell let out a giggle and quickly tried to mask it with a cough.

"The *three* of you may leave now," the queen continued. "There is feasting and celebrating which we all should take part in. Guards, you shall not be needed. The Prince and Killian will make sure our new Eloria doesn't get into anything unwanted." Without another word, the queen turned away. The Prince, Killian, and Sorrell all bowed and began making their way down the stairs.

"Eloria," the queen said.

Kaylin felt a weight settle on her body when the queen spoke her new name. She took a step towards the queen and did her best curtsy.

"Eloria," the queen whispered to her. "It is a name of legend in this land." The queen bent down so that her face was even with Kaylin's. Her wings and hair fanned out around her. Kaylin was in awe of how majestic this woman was. Truly she seemed like an angel. "Eloria. The name belonged to another once. New names are not simply chosen, they are given as well. It is said that a name comes to your mind that represents your true nature. That you choose your true name by divine intervention." She looked thoughtfully at the young girl, "You will learn about a war, dear one. A war that we are still fighting to this day. Please be careful who you trust. All of us here are people of this land, but I cannot guarantee your safety or your return home."

Kaylin locked eyes with the queen, "I do not think I want to return."

Her red-blonde hair fell over her shoulder, "I cannot promise that you may remain either."

Her eyes looked sad when she said this, as if she knew the pain Kaylin felt. The queen's gaze moved to her arms, as if she could see where Kaylin's cuts had been. Tears gathered as memories of the screaming and hitting flashed through her mind. She felt a surge of guilt, pain, and pity.

The queen reached up as if to wipe away her tears but stopped. She smiled and lowered her hand. Her wings gave a little flutter. Kaylin's hair blew slightly from the wind they created in that small movement. The queen turned back to her other guests and Kaylin hurried down the steps to her new companions.

The Prince and Killian were speaking privately to one another by the doorway. Sorrell stood at the bottom of the stairs waiting for Kaylin.

"Come with me," Sorrell said excitedly. "That didn't go exactly to plan, but close enough! The celebration continues and we don't want to miss it!"

She took Kaylin's hand and pulled her outside, sweeping past the men who seemed not to notice them leaving. Kaylin had a hundred questions about to burst out, but the music and smells hit her like a wall as they entered the throng of people. Crushed pine, lavender and some other scent she couldn't name seemed to fill the air of the forest. The violins and reed pipes worked their magic once again and Kaylin couldn't help but feel euphoric. The questions she had melted away.

Though her spirits quickly elated, her body was spent from nerves. She and Sorrell joined the throng of dancers and Kaylin's mind grew hazy and blurred. She was having fun, she knew that much, but she could hardly make out the words people were saying or respond back to them. Things began to blur together as she entered a trance-like dream. The last thing she remembered was following Sorrell up a ladder, listening to her giggle as she stumbled through a door leading inside a tree.

***

"How could you keep this from us, Sorrell? We've been together for years."

"Keep your voice down, my Prince," she snapped. "The others will hear you."

The celebration was wearing thin and fewer people were feasting and drinking. The sky was already turning pink and blue from the morning sun.

"I don't understand. All this time and you never told us? Don't you think of all people I should have known?" The Princes' voice was desperate. "That prophecy is about me. It's my life! You tampered with it the moment you brought her here."

"I had to. It was time for her to arrive in this world and it was my job to bring her here."

"How did you know? Who told you that was your duty?" his voice shook with anger. "We returned from the front lines a month ago. Were you tampering with other worlds then too?"

Killian made his way through the small groups of people until he saw the Prince's tall, blonde head bobbing across the way. He pushed through a hefty group of Builders, begging pardon as he did.

The Prince noticed him approaching. "We will discuss this later. I'm hurt that you didn't consider me before changing the fate of our world. It's something I would have liked to know about."

"Everything all right?" Killian approached them.

"We were discussing the recent changes to our group dynamic," the Prince shot a glance at Sorrell.

"It's done now," Killian said. "If the queen wants the girl to learn of our people then it will be as she commands. Where is she?"

"Eloria is asleep in a guest house. Our celebration seemed to have a strange effect on her. She was hardly coherent after a few songs."

"Don't call her that."

Sorrell looked up at Killian, "Eloria is her name. It was given to her by the Creator. I will call her by her destined name."

"Someone must have told her what to say," Killian crossed his arms in thought. "There's no other explanation on how she would know that name."

"Why can't you accept the truth?" Sorrell gawked. "That is Eloria! That is the Eloria from every legend we ever heard growing up. The Prince will do his part, she will save our world, and we all get to go back to our lives as usual. It is all happening according to the prophecy, so don't belittle what I have done."

The Prince rolled his eyes, "There is no going back after the time of Eloria."

"That," Killian pointed towards the forest, "is *not* Eloria. She knows nothing of this world. She has no magic, she cowers at danger, and it is clear she won't be outrunning any enemies. She could hardly get up the stairs! Did you see her, Sorrell? Did you even look at the girl, or were you too busy celebrating your own victory, as usual?"

"That's enough, Killian," the Prince commanded. "For a Guard your eyes have been blind tonight. She may not seem like the Eloria from our legends, but did you see how the people looked at her? Yes, the girl is scared and naive to our ways, but the people saw hope. Didn't you see the light in their eyes? They saw a stranger from a new land with endless possibilities. For the first time in our lives, we have a chance again. Rumors spread down from the mountains and people are afraid of what they hear. Now we have a weapon to use against the enemy. We have Eloria."

"She will need training, obviously," Sorrell sighed, "We will acclimate her to this world. The three of us are strong, like the queen said. We can teach her the ways of our people and how to fight. With that, she can wake the dragons and lead armies."

The Prince shared a weary glance with Killian, "It's more than giving a speech and wielding a sword, Sorrell. You know the prophecy. She will be turned into someone else… she will be transformed into some*thing* else. In order to make the prophecy come to pass, I'll have to do things that will change us both. We will be giving up everything in order to make the prophecy come to be. Are you really asking me to give up everything for her?"

Sorrell's gaze was unwavering, "Yes, my Lord Prince. I would have you fulfill the prophecy."

The Prince looked to Killian, "And you? You're my Guard until the very end, no matter what becomes of myself and this Eloria. That was the Choice you made. Would you see me do it?"

"I do not know, sire," Killian's voice was solemn. "The fate of our world rests with her and yet it has become the duty of three to guide her to that fate."

Sorrell looked to the two men before her. Both noble and strong, she hardly remembered the last time they were incapable of an assignment given by their Houses. Now, they faced their greatest challenge.

"I didn't think it would be like this," she whispered. "Once Eloria arrived, I thought she would be taken to the castle. I didn't realize it would fall to us… to either of you… to create the Eloria we all dreamt of."

Killian shook his head, "It is what it is. We take it one day at a time. We should start at the Ocean and the girl can apprentice with the House Masters there. We will teach her our ways, but for now," he looked deeply into each of their eyes, "We will *not* tell the girl of the prophecy. She is here to save the world, and that is all she needs to know."

"But if..."

"No, Sorrell," the Prince interrupted, "Killian is right. We will not tell her of the prophecy until I say the time is right. You have brought this trouble to us and now you will leave it for me to decide how it is played out."

"I understand," she sighed.

The Princes' voice grew soft, "You are still one of us, Sorrell, but you must understand how different you must seem to us now. For you to have done this without a whisper of it; when we have been so close.... you are not the woman I knew."

Sorrell was unable to meet the Prince's gaze.

"But I trust you did it for the right reasons and I still trust *you*. Now we must work together, as we always have, to live through this."

"Yes, Highness," she whispered.

"You need to speak with the queen," Killian said to the Prince. "She summoned you some time ago and we should let her know of our plans. She has yet to share her decision on Sorrell's punishment. We'll buy you a few hours of sleep if you wish. I'll wake you when we're ready to begin."

Sorrell quickly left them. The Prince shared a weary glance with Killian and they made their way to the twisted trees. They hurried up the steps, taking them three at a time. Entering the Great Room, Killian saw that most of the Queen's House had left. Only two or three of her closest advisors remained.

"My Queen," the Prince said as they approached.

He gave a slight bow with his chin. Killian took his usual place behind the Princes' left shoulder.

"Thank you for coming, if not so quickly. I have had time to discuss the situation with my House and with the king. Sorrell's actions have gone too far."

The Prince's muscles tensed. Killian saw the worry on his face. The Prince had grown quite fond of Sorrell, even protective, over the years they'd been together. Their travels among the outer lands, keeping the boarders safe, had created a strong camaraderie between them. Sorrell was a good fighter and had an easy smile, much like the Prince. Not that it was Killian's place to judge, but he was glad when the Prince seemed to favor her over many of the other women.

Too bad he won't make a move, Killian thought.

The queen took another step towards the two men, her wings rising a bit higher to keep from dragging on the floor. "We do not see any evil in the girl's heart and believe her intentions were pure. She is, however, hiding something from us. There was no curiosity in her eyes when we spoke earlier. Sorrell clearly knew what she was doing when she brought that girl here. Either way, she will not be punished for now."

The Prince's shoulders relaxed, "Thank you."

"As I said earlier, the three of you will guide Eloria and teach her our ways. With this girl's appearance, it seems our war is coming to its peak. Evil has been pushing against our borders for years. We do not have the power to hold them back much longer. With the appearance of Eloria, we can only hope it will tip the scales in our favor before it is too late. Do you feel equal to the task at hand?"

The Prince nodded confidently, "With Sorrell and Killian, we should be able to help her understand and learn. Each of us have our unique strengths. We will teach her."

"Very good. I trust that you will do well, as always," the queen smiled to him. "As for you, Killian. Step forward."

Killian stepped to the Prince's side, bowing his head.

"Do you understand why I've assigned you this task?" she asked.

"I understand," he scoffed.

The advisors across the room cleared their throats.

"I understand, *my Queen*," he corrected.

She nodded, "I hope so. It is important that you help this girl learn."

She placed a gentle hand on Killian's shoulder. Looking into her eyes, Killian didn't see the queen anymore but a mother worried for her child.

"Will you protect my son and keep him safe?" her voice was soft as a whisper. "Eloria… we all know what it means."

Her eyes searched into Killian's wild green gaze. Like so many times before, the queen wondered how this dark haired boy had such light eyes, so much lighter than that of his parents.

"Protect my son from harm, and protect his heart above all else," she said.

"You both know the prophecy," one of the queen's advisors approached. "Since you lay in your parents arms they have sung the song of Eloria. The enemy is upon us even now. Though their deathly creatures wait among the mountains, their birds spy from above, catching every whisper. They expect Eloria to be a great weapon, with powers beyond anything this world has seen." The man glanced nervously at the Prince, "Meaning no disrespect, but it is clear she is quite deficient. Deficient of magic. Deficient of Guard skills. Deficient of great powers. Deficient of…"

"Everything…," Killian mumbled at the Prince's side.

The queen shot daggers in his direction.

"We all understand your meaning, sir," the Prince inserted. "She needs training."

"They will expect us to take Eloria to the palace, where she is safe and hidden until we decide to use her as a weapon. That is why we have decided to do the opposite. We will parade her through the land, letting everyone see her at your side. Let rumor spread that Eloria has come, and with our brave Prince, she is being Transformed so that they may lead us to peace and triumph over our enemies! In the meantime, take her to each House for training. Once she has learned every skill, bring her back to the palace. If the prophecy holds true, she may hold the greatest power we've ever seen. Use this time to teach her all that you can, as quickly as you can. We know how she'll get her powers, but I do not recommend beginning her Transformation until she has trained at every House. She must know of this world before those powers are available to her. And we must know if she stands with or against us."

"That may be difficult," the Prince said.

"The transformation or the training," Killian chuckled.

"That is enough!" the queen spat.

The tree surrounding them creaked as if swayed by a strong wind. The advisors slowly withdrew from the queen.

"You will take this seriously, young Guard," she scolded. "How proud you seem to think you are compared to this Eloria. What is it that bothers you so?"

Killian dropped his eyes to the floor.

"Speak up!"

"She cowered," Killian mumbled.

"Excuse me?"

"When the Guards surrounded her she cowered."

He glanced to the Prince for help but none came.

"The girl begged for her life with no sense of honor whatsoever. Anyone can see that she is physically incapable of protecting herself. Letting her go through the normal routine of apprenticing is one thing, but she has been found wanting both physically and mentally for her role ahead."

"Speak plainly, Killian."

"If she were to run from her enemies, she would be slaughtered like a boar on a hunt. Screaming and stumbling."

"Very well then," the queen lifted her chin, "I make you solely responsible for Eloria's combat training."

It was now the Prince who fought to contain his laughter.

"My Queen?"

"You will create a regime for Eloria and train her accordingly. This will be done with little to no assistance from my son or the lady Sorrell. I believe I'm correct in saying that you were the top of your class, Killian? And that you've completed the trials, being declared a Master by the time you were a year past your own Choosing Ceremony?"

"Yes, but my position requires it," Killian defended. "It is my duty to be no less than a Master, as is my vocation."

"Quite true," she smiled. "Thus, I expect Eloria will be one of our finest warriors by the time you return her to the palace."

"Pick up your jaw, Killian," the Prince chuckled. "It will be as the queen commands. I'll make sure of it."

"Be safe and wise," she spoke with a gentle voice. "If your need grows dire, seek out a dragon."

"We will go to the ocean first. After that the forest so that she can train with the Mages."

The queen nodded in approval, "Be safe and sure. Take care of each other, but be weary of the girl."

Killian and the Prince both bowed before leaving the queen. When they emerged back into the clearing the Prince stretched his limbs, taking in the morning.

"This shall be exciting," he said with a smile.

Killian rolled his eyes, "Why do you make everything a game?"

"If I don't, I will be as melancholy as you."

He gave his friend a shove. Killian quickly regained his balance and waved the Prince away.

"Go get supplies. I'll check on our weapons."

"Killian, please," the Prince made a pouting face. "Guard my heart," he joked.

"Don't mock your mother!" Killian smiled, "Besides, I already know where your heart lies."

"Ha!" the Prince lunged for him.

Killian neatly dodged his comrade's large frame and trotted away, ignoring the Prince's taunting faces. After gathering their weapons and armor, he made his way to Sorrell's tree. His humor had quickly left him. With the night's events, he was anxious to leave the Ceremonial Woods.

He swiftly climbed the ladder and stood on the edge of the balcony, contemplating what the next few weeks may hold. Killian had prepared his whole life for Eloria, knowing she might come during his time. But the strange girl inside the tree couldn't be her. She looked weak and scared.

Not the stuff of legend, he thought.

When he saw her at the Choosing he had immediately noticed she was different, and he had been curious. Now, he was angry and annoyed with it all.

They're only stories, he thought, *and I have no intention of letting them become anything more.*

CHAPTER 6

Red and orange hues flashed over Eloria's field of vision. Warm light covered her face. She smiled happily as the colors changed behind her eyelids. The leaves outside rustled in a light breeze. Birds were singing merrily. Squirrels quipped back and forth to one another as they ran along the tree branches. She sighed in complete bliss. She retraced her steps from the long night, using it as an excuse not to fully wake.

She hardly remembered the party, except that she had danced for most of it. The queen she certainly remembered. With her majestic wings and long red hair, Eloria imagined she would never forget such a woman. She thought through the Ceremony and all of the faces she had seen. Then she remembered Sorrell finding her in the forest. The joy she felt at being in a new world.

No, that's not all. Before Sorrell found me, there was that man. The one who sat on the boulder, she thought to herself.

She watched the image flash in her mind. A blurry memory of a man who sat on a large rock. The moonlight had outlined his figure and as he leaned forward, she thought she had seen... wings.

Identical to the queen's wings, she thought. *Maybe they are a different race or species from everyone else. How many species are in this world?*

The warm light on her face disappeared, cast away by a cold shadow.

"It's almost mid-day," a familiar voice said. His tone seemed unpleasant. "You've slept too long. Get up."

Eloria slowly opened her eyes. Upon seeing Killian's face she immediately cringed. It wasn't that he was unattractive, quite the opposite. Eloria thought she could stare at him all day without growing tired of his handsome features. He was exactly the kind of man she always dreamed of, if she was ever popular enough to be noticed. Killian, however, seemed unhappy by her very existence. His disgust of their situation certainly hadn't improved throughout the night.

"Hi," Eloria's voice cracked. She blushed and cleared her throat. "How are you?"

"If you aren't out of this tree by the time I return with the Prince, we're leaving without you," he grunted.

He trudged out the door.

Manners! she thought.

Beverly would have delighted in teaching him proper decorum.

Eloria rubbed her eyes, taking in her surroundings. They were in a hallowed out tree. It was round, with smooth walls and a finished floor. Everything inside the room was made from an article of the forest. She lay in a branch framed bed with a cushion that seemed to be filled of feathers and cotton. There was an animal hide covering her but she did not remember falling asleep with it there.

She was directly across from the room's open archway which explained the sunlight shining in on her. There was also a carved stairway leading up to a human sized nest. To her right was (from what she could tell) a kitchen. It had a dark wood counter and a small clay fire pit with a sort of tea kettle above. Next to it was an indentation that looked to be a wash room of sorts.

"Good morning," Sorrell smiled groggily.

She slid smoothly out of her nest like bed.

"I guess I overslept?" Eloria asked.

Sorrell waived a tired hand, "Don't mind Killian. He can't contain his excitement is all."

"Excitement?"

Sorrell shrugged, "He loves waking people from pleasant dreams. He lives for early mornings."

"I take it you know him rather well?"

Sorrell yawned. She waved Eloria to the adjoining room in the tree. There was a pitcher of water and a fixed basin with a hole in the bottom.

"You can wash here. Do you know your plants?"

"Uh... no. I don't know much about them."

Sorrell pointed to three potted plants next to the basin, "The dark green leaves are mint. They will freshen your breath and help your teeth. Rub them against..."

"I actually know what mint is. We have that in our world."

Sorrell nodded, "The round leaves can be broken in half and used to wash. The leaves will exfoliate and the sap will cleanse your skin. After that, use the yellow buds from the third plant on your skin. It will soak in and keep you from drying out."

"Toothpaste, soap, lotion. Got it."

Sorrell gave her a quizzical expression, "New clothes were brought up for you. We can throw your old ones out if you wish, or take them with us."

Eloria glanced at her hand-me-down sweater, "I suppose I could leave them."

"That's fine, but you still need to take them off to get clean."

Eloria was all too aware of her body and its imperfections. She quickly sized up Sorrell. She was thin without being anorexic, had well toned muscle, and her skin was perfectly tanned and pore-less. Sorrell was the sort of girl that would model for gym advertisements in the other world. Eloria tried to fight off her

74

own self hatred. She had a pudgy stomach and muffin top hips. Despite the jokes from her sister, her bust had remained small and unnoticeable throughout her high school career.

"If you would rather, I can explain?" Sorrell asked, noticing Eloria's hesitation. "I am not sure how your people wash but here it is a common thing."

"Oh! No, we shower… er wash, every day. It's only that we don't usually do it in front of one another," Eloria explained.

Sorrell's eyes lit up with understanding. She handed the large leaf to Eloria then made her way out of the tree. Eloria quickly washed and donned her new clothes. She combed her fingers through her hair, trying to make it somehow look presentable without her usual styling tools. When Sorrell returned, she followed suit. The clothes provided for Eloria matched Sorrell's. Once they were dressed, Sorrell pulled two satchels out of the wardrobe.

"These are already packed for our journey. There are more clothes inside. Food will be provided to us wherever we go but I packed snacks," Sorrell winked.

"Where exactly are we going?" Eloria asked as they each laced up a pair of boots that extended to their knees.

"Everywhere," she answered, reaching back into the wardrobe. She pulled out a series of belts and weapons. She strapped one belt across her chest and another around her tunic, a sword dangled from her hip. Two more small belts with sheathed knives went on her right thigh.

Eloria watched with apprehension, "So, I'm assuming this war that the queen mentioned is pretty close to home?"

Sorrell shrugged, "I travel with the Prince which means I must always be prepared. As part of the Queen's House, you learn to fight like the Guard."

She pulled out a bow and quiver next, securing them around her. With a smile, she handed a tunic belt and a thick, wool-like wrap to Eloria.

"I don't think I am qualified for any sort of weaponry," she hastily refused.

"You won't get any yet, but you still need these."

Sorrell wrapped the cloth around her like a short cloak and belted it to her tunic. She looked Eloria up and down then gave a curt nod, walking out of the tree.

Eloria followed and found herself on a small balcony made of green branches and reeds. They were bathed in sunlight upon exiting the tree. People moved below on a well trodden path that led through the thick forest. Some hurried about with carts and large totes while others milled lazily, conversing with one another. Eloria noticed that they were not far from the clearing where the celebration had taken place.

Staring up at them was Killian and the Prince. They were both adorned with new clothing and weapons. They each wore tall boots with swords at their sides. Over Killian's tunic was a leather vest that laced up the front. He wore two knives like Sorrell's. A short, cloth cloak wrapped around him almost identically to Eloria. The Prince was dressed similarly but with knives lining his side and two short swords on his back.

Sorrell waved to them and quickly descended a rope ladder, swinging gently in the breeze. She ran to the Prince's side and began talking to him excitedly. Killian grunted something then looked annoyingly to Eloria.

Eloria peered cautiously over the side of the balcony. It was at least three stories from the ground below. She adjusted her satchel with mock confidence. Getting on her knees, she extended her leg, searching with her foot for the first rung. When she couldn't find it, she turned around to try the other way. After feeling like a

76

complete idiot, she turned her back once again and carefully let one foot fall until she finally felt rope.

She sighed with relief and began to lower her other foot. Quickly she realized there was nothing to grip, her body began sliding off the balcony. Her leg went through the hole in the ladder as she grabbed the edge of the wood. Holding herself up with her finger tips, she quickly looked down, searching for the ladder's rope. She extended one hand to grasp through the air in a desperate attempt to find something to hold. Slipping fully off the balcony and using her leg to not completely fall, she finally grabbed a length of rope. Shaking and embarrassed, she pulled her leg out of the hole and made her way down the ladder.

She half stumbled, half fell to the ground. The Prince and her reflection-self hadn't seemed to notice the embarrassing descent. Killian's expression told her that he was not amused. She adjusted her belt, self-conscious of her new clothes and tight pants.

"Please tell me that was a joke," he said to her.

"I've never used a rope ladder before...," she mumbled.

"Let's go," he sighed, speaking more to the others than Eloria.

The Prince broke off his conversation with Sorrell and gave Eloria a kind nod. Sorrell and Eloria followed, joining the steady flow of others moving about the trees. They only walked a short ways when Killian led them to a cluster of round tables and stools in the forest clearing. They each took a seat and dropped their packs to the ground. People walking by acknowledged the Prince with short, formal greetings or quick bows. He smiled kindly at each of them and wished them a good morning. Sorrell seemed used to this behavior. She would nod kindly to each person. Killian ignored the greetings completely.

"Morning, young company!" a solid, tall man said as he walked to their table. "What can I provide you with?"

"A light spread if you please," the Prince said to the man. "We have traveling to do today."

The man disappeared into a hollowed tree. When he emerged, he held a tray filled with an assortment of fruits and greens. Eloria immediately recognized strawberries, blueberries, lemons and limes, spinach, kale, and apples. The rest of the platter was foreign to her. The man sat the tray upon the table and everyone thanked him, including Killian. They reached for their breakfast and ate hungrily.

Eloria watched the tray wearily, debating what to do. She was a picky eater. It always made these moments awkward for her. The only edible thing on the table, in Eloria's mind, were the apples. For a brief moment she thought about trying something new then thought better of it. She didn't know if spitting out food was considered rude in this world. Her mother would have certainly scolded her for it back home. She picked up a small red apple and wiped it with her tunic, in case in hadn't been washed.

The Prince noticed her behavior. He felt a pang of guilt for this young girl who had travelled so far from her home.

"Eloria, how was your sleep?" he asked through a mouthful of blueberries.

"It was very nice, thank you," she replied, taking a small bite of apple.

It didn't sound satisfying, but she guessed that lunch may still be a few hours away and she had to eat something.

"I'm glad to hear it!" he smiled. "The guest houses of the forest are always hospitable. I hope you will enjoy the next few as well. I am quite excited to teach you about our lands. Each region has much to offer."

Eloria abandoned her apple, "How is this working exactly? Are there books I need to read, or are we going for some sort of tour?"

"The queen wishes for you to be fully integrated," Sorrell explained. "We are going to travel to each region and help you apprentice for the seven Houses. It should be fun! A few months to travel and relax..."

The Prince reached for another handful of blueberries, "It will be hard work, don't get us wrong, but as we've already apprenticed before, it will be our main duty to assist you. There is history that you are lacking so there will be much to cover between Houses."

"Wait, there are seven different Houses?" Eloria asked.

"Yes. There are the Builders, Healers, Guards, Farmers, the House of Beasts, Mages, and the Queen's House. We are to visit them all until you learn each skill."

"But...that will take months!" Eloria gawked.

"Did you have plans?" Killian asked as he studied a strawberry. "Because some of us did. Thanks Sorrell, by the way, for bringing her here. I'm glad you got bored and had to cross over to another world so you could get a holiday."

His voice dripped with sarcasm. The Prince nudged him which caused Killian to teeter on the edge of his stool. He regained his balance and scowled at the blonde man's muscular frame.

"Don't mind Killian," the Prince said, scowling back at him in jest. "He's upset the queen assigned him. Too bad you're my Guard, eh?" he punched him playfully.

Killian shrugged him off and threw a strawberry top across the table.

"So if we're going to be spending all this time together, what do I call you?" Eloria asked the Prince. "If that's alright to ask... Sire."

She tried to sound respectful but could tell from Sorrell's face that she was failing.

"You may call me 'the Prince,' of course," he said nonchalantly.

Eloria rolled her eyes, *He can have a title of 'the Prince' as a name but I couldn't have been called 'the Doctor'? We could have avoided all this trouble if they had let me go with it.*

"May I ask another question?" she wondered.

He nodded for her to proceed.

"I noticed that the queen had, well, wings. Are you her biological son or something else? Because I notice that you don't... er...have wings that is."

To all of their surprise, Killian burst out in laughter, spraying the Prince across the face with strawberry juice. His laugh was deep and true. Eloria immediately thought of long, summer days with a warm breeze. His deep sound resonated inside her and filled the forest around them. Hearing his laughter made her feel more at ease and she smiled too.

The Prince wiped the juice off of his face with a glare.

"No, I am her son," he spat in Killian's direction. "Every future king or queen that is born into the Royal family spends a few years 'walking among the people,' as we call it. It is the goal that the prince or princess apprentices among each House as the others do. We learn the ways of the people. No man or woman can command a nation without first being a part of it. Generations back, the Mages created a way for us to hide our wings. This helps there to be fewer barriers between me and everyone else. Without realizing it, you are more likely to see me as an equal since I do not have a major physical difference."

"Are they still there? Simply invisible?" Eloria asked, unable to contain her questions.

The Prince laughed, "Of course they are still there. The magic lets them sort of... fold into me and remain unseen. It is difficult to explain but they are not invisible, they are simply hidden."

"Have you seen them?" Eloria asked Sorrell.

They looked at one another comically.

"I met Killian and the Prince when I was young. The Prince had already began his time among the people so no, I have not seen his wings. Killian grew up in Kien Illae and knew the Prince when they were children. He has seen them many times."

"How long have you all known each other?"

"We met when I was a little girl," Sorrell explained. "They're both a few years older than me. We apprenticed together before our Choosing Ceremonies, though. Killian went to the Guard and later became the official Guard to the Prince. I became part of the Queen's House. We've had assignments together off and on for the last few years."

"Why do you have guards?" Eloria couldn't help herself.

"I'm the Prince," he said with a shrug. "Why wouldn't I?"

He popped another blueberry into his mouth. Eloria wondered if perhaps all popular people thought of themselves that way. He's important, why shouldn't he get whatever he wants? Killian stuffed greens, lemons, and limes into his pack. The Prince did the same. Sorrell began squeezing lemons into everyone's water skins. Feeling awkward for not doing anything, Eloria grabbed the best looking apple she could find and slipped it into her own bag.

"I'll take lead," Killian said, briskly leaving the table.

"Fine by me," the Prince grunted as he swung his pack around his shoulder.

He quickly turned to help Sorrell with her pack then followed after Killian. Eloria skipped up to Sorrell as the boys began discussing routes through the forest. The sun was high above them and Eloria guessed it was somewhere around noon.

"From what I can tell, people here don't care too much about the time? Staying on schedule and whatnot?"

"I suppose that is true," Sorrell smiled. "Tasks and assignments for one's House are to be done in accordance with their deadlines and expectations. Overall, we find no need to rush if something is not urgent. As we are simply traveling. There is no hurry. We will be teaching you along the way. Many others that you see traveling this road are retuning home from the Choosing Ceremony. They all must go back to their respective duties."

The path was fairly easy to navigate despite the large trees and roots that rippled across the ground. Eloria knew the small hills would wear her out within the hour. She was at a physical disadvantage compared to the rest of her athletic party. Already she was slightly out of breath from their brisk pace and the weight of her pack. People continued to greet them as they made their way about the trees. The Prince always flashed them a pearly white smile and a happy greeting in return. His blond head gleamed in the sun in stark contrast to Killian's dark mass of wind blown hair.

"What's with this Killian guy?" she asked Sorrell as they weaved in and out of the other travelers.

"What do you mean?"

"He's... stoic and.... not nice."

"Of course not!" Sorrell objected. "Well... I suppose he has been a little short fused today. He's not happy that he got scolded by the queen. You probably aren't helping the situation much either."

"What did I do?"

"Oh, it's not your fault! It's my fault more than anything. Actually... why isn't he mad at me?" she pondered. "Understand that Killian is a Guard. More than that, he's personal Guard to the Prince which means no one is closer than those two. They are like brothers. It's his purpose in life to guard the Prince and protect him. We are at war and Killian takes that very seriously."

Eloria glanced at the happy faces around them. Children laughed as they raced by their parent. Adults smiled graciously to one another.

"The queen mentioned a war too. Besides the weapons you carry I have seen no other signs of violence. Hardly anyone else at the Choosing Ceremony wore weapons that I could see."

"We'll tell you all that you need to know in time."

"I still don't understand Killian's attitude towards me. Last night at the Choosing Ceremony he gave me the weirdest look, and that was before I had even really met him," Eloria whined.

82

Sorrell waved a flippant hand, "It's not you, per say, that he's upset with. It's that you are an unknown entity. No one has ever called upon their reflection and brought them into this world. It's been centuries since another world has been tampered with. Killian doesn't know if you are a threat. He's protective and slow to trust others."

"Why did you bring me here?" Eloria inquired. "Last night the queen seemed to think you have some big plan in place. Do you have an ulterior motive?”

Sorrell smiled.

"Since it's about me, can't I be in on it?"

She shook her head, "You will find out in the end. I, myself, am only a single leaf among the many trees."

I am a leaf on the wind, watch how I fly, Eloria heard the words echo through her head.

"What is that?" Sorrell asked, stopping to look inquisitively at Eloria. "Those words you thought of..."

“Oh! I forgot that you could... er... hear me like that. It's just a quote from a show. It got cancelled, but it was one of the best.”

"I am a leaf on the wind," Sorrell pondered. "It is beautiful, but sad in a way. I am not sure how."

"Spoilers. Anyway, back to the scowling wonder," she nodded towards Killian, "I think he plain doesn't like me."

"That's ridiculous. Killian has a very compassionate heart."

As she was about to reply, Eloria tripped over a tall root. She sprawled face first into the grass and dirt. Her palms scraped over the earth as she attempted to stop her fall. Her pack swung off her back. Sorrell rushed to her side. Eloria fumbled to her feet in a hurry to wipe the dirt off her new garments.

“Are you alright?” Sorrell looked her over. “Your pack must be too heavy for you. I forget that this is all new to you. I apologize for my negligence.”

Eloria saw two large grass stains on her new pants. Small specks of blood began peeking out of the skin of her palms.

"Everything okay?" The Prince asked.

"It's fine, I'm fine. Let's keep going," Eloria did not want to draw attention to herself. She was not used to being fussed over.

Sorrell went for Eloria's pack, "Let me carry this for a while. I will hardly notice the extra weight."

The Prince trotted to her side.

"I'll get that!" he also reached for the pack. "I should carry the extra weight, not you Sorrell. It wouldn't be right."

Sorrell was about to object when Killian snatched the pack and tossed it in the air. Eloria barely caught it as it hurtled towards her face. The blood from her hands smeared against the fabric leaving a bright red stain.

"She can carry her own supplies," he grunted.

His eyes quickly sized her up, making sure she was able to walk then he turned and paced away. The Prince followed without comment. Sorrell gave Eloria an apologetic look.

Oh yeah, compassionate and kind. That's exactly what he is, Eloria hoped Sorrell was still listening to her thoughts.

CHAPTER 7

They walked in silence for the rest of the day. It was easy for Eloria to discover that her new comrades were not much for ongoing conversation. She took in as much of the scenery as she could. The tree houses had grown more scarce as had the hollowed out bases where shops had resided. Many others journeyed the same path. As the sun's light diminished, the hustle and bustle of their road dwindled. The small ensemble approached another throng of tree houses, and it was the Prince who called a halt.

"Perhaps this is a good place to rest for tonight, eh Killian?"

"I, for one, stayed up far too late last night," Sorrell yawned.

They found a few open guest houses, which were built into the bases of trees this time. The girls claimed a tree for themselves while the men sauntered into one of their own.

Sorrell was tired enough that she didn't bother unbuckling the armory still about her. Although Eloria's body ached, she didn't feel like sleeping. Her mouth was dry from lack of un-lemon squeezed water and her stomach slightly rumbled. Her sustenance for the day consisted of one apple and a mint leaf. Sitting against the tree, Eloria gazed up at the leaves and sky as it slowly changed from the burning red of sunset to the pale blue of twilight.

A twig snapped a short distance away. Eloria was surprised to see Killian standing outside his own tree. He looked at her curiously before sharply walking in the opposite direction. Eloria tried to dismiss him from her mind, not wanting to ruin the peaceful evening. The stars began to shine when she finally felt herself nodding off. She lazily went back into the tree house to fall asleep in her bed.

When morning came, Eloria watched as her companions pulled out their greens and fruits that they had stashed from breakfast the day before. Unfortunately for Eloria, no one made any attempt to get anything new for breakfast.

She reached into her own bag and pulled out the apple she had taken earlier. If anything, she wished they had been given grapes and bread. She figured she could eat those all day and survive. Her mouth watered as she thought of a warm loaf of freshly baked bread and sweet purple grapes.

Her companions were silent as they ate. They drank in the morning sunlight as much as Eloria. The warm rays felt cozy and tingly on her skin. The soft breeze was cool enough that the temperature was perfectly comfortable. Killian was popping bits of a strange fruit into his mouth, staring up at the leaves as their shadows danced across his face. The Prince had more blueberries and Sorrell chewed daintily on spinach leaves.

"Alright then," the Prince said. "It is time for you to learn about this land." He faced Eloria with a grave expression. "You are going to learn everything about us. Loraillvon's culture, history, skills, and ourselves. The three of us," he said glancing towards Sorrell and Killian, "already know each other well. We know each others' strengths and weaknesses. We know each others' hearts."

"So you are like best friends forever?" Eloria joked.

"This is not a time to make fun," Sorrell scolded, her tone seemingly more mature, much like the Prince's. "We have known each other for quite some time. Killian and the Prince even longer.

What he means is that the queen chose us because we know how to work as a team and we need to integrate you not only into this world but to its people as well."

"During our time together you will learn to understand us, as we will with you," the Prince said. "Sorrell already has a unique connection to your mind so your understanding of one another will grow the swiftest. In our culture, we use our comprehension of each other to complete our goals and accomplish tasks to the fullest of our abilities. If you wish to stay, you must learn to do this as well. The queen has high expectations on your level of understanding and communicating by the time we are summoned to her."

Eloria nodded, "Then teach me. I want to learn everything so that I may stay."

"We will start by sharing our history. I do not know about your world, but here we cannot simply tell you the story, you must experience it as well. Have you ever noticed how music manipulates your emotions? Certain instruments can make you sad or frightened and some notes when played in harmony create feelings of happiness? That is how we must tell you of Loraillvon. Sorrell has told me that music affects you differently. That is how it is supposed to be."

To Eloria's surprise, Killian spoke, "We know that there are other worlds and that they are similar to ours although we cannot see them. You are from such a world. Like our world, there was a point where it did not exist. At the beginning of time and before all things, there was nothing. No darkness or light. No earth or water or living creature. Our Creator existed but He is outside of all things such as time and physicality. Our minds cannot fathom His existence or goodness and this is how it should be. First, He created the worlds which were made of water. With this act, He also created His home, which we call Heaven, and He filled it with angels."

"Like the queen?" Eloria asked, excited to hear about the winged creatures.

Killian shook his head, "She is not an angel. Angels look completely different."

"How do you know?"

Killian glanced at her with annoyance, "Because I've seen them, and they look completely different. Now be quiet and get your bag."

Eloria snapped her mouth shut and reached for her bag as instructed. She swallowed the last of her apple as the group made their way to the main forest path. The Prince took the lead this time. Killian walked next to Eloria. He kept a comfortable amount of space between them. Sorrell followed behind. Looking eagerly to Killian, waiting for him to continue, Eloria kept silent. He watched her closely, not trusting her to keep her mouth shut.

From behind them, Sorrell sang out a clear, high note. The sound pierced through the air, and the trees seemed to shiver. She held the note so long that Eloria wondered how she maintained her breath. When she released the sound, it echoed among the trees. She began to sing again. Eloria listened to the melody and could feel the hope and joy within the song.

"The Creator spoke and light came to be," Killian said.

Eloria was entranced by the way his mouth moved. The words sounded like an instrument of their own.

"He named the light and the darkness and thus created time. When He spoke again, it was to separate the water from water. It created an expanse that He called sky," Killian sighed the word as he said it.

Sorrel continued her song that echoed throughout the forest. As other people along the path heard, they joined in with her singing. Other harmonies melding with Sorrell's.

"The Creator again made a distinction between water and water, having earth emerge from between the waves," Killian continued. "Upon the earth and within the water He created plants and vegetation, each with a specific purpose. With His next words, He created the sun and the moon, for light and dark needed a source besides Himself. The sun and moon now distinguished day from night and all the times in-between."

From ahead, the Prince began to sing a song that was different than Sorrell's. His voice was low and rich but the melody was slow in comparison to her tune. As he sang, Sorrell began to sing in and around his notes, melding the two songs into one.

Killian spoke in rhythm, "With another word, The Creator made animals to populate both the sea, the land, and the sky. But as they were not angels, all creatures were molded to make land and water their home. His final word created man and woman, for man was not to be alone and one without the other was unbalanced. He created them in His likeness, giving them the ability to imagine, invent, and create. Thus the creation of Loraillvon."

The song continued and Killian sang about the first civilization, or Community as they called it. He spoke of how they spread across the different regions, learning from the Creator about the plants and animals from each place.

Then a dark time came when the people turned away from the one who created them in order to gain power for themselves. They corrupted their resources by using plants and animals against their original purpose. The people entered other worlds and interfered where they didn't belong. At this point, the music grew sad and Eloria felt devastated for the people that Killian sang of. She wanted to scream out for them to stop. She felt the dread that the song played out.

Killian told of how the Creator wanted to destroy the world because of the wicked ways of the people, but He found a young man who still believed in Him and wanted to learn the righteous ways of living. The boy imagined inventions and creations that healed and nurtured instead of destroyed. Because of this, the Creator replenished the water and earth with life. He set laws for the people of Loraillvon that restricted their abilities. He gave each of them a specific gift and vocation that would serve the land, not themselves. When the people realized how far they had fallen from His grace, they reconciled themselves to the new law. Sorrell and the Prince's melodies lightened and their voices continued to play back and forth, telling a story of rebirth and sorrow.

"After seeing other worlds, the people asked to have someone to lead them. A king," Killian said, his voice sounding as melodious as the songs around them. Eloria couldn't tell if he was speaking or singing. "Although the Creator told them it was unwise, He conceded and gave them a king. He chose the man that was most humble and wise. A man that honored the Creator above all else, even himself. So he was set apart from the other people by giving him new gifts and abilities. The Creator gave him a new name: Seraphim. Meaning an angel-like being. The king was given wings, control over the wind and weather, and he also had the ability to see things that others could not. This way the king would know what was from his world of Loraillvon and what was foreign. The Creator said that when he found his life partner, she would grow to be like him. Their children would continue their line, always to be Seraphim. Different than the rest and set apart for a purpose. This is why we have the Choosing. It is when our Creator gives us our vocation and we choose a new name for ourselves."

As he sang, the Prince glanced back at Killian and they exchanged a look that Eloria couldn't identify. Sorrell noticed it too. Her voice wavered for a moment.

Killian continued, "Though most people had seen the evil that they had brought onto the world, not everyone did. There was a group that believed they were more powerful than the Creator because they could tamper in other worlds. They did not wish to follow our Creator's law. They despised Seraphim, the king, for having gifts and powers that they could not. They hated our Creator for what He had done. They decided to sever all bonds with Him and destroy anyone who followed the Creator.

"Though His people had done wrong, the Creator forgave them and came to Loraillvon himself. He came as man, with the same vulnerabilities and weaknesses of any man. He came to our world to rescue the people from the evil. He came to teach them how to live with their new gifts as well as save them from those that wished them harm. In the time He spent with them as a man, He went to the most humble and selfless of everyone. They became the most blessed and honored by Him. To King Seraphim, He sent an angel as His ambassador.

"After establishing six of the seven Houses, the Creator went to the Evil Ones and gave His life to protect His people. It was the ultimate sacrifice for, although He ascended into Heaven, He first endured torture and bore the pain of all the world. Past and future. As He was dying, all of the evil of the world was cast upon Him so that the Creator might forgive those who had slain Him and offer them a second chance."

Sorrell's song was mournful. Eloria saw that she cried silently as she sang. Even the Prince discreetly wiped his eyes as he led them onward in trail and song.

"After the sacrifice of His life, our Creator withdrew to Heaven, vowing to never come to this world again until it was time for all to join him in Heaven. He only speaks to us in small ways now; a stirring in our heart that leads us to the right path, or in the Choosing of our new names when we come of age. All else goes through His ambassadors, the angels, then to the king. Since the time of His death here on Loraillvon, our people have dedicated their lives to living as the Creator intended.

"We sing to His glory and thank Him for the beauty that surrounds us. We strive to take care of one another and fulfill our purpose. The Royal family follows the example of His earthly life by sending their own son or daughter to live among the people. Not only is this to learn about the world but to guide each House as the Creator instructs."

Sorrell and the Prince did not end their song. Killian went on to tell more about the people and how they spread through the different regions of this world. Some areas belonging to the Evil Ones and some to those who followed the Creator's law. They walked through the forest, singing and speaking the tale to her. Time passed but her mind only saw images of the stories they told.

Finally, their songs slowed and Killian told the story of a fisherman who lived at the sea. The fisherman had left the community as a young boy, afraid of the evil that corrupted them. He lived alone and made friends with a whale that became his sole companion. One day, the Creator sought out the fisherman and asked him for a meal. The fisherman obliged and, knowing that it was the Creator appearing to him as a man, left his hut to travel with Him. Everyday the fisherman thought of his friend, the whale, and he asked the Creator to protect the whale. He asked that the whale not feel alone while the fisherman was away.

In the end, the fisherman followed the Creator to the spot where He was sacrificed. The Evil Ones let the fisherman live so that he might tell others of their power. Instead, the fisherman traveled to all the lands within Loraillvon and told the people of how the Creator sacrificed Himself to die in order that they all would be given a second chance. He told the people about the Creator's love and generosity. He spread the news of what the Creator had done for them, but every day he thought of his whale. He asked the Creator to keep the whale from being lonely. When the fisherman knew he was growing too old to travel, he went back to the sea to find his friend.

The Creator blessed the fisherman for speaking the truth about His death. As a gift to the fisherman, He gave intelligence to a third of all mammals in this world. The Creator sent an angel to the fisherman's hut and it told him of the Creator's gift. The angel taught him how to use his mind to speak to the beasts of the land and sea. The angel told the fisherman that he was to create a new House. All who Chose this House would communicate with the beasts and tend to the animals of each region. When the angel left him, the fisherman went to the ocean to find his old friend, the whale. Once they were united, they were able to 'speak' as true friends. Killian explained the difference between beasts and animals. Those gifted with intelligence by the Creator were not to be hunted or harnessed. They were friends to the people and served their Creator as man and woman did.

"And that," Killian said, the rhythmic patterns leaving his voice, "is how our world was created. It is also how the House of Beasts was founded. Its origin place is the ocean, where all go to apprentice in the craft."

"Wow," Eloria sighed. She felt many different emotions still lingering from the power of the music. "It's similar to the Bible."

"What is a Bible?" Sorrell asked. "Is it like the fisherman?"

"Oh, no. It's like a big book that talks about God and how the universe was made. It covers creation all the way until… well… Roman times I guess? I guess it's like your story of creation but instead of songs, a bunch of prophets wrote it down. You could say it's one of our holy writings, but it is so similar to yours! My people were… a lot worse… and still are."

"We believe that our Creator created all worlds," the Prince shrugged. "We should stop here," he motioned to a clump of trees ahead. "There are a few guest houses. Let's see if any are available. Many travel looking for beds."

Eloria hadn't noticed that dusk had fallen. Killian adjusted his pack and joined the Prince.

"You have a beautiful voice," Eloria complimented Sorrell. "I've only dreamt of being able to sing so nicely!"

"With time you will learn the song too. After that you can help in retelling our history," she said with a smile. "Did you enjoy Killian's telling of it?"

Eloria nodded, "His voice sort of… flows differently than everyone else's. The way he forms words adds more power somehow. He almost affects you when he speaks. Have you noticed that?"

Sorrell looked inquisitively to the men ahead of them. "I had not noticed that about him. Perhaps you see more than we thought, Eloria. Thank you for being honest with what you heard. I am always too busy listening to the Prince's song that I forget to listen to Killian. He was always the best at it though. The Prince and I prefer song."

The small company approached a clump of trees with ladders and balconies. Sorrell explained that they had clusters of guest houses throughout the forest due to the annual ceremony. In the forest, there was always a place to stay if you knew where to go. The Prince hurried up a ladder and knocked on the door to the hollowed room inside. He inquired after available rooms for the night. Once he got his answer, he gracefully descended the ladder to rejoin his group.

"There is one house available. The path has been well traveled today and most are full. It's off this way."

It was a long trek until they came upon the empty tree house. Sorrell and the Prince scurried up the ladder, followed closely by Killian. Eloria approached the ladder with hesitancy. Her hands still stung from her fall the day before and her muscles were tired from walking.

With reluctance, she grasped the wooden rung. Unlike a normal, solid ladder, this rope ladder swung back and forth as she climbed. When she neared the top there was, once again, nothing to grip. She grasped onto a plank of wood that served as the balcony floor. As she started to pull herself up a splinter slid into her skin. Without thinking, the surprise of pain caused her to let go of the balconies edge. She felt her heart skip a beat as she tipped backwards. A hand shot out and grabbed her around the wrist, lifting her to the floor where she swung her legs onto the balcony. She sat there, catching her breath from the adrenaline rush. Killian knelt across from her, his hand still wrapped around her arm.

"Thanks!" she looked up at him.

His green eyes stared back at her. She felt another jolt of adrenaline rush through her veins, her breath catching in her chest. Those eyes seemed to pierce into her very soul. He was looking at her the same way as when she first saw him at the Choosing Ceremony. Blood flushed her cheeks.

"Do we need to lower you down in a basket?" he asked.

She couldn't tell if he was joking or serious. Either way she was embarrassed, yet again, by her obvious lack of physical ability. Killian dropped his pack on the floor.

"If they ask, I'll be back shortly."

In one graceful motion, he stepped off the balcony and landed in a light, crouching position on the earth below. The muscles on his arms flexed as he stood, casually walking away amongst the trees. Eloria quickly realized she was gawking and closed her mouth.

Show off, she thought. *What is with that guy?!*

She went into the tree to join the others. Inside, Eloria saw that this room was almost identical to the tree she had stayed in the night before. Instead of a bed on the floor, there were two nest-like structures above them. Sorrell had a small fire kindling in a clay stove against the far wall and the Prince was grinding leaves into a kettle. Eloria stood aimlessly. Sorrell moved away from the fire, giving him a wink as she did.

"The house was stocked before we arrived," the Prince said. "They provided dinner for us. Speaking of, where's Killian?" he glanced out to the balcony.

"He said he would be back soon," Eloria answered.

Food!

Eloria could hardly wait to fill her stomach. The one apple she ate had not sustained her. She hurried over to the Prince and looked at the tray that he pulled from a cupboard. Greens, sprouts, and fish. Her heart sank. While she loved meat, fish was not on her personal list of edible foods.

"Dinner under the stars?" he said with a grin.

He took the tray to the balcony and the two girls followed, Sorrell bringing their water skins along. The ledge was large enough for five or six people to sit comfortably despite the lack of railings. Eloria sat next to Sorrell. They could see Killian's dark figure a little ways off, heading back towards them. Not wanting to wait, they dug into the food.

Eloria picked up a bit of sprouts and popped it in her mouth, hoping she would like it. Immediately her tongue rejected the texture and taste. She turned her face away so the others wouldn't see her cringe. Forcing herself to swallow it, she fought the gagging reflex in her throat. Eloria reached for a water skin and began to chug. The bittersweet taste of lemon soaked her tongue. Water came spewing from her mouth with a choking cough. The others looked at her curiously as she continued coughing.

"Sorry," she said between coughs, "choked on…," *cough*, "some water," *cough*.

Her eyes teared up. She finally sat back and abandoned any hope of eating or drinking while in this world. Killian's head popped into view from the balconies edge.

"Who's dying?" he asked, gracefully swinging his body onto the platform.

"No one," Sorrell covered. "I choked on some water."

96

Killian grunted, no longer interested. He sat next to the Prince and scooped up fish meat. Eloria was silent throughout the meal while the other three talked about their journey ahead. They discussed routes and best places to camp each night. Eventually Sorrell announced she was tired and stood to go inside.

The Prince hit Killian on the arm, "Only two beds. We're on the floor."

Killian nodded in agreement. Eloria opened her mouth, already knowing the appropriate thing to say. Her mother had trained her well on manners, and even if it was a lie, Eloria was never to inconvenience someone else.

"You don't have to do that. I can sleep on the floor if you want the bed."

Both men stared at her, somewhat confused.

"No," they said in unison.

The Prince stood and wished them a good night, following Sorrell into the room. As soon as he disappeared behind the door, Killian rummaged through a bag next to him. Eloria ignored him and looked up at the stars. There were more in this sky than in hers back home. She wondered if that was another reason the forest was so well lit.

"Here," Killian reached his hand out to her.

"What?"

"Take it."

She eyed his hand cautiously, seeing his silver ring glint in the moonlight. She wondered what he could possibly have to give her. She reluctantly held out her palm and a stem-full of grapes fell into it. She gasped. Seeing her expression, he reached back into the bag. He pulled out a small roll of bread, about the size of his fist. She stared at him with wonder as she accepted the bread.

"I noticed you didn't eat today, or yesterday."

"I had an apple," she said without thinking.

He laughed sarcastically, "Right. I'm sure that will hold you over for a few days."

He reached into his bag one last time and tossed over a small block of cheese. Eloria felt as if it were Christmas morning. She took a bite of bread and moaned out loud. It was warm inside.

Freshly baked!

"Thank you," she said quietly.

Killian had clearly waited until the others had left to give her the food. She wondered if it was for her sake or his.

"Don't get used to it," he said, back to his cold demeanor.

Despite his attitude and blunt tone, his voice was still like music. They sat in silence while she ate her private meal.

"You're right. I didn't really eat," she said, attempting to break the silence between them. "I'm sort of a picky eater. Foods that I don't like back home just make me gag. There's usually plenty of options and if I don't like something then I go without for a few hours."

"Sorrell didn't notice your hunger, but she heard you thinking about your favorite foods. We don't eat much else besides what you have seen, at least not while in the forest. If you starve yourself, you won't be able to keep up. Grapes are rare in the woods and bread disappears when the guest houses do, which is tomorrow."

Eloria nodded in understanding. She had to suck it up and start eating or she would starve. She savored the last grape as she pondered what their future held in store for them.

"Killian? What does Eloria mean?"

She glanced over and saw a shiver run through his body.

"It means you," he replied. "It is your new name."

"At the Choosing Ceremony, you looked at me and said the name. But..." she struggled to find the right words. "You said it as if you already knew it. Everyone seems to know it except for me. It sort of popped into my head. But you said the name as if you knew her. Whoever Eloria is or was, you looked right at me and said the name like it was familiar."

He stared ahead, his eyes in a blank gaze to the forest spread out before them.

"I know I probably don't make sense, I'm sorry. I thought that since everyone else knows the name, maybe I should too. Sorrell admitted that she won't tell me much, I have to 'find out at the end,' whatever that means…"

"She said that?" he looked at her with a raised brow.

"Uh yeah. Technically I asked her why she brought me here then she said the stuff about waiting until the end. But I'd still like to know what the name means."

"It was the name of our first queen," he said quietly. "She married King Seraphim and became the first Queen Transformed."

Eloria raised a quizzical brow, and he remembered that this was all new to her.

"In the story of creation, we told you how our Creator changed the first King. He gave him wings, control of the wind and weather, and… other things," his voice drifted off as if he was bored with the tale. "Well El…," he stopped before saying the name. "She… was the woman that King Seraphim married. As he fell in love with her she began to change. Once they were united, she was full Seraphim, just as he was."

"Is that it? No offense but what's the big deal about having the same name as the first queen? Did she do anything cool?"

"There's a legend that says another of that name will arrive when evil rises to power once again." He stretched his arms out in front of him, seemingly bored. "You basically walked in from another universe and announced the destruction of our world."

What a way to kill a party, she thought.

Killian handed her the empty food tray, "Put this inside. Your bed will be on the left." He looked down to the ground, itching to make the jump again. "Don't step on the Prince on your way in. He's sleeping on the floor."

"Uh, ok. What are you going to do?"

"Keep guard. Someone has to be ready if you fall down the ladder again."

Any brownie points he just gained… lost! she thought with a streak of anger.

She stormed inside then quickly remembered to tiptoe around the Prince's sleeping figure. She silently placed the tray on the wood counter, then made her way up the wood carved steps leading to one of the nest beds. She sank into the feather and cotton cushions and immediately felt relief.

Another day of a new world complete. She would do better tomorrow. She had to. Drifting off to sleep, Eloria thought of talking whales and singing angels.

CHAPTER 8

She heard large boots stomping towards her. The floor shook with each step. The room was dark, but she could make out Justine in the bed across the room. She slunk under her covers. A man as big as a giant crossed her line of sight and walked to Justine. He drew his hand into the air, preparing to strike.

Eloria tried to shout and warn her. Did Justine see him? Did she know what was coming? Eloria opened her mouth but no sound came out. He brought his hand down and she heard a bang. Another bang. He hit her in a rhythm that began to quicken. After a moment Eloria realized it wasn't a banging noise at all but the sound of wings flapping. Large wings.

She sat up, trying to scream out to Justine, to help somehow. The giant man turned on Eloria instead. She froze. It wasn't Justine in the bed, it was Sorrell. She was curled into a ball with tears streaming down her cheeks. Her face was red with… blood.

Eloria stared, horrified as the man came at her. He wrapped his hand around her throat and lifted her off the bed. She swung her fists to get free but her hands bounced off of him as if they couldn't make contact. The more she tried to hit him, the slower her arms moved. It was as if they were stuck in molasses. He lifted her off her bed and threw her into the air.

The wind whipped her hair about her face. She was falling. Something was on her wrist, squeezing it tightly. She looked up to see a faceless man with wings, holding her arm, trying to save her. Before she could see his face, her arm slipped out of his grasp and she was falling once again.

Gasping for air, Eloria bolted up, reaching for anything around her to keep her from falling. She cried out, tears streaming down her cheeks. The room was dark, she couldn't see anything. She heard someone screaming on the other side of the room.

It was a dream, only a dream. He's not here. He won't hurt you, she thought to herself as she struggled to breathe. *Who is screaming? Are we in danger? What if he's here!*

She was still gasping for air and struggling not to scream herself when candle light filled the room. Killian was shrugging on a tunic with one hand and had his sword drawn in the other. The Prince dashed up the steps to Sorrell's bed as Killian ran to Eloria's.

"What happened?" he shouted to her.

From below, two more candles burst into flame and the room filled with a soft glow. Eloria's hands were grasped, white knuckled, around a branch of the bed frame. She was still struggling for air, unable to answer Killian. She looked across the room to Sorrell. Her reflection-self was staring back at her with eyes that looked wild. They were filled with tears but none fell. For the first time, Eloria was afraid of Sorrell. She looked like a wild animal about to attack anything that moved.

"Was that you?" she gasped.

Eloria nodded. She felt sick to her stomach with guilt. The fear from the dream still tore at her thoughts. Sorrell had seen it all. Their minds had been linked even while they slept.

"Why didn't you do anything?" Sorrell growled. "How could you not *do* anything?"

Eloria shook her head unable to speak. Visions of that man flashed across her thoughts, his fist falling...

"Stop it!" Sorrell screamed at her. "Don't!"

Eloria tried to keep the memories from reappearing. *Think of something happy.* She saw the winged man, holding her midair. Sorrell gazed at Eloria then turned to the Prince. She looked at him curiously then back at Eloria. The wild look slowly left her eyes and her body relaxed.

"I don't understand," the Prince said helplessly. "What happened? Are you hurt?"

He reached out, as if to check Sorrell for injuries.

"It was a bad dream."

"A dream? Are you sure?"

She gave him a weak smile, "Sorry if we woke you."

Killian glanced back to Eloria with a distrustful eye.

"We were switching shifts," he said.

The Prince rolled his eyes and reluctantly walked back down the steps.

"We aren't switching shifts," he corrected. "Killian simply won't sleep unless someone is on watch. Therefore, I'm now on watch so that he can get rest."

"Such a selfless Prince," Sorrell joked.

He smiled at her comment, "It's madness. No one needs to keep watch when we're still in the Ceremonial Woods."

"Killian's the expert," Sorrell fell back into her cushions.

Killian opened his mouth to argue but the Prince held up a hand, hanging his head in defeat.

"I know, okay? I'm on watch."

The Prince walked out to the balcony as Killian began blowing out the candles. Eloria released the branch from her death grip and carefully found her way down the steps. Killian glanced her way but otherwise ignored her. She did likewise and made her way to the balcony. The Prince was sitting with his legs out in front of him, leaning back on his elbows.

"Sorry again," Eloria smiled.

"Hello," he kindly acknowledged her.

She sat a little ways from him and stared out at the forest. She breathed in the night air as deeply as she could, filling her lungs. Her body slowly stopped trembling as the memories seeped from her mind.

"So, bad dream?" the Prince asked, breaking the silence.

"Yeah…."

"It must have been pretty awful. Sorrell was ready for a battle," he laughed.

"It was."

He turned his attention back to the forest.

"Don't feel too bad. You can't help that there's a connection between you, and it's nothing you can control. After a certain age we stop dreaming. That is probably what surprised Sorrell the most."

"No, I don't think that was the surprise."

The Prince didn't question it but stared into the forest beyond.

"In the creation story, the people became corrupt when they began tampering with other worlds," Eloria said. "That's how evil entered their hearts and they turned away from your Creator? They became the Evil Ones."

The Prince lifted an eyebrow.

"Sorrell tampered with another world," Eloria let her words sink in. "She brought me here. In your mind, does that make her an Evil One? Is her heart corrupt?"

The Prince took his time to reply, choosing his words with care. "Evil entered their hearts when they wanted to be separated from the Creator. They tried to harness His power and be better, or what they thought was better. The Creator *is* the Creator. He has spoken all things into existence. He alone creates life and death. No man or woman could ever have that power. It is unfathomable to truly believe it could be within our reach. The Evil Ones became evil from looking into the other worlds and lusting after them. Their minds became jealous, greedy, and their hearts darkened."

He glanced into the room behind him where Killian and Sorrell slept.

"If Sorrell had evil intentions, the queen would never have allowed her to go free. She would've been taken to the king. You as well, I imagine." The Prince gazed dreamily up at the sky, "Sorrell's intentions were pure and good. She broke the rules, yes, but she did not do it out of selfish desire. The queen felt something change, the air in the forest was different."

"Like a disturbance in the force."

"She sent me to find out what was wrong. That was when I found you and Sorrell."

"What does Eloria mean?"

The Prince smiled, "I think you already know."

"Killian. He told me what he thought I wanted to hear but... there's something else. He won't call me by the name. Why not?"

The Prince had a playful look in his eye, "He didn't tell you everything because we had decided to wait."

"What is it? Am I an awesome, Xena warrior who can summon the Titans or something?"

"You say the oddest things. Your world must be interesting indeed."

"Not like here," she sighed.

"There is a prophecy about you, Eloria. I don't think you should hear all of it yet, but I suppose I can give you a piece of it tonight. Killian told you about the first Queen Transformed, the first Eloria?"

She nodded impatiently.

"The legend says that evil will rise again when someone arrives, claiming the name of Eloria. This person would be of another world and she would either destroy or save us."

Eloria was taken aback, "Killian said I already 'announced' the destruction of this world. Are you telling me I can help save it from the Evil Ones?"

"Of course," the Prince replied. "It all depends on who you fall in love with."

Eloria choked in surprise, "Excuse me?"

The Prince laughed, "I know, it sounds ridiculous. I thought it was a fable too until I saw what happened at the Choosing Ceremony. The legends say that when Eloria arrives, she cannot fall in love with anyone but the line of Seraphim or all will be lost. To sum up, say hello to your new life partner," the Prince extended his arms for a hug.

Eloria shook her head in disbelief, "You have got to be kidding. This adventure just turned into a chick flick?"

The Prince laughed, loud and deep, letting his arms drop. "Am I not suitable for you? Did the legends get it wrong?"

"No offense, your Highness, but I hope you have a brother because you...," she pointed a finger at him, waggling it up and down, "... are not my type."

"Excuse me," he said in mock offense, "What's wrong with me? I'm perfect! I'm the Seraphim Prince, thank you very much."

"As I said, no offense, but you're all... muscly and big," she looked at his huge biceps and cringed. "My sister Justine would go for guys like you, but not me. I'm more into the nerds. Football players are weird and bulky. Seriously, do you have any brothers?"

"I don't know what a fat-ball player is, but I am an only child. Well, Killian is adopted into my family. He could count as my brother."

Eloria made a gagging face, "Never mind. It's you and me after all."

"Honestly, I think your sense of man might be askew. I am perfection," he grinned comically. "Who wouldn't want to be united with me? My looks alone make every girl swoon."

Eloria admired his light mood. Her worry faded away.

"Your wings are handsome, but seriously, stay away from me with any romantic intentions," she joked.

"My wings?"

"Yeah, they're pretty cool. I mean, you were this hazy blob when I saw you but they looked awesome. I don't think they need to be hidden. Be yourself and everyone else can get over it."

"When did you see me?" he asked.

"When I first came here."

He looked at her bewildered, trying to make sense of what she was saying.

"It's alright," she laughed, "I don't think you saw me. I had just... gotten here. My vision was hazy and I couldn't even move. I only saw a blurry outline of a man with these huge glowing things and I guessed they were wings." Eloria extended her hands, trying to illustrate the size of the wings. "Anyway, you know what they look like. I wanted to say that they seem wonderful, and I'm sorry you have to hide them. I would still think of you the same way if I could see them now."

"I appreciate that. I hope that's true for others as well. It won't be long until I take my place beside my parents. My wings will be on display for all to see."

Eloria stood to go back to her bed, "If I'm not out of place in saying it, I think you'll make a great king. However, there's simply no way I can fall in love with you; the world would definitely come crashing down. Can I trust that you won't fall in love with me?"

"You have my word. But, strange as it may be, you are my type," he grinned.

"Back off, Hercules. Your superhero good looks are making me sick."

"Thank you, Eloria. You are too kind."

She slipped into the darkness, snuck past Killian wrapped in furs on the floor, and climbed into her nest bed. She was grateful for the Prince's light hearted mood, and knew he would be a good friend. If he wasn't worried about her destroying the world, then she wouldn't be either. All she had to do was not fall in love. With all the perfect people around her, she doubted that would be a problem. Confident that there would be no more dreams, she let her exhaustion wrap around her.

***

The Prince woke each of them a little after sunrise. He and Killian went out to get more supplies while Sorrell and Eloria washed up. When the girls were dressed, they refilled the water skins. Eloria helped Sorrell make an ointment from the contents of the tea kettle that the Prince had filled the night before. Sorrell stored it in her pocket then they made their way to the balcony. The boys were below, talking by the ladder.

"You can come up," Sorrell shouted to them. "We're done."

The Prince and Killian gracefully made their way up the ladder.

"Breakfast is below, see you in a bit!" the Prince said, pulling a cotton towel from a hook inside.

Sorrell went down the ladder with ease. Eloria turned to follow her but threw a weary glance in Killian's direction. He had his arms folded, leaning against the outside of the tree. He stared at her.

Eloria's cheeks flushed with embarrassment, "Are you going to watch?"

"Do I need to get a rope and a bucket?" he snapped at her, not trying to be funny. "You'd probably snap the rope anyway."

She shook her head with frustration and began her awkward climb. She already decided that if she couldn't get on the ladder in ten seconds or less then she would fall from embarrassment. Anything would be better than putting up with Killian's disapproving looks. Luckily her foot found the slot of wood immediately and she reached out to hold the rope.

Success! She shot Killian a smug glare and made her way down.

At the bottom, their packs were laid out with rolls of animal fur and blankets attached. Killian's sword and a few other weapons lay next to his pack as well as a bow and sword next to the Prince's. Sorrell went straight to her pack to place the ointment inside. She began putting her small knives and bow in place on her person. Eloria looked at her bag, checking out the furs. She could already tell that it meant extra weight to carry for the day.

"We'll be leaving the guest houses for a while," Sorrell said. "The blankets are for sleeping on the ground."

"Oh lovely."

"There should be a pair of gloves in your pack, go ahead and pull them out."

Eloria flipped open the cover to her bag. Sitting perfectly on top of her clothes was a piece of bread and a small stem of grapes.

Killian, she thought with a sigh.

She snatched them up and quickly pulled out the pair of gloves. Sorrell had moved on to the tray of food a little ways away so Eloria took a bite of her roll. It was slightly warm in the center which told her it wasn't leftover from last night. She popped the grapes in her mouth then returned the remaining half of the roll to her pack, saving it for later.

She plopped down next to Sorrell and began lacing up her boots.

"We need to talk about the dream," Sorrell said as she scooped the pit out of her peach. "Why couldn't you fight back?"

Eloria shrugged, trying not to think about it, "For some reason I can never hit people in my dreams. There are times when I'm being kidnapped or attacked, but I can't do anything. It's like something is holding my arms and legs back."

Sorrell nodded, "I've heard of it happening before but I had never experienced it myself."

"When I saw you on the bed after he hit you, what perspective did you have?"

"I saw it from your eyes. When you saw me on the bed, I was looking at myself too."

Eloria felt relieved. She had worried that perhaps Sorrell had seen the dream from a different perspective than her own.

"Today you will begin learning how to fight. If you can't hit someone in a dream it is because you haven't hit anyone in reality. You are afraid of pain?"

"Of course, who isn't?" Eloria answered.

She took a bite of her peach, "Alright, hit me."

Eloria wondered if she had gone crazy, "I'm not going to hit you!"

"Why not?"

"Why would I? It's ridiculous," she scoffed.

"Eloria, you have to be strong in this world. If you cannot fight then you cannot survive. That starts with hitting someone. It may not be nice, but that's the way it is. Put your gloves on."

Eloria stayed put, shaking her head, "I'm sorry, but your way is stupid. If some bad guy comes running up to me then I'll hit him if I have to, but I am not going to hit you for no reason."

Sorrell started bouncing back and forth on her toes like a boxer. She put her fists up by her chin and punched into the air.

Eloria smiled but didn't move. "I'm not doing it."

Sorrel kept bouncing and punching. "It's not like you could hurt me, your tiny little muscles would only give me goosebumps at best."

Eloria laughed and watched as Sorrell made moves that resembled kickboxing.

The Prince climbed down the ladder, watching them curiously. "What's going on?"

"Eloria," Sorrel said, kicking her foot above her head, "Has never hit anyone. And she's afraid of pain."

The Prince looked at her in disbelief, "Really? Not even as a child?"

She shook her head, laughing as Sorrell threw a punch his way. The Prince caught her fist and threw it towards the ground. Sorrell giggled and continued jabbing the air.

"Hey!" Sorrell shouted excitedly, "Hit the Prince! He's huge and full of muscle. There's no possible way you could feel bad about hitting him. Nothing that *you* do could hurt him."

Eloria stood, "Fine, but don't send me to prison for knocking out a member of the Royal Family."

He laughed, "Hit me wherever, but not my face. Have to keep that looking pretty."

She gave him a light tap with her fist into his chest.

"Well she knows how to make a fist, that's a start," he looked at her hand pathetically. "Seriously, hit me."

"I did! Can't you let it go? I'm not going to hurt anyone alright? Besides, it's not like hitting either of you would really do anything."

Sorrell bounced towards her with a smile. "What if I hit you first? Then you have to hit me back, to make it even. You'll begin learning how to harness pain and how to fight back."

She shook her head.

"Eloria, you have to learn and this is how we do it. In our apprenticeships, if we wouldn't do it willingly, our Master would get us angry until we harnessed it into an attack. It's part of the training that we all went through."

"That's great for you," Eloria said sarcastically, "But I'm not doing it. Even if you do hit me."

"Well I'm not going to hit Eloria," the Prince laughed.

"I will," a voice said from behind her.

CHAPTER 9

Eloria turned to the voice. She saw Killian's face for a brief moment and then gasped. His fist slammed into her stomach so hard she swore a rock had been punched through. The wind was knocked out of her, and she began to crumple to the ground. Killian caught her before she hit the dirt. Her eyes watered with pain as she stared at the grass, trying not to throw up the bread and grapes she had just eaten. After a good long cough to get her breath, she pushed Killian away from her.

Sorrell had stopped bouncing and looked at Killian with disbelief. The Prince couldn't decide if he should laugh or be concerned, so he stood with his jaw hanging open.

Killian shrugged, "Someone had to do it."

"You stupid… idiotic… fracking skin job!" Eloria yelled. "What is wrong with you?!"

"Oh come on," Killian smirked, "We had to find someone you don't like." He grinned at the Prince, "How could you not think that was a good idea?"

The Prince looked at Eloria then back to Killian, "She's not from here so we were trying to take it slow. We thought that…"

Eloria stopped listening. She was confused enough by Killian's mixed signals. He was rude all day then nice by giving her food. Hot and cold, back and forth. Now throwing a punch?

She was brimming with anger and decided to take advantage of the situation. The Prince and Killian were arguing back and forth. Eloria had never hit anyone, but she had no problem with tackling. She took a deep breath and lunged.

She caught him around the waist, knocking him to the ground. She lost her balance and rolled away, but hurried to her feet the moment she gained control. Without thinking, she threw a punch at him. Killian had already rolled into a low crouch and he easily leaned away from her fist. Grabbing her wrist, he pulled her up in one smooth motion. He moved as if it were a dance instead of a fight. Eloria swung with her other arm and caught him in the side. To her disappointment, Killian hardly seemed to notice the hit. He took the wrist he was holding and placed it against his ribs.

"Here," he said. "Hit me here."

She used her other fist and threw a swing at his face. He ducked easily away and grabbed that arm with his free hand. Though she struggled against his grip, he hardly seemed to notice her efforts.

"Hit me here or don't hit me at all," he said with frustration, tapping her fist against his ribs.

Eloria didn't care anymore. She wanted to hurt him. She pulled back her fist from his body and jabbed him with it. He didn't let go of her wrist, but he didn't soften the blow either. He let her hit him as hard as she wanted. She felt her knuckles push into his body and pain surged through her fingers. He grunted and flexed his body against the blow so that the force wouldn't move him. She pulled away and he released her. She immediately cradled her left hand, the knuckles throbbing from the hard contact.

"That was interesting," he smirked.

"Don't talk to me," she spat.

"You really tried to hit me, that was sweet."

Maybe one more, Eloria thought.

She balled up her fist. To her surprise, the final effort caught him off guard. She clocked him square in the jaw. His face slid off her knuckles and he stumbled away. Eloria cried out in pain. She fell to her knees, holding her hands out in front of her. She looked at her punching hand in horror as she saw that one finger was strongly misshapen.

Sorrell stood frozen in place.

The Prince was jumping up and down, laughing, "She hit you! Killian, she actually hit you!"

Killian rubbed his jaw with an annoyed expression.

"Yeah, I know," he snapped.

The Prince began cheering. Killian knelt in front of Eloria. He slowly reached for her hand.

"No!" she gasped as tears streamed down her face.

It hurt so badly. Killian looked down at her, feeling sorry now for what he had done.

"If you promise to trust me, and not hate me, I promise to make the pain go away."

Her anger had subsided the moment she sucker punched him. She was confused by him and certainly didn't like him, but hate? Embarrassed for crying, but overwhelmed by the pain, she nodded.

"I don't hate you," she whispered.

"Sorrell, get the ointment," he ordered.

He gently turned Eloria's hand so the palms faced the ground. Sorrell knelt next to them with the small container.

"You broke your finger," Killian assessed, "but the pain will go away quickly enough. Take a deep breath. It hurts, but the pain will end. You have to always remember that the pain goes away. Don't let it define you. This is not how your life will remain. Pain is nothing to fear, only something to grow from."

He popped her finger back into place and Sorrell quickly spread the ointment over both of Eloria's hands. Immediate relief spread through her hands. Within seconds, all pain was gone.

"Thank you," Eloria gasped.

"You did great," Sorrel smiled.

Killian walked away, picking up his weapons and pack. The Prince did the same and Sorrell quickly helped Eloria up. They grabbed their bags and followed after Killian.

"Will it always be like this?" Eloria asked.

"Once you learn to do it right, you shouldn't break any fingers."

"No, I mean the way we start to leave without anyone saying 'it's time to go.' What if I wasn't ready?"

Sorrell laughed and they began their trek through the woods. All day they walked and all day Sorrell and the Prince explained the basics of fighting and the proper ways for Eloria to use her body for different techniques. They didn't stop for lunch but ate as they walked. Killian kept them at a brisk pace and navigated their way among the trees. Despite their continuous exercise, no one perspired or got too warm. Eloria wondered how the Prince, with so much more body mass than his companions, didn't generate more body heat than the rest of them. She chalked it up to him being angel-like.

They did not stop until the sun had set, at which point Eloria was exhausted both mentally and physically. She did her best to remember everything they had taught her, but it was all so foreign to what she was used to learning. Standard text books on math and grammar was a little different than knowing when to use your palm to break someone's nose or a fist to damage an organ.

Killian scouted out a flat patch of earth for them to sleep on and they unrolled their blankets. To Eloria's surprise they didn't light a fire since it wasn't cold and they had no other purpose for it. She learned that there was a strategic pattern that they must use in making camp. When they slept, their heads had to be at the center, near one another with their feet pointing towards the open forest around them. They were spread out enough to feel a sort of privacy, but their blankets were evenly spaced. Once they had their blankets and furs laid out, each of them went to sleep except for Killian. He had declared first watch and stationed himself by a small tree not too far from his own sleeping spot.

Eloria tried to sleep but despite her exhaustion, she couldn't get comfortable on the hard ground. She tried reviewing everything she had learned but gave up, not being able to keep her mind from wandering. She looked over at Sorrell and saw her slow, steady breathing. Eloria wished she could join her in peaceful unconsciousness. A rock or hard clump of some kind poked into her side. She sighed and turned over, trying to find a comfortable place. She finally settled and gazed into the forest ahead of her.

Killian sat on a fallen limb with his back to her. His wild, dark hair swayed in the breeze. His cotton tunic blew across his back like ripples of water. With the moonlight shining down, Eloria thought she could see his body beneath the fabric. His shoulder blades stuck out as if he were stretching. He glanced towards her and she quickly closed her eyes, pretending to be asleep. She waited for a while before peeking out again.

Killian was standing, staring out into the forest. He drew his sword from its sheath. He positioned his feet and bent a knee while bringing up his sword, elbow back by his ear. The sword was parallel to the ground and gleamed in the moonlight. He held the position for what seemed like minutes. Eloria could see his chest rising and falling, breathing in the night. He began whispering to himself. She strained to make out his words but he was too far away. She wished she could read lips, but even that seemed to be a long shot.

Without hesitation, Killian began a succession of different movements. He fought against an invisible enemy, whispering all the while. He moved so quickly and smoothly that Eloria could barely keep up with his motions. His feet moved but he never crunched a leaf or snapped a twig. The forest remained silent with only the occasional hoot of an owl. There was a slight *whoosh* as his sword cut through the air. His feet danced with the rehearsed choreography. His muscles flexed with each motion and his posture remained perfect. His eyes were focused and sharp. After a while, Eloria drifted off watching him fight his way through the forest around them.

The next day began before sunrise. Sorrell shook Eloria's shoulder in a gentle greeting.

"Time to practice," she said cheerfully.

The Prince handed Eloria some kale leaves and a water skin. She grimaced as she stuck the leaves in her mouth, chewing quickly. Killian approached her next, with his sword in hand.

"We will scrimmage every morning before the sun rises. You need to learn how to handle yourself and your weapon without thinking. Your body must learn to move on its own, do you understand?"

Eloria yawned.

Killian began explaining to her the stretches and warmups she had to do each day. Sorrell joined them to help Eloria with proper form. After thoroughly teaching the stretches, Killian progressed with hand to hand combat. Sorrell assisted by correcting her form as she went. She would rotate her hips or adjust the angle of her arm. Finally, Killian went over the basics of how to care for weapons and properly hold a sword. After that, they packed up and went on their way.

Killian led the group once again, his part in teaching over for the day. The Prince and Sorrell continued to explain theory and techniques of fighting. They also began pointing out the different types of trees and vegetation as they walked. They marked how each was different from the others and what its purpose was. All day this continued and after the sun set, they made camp once again. Eloria spent each night reviewing everything she had learned. She would fall asleep watching Killian whisper to himself from a distance while he fought his invisible enemy.

For days they continued this pattern. Wakeup, train, walk and learn, sleep. No path guided them, only trees. After a few days, Eloria noticed that the trees had grown smaller. They resembled the trees she knew from back home and their canopies didn't stretch quite as high. Everything they ate was from the vegetation around them. Mostly berries and leaves, they could eat their fill but it lacked in variety. Killian always had them make camp a short distance from a stream. They were able to wash and refill their water skins. To Eloria's joy, it was pure water with no lemon juice squeezed in.

After a time, Eloria stopped counting the days. All she knew was that they were headed to the Ocean Region. After that it would simply be more traveling through the forest. So the days wore on. Her body became stronger and her mind was filled with knowledge. She began to notice muscle where there hadn't been any before and some of her fat was starting to burn away. She knew it was from the lack of carbs and sweets that her diet had consisted of back home. Justine had always told her to eat more green food if she wanted to get rid of her muffin top. For the first time, she regretting not listening to her sister's advice.

One day, Sorrell pointed out webs of moss hanging from the trees above them. They were getting closer to the ocean. The pines began to disappear and the moss covered trees took their place. The air grew warmer but the breeze also grew cooler, maintaining a perfect temperature wherever they went. Here and there, they even spotted something that resembled a palm tree with fruits hanging high above.

When they passed by such a tree, the Prince shimmied up with ease to cut down the fruit. It had an outer shell similar to a coconut but the inside was a purple and blue grapefruit. That night, Eloria ate what the Prince called 'fruit meat' and drank juice from the splintered shell around it. It was tangy and bitter, but she was happy to have something in her mouth besides leaves.

As they laid to sleep one night, and Killian took his usual spot away from camp, Eloria leaned over to Sorrell.

"I've been watching Killian practice his sword at night," she admitted. "He does this weird thing where he talks to himself. Have you ever noticed that?"

"Of course. We all do it," she shrugged.

"Obviously everyone talks to themselves but he does it for a really long time," Eloria explained.

"He isn't talking to himself," Sorrell giggled. "He's talking to his Creator."

"Why would he do that? If it's God then can't he just.... hear his thoughts?"

"Well... I can hear your thoughts but I still prefer you say them out loud. Wouldn't you? When the Creator spoke, that is how all things began, so we speak to Him as well. There is power in spoken word. Once something is said, it comes alive. It cannot be taken back or destroyed."

Eloria contemplated what she said.

"But the Creator is like... really old. Isn't He more of a legend?"

"Like you?" Sorrell lifted an eyebrow. "Wasn't Eloria a legend? Yet here you are. Many in this world think as you do, that the Creator is simply an old story or legend made up to explain the beginning of the world. They still live by the law but they do not know Him. The three of us," Sorrell nodded to Killian and the Prince, "We have seen things."

"What sort of things?"

"As part of the Queen's House I had to do extra training at the House of the Guard. Our Houses overlap sometimes and my position required me to understand more advanced combat. The Prince chose a group of us, both from the Guard and the Queen's

House, to travel with him to the outer lands. There were rumors that the Evil Ones had been attacking villages that bordered the Barren Desert. The king thought they were up to something new, something that we hadn't seen before.

"So we journeyed to a village that we heard had been hit hardest. When we arrived, there were dead bodies but all of the houses were empty of any other people. Either the villagers had fled or they were taken by the Evil Ones. When we looked around for evidence of which, we found… strange creatures hiding among the shadows and in the rafters. They were beasts and animals, deformed and vile things." Sorrell shivered as she remembered. "I can't really describe them. They were… changed by potions and transfigured. They struck fear into our hearts and minds the closer we got to them. All we knew was that they had been turned into something new. Something we had never seen before. The beasts, who had intelligence, spoke to us when we captured them. They told the Prince that they would destroy the line of Seraphim, that the Creator was wrong to have blessed him and not the others. The beasts cursed the Creator and cried out in hate against Him. After that day, we called them the Deformed.

"I had never given much thought to the Creator. To me He was only a story too. But that day, when the deformed beast spoke of Him, it spoke with no doubt of the Creator's existence. That's when I knew He was real. If the vilest creations of this world held a purpose of nothing more than to hate the Creator, how could He not exist? I have spoken to the Creator ever since, trying to know Him, and let Him know me, better."

Eloria thought about her words. "In my world there are many different religions."

"What is religion?" Sorrell asked.

"It's…," Eloria had never thought of how to explain it, "Well there are different beliefs in different creators and histories. Some people believe in one kind of creator and some people believe in another kind."

"How do your people know which is the true Creator?"

"We don't know. We've fought many wars trying to prove one religion better than another. So many people believe different things. But there is one book, the Bible, that's been around the longest, supposedly. My mom went to a Christian church when she was a little girl. She tried making me go on special holidays and stuff too. There's a verse... er there's a line in it that says 'If you believe in the one true God that's good, but even the demons believe that and they tremble in terror.' It was something like that."

"'Demons believe...'" Sorrell whispered. "These creatures we found, they would be your demons I think. It means that it's not enough to only believe in the Creator, but one must also know Him."

Eloria nodded, "It sounds like it. Does your Creator ever talk back to you?"

"No, He only speaks to us through His angels now. The Prince and Killian have seen the angels but they do not speak of it. I think their first encounter with an angel is when they truly believed."

"What happened to the creatures that you found in the village, the Deformed?" Eloria asked.

"We killed them," Sorrell said bluntly, looking away. "They would have harmed others and we couldn't allow that. It is terrible what the Evil Ones did to them. They took beasts that were good and turned them against their purpose. They made them into weapons and warped their minds and bodies."

Sorrell let her mind drift away, the memories flashing before her.

"It rained that day. It was the first time I had ever seen the Prince cry. Killian too for that matter," she thought aloud. "The Prince's tears caused clouds to cover the sun and water fell upon the earth. He was devastated by what we had seen. He cried for the lives we had lost, and for the beasts that had been corrupted. The rain did not stop until he slept."

"He made it rain?"

"The Royal Family has influence over the weather, remember? Have you seen anything but sun since you arrived?"

"I hadn't thought about it but no, I haven't."

"They can control the winds and the weather. It rains when they cry, and it storms in their wrath."

"I wonder what would make it snow…," Eloria thought.

Sorrell went to her furs. As she laid down she said, "The Creator still speaks to us in different ways. At my Choosing Ceremony, He gave me the name Sorrell. I could think of nothing else but that name, even though I had never heard it before that night."

"That happened to me too," Eloria said.

Sorrell nodded, "That was the Creator. He still guides us, in subtle ways. If you find yourself watching Killian again, remember that his conversation is his own. It's between him and his Creator. Don't try to listen in, it's not meant for you."

CHAPTER 10

A twig snapped and Killian glanced back. The Prince stumbled toward his Guard.

"My turn," he mumbled, still half asleep.

Killian couldn't help but smile as the Prince plopped down next to him.

"Perhaps I should stay with you for a little while," Killian said, "At least until you are aware of yourself."

"At your leisure."

They sat listening to the stream gurgle a little ways ahead of them. Though it had been a few hours, Killian's arms were still tired from his sword play earlier, and his thoughts still lingered on his conversation with the Creator.

"So…," the Prince groaned, stretching out his arms and legs. "What are we going to do about Eloria?"

Killian rolled his eyes.

"Yeah, me too," the Prince sighed. "We are at the ocean's border and tomorrow we enter back into Community. Everyone knows the legend. They're going to be watching me."

"By 'me' are you referring to your arranged marriage to Eloria?" Killian clarified.

The Prince shrugged, "She's not interested and that is fine by me. She's a great girl, and she fits into our little group, but there's nothing but camaraderie between us. Besides, I don't want to give Sorrell the wrong idea."

"I know you don't. Honestly, I don't think you are giving her any ideas right now, that's the problem. You've got to do something or the line of Seraphim dies out with you," Killian joked.

"I'm serious, Killian," the Prince said. "Anyone who believes the prophecies about Eloria will be expecting something between us. I'm not sure how to play this one out."

Killian saw the worry on his face.

"Sorrell knows the prophecy of Eloria, maybe better than us by now. Don't forget that she's the one who brought her here," Killian pointed out. "It shouldn't be any surprise to her if Eloria falls in love with the prince."

"So do I forget about Sorrell? I do not believe the prophecy determines our fate but I do not want to cause the people to be afraid. Many of them have been waiting for the time of Eloria to arrive," the Prince sighed, his breath shaking ever so slightly.

"Be yourself. It's no one else's business. They can make whatever assumptions they want to. You can fall in love with whoever you want to."

"What about you?" the Prince turned his broad shoulders in Killian's direction.

"What about me?

"You still won't say her name. Eloria."

Killian shivered when the Prince said it.

"I saw you sneaking food into her satchel back when we were in the Ceremonial Woods. You seem to enjoy yourself during training each morning. I know they can't see it, but I do. You've agreed that Sorrell is off the table, so that leaves one woman."

"There's not one woman left, there's a whole world of women out there. Besides, she's weak and lazy and slow to learn. Not my type."

"Is that why you are trying so hard to avoid her?" the Prince asked with a grin.

"She's strange."

"Strange isn't a bad thing," the Prince pointed out.

Killian leaned back on his elbows. The Prince watched him, wondering what he really thought. Killian had always been quiet about his thoughts and kept to himself. Even after they had Chosen each other, to protect one another and stay together as brothers, it still took the Prince a long time to get anything substantial from Killian.

"I think that if I fell in love with her, the world would certainly come crashing down." Killian plucked a piece of grass from the earth and studied it between his fingers.

"That's funny. She said almost the same thing about me. However, I think her meaning was a bit different than yours."

Killian looked up to see his friend grinning ear to ear at him. He threw a handful of grass at him. "Go splash some water on your face. You clearly need to wake up."

The Prince shrugged, still smiling, and clambered to his feet. Killian walked to his own bed. He glanced at Eloria as he passed by. She slept peacefully with her hair unfurled behind her. Though he tried to ignore it, something seemed different about her. He thought she looked stronger and at the same time, more vulnerable. He hadn't noticed it before, but her skin looked healthier. Not pale and hollow like when she had first arrived. Her hands were blistered from being new to combat. Her hair had gained a tint of red from being in the sun. It reminded him of the queen's strawberry-blonde hair.

He climbed under his furs, upset with himself for noticing her the way that he did.

"Your will be done, Creator," Killian closed his eyes.

***

125

Eloria woke with a start. She shot up from her blankets, eyes burning as she looked around the forest with fear. The sky was a pale pink with the sun sitting on the horizon, barely risen. The stream curdled but nothing else seemed to move. Eloria noticed there was no breeze, the leaves among the trees stood oddly quiet.

"Sorrell!" she whispered urgently.

Reaching over to Sorrell's bed, she pressed on the blankets only to find it empty. She looked to the next bed over. The furs were carelessly cast aside as if its tenant left in a rush. Sorrell and the Prince were gone.

Killian still lay asleep under his furs. His chest rose and fell gently beneath the blankets. Eloria glanced around the forest, looking for what had woken her. She crawled out of her warm bed and inched her way to Killian. Her eyes scanned the tress with every breath.

"Killian," she whispered, placing a hand on his back. His eyes opened. Before she could blink, he rolled into a low crouch, drawing his sword out to his side. The blankets slid quietly off his back as his eyes jumped from tree to tree around them.

"Whoa!" Eloria exclaimed, forgetting to keep her voice down.

She was still on her hands and knees, with one hand extended towards him. She quickly dropped it, feeling her cheeks flush with embarrassment.

"I heard something," she whispered.

He nodded once, still watching the trees. A deep, throbbing sound vibrated the air around them. An animal growled from a distance away. The noise reverberated through Eloria's body and for the first time since arriving in the new world, she felt cold. Goosebumps covered her arms and she began to shiver uncontrollably. The cold seeped into her bones and they began to ache in pain. When the noise from the forest ceased, the cold pain in her body grew.

126

"Look at me," Killian whispered, his eyes turning to hers.

"What's happening?" she replied through chattering teeth.

He smiled, even though the girl's eyes were full of fear. His deep green gaze pierced through her like it had so many times before. There was something new about his look.

"Do not be afraid," he said, not caring to whisper anymore. "Pain is nothing to be afraid of; it fades. They were created to fear, we were not."

"Who is they?"

Killian stood and gave his sword a large flourish. He paced in a wide circle around her, his eyes always searching the forest. His head snapped when he caught movement behind a tree. Eloria quickly turned to follow his gaze. There was something dark lingering, too far off for her to see. Her body shook with cold and fear.

"Eloria," Killian said.

Warmth ran through her veins at the sound of him speaking her name. She remembered the sun and its warm light. She savored the musical quality of his voice. The cold began to seep away.

"Try not to be afraid," he stepped between her and the dark shape.

The dark creature moved, slowly circling nearer to its prey. Killian followed its movements, keeping himself between Eloria and the beast. She tried to peer around him, to get a better look, but it was too dim without the sunrise and the creature was far enough away that she couldn't make it out.

"If I die here, what happens to me back home?" she asked. "Before, when Sorrell tried bringing me through, I sort of passed out. I think if I die now, I end up back on the floor of my bedroom."

Killian didn't answer, only followed the beasts movements. It was closer now, close enough that Eloria could see it clearly. A strange, misshapen bear stood amongst the morning fog. Its arms were too long for its body. Bones jutted out of its hide as if it hadn't eaten in weeks. Instead of thick, dark fur it wore a pale grey coat with balding patches. The skin looked yellow as if it were diseased. Another snarl rippled through the forest and saliva dripped from its mouth. She understood now why they had been named the Deformed.

"Killian...," she whispered. "Killian, I don't want to go back."

"You won't," he said.

The Deformed let out another deep, low growl that was more furious than the last. Killian moved as the monster did, charging at one another through the thin trees. With his sword extended at his side, Killian sprinted headlong to the Deformed. Before they reached one another, he veered and swung his blade across its side. Blue blood splattered across the ground. It bubbled and hissed like acid, eating away at whatever it touched.

The bear snapped its jaws at him, turning back in his direction. The creature moved faster than it appeared, throwing a long, tanned paw at his foe. Killian knocked it aside then suffered it another blow. It retracted away from him with a nasty hiss. They circled each other, both waiting for the next strike.

"Eloria!" Sorrell's voice shouted out behind her. She and the Prince were running their direction from the opposite side of the woods. Sorrell's bow was notched in her hands and the Prince ran alongside her with two short swords. He looked like a statue of Achilles. His arms bulged as he flexed. The Prince looked excited for a fight.

"My knives, Eloria!" he shouted to her. "Pick up a knife!"

The Deformed's attention was diverted. It dodged Killian's blade and swung its claw, catching him in the chest and knocking him into a tree. The creature immediately set its sights on Eloria.

She locked eyes with the creature's red pupils and froze. It ran for her, gnashing its teeth and bleeding onto the earth below. Sorrell shot two arrows into its shoulder but it neither slowed nor stopped. Eloria snapped her eyes away from the beast and searched for the Prince's knives. She found one, peaking out from under his leather pack. She gripped it the way Sorrell had taught her. Sorrell continued firing arrows into the creature but they were too far away. Eloria knew no one would reach her in time.

The sky lit up like midday. A bolt of lightening ran across it and struck the ground, barely missing the deformed creature as it ran. Sorrell cried out in fear. She stumbled back, staring up at the clouds that had appeared above them. The Prince gained speed, his arms pumping furiously at his sides. Killian ran to Eloria as well, faster than the Prince because of his light figure. Thunder shook the ground and rumbled through the air. The earth beneath their feet trembled and Eloria struggled to keep her balance.

Another bolt of lightning flashed down, striking the earth directly between her and the creature. She could see the static electricity spread into tiny lines before they withdrew back to the clouds. It disappeared into the sky. Eloria saw the bear, leaping through the air towards her.

The Deformed landed two feet from her. It moved swiftly, standing on its back paws and swinging a large claw. She managed to duck the first blow and raised her knife to the second. She felt the blade slide into its skin. Acidic blood spilled over the knife and down her arm. Eloria lost all feeling as the blood bubbled and hissed against her skin. The blade dropped from her hand and she screamed out in pain. Thunder rumbled through the sky and the ground shook, harder than before. She lost her balance and fell to the blood soaked dirt.

The Prince and Killian reached the Deformed at the same time. Killian leapt into the air, moving his sword to strike. The Prince lunged, his blade thrust forward. With a loud scream, the creature was finished. Killian knelt on the bear's back, his sword sunk to the hilt. The Prince withdrew his own blades from its chest. He wiped them against the ground to clean off the boiling blood.

Killian gave him a curt nod, both their chests heaving. Killian removed his sword from the carcass and lightly kicked off its hide, backflipping to the ground.

"Eloria," the Prince hurried to her. "Are you alright?"

She cradling her arm tenderly, "My arm. It's burning."

She held it out for him to see as she held back tears. Her sleeve had burned away and the skin was blistering. A blue-red slime dripped from the wound.

"Sorrell, get the ointment," he shouted. "Did it say anything to you?"

"What do you mean?"

"The creature, did it say anything to you?"

She looked back at it, confused. "It growled at us."

"Where were you?" Killian chided the Prince.

"Sorrell was on watch and thought she heard something. We decided to run the perimeter."

"You should have woken me," Killian spat angrily. "If the girl hadn't stirred from the fear it might have gotten her."

Eloria glanced up in disgust, forgetting her pain. "Excuse me, but I have a name."

"Killian you could have killed that thing with a hunting dagger if you wanted to. You know that as well as I. Don't act as if you were actually in danger."

"We put her in danger by splitting up. This is not about *my* skill. It's about *her* lacking any. She doesn't learn! That thing would have killed her!"

The Prince's eyebrows furrowed and his eyes narrowed. Thunder rumbled through the sky as he stood against Killian.

"We did what we thought was best. You may be a Guard but do not make the mistake of thinking I don't know what I'm doing. The Deformed is dead with little injury. Leave it be."

Lightening lit the clouds above them. Killian and the Prince glared at one another before the Prince finally knelt back down to Eloria.

"What happened to you?" Killian scoffed as Sorrell approached them with the ointment.

"Leave it be, Killian!" the Prince said angrily.

Sorrell looked down with shame, "I've never seen the lightening before, only heard about it in the stories. I'm sorry. I thought it might be Evil's magic, like the Deformed."

"It's alright," the Prince placed a hand on her shoulder. "There's a reason it belongs with my anger."

Sorrell spread the ointment across Eloria's arm and the blisters disappeared along with the pain.

"You were angry this time?" Eloria wondered. "Why weren't you sad?"

The Prince glanced at Killian but Sorrell was the one who spoke.

"I told her of the creatures. I also mentioned the rain."

"The first time I saw them," the Prince explained, "it was terrible. When we realized what had been done to the beasts and animals… none of us could believe it. The evil that was inflicted on these poor creatures was a tragedy. We have seen them many times since then but never past the mountains. It is strange that it was able to get this far."

Killian spoke, "He told me that rumor of the second Transformed had reached them. They are seeking out the Prince and his new companion."

"We need to hurry to the ocean. We can send word to the king and queen from there."

The sky began to clear and the sun rose above the horizon. When everyone had their furs tied and packs on, they walked in the direction of the ocean, leaving the deformed carcass behind them.

"By the way," a smile spread over the Prince's face. "Good morning, everyone! Happy to see you alive this fine day."

The sun was past mid-sky when they left the forest behind them. The constant surrounding of trees faded away and they stepped onto a white, sandy beach. Eloria took a long, deep breath. She hadn't been near the ocean since she was a small child. She had almost forgotten the smell of the sea. The sun beat down on them and the waves gurgled as they slid over the beach. Eloria's heart felt like it was going to burst from happiness.

"I must have brought us further down than I thought," Killian gazed down the stretch of sand.

"And that is why you're only a Guard," Sorrell teased.

She dropped her pack and ran into the ocean water. The Prince watched her, chuckling in his low voice. Eloria and the Prince shared a glance then ran after Sorrell. The water was surprisingly warm as she sprinted across the rolling waves. She ran as quickly as her sore muscles would allow, immediately tasting salt as water splashed across her lips. She ran across the shoreline, forgetting all of her worries from the morning.

Sorrell and the Prince ran ahead of her, kicking water at one another as they laughed merrily. Eloria unlaced her boots to feel the sand squish between her toes. She lazily walked through the shallow waves. The wind whipped her hair around her face. She let herself fall into the soft, warm sand.

"Wow!" she giggled.

Killian's shadow fell across her face. "What's wrong with you?"

"Nothing," she said. "It's freaking awesome! I haven't seen the ocean in years."

"Is the water effecting you? The way our magic did at the Choosing Ceremony?"

Eloria frowned, shielding her eyes to get a better look at him. "Don't you ever have fun? Besides doing it at my expense?"

He shrugged and sat next to her.

"Wouldn't it be amazing to see a whale jumping? Do you think there are any around here?"

"They don't come this close to shore. I doubt you'll see one."

"Buzzkill," she whined.

Further down the beach, she noticed a rocky peninsula with a building at the end. She wondered if they had light houses in this world. Closing her eyes, she lay in the sand, listening to Sorrell and the Prince's laughter. They were still further down, throwing water and sand at one another. Seagulls cawed above them. Eloria began humming a random melody. After a little while she dozed off, fading in and out of consciousness.

"They're here," she heard Killian say.

Opening her eyes, she was surprised to see the sun hanging low in the sky with purple streaks cutting across the blue horizon. Killian had taken his boots off and they sat neatly beside him. His pack lay against him as a backrest. Eloria looked down the stretch of sand to see a large group of people speaking with the Prince and Sorrell. They bowed to him the same way Sorrell had the first night Eloria came to the forest.

"Who are they?"

"People of the Ocean. Mostly those from the House of Beasts and Healers. This is their origin place. Gather your things," Killian said as he picked up the Prince's belongings as well as his own.

Eloria did as he said and scooped up Sorrell's pack and bow. When they reached their companions, Killian bowed to an elderly man at the front of the clan. He wore a long white braid and had tanned, leathery skin. He looked very fit for his age and his eyes matched the sea-foam green of the ocean. Eloria took her usual place beside Sorrell. Both she and the Prince were still dripping wet but the smiles had faded from their mouths. As Eloria approached, all eyes followed her.

"The queen sent a messenger ahead of you. Apparently the great Eloria has come to our world at last," the man said to the Prince.

"She has."

"The rumors have spread since the night of the Choosing Ceremony. Many are curious to see the girl who Chose the name of the first Queen Transformed." The man cast a leery eye towards Eloria. "We are honored to help her apprentice among our Houses."

"We encountered a troubling foe in the forest on our journey here. I need to contact my family as quickly as I can," the Prince said.

The old man nodded, "We are happy to help the Prince in any way. A feast is being prepared in your honor. In a few short days we shall celebrate in the halls of Seraphim and Eloria!"

The Prince winced at the old man's last words but no one noticed. The crowd swarmed around the four of them. They offered baskets of fruit and fish, welcoming them to their Houses. People took their satchels from them and Eloria noticed that Killian refused to hand over his sword.

Ever the paranoid protector, she thought.

Sorrell gave her a small nudge, apparently agreeing with her. They walked over a mile down the stretch of beach. Despite the hot sun, Eloria noticed that the breeze was ever present, cooling her skin and causing her hair to blow. They came upon a large village, filled with huts made of wood and reed. The roofs were constructed from palm leaves. Many structures didn't have walls, only supports and coverings. Beyond a throng of palm trees, Eloria saw a large mansion made of stone.

"The Healers' House," Sorrel said to her.

Further down still was the rocky peninsula that Eloria had seen earlier. At the very end was a sort of palace made of large rock as if it had grown from the very earth. Beside one of the castle towers, built high into the structure, was a glass dome. It looked out to the sea beyond. Eloria could only imagine the view it would provide. The glass glinted in the sun, acting as a beacon to any who caught its rays.

"That is the first palace, Kailani. It means 'sea and sky.' It was built by the first king, Seraphim, shortly after he met Eloria. He wanted to create a place where they could feel close to the Creator and where they could fly freely."

"It's beautiful," Eloria replied.

"Wait until you see inside."

"We can go in it?"

"Of course! That is where the feast will take place in a few nights. You are about to see a whole new style of Community," Sorrell winked. "The people of the Ocean Region love to lavish on the Royal Family. They throw large celebrations and feasts whenever the king or queen visit. The time we spent here as apprentices ended up being more like one big celebration. They wouldn't leave the Prince alone and he loved it."

"Don't remind me," the Prince said with a grin, clearly not bothered by all of the attention.

Everyone around them kept trying to ask questions. Eloria felt like she was Princess Leia walking amongst the Ewok. Although she knew they were trying to be welcoming, she had to keep pushing through people to keep up with Sorrell.

"Party island," Eloria said to herself, "this should be interesting."

"The House of Healers is going to provide us hospitality. We will dine with them then be left alone for the night. You will need your rest. We continue training again in the morning."

The crowd of people grew larger as they made their way to the House of Healers. When they reached the steps, leading to a giant archway, everyone waited while the old man and his guests made their way up. Sorrell took Eloria's arm and led her through the open arch into the main room. They heard a loud cheer rise from the crowd and turned back to look. The Prince was holding up a hand, waving to everyone on the beach. The people shouted greetings and words of welcome. When he held up his other hand, waving happily, they hollered more loudly. Killian grabbed the Prince by his collar and pulled him into the building.

You weren't kidding, Eloria thought.

"I could never joke about his love of affection," Sorrell smiled.

CHAPTER 11

Eloria admired the building around them. They stood on a marble floor with exotic flowers growing in large pots scattered throughout out room. The space was a gathering place for many different hallways that branched out in various directions. A grand staircase rose from the marble in front of them. There were chairs and couches made of what looked like drift wood with feathery cushions. Men and women strolled through the room, smiling kindly as they passed.

A woman approached them and bowed to the Prince. Like the others, she had tan skin and she wore a blue cotton dress.

"Good day. I am Vineeta. We have rooms prepared for you where your belongings have be taken. If you would follow me, I can take you to them so that you may change."

The woman led them up the staircase. They traveled through a long hall until she stopped at the last door. Opening it, she bowed again.

"This is the common room and there are separate sleeping and wash rooms for each of you," Vineeta said. "The Prince's room is here," she motioned towards what looked to be the grandest of all the doors. "Eloria may have the room next to his," she grinned.

"Thank you," the Prince said quickly, glancing to see Sorrell's reaction. "We appreciate your kind hospitality. Please send our gratitude on to your Masters."

He ushered her out, closing the door behind her.

Killian tossed a piece of half eaten fruit onto a chair and walked into one of the rooms, closing the door behind him. Sorrell took Eloria's hand and went into her designated room.

Inside was a large canopy bed with posts made from pale shells. There was a fireplace across from it and a small desk next to the window. From the window, they had a clear view of Kailani. Eloria could see a small path that led from the beach to its gates. Sorrell opened an elegantly carved chest that sat next to the bed.

"Put this on," she handed a dark blue dress to Eloria.

"Is it a formal dinner?"

"That will come later," Sorrell pulled out a dress for herself. "This is what most Healers wear. They are kind to provide us with so much. It is their custom to always change before the final meal of the day."

Eloria began undressing.

"We haven't talked about the House of Healers. What do they do exactly?"

"They are responsible for many things. They provide hospitality, look after the needs of those around them, and they study the art of healing and comfort. They help those with physical and emotional pain."

"Like a doctor or therapist?"

"They help people with loss after a loved one has died. They comfort children who worry. If you are injured in battle and need care, they know the most about saving lives and healing your wounds. They are the humblest of us all because they put everyone's needs above their own. It is said that when the Creator walked among us, He spent most of His time with the Healers."

Eloria nodded with understanding. Healers were the doctors and mothers of their society.

"This is their House but it is only for guests and apprentices," Sorrell continued. "The Healers themselves live in the small huts along the beach."

Sorrell helped Eloria lace up the back of her dress and vise versa. They brushed their hair with a small comb they found before leaving the room. The boys were already waiting for them. Also in blues, they wore light cotton shirts that buttoned up the front and long pants.

"No dress for you?" Sorrell joked as they entered the room.

The Prince smiled. "I asked for one but they said I had to try to humble myself. I can't be allowed to look better than everyone else."

Killian rolled his eyes. "Enough jokes. Let's go."

"Believe it or not, Killian fit in best with the Healers when we apprenticed," Sorrell quipped. "He never thought of himself, only wanted to make others feel better."

"With the way you both make fun, you are clearly made for each other," Killian shot back. The Prince glared at him. Eloria thought she saw a blush come over Sorrell's cheeks.

They followed him out of the room and down the corridor. When they entered the main hall, Eloria noticed a long table had been placed in the middle of the archway that led to the beach. Men and women in blue were setting trays of food and filling glass chalices. Others stood about in groups talking with one another. When they descended the stairs, everyone in the room turned and bowed to them. The Prince smiled and bowed in return. Vineeta appeared and escorted them to the table. As they walked across the lobby, everyone in the room fell into a line behind them.

Killian and Sorrell were given seats in the middle of the table and the Prince took the head seat. Eloria was escorted to his right hand side. She was grateful that she and the Prince had gotten to know each other well, otherwise the dinner may have been an awkward affair. It felt strange without the four of them close together. Since no one else seemed to mind she kept her thoughts to herself.

"They take the Eloria prophecy pretty seriously, huh?" she whispered to the Prince as they all sat.

"You have no idea," he grinned. "Just play along and no one has to know. We're only dooming the world right?"

She laughed, nervously. "Hey that's only if I fall in love with someone else, right? No big deal, I haven't seen any men of my type yet. The world remains safe."

"If you do have a secret affection for me, don't worry, it's normal," he winked at her.

"Are you seriously not worried about the prophecy?"

As he looked at her, Eloria knew this was one of those rare moments when the Prince was being serious, "I am not. I fell in love with someone long ago and I don't believe the Creator would let this world be destroyed because of it. He guided my path and I follow it."

Eloria smiled, "Then we are officially friend-zoned."

"Zoned?" he asked.

Before she could answer, a man approached them, taking the seat across from her. He tapped his chalice and a hush fell.

"We welcome our most honored guests: his Royal Highness and our new Eloria."

Eloria slunk down in her seat as everyone smiled in her direction.

"May they learn, grow, and find the Creator's joy while here at the Ocean," the man raised his glass to them.

With that, everyone began eating in fellowship. For the first time in weeks Eloria saw bread, grapes, and meat other than fish. She quickly grabbed a stem of grapes and popped one in her mouth. It tasted surprisingly good compared to the greens she had been eating on their journey. Its flavor was almost overpowering.

"Killian requested them on our way in," the Prince leaned toward her. "Which is odd because he never really enjoyed grapes before."

"Eloria," the man across the table spoke up. "How have you enjoyed your time here so far?"

She glanced at the Prince for direction but he looked at her with mock curiosity.

"It's been different," she said slowly. "Your food is.... rare... where I'm from. We also do not use your kinds of weapons."

Help me, she hoped that Sorrell could hear her thoughts from across the way.

"We've been traveling with companions," the Prince interjected. "My Guard and a woman from the Queen's House. They have been essential in Eloria's learning."

"How wonderful," the man smiled, sipping at his drink. "How have you enjoyed their tutelage?"

"Sorrel has been wonderful to learn from. I admire her greatly. She is a strong fighter and I can tell she cares very much for others. She and the Prince have ingrained almost every plant into my memory and they began teaching me of the animals before we arrived on the beach this morning."

The gentleman nodded, as if she had answered correctly to his inquiry. "What of the other young man? I hear he has quite a reputation among the Guard."

"Killian is nice," she cringed. "His methods are a bit more... straightforward I suppose. He seems very determined to see me do better, especially when it comes to training with the sword. He has protected the Prince and the rest of us very well."

"How wonderful," the man said again. He shoveled a fork full of fish into his mouth. "Perhaps I shall join everyone in watching your training tomorrow."

"I beg your pardon," Eloria coughed.

"Well everyone here is very excited to meet you, dear Eloria," the man said with a smile. "I'm sure the Prince has explained the legends and prophesies about you. We know that you are to be exceptional. Naturally, people will be watching your morning training routines and lessons among the Houses. Perhaps you could teach *us* a thing or two."

Eloria's eyes widened with fear. The Prince quickly shoveled food into his mouth. The man turned to a short woman next to him and started up a new conversation about fishing nets. Eloria remained silent for the rest of the meal, imagining the horrors that tomorrow would hold. She glanced down the table and saw that Sorrell and Killian seemed to be enjoying themselves well enough. Sorrell had a kind smile on her face as she spoke with a women across from her. Killian spoke fervently with a gentleman next to him, as if in a debate.

After much eating and conversation on everyone else's part, people began to drift away from the table. Some stayed in the room and conversed in small groups while others left for their homes. Sorrell got up with the first of the drifters and went back up the stairs. Eloria tried to follow after her but the Prince stopped her with a quick shake of his head.

He didn't explain but she stayed where she was, staring at the waves as they crashed upon the sand. After another half hour, the table had mostly emptied. The Prince gave Eloria a curt nod and they rose from their seats together. Killian quickly hurried from his chair when he saw them rise. Everyone in the room turned and bowed. He returned the gesture and gently took Eloria's elbow, guiding her to the stairs. Killian followed and they climbed up to their rooms.

They were all tired when they got to the common room. After so many days of only the four of them in the forest, the extra company felt a little overwhelming. Eloria walked over to Sorrell's closed door and lifted a hand to knock.

"Don't," the Prince said. "Let her be for a while."

Eloria dropped her hand and looked at the door, wondering if Sorrell was alright.

"It's been a while since any of us have had time alone," the Prince explained. "Sorrell always had to be alone to gain her energy back. I think we could all use some time to ourselves this evening."

The men each went into their own rooms and Eloria followed suit. As she closed the door behind her, an overwhelming sense of exhaustion and loneliness fell on her. She pulled back the blankets and fell into the bed. The cushions felt wonderful and she saw that there was a skylight above her. The large window built into the roof gave her the greatest view before falling asleep. The sky was a light blue and deep purple from the sunset. She smiled and drifted to sleep almost immediately.

A moment later she woke. Had a door opened? Was it Sorrell? She opened her eyes and saw that the sky above her was a deep black. The stars' shining light filled the room. Eloria realized that she must've been asleep for a few hours. She turned and closed her eyes again. Sleep did not come. She tossed and turned before finally abandoning all hope of rest. Wandering around the room for a while, she went to the window and looked out. The moon and stars were reflecting off the ocean with brilliance. There was no one on the beach and the torch light below was dim.

Turning away, she walked quietly to her door and peered out. The common room was empty. Everyone's door was shut. She crept into the room and tiptoed her way into the corridor. Empty. She quickly made her way out of the mansion and to the beach. The smell of the sea filled her nose and she smiled, wide awake. She walked down the shoreline towards the rocky peninsula, letting her toes drag in the sand. She watched the waves go back and forth, folding over her feet then back again. She felt a strong urge to run into the sea and float the night away.

Whoosh.

Eloria's chin jerked up. She heard the sound between the crash of the waves.

Whoosh.

She saw the moon glint off of something further down the beach. A sword.

Whoosh, whoosh.

It flashed in the moonlight, attacking an invisible enemy. Holding the sword was a dark figure with wind blown hair. Eloria shook her head in dismay.

Killian.

Some things don't change, she thought.

Sneaking her way up the shore, she inched closer until she was comfortably able to see him without being noticed. There was a small mound of boulders further up shore. She sat by one, curling her knees up to her chest and resting her head against the rock. She watched Killian do his sword dance, his hair and tunic blowing in the night's breeze. Round, slice, twirl, side step, thrust. Her eye lids grew heavy. She closed them, listening to the sound of his sword slice through the night sky and the waves slide upon the sand.

***

There was a pounding in her ears. Some loud noise that wouldn't go away. She thought about opening her eyes but gave up.

Boom boom boom.

Moaning, she turned over in her bed, dragging the blankets over her head. *Wait... blankets?* Her eyes snapped wide, looking at the white covers around her. When had she gone back to bed? The last thing she remembered was watching Killian on the beach.

"Eloria?" Sorrell's voice said through the door. "Are you alright? I'm coming in."

The door opened and Sorrell stepped inside, peering around the room.

"Morning," Eloria croaked, still trying to wake up.

"I've been knocking for ages! What are you still doing in here?"

"What are you talking about? I'm sleeping."

"You have training this morning!"

"No I don't," Eloria mumbled, slipping back into a nice dream.

Sorrell reached over and whipped the blankets off of the bed, "Killian has been waiting since sunrise. It was the only time to train without people watching. Now there's a huge crowd waiting to observe you."

"What?!" Adrenaline shot through her system and she jumped out of bed. "No, no way! I'm not training in front of a bunch of strangers. All I know are poses, not actual moves. Killian will kill me!"

Sorrell rolled her eyes as she pulled clothes out of the trunk. "Killian won't hurt you. He knows you're new to it all."

"Killian took a cheap shot and sucker punched me, in case you forgot."

"Well yes... but it was only that one time."

Eloria snatched the clothes away from Sorrell and quickly changed into a blue pair of pants, tunic, and her usual boots. Without bothering to lace them she ran to the washroom, snipped off some mint leaves, and sprinted out the door. Sorrell followed, shouting something inaudible after her.

Eloria ran through the corridor then swung on the stair post, taking the steps two or three at a time. She saw Killian standing at the bottom and her heart skipped a beat. He looked upset. She was halfway down when she felt her boot lace get caught beneath her. Her foot slipped out behind her and she tumbled down. She fell over herself and flew off the stairs, rolling across the floor. When she gained control, she hurried to her feet.

"I'm here," she said, looking dizzily around to Killian.

"I can see that," he said.

Her eyes blurred and the floor spun beneath her. She suddenly felt a pang of fire shoot up her shoulder, backside, and something on her head was moving. She reached up and felt a warm liquid run down her fingers. She looked at her hand and saw blood.

"Oh," she said with surprise. "I'm ah…." she sat back down. Her eyes tried to focus to stop the ground from spinning.

"What did you do to her?" Killian asked Sorrell, who had caught up.

"Nothing. She was in a hurry. Perhaps you should work on her coordination and balance today?"

Eloria reached out for Sorrell's arm but missed. "Would you get that ointment stuff? I think that would really help right now… except for my pride."

"No," Killian said, motioning for Sorrell to help her up. "You are afraid of pain, which is why you hold back during training. It's why you cowered when the Deformed came at you. You need to experience pain until you no longer fear it."

Eloria was not thrilled with Killian's attitude. Sorrell lifted her to her feet and they made their way outdoors. Killian led them down the steps and they walked to the peninsula, passing huts and groups of people. They were greeted as they walked by. Sorrell waved and spoke with the people seeing as Killian and Eloria didn't seem particularly friendly. After a time, they turned and, to Eloria's horror, there was a large group of men and women gathered, all robed in blues and greens. As Killian approached them, they moved aside and formed a large circle where he stood. Excited whispers began when they saw Sorrell and Eloria. There was a wooden table behind Killian filled with weapons.

Real weapons, Eloria thought. *These aren't sticks to practice with. He literally wants to kill me.*

"He does not," Sorrell answered. "Besides, you won't use weapons for a few days still. This is how we all have learned. Focus and you will do well."

Eloria stepped into the circle of people and they all fell silent. She walked over to Killian and waited for instructions. The tail of her spine was still throbbing and her shoulder felt severely bruised. She could see people staring at her forehead where it was scraped and bloody from her fall.

"Sorrell and I have taught you the basic positions for fighting without weapons. In battle, there are times when you have nothing but your body to fight with. Today, you will learn to put those positions into motion."

Killian began calling out difference poses that Eloria had learned. She struck each of them quickly and smoothly, keeping in mind the times that Sorrell had adjusted her angle or rotation. Her muscles remembered most of them automatically but some were still a struggle. He began shouting them out more quickly, repeating some and throwing in ones he hand't used yet. She felt ridiculous as people watched, whispering to one another. She was sure they were critiquing her form and lack of grace. Killian's pace quickened and she did her best to keep up. After another few minutes, he stopped and called Sorrell into the circle.

She danced across the opening and stood opposite of Eloria.

"We will do the same thing again," Killian said. "This time, Sorrell will counter you. Watch how she moves. Look for a flex of her muscle, a twitch in her limb. This will be your clue to how your opponent will strike. Learn how she moves and how she thinks and you will be able to predict the next move before she makes it."

He shouted a motion and Eloria began to move, her right knee extending into the air. Sorrell attacked at the same moment, her own leg blocked by Eloria's knee. Her right hand shot out towards her chest and Eloria's arm swept across her body, knocking Sorrell's fist away from its target. The pose was completed. Eloria dropped her arms and smiled at Sorrell, proud of her first successful block against someone. Killian shouted for another motion. Sorrell winked and moved so quickly that Eloria spun and fell to the ground. Her mind hadn't even identified the move or what had knocked her down.

"Too slow," Sorrel said with a smile.

"But...," Eloria rubbed her sore backside, "I didn't even get a chance to..."

Killian shouted out something else and Sorrell somehow lifted Eloria back up before knocking her to the sand once again.

Her back hit the earth and she felt the air get knocked out of her. She coughed and remained on the sturdy sand, wondering if she was safe there or if Sorrell could someone throw her into the air from this position. The people around them murmured aloud to one another and some even dared to giggle.

Sorrell extended a hand and gave a weary smile, "Sorry."

Eloria gave her a cautious eye but accepted her help. She wiped the sand from her clothes and felt the blood rush to her cheeks.

"Again," Killian said.

They took their positions and began again. Each time Sorrell used her speed and strength to knock Eloria to the ground. There were a few times that she intentionally let Eloria win but once Killian noticed, it became less and less. This went on for most of the afternoon. Eloria did her best to move quickly and remember her training, but Sorrell had much more experience. She was sweating and had been covered in sand from head to toe. Her limbs were sore and the sweat trickled into her eyes. Sorrell finally backed down, not wanting to wear out her companion any further.

"I'm done," she said to Killian.

"She needs to continue. There hasn't been one blocked attack yet. She's not in pain, she's just tired."

"It's time to finish Killian. The feast is in a few days and they expect Eloria at the Prince's side... with a functioning body."

He shook his head, "It's not my fault she slept so late. The dangers in the mountains are more important than a party. She needs to use this time to learn. Did you forget, Sorrell, that she's supposed to save our world?"

Sorrell glared at him. This was clearly not a joke to either of them.

"Perhaps you brought the wrong girl," Killian continued. "Let me find you a reflection and you can try again," he shot at her.

Sorrell shook her head, furious with him. Turning on her heels, she stormed out of the circle, pushing past the crowd as she went.

Killian's body didn't relax as he walked to Eloria. His muscles were tight and she could see his veins pulsing. "Get up," he commanded.

She struggled to her feet and looked at him with dismay. He squared his shoulders and put a hand behind his back, the other extended as if to block her.

"Are you seriously..."

"Try to hit me," he interrupted her.

"Killian, I don't want to play this game."

"This is not a game. Sorrell says you are too tired to defend yourself so now you are on the offense. Try and hit me."

Eloria moaned. Though he had said otherwise, she thought it was only a sick game to get her to look bad in front of everyone. She didn't understand why Killian disliked her enough to humiliate her.

She scrolled through the different attacks she had learned in her mind. Choosing one, she moved as quickly as she could to hit him. Blocked. She tried again, this time thinking of ways that she could confuse him or surprise him. Blocked and blocked. They continued like this for some time. People began leaving the crowd, deciding they had other ways to occupy their time. Eloria saw looks of disappointment and worry cross their faces. She felt useless.

She began to stumble around the circle, barely able to keep her body upright. Her limbs were exhausted and her mouth was parched. Her punches were feeble and her body moved like a piece of seaweed in the ocean's current. She began watching Killian's motions instead of focusing on her own. When her arm went out, she could see the definition of his muscle as it flexed to deflect her blow. His hair would sway and his tunic rippled over him. His foot would adjust ever so slightly to maintain his balance. Her tired mind was reminded of his dance. She saw a flashback of Killian moving on the sand, swinging his sword through the sky and piercing the air. His feet had kicked up the sand and his sword has slid through each tiny grain.

His sword play! she remembered.

There had been so many nights of watching him that she hadn't remembered that it was only an advanced form of combat. Each twirl and thrust was simply an attack that he had been practicing. She had watched it so many times, surely she could replicate a move. It could throw him off.

In a desperate, final attempt, Eloria envisioned her next move. She was exhausted and Killian was pumped with energy. Without a sword, she improvised how her arm would move, acting as the blade. She had to do it just right. She counted to three and lunged at him.

Thrusting her right arm at his chest, he easily blocked it, pushing it aside. She used the force of his deflection to propel herself into a spin, lowering onto one knee and swinging her body around. As her body rotated to face him again, she caught the back of his knee with her arm, sweeping it across her body with every bit of strength she had left. Killian's foot flew into the air, kicking up a spray of sand. He fell to the ground in front of Eloria.

She froze in disbelief. Her arm still extended and her knee in the sand. Killian rolled out of the fall into a crouch like she had seen him do before. He looked at her with his wild green eyes. To Eloria's surprise, he was smirking.

"Somebody has been paying attention," he said quietly.

He stood and extended his hand to her. Proudly, she took it and stood, still looking into his eyes with a smile. A warm tingle spread across her palm as they touched. The thin line of people around them were silent, as shocked as Eloria had been. From behind her, a young boy hooted in joy and jumped into the air. Everyone else immediately burst into shouts of surprise and excitement, applauding the two fighters. Killian looked at the crowd around them and for the first time, Eloria saw him truly smile. It was not a smirk or joke but a pure smile of pride. He looked back to Eloria's face, a new sort of recognition in his eyes.

"Again," he said.

Eloria's heart dropped, "Are you kidding me?" But her body was pumping with excitement from her achievement. She was sure she could never pull that off again, but she didn't feel as exhausted as she had ten seconds ago.

They continued. She tried a few more of Killian's moves but was blocked at every turn. He knew that she wasn't as limited as he had originally thought. Eloria mixed the simple, beginner moves with Killian's sword technique. They went on until the colors of sunset touched the sky. In the end, she was only able to hit him one other time before evening came. It was a simple fist into the shoulder. Although it had been intended for his chest, Eloria's tired muscles missed completely which is why he failed to defend it. It hadn't knocked him down or even caused him to flinch, but it still counted as a hit.

When Killian called it, the people dispersed, chatting happily among themselves. Eloria chugged some water and fell into the sand, finally able to get off her feet and relax.

"It would appear last night wasn't the first time you've watched me practice," she heard Killian say.

Eloria instantly remembered waking up in her bed this morning but not knowing how she had gotten there. The last thing she could recall was Killian gleaming in the moonlight a little ways down the beach. Blood rushed to her cheeks. She sat up to explain but he was gone. With a sigh, she made her way to the Healer's House and straight to bed.

CHAPTER 12

For three days Killian made her train in hand-to-hand combat against Sorrell. She slowly improved and became a closer match to Sorrell's skill. Each morning she woke up more sore than the day before. Her muscles screamed in anger when she swung her feet from the bed to complete her assigned stretches.

Whenever she woke in the middle of the night she roamed the beaches. It was always her hope to see Killian practicing his sword, but he had disappeared. She wondered if he was angry with her for spying. It wouldn't be unlike him. The only time she saw him was during morning training. Even then, she only sparred against Sorrell while Killian barked out instructions.

She woke each morning at sunrise to begin her training. There was always a crowd waiting for her when she arrived to spar. It had become a show to them. Would Eloria land a hit today? Maybe two or three? After sparring, Sorrell took Eloria to the Master Healers where she apprenticed.

Her time was spent learning basic first aid, names of the plants used to heal, and helping those around the ocean villages with their everyday needs. Sorrell explained that these chores were to help them notice the little things and find joy in humbling themselves to others. The Masters taught her to meditate and think of her actions and words each day, challenging her to see them from the perspective of others. Because of her unique connection with Sorrell, it became Sorrell's duty to sit and listen to her thoughts during meditation. She would determine whether or not Eloria succeeded.

Eloria didn't mind the chores and training. It was peaceful and gave her mind and body a chance to rest each afternoon. The meditations, however, became somewhat problematic. She and Sorrell would spend the evenings sitting on the beach and staring out to the ocean. Eloria would think through her conversations each day, trying to determine if she had been polite, truthful, and conscientious to those she had interacted with. After a few minutes her thoughts would stray to other things. Mostly she worried about the prophecy and the comments she had heard from others.

They don't like my progress. They look at me with such disappointment, and what if the queen finds out? I'm not doing well and they'll find a way to send me home, despite the prophecy.

"Don't think that way," Sorrell would say. "The queen knows that it takes time. She will not summon you this soon. You are supposed to apprentice at each House. They will wait to evaluate you until you have been properly taught. Now, try to refocus your mind."

With a sigh, Eloria would try again. And again. And again.

What about the Prince? Everyone is looking for two perfect love birds and there's no way that is happening. I've basically already doomed this world and the Prince doesn't seem worried about it. Everyone else is. That big feast is coming up and I know it's all about Eloria and Seraphim. The first king and queen. What happens when this Eloria can't lie to everyone?

"You worry so much! Stop making yourself a victim. The Prince believes he can choose who he loves and create his own future. Won't you learn from his example? The prophecy was not spoken by the Creator, it was.... Well you will find out soon enough at the feast. Please, Eloria, focus."

So the meditation continued each day, always with Sorrell trying to qualm her fears and keep her mind in line with the day's training.

On their seventh morning at the ocean, Eloria was instructed to choose a sword for her sparring lesson. She and Sorrell would begin training with real weapons. Despite her enthusiasm, Eloria did no better with a sword than she had the first day with her fists. It was a whole new style of fighting and she was back to square one. Sorrell was skilled enough to never truly harm Eloria, but only suffered her with blunt hits that caused major bruising. The ointment that Sorrell had once used was no longer an option. Killian made sure it stayed safely hidden unless there was a broken bone or deep cut from one of the swords, which was rare.

Their first day of swordplay ended up being another full morning's work. When lunch came, Killian declared that she would not leave the circle for her Healing training until she used correct form with the sword. It was supposed to be her last day of training with the House of Healing. She knew this meant she could lose precious time to learn.

When the crowd dispersed to eat, Sorrell left to inform the Healing Masters of their new schedule. Eloria plopped herself onto the table of weapons and peeled back a banana. Killian's unsatisfied attitude had made her grumpy and impatient. She was sick of being embarrassed in front of all the onlookers, and she couldn't handle another black and blue bruise. Most of her body seemed to be covered in them and some were a strange yellowish color. Sorrell's patience was the only thing getting her through these long sparring sessions.

"Time to begin," Killian said, setting down an apple.

Eloria glanced around the beach, "Sorrell isn't back yet, and I haven't eaten."

"You can learn without Sorrell. Besides, she has been going easy on you. She doesn't need to read your mind to know how you

155

try to attack or block. You are too slow and obvious with your movements. We need to put you in the element of battle and see how you really respond."

She made a loud gulping noise as she choked her bite of banana, "How do you mean? You aren't sending one of those creatures after me, are you?"

"Of course not! Do you think we keep Deformed locked away for sport? You will be fighting me," he swung his sword through the air with a flourish.

"Oh no...," she said with a half laugh, half cry.

He came close to her, leaning into her body in a way that seemed far too intimate, especially for him.

"Are you afraid of me?" he asked.

His green eyes were bright, mirroring shades of the ocean as he searched her face for an answer.

"Are you afraid of me?" Killian asked again.

She nodded slowly, "Yes... I am."

For a moment, disappointment swept over his face. As quickly as it came, it disappeared.

"Good," he said, pulling away from her. "Then it will be like battle."

She quickly grabbed a sword, remembering how he had struck before without warning. She stood ready to defend herself as he meandered in a lazy circle around her. There had been a few people that morning to watch their training, and they looked up from their lunches and watched with curiosity as the two moved.

Eloria kept her eyes on Killian's midsection so that she had the best vantage point to see his feet and his sword hand should they move. Even though they both were using single handed blades, Eloria had to use both her hands to keep the sword upright in defense. There was no sword light enough for her to handle with only one hand which gave her yet another disadvantage. Killian continued to circle her, watching her feet for proper form and watching her eyes to try and figure out her intentions.

Killian knew what Eloria must have thought of him, but he had to teach her. She had to learn quickly. She had to be able to defend herself. He remembered when the creature had attacked her in the woods. Killian knew that neither he nor the Prince would make it to her in time. In that moment, he had truly thought she would die. He had been angry at himself for not doing better, for not being able to protect her or teach her to protect herself. Since then, Sorrell had begged him to go easier on Eloria. She argued that no creatures could get as far as the ocean and they had nothing to worry about. Killian knew she was right, but he also knew that they were headed back to the forests soon. No one knew the dangers that would find them there. He had to make sure Eloria was ready.

He advanced, moving slowly. Eloria stumbled back, almost losing her balance. He thrust out in that moment, his sword nicking her thigh and whipping her blade from her hand in one smooth motion. She gasped and put up her hands, palms facing him. He lowered his blade in confusion.

"What are you doing?"

She looked at him with dismay, "I'm showing that I am defenseless. As in 'don't attack me because I am unarmed.'" She didn't bother mentioning the burning sting on her leg where she was now bleeding. Killian wouldn't care about the pain but would just tell her to fight through it.

He sighed, "What do you think the last five days have been about? Your body is still a weapon, whether your sword is in your hand or not. If you lose your blade then continue to attack and defend yourself, don't give up."

She nodded but doubted her ability to defend herself against Killian's scabbard let alone his sword. She picked her weapon up from the sand and they began again. This time when he attacked, she was able to defend two moves before suffering another strike to her arm. The next time, she blocked once and attacked herself. Her move was easily defended. Killian didn't give her time to recoup but went on the offense once again. He stepped to her right, beginning to extend his arm but it was a fake out. Eloria turned to block but realized too late that Killian had already brought his sword to her other side. The edge touched her skin just enough to open a long line of skin down her back.

Eloria cried out in pain. She felt blood spill from her wound and soak into her clothes. She stumbled quickly away from him to try and regain her composure before he struck again.

"Killian wait!"

"I'm intentionally slowing down for you," he said, pacing the empty space. "You need to move faster, you need to watch me and predict my movements."

"I can't, okay?" she fumed at him.

"You must if you want to learn. Stop tripping over yourself and use your sword as an extension of your arm, the way I've told you."

"Your way sucks Killian, I'm done!" Eloria threw her sword to the ground. She knew she was acting childish, and the Healing Masters would disapprove, but she didn't care. Even if she was afraid of him the answer wasn't to hurt him, it was simply to stand up for herself and be done with it.

"The Evil Ones won't stop to listen to you talk, and they won't care if you are defenseless. Get your weapon."

"No!" she yelled. "I'm done. Get it through your idiotic head that I'm not doing this anymore. You beat me up like this and pretend it's helping me? Don't you get it? It doesn't matter how well I fight. None of that matters for me. I'm Eloria. All that people care about is who I fall in love with! Do you know how lame that makes me sound? Doesn't it bother you that I'm not madly in love with the Prince right now? Have you noticed that we're not riding horses off into the sunset? Because everyone else noticed a long time ago. Everyone's talking about it. How Eloria came and destroyed the world!"

She took a step towards him, not caring about his sword. His eyes seemed to fill with fire as he looked at her.

"No one cares if I can fight because I've already destroyed them! I'm already killing everyone here simply because I'm not in love."

Her body shook with anger and exhaustion. Her back stung from the last slash of his sword.

"I hear them whisper when I walk by. I see their faces when we train. No one wants me. No one believes in me. I'm the wrong girl. I'm not the Eloria that they wanted."

"Get over your selfishness," he spat. "All you worry about is yourself. Who cares what everyone thinks about you? Have you even glanced at Sorrell?" He thrust his sword into the crowd and the people parted away, showing Sorrell standing among them. "Have you tried, even once, to hear her thoughts the way she hears yours? She brought you here for a different reason than the prophecy, but that's all you think about! She saved you from your world, but all you care about is everyone's expectations. The Prince could care less about your destined love for each other, but it is all *you* are focused on. If you want him so badly, go get him! If you are so scared of destroying our world then *do something* about it. In the meantime, while you sit and worry about only you, I will teach you to fight. I will do my duty. Because I need you in Loraillvon. I need you to survive, Eloria."

A tingle went up her spine. A warm sensation ran through her skin.

"The prophecy is bigger than you, or me, or Sorrell. You need to know how to stay alive before you think of how everyone dies, Eloria."

"Don't say my name," she whispered.

"You are here for reasons besides yourself, and you need to realize that before someone gets killed. We are all trying to help, but you don't even want to help yourself. Eloria, you have to start working for what you want."

She looked up to find Killian standing close to her. His arms hung limply at his sides.

"Don't say my name," she whispered. "You never say my name."

"Killian!" they heard Sorrell shout.

He closed his eyes, turning towards her. The small crowd of people had grown larger as they all stared in silence at the scene before them.

"You are both done," Sorrell stomped towards them.

"Explain it to us, Sorrell," he fumed. "Explain to us why you brought her here and explain to her what she really needs to know about you, because it's clearly keeping her from understanding. And if she doesn't understand then the queen won't let her stay."

Eloria stepped back in fear. His words hit her like a hammer. She wanted to stay, she *had* to stay.

How could I be so stupid? she thought. *He's right. The queen is going to summon me, she is going to send me away! I can't go back, I have to learn no matter what. I have to stay. Why haven't I been trying? I've only been complaining. They'll send me home.*

"Stop it," Sorrell commanded. "You were angry and spoke out. You have not lost your chance here. And you," she turned back to Killian. "Since when do you care if she stays or goes? You've been mocking her from the beginning. You've made everything more difficult for her transition to this world."

He stood like a stone in the sand.

"The feast is tonight," Sorrell said, taking Eloria by the arm. "And I think you both need the day to work on your attitudes." As she pulled Eloria away, her eyes fell to the long cut down her back. "Killian!"

"What do you expect Sorrell? We were training!" he defended.

160

She shook her head in frustration, "This will ruin her dress!"

CHAPTER 13

Sorrell stayed glued to Eloria's side the rest of the day. They used the ointment to heal her most recent scars and bruises. Despite the fact that Eloria missed the rest of her Healer training, they took time to meditate anyway while in Eloria's room. She knew that Sorrell was trying to keep her and Killian apart and appreciated her understanding.

Eloria didn't understand him and she couldn't figure out why. He pushed her harder than anyone else expected. Even Sorrell and the Prince seemed against his method of quick study. For as much as he wanted her to learn, he never took the time to truly explain things. It was all about combat and action. He never simply spoke to her like the night in the tree house when he had brought her food. But despite these things, she couldn't get over the way he would look at her. At times, his eyes would change from their usual serious demeanor and become intrigued and protective. These were things that he never displayed in any other way.

Then there's how he never says my name...

"What do you mean?"

"Oh," Eloria jumped. Sorrell was rubbing flower petals into her hair. Apparently it was a beauty treatment of sorts. She hadn't realized that Sorrell was listening to her thoughts again. "I was just thinking..."

"I don't mean to pry," Sorrell apologized. "Sometimes your thoughts are as clear as if you were saying them aloud. Other times I can't hear anything. Once you train with the House of the Beasts, you will understand. The way I can speak and listen to them is similar to how I hear you."

"Are you calling me an animal?" Eloria laughed.

"Beast," Sorrell corrected, "Animals do not have intelligence like that. What did you mean, about Killian not saying your name?" she asked.

"Well have you ever noticed? How he hardly uses my name? Every time he talks to me… well it's subtle but he never says 'Eloria.' When he has it's only during moments of stress like when we were attacked by the Deformed or earlier during our argument."

Sorrell thought about it for a moment. "I hadn't noticed, but I suppose you're right."

"Isn't it odd?" Eloria asked.

"Not necessarily. People's new names are supposed to be more than just a calling or a label. Each name means something and they are supposed to reflect the essence of ourselves, our true selves. Perhaps he doesn't see you as Eloria so he cannot bring himself to call you by that name." She didn't sound confident in her own explanation. Eloria could see that her mind was distant, as if she were thinking about something else entirely. It was as if Sorrell always had some puzzle in her head and she would gaze off to fit pieces together.

"Well what does Eloria mean?" she wondered aloud. "Maybe if I knew, it would help me be better. Is it something like 'loved by royalty' or 'savior of worlds.'"

Sorrell laughed, "Not at all. Eloria means 'to whom the Creator has given victory.'"

"Huh," Eloria thought about it. "I've not felt victorious yet. What about everyone else's names? Obviously we know what 'the Prince' means... no guessing there."

Sorrell smiled and shook her head, "He has a real name too. No one uses the names of the Royal Family though, out of respect, so we call them the King, Queen, and Prince."

"What about you and Killian?" Eloria asked, rubbing flower petals on her skin and enjoying the aroma as it filled the room.

"Sorrell is a complicated name. It means 'girl of reddish brown hair.'"

Eloria nudged her playfully, "Come on, tell me."

"I'm being perfectly serious," she giggled. "That is what my name means. Thus, I have completed my journey. The true nature of myself is reddish brown hair."

Both girls laughed and Eloria couldn't help but still feel a pang of jealousy. Sorrell's hair was a beautiful auburn brown. Eloria always wanted hair that beautiful and shiny. Unfortunately she was stuck with her dirty blond, boring look.

"What about Killian?" she asked. "Is it 'to serve and protect' or 'to scowl and scold.'"

Sorrell's face grew more solemn, "It means 'the church.'"

"I didn't know you had churches. We haven't passed any have we?"

"No, a church is not a place, it is a people. The church is all those who believe in the Creator, the one and only Creator. It is a body of people who truly believe in Him and speak to Him with understanding. Killian takes this very seriously. He has worked hard over the years to earn his name."

"How does he earn 'the church?'" Eloria didn't understand.

"Killian would need to explain it to you himself but from what I've seen, he strives to be the best person he can for the Creator. He does his best to know Him and to help others who do not understand fully. In a way, he is a Healer for people's hearts and spirits."

Eloria chortled, "I'm sorry but I cannot see it. Killian?"

"You have only seen him as an instructor and the Prince's Guard. Try to watch him with new eyes, like the Healers have been teaching you. Watch him among the people and when he's alone. Killian keeps a lot to himself but he shows quite a bit through his actions, if not his words."

Eloria doubted what Sorrell was saying but thought about it nonetheless. Perhaps she would take a glance here and there while they were at the feast, but she didn't want to spend any more time thinking of Killian than she had to.

Sorrell brought Eloria's dress for the feast. She explained that it had been made by the people of the Ocean to honor the second Queen Transformed...or so they hoped. The dress was made of a light, sea-foam colored silk that rippled like the waves as it moved. The fabric was soft in her hands but she feared her calloused fingers would snag the fabric. Sorrell assured her that the dress would not snag or tear throughout the night but Eloria still held it gingerly as she donned the gown.

It fell to the floor and trailed slightly behind her. The top was cinched with sapphire, emerald, and diamond stones sewn in. They traveled in a pattern down the front and disappeared in a line around the back. There were straps that wrapped around from her shoulders to under her arms, holding it up due to the open back.

"It's beautiful, but why is there no back to the dress?" Eloria wondered. She had never worn anything so revealing before and she could imagine her mother's scoldings.

"Eloria is the name of the first Queen Transformed. The prophecy says that the second Eloria would also be transformed because of her love for the Seraphim Prince. They left the back open for your wings."

Eloria laughed, "I wouldn't mind wings if they would cover me. I feel so… exposed."

Despite the open back, Eloria loved the dress. It displayed her body perfectly without being too form fitting or tight. The fabric was so light that she felt almost naked. Sorrell took her hair and created a loose braid that wrapped around her shoulder. She wished she could see herself in a mirror.

Sorrell's dress was similar with a deep blue hue and silk fabric. Instead of going to the floor, her dress was slit at her side slightly above the knee. The fabric flowed around her when she moved and it fell into a train in back, slightly longer than Eloria's own dress. It was gorgeous on her. With her perfect body and hair, she looked like a supermodel.

"Now there is one thing you need to learn before we go to the feast," Sorrell said as she quickly braided her own hair.

"Please don't tell me I have to fight someone wearing this," Eloria moaned.

Sorrell giggled, "I'd never subject you to such torture, but you do have to dance. Which is very much like fighting but hopefully, for you, less bruising."

She walked to the door and opened it to the common room. Waiting in a chair was the Prince. He was already dressed for the feast himself with a silky blue shirt and dark pants. His golden hair was perfectly placed and he flashed a pearly white smile at them as they entered.

"You both look magnificent," he said, staring at Sorrell.

She blushed and Eloria felt her happiness.

"The Prince is the perfect partner for dancing," she quickly said, motioning Eloria to him. They went to the open area on the floor and he bowed. "He will teach you what you need to know before we leave."

"This feast is like a ball?" Eloria felt her heartbeat quicken. "I enjoy dancing, but I think we can all agree that I'm not a quick learner."

"You will be fine," the Prince said, taking her hand in his. "Any man that you dance with will lead and guide you. All you have to do is feel the rhythm and allow yourself to be guided."

He placed a gentle hand on her back and smiled. Applying a slight pressure to her hand, he stepped towards her and she stepped back. He rotated and she felt his hand guide her by pulling against her back, leading her towards him. He spun her with a slight push and nod then brought both their hands into a twist as they walked in a circle. With another small nudge, their hands unwound and they both spun, bringing them back to their original position. He continued in this way, applying a gentle pressure to her hand or back to guide her around the room. After about an hour, she understood her footing and was gliding around the room, laughing with Sorrell and the Prince. She let go and stepped away with a curtsey.

"That was wonderfully done," he said with a smile. "Shall we?"

He extended an arm to both Sorrell and Eloria. They accepted and left the room. At the top of the stair, Eloria was shocked to see the lobby below filled with men and women dressed in their finest. They all bowed when they saw the trio. The Prince escorted the ladies down. The crowd parted as they walked, making their way to the beach below. Eloria hesitated when they approached the sand. She hated to get the dress dirty. She looked to Sorrell and saw that she walked onto their sandy path without a second thought. Eloria quickly followed and saw that the sand did not stick to either of their dresses. She wondered if they were made with some sort of magic.

As the others followed them out of the House, many picked up torches and lit them in the fire pits beside the stair. The sun had not yet set but Eloria guessed it would grow dusky soon enough, and it wasn't a short way to the palace of Kailani where the feast was to take place. As they walked to the peninsula, the people began to walk alongside them with their torches.

A small boy began to sing out a song. He smiled and skipped ahead of the Prince as he did. His voice rang out over the crowd as he sang about the beauty of the sea and the friendship of the whales. One by one, the people began to sing with him. Harmonies floated in and around the young boy's melody and even Sorrell sang along as they walked.

"Isn't Killian supposed to be here?" Eloria whispered to the Prince.

He shrugged, "Killian does what he wants as long as he thinks I'm safe. He'll be at the palace at some point. Lurking in some corner to avoid dancing I'm sure."

"Will we get to go to the room made of glass?"

"I'll get someone to take you," Sorrell replied. "It's sort of... off limits to most people."

The sun was setting when they reached the peninsula. Eloria felt like crying at the beauty around her. The sky was painted pink, blues, and purples. The peoples' song filled the night and their torches created a winding path of light behind them. The gates were open and she could see light peaking through the curtains of all of the windows above. Trying to soak up every detail, Eloria followed her friends as they walked through the marbled doors.

The room they entered was more beautiful than Eloria could have imagined. The ceiling was so high she had to squint to make it out. Chandeliers hung down from above on ropes as large as tree trunks. They were filled with candles and glass, reflecting their light all about the room. Ahead of them was a staircase that split in two and met at the second floor. The stairs were made from pearls and the railing was solid gold. The floor was decorated with rich green and blue tiles that designed a mural of a dolphin at sea.

The Prince gently pushed Eloria along, up the stairs. The second floor was as beautiful as the room below. Its ceiling was just as tall and the floors had the same decorative tile. It was a large room with tables of knobbed wood set throughout the space. Hundreds of people were already inside, sitting at tables, talking in groups, and admiring the room as Eloria was. In the middle of the ballroom, Eloria heard a noise akin to an orchestra.

"It's rather extravagant for our humble Healers," a voice said from behind her.

Killian stood close to her, wearing an outfit almost identical to the Prince's but with a fitted jacket. He, of course, had his sword strapped to his hip. His hair had been managed and styled for the occasion to not look so wild and windblown. The simple ring on his hand even looked polished for the occasion. As she looked up at him, she caught the scent of something akin to cologne. She swooned slightly, reminded herself it was Killian, and quickly regained her composure.

A tall, slender woman with a long wooden staff stood in the center of the room. She had sun bleached hair and a stern face. At the sight of the Prince and his party entering the room, she thrust the butt of her staff into the floor below her. A low, booming noise echoed through the hall and everyone fell silent, turning to face her.

"People of the Ocean," she said with a raspy voice. "Those from the House of the Beasts, Healers, Builders and Guard. People of the Queen's House, the Farmers and our Mages. We join together to celebrate a member of the royal family who is among us. We also gather to extol the arrival of our second Queen Transformed, the prophesied Eloria. May she feel welcome in the halls of her namesake and find peace by the ocean and sky. We thank Eloria for the good fortune that she will bring us through the prophecy's words. Let the celebration begin!"

The woman knocked her staff on the ground once more and fireworks exploded at the peak of the ceiling. Streamers fell from the chandeliers and the people shouted with cheer. The musicians across the room began playing a joyous tune and everyone returned to dance and feast.

The Prince led Sorrell and Eloria to a large round table where they sat. She was introduced to the others at the table including the woman with the staff who, she learned, was the Head Mistress of the House of Beasts. She seemed particularly interested in Eloria and Sorrell.

"My name is Fauna," she told them, setting her staff against the table as she gathered food onto her plate. "The Healing Masters tell me that you can hear each others' minds?"

"Not quite," Sorrell answered. "I can hear Eloria, but she is unable to hear me."

Fauna nodded, "This is due to her lack of training. Has she spoken with a beast?"

"Not so far."

Eloria listened curiously as they gathered food onto their plates.

"Sorrell, do you block your thoughts from her?" Fauna asked.

Eloria was surprised by the question. When Sorrell didn't answer, she was even more shocked.

"Do you mean that she isn't letting me hear her?" Eloria asked Fauna.

"Not necessarily," she waved her fork as she spoke. "You need proper training from my House in order to hear the words of beasts and the thoughts of your reflection counterpart. However, in moments of high emotion, it would be my guess that you would be more likely to hear her, unless of course, she was blocking you. With Sorrell's level of training, that would be an easy thing to do."

"We have had few enough times where that would be possible," Sorrell replied with a curt smile. "Even in those times, my thoughts are my own."

They ate silently, listening to the music and watching all the people around them. A man across from Sorrell struck up a conversation and Eloria listened as the whole table began to debate the process of exportation by the Farmers of the Ocean Region.

After their plates were empty, the Prince stood from his seat. "Please excuse me, I have a few people I need to pay my respects to. Sorrell would you join me?"

Sorrell excused herself from the table and quickly followed after the Prince. They snuck into one of the many halls that parted away from the ballroom. After a few minutes walking, they turned a corner and entered the old throne room. Killian sat with his legs dangling off the armrest of the first king's royal seat. His dark figure glowed atop the large dais.

"Remove yourself," Sorrell snapped at him. "You're being disrespectful."

Killian rolled his eyes but did as he was told, stealing away from the pearl laden throne.

"This is the most inopportune time," Sorrell complained. "There are too many ears."

"One of us is with Eloria every moment of the day," the Prince said. "This is the only time we could all slip away without causing suspicion. How is she doing, Sorrell?"

"She's tired and defeated. Eloria's mind is constantly worrying about what the people think. The crowds watch her every morning during combat training and it's clear they are losing faith."

Both looked to Killian.

"I'm not to blame," he scoffed.

"An apprentice is only as good as the Master."

"Keep your royal wisdom to yourself, highness," Killian grumbled. "She is lazy and does not learn from her mistakes."

"It doesn't help that we point out her flaws," Sorrell argued. "Eloria dwells on your insults Killian. They are tearing her apart."

"It's good to know she's listening."

The Prince gave a long sigh. "I received word from Kien Illae. My parents and the Queen's House believe the enemy has eyes on us. They are getting information on Eloria somehow. The Deformed are taking more territories in the mountains, and word of Eloria's coming has not deterred them. We need to change our tactics, let them think Eloria is losing the advantage, that she is not ready for battle. Perhaps they'll slow their advances, give us time to actually teach her something worthwhile before this war. Perhaps she'll give the Evil Ones a nice surprise once they do meet her."

"That's easy enough," Killian adjusted uncomfortably in his dress coat, "It's true enough right now anyhow. She is a losing advantage to us, after all."

Sorrell gave him a threatening look.

"Fine! I'll adjust my training," Killian caved. "We'll limit when the people are allowed to observe. Not many are coming to watch at this point anyway. Let those who come see her fail. Then in private we'll try a different approach. I will even feign a few hits if it helps her self-esteem."

"That will keep her hopes up. I only hope your pride can take it."

"My pride is none of your business, Sorrell," he shot back. "Now off to the party with you. Our dear legend shouldn't be left alone."

"Did you actually comb your hair for this?" Sorrell mused as she left the room.

The Prince lowered his voice, "We need to do more, Killian. More than teach her our ways and how to fight. No one is believing the ruse of Eloria and I being in love. The prophecy hinges on that fact. If there are spies among us, then let them believe the prophecy is turning in their favor. Let's convince them that Eloria is not falling for the Seraphim Prince."

Killian understood his meaning, "It won't be fair to the girl."

"Has any of this been fair?"

"She seems to be enjoying herself... for the most part," Killian smirked.

"Either way, the enemy needs to believe the prophecy is turning in their favor. They need to think we're failing, at least until we gain an advantage. It will be our only way to gain the element of surprise over the Evil Ones."

"Let them think they are winning this war. If there are spies among the trees, it will be the only way."

"Sorrell would need to remain unaware."

"Yes, you should save face as well."

The Prince straightened. "I am sorry it has come to this so quickly. Are you sure you are willing to move forward?"

"Thanks for considering my feelings," Killian jibed. "I'll be fine."

"You understand what needs to be done?"

Killian knocked his boot against the wall, "Yes, I know what to do."

CHAPTER 14

"Eloria, would you like to dance?" the Prince extended his hand. "I'm sure the people would love to see us among them, swirling through the crowd."

"Oh, of course," Eloria replied, although she had hoped to continue her previous conversation with Sorrell and Fauna.

"Fauna, please be kind to my companions," he said with a smile. "Sorrell, come find us in a bit. I should like to dance with you as well."

He pulled Eloria away and they glided through the crowd, heading towards the other dancers. People greeted them as they passed and the Prince gave each of them a kind smile. When they reached the dance floor, everyone cleared and waited for them.

"Ignore them," the Prince whispered to Eloria. "It's tradition for members of the Royal Family to take a first dance alone. They'll join back in soon enough."

Eloria gulped, "Don't let me trip on my dress, okay?"

"Of course," he said with a wink.

As usual, the Prince was keeping things light and fun. With a smooth motion, he began their dance. Due to her nerves she stumbled at first but he made a steady partner and quickly got her back instep with the music. The musicians played on string instruments unlike the reed flutes of the forest. Their music was smooth yet intricate with melodies and dissonance that played in and out. Other dancers slowly joined them on the floor and Eloria began to enjoy herself. After three songs, Sorrell approached them, looking happier than Eloria had seen her in some time.

"Eloria, please excuse me," the Prince said with a bow.

She saw the look in his eye and understood. She gave Sorrell a quick smile and left them on the dance floor. She rejoined the group of House Masters at her table and ate more of what she considered a fine meal while Sorrell and the Prince danced on. After some light conversation, the Masters left the table to mingle with others. Eloria was left to gaze at the room around her and watch the people as they enjoyed the celebration. She hummed along to the music, feeling the familiar daze of the instruments' magical effect.

"Come with me," Killian's voice whispered in her ear.

Her body tensed in surprise, but she stood and followed him through the crowds of people.

"Where are we going?" she asked, lingering in the room before following him further.

"There is something you need to see," he shrugged.

"That's not exactly an answer," she mumbled, slowly following him. She looked back to the people at the feast but no one seemed to notice them leaving.

Killian led them down a series of passages and Eloria began to worry about ever being able to find her way back. To her surprise, all of the halls were lit and she could see light under the doors that they passed.

"I thought Kailani was empty," she commented. "But all of the hallways are clean, and I noticed lights in the windows when we were making our way here."

"There are caretakers for Kailani that keep it preserved and habitable for occasions such as these. The feast will last most of the night so there are rooms prepared for guests and House Masters if they wish to stay here after the celebration."

They turned a corner and came to a blank wall with a large framed canvas. There was script on it with long, curling letters. The calligraphy was beautiful and Eloria wondered if this was a skill she might pick up during her training.

"This is the prophecy of Eloria. The original text that was scribed as the dragon told it."

"A dragon?" Eloria asked with surprise.

Killian nodded, "It was an ancient dragon that spoke of the arrival of the second Eloria from another world. He arrived here when our people first began tampering with other worlds. He still lives. It will be an interesting conversation when the two of you meet," Killian wondered aloud. "His life is mostly sleep and dreams now, but he has his home in the mountains by the king's castle, Kien Illae. When the dragon spoke the prophecy it was scribed to this canvas. It has hung in Kailani ever since."

"No one has told me the prophecy," she awed. "The Prince told me part of it but I knew there was more. What does it say?"

Killian looked to the canvas and read:

From a world of reflection, Eloria returns
When Evil rises and the world be burned
She shall love Seraphim wings or doom will she bring
A death to come that will change all things.
On winds they fly to the desolate place
Where a Queen Transformed finds Evil's true face
On black wings they die and fall
When he follows her to Qwells Vraugh
Where feathers and scales reign down
Love of another face will be found
The people will be with fear
When the time of Eloria draws near

They stood silently while Eloria ran the words over in her head, trying to understand their meaning. "I can see why no one recited it to me," she stated. "It's terrible. It doesn't even rhyme well. What, exactly, does it mean?"

Killian shrugged, still gazing at the canvas, "No one knows. That's why there is so much mystery surrounding you. We have never heard of a place called Qwells Vraugh and Evil's face has long been known to us. We know where they are and who they are. They're people like us, bu they don't honor the Creator."

"Why hasn't anyone asked the dragon about it? The one who said these things."

"Many kings have tried. We once fought alongside the dragons and, though we still have a good relationship with them, they refused to continue in our war against the Evil Ones. This prophecy was all they gave us as help and we are left to guess at their words. The dragons sleep now. They have for centuries. Only a few remain awake to watch the world. It is mostly the young ones, only a few generations old. The Royal Family keeps in contact with them in case they ever choose to wake again."

"The Prince mentioned once that he thought I would come in his time. How did he know? There's nothing here that mentions a time or name."

"I told Sorrell you would only ask more questions if you saw this," Killian sighed. "The Royal Family has only had daughters for generations. There were many sons after Seraphim, and even after the dragon gave us this prophecy but for many generations now, only princesses were born of the Royal Family. When the Prince was born, the first male Seraphim for generations, the prophecy was brought back to light. He has grown up being told that Eloria will come to him. He grew up believing he was already betrothed to this woman from another world because that is all anyone spoke of. His mother, the queen, wouldn't hear of it but she couldn't stop the whispers. It wasn't until he met Sorrell that he truly believed he could write his own destiny, that maybe the prophecy was for a different male heir."

"Then I showed up."

Killian nodded, "Then you arrived. Because of Sorrell, everything is happening as people predicted."

"Well... not everything," Eloria said. "I'm not falling in love with 'Seraphim wings' and no one has died."

"'A death to come,'" Killian corrected. Eloria raised an eyebrow at him in curiosity. "The Prince used to make me recite it to him when we were young. He wanted to know everything he could from this prophecy."

"Why didn't you tell me before?"

"This place has power in it. The Prince thought it was best that you heard it here. Sorrell agreed with him."

Eloria shook her head. Sorrell seemed to know a lot about what was best when it came to Eloria. She wondered again what Sorrell knew that everyone else didn't.

"Come with me," Killian said. "There's something else you need to see."

"How do you know about all of this? How do you know your way around?" Eloria asked.

"I was not the best at following rules when we apprenticed with the different Houses. Whenever there was a feast, I would slip away to anywhere they said we couldn't be. You learn a lot that way."

"Will we get into trouble?" she asked, nervous to follow him.

"You are a long honored prophecy," he said with a smirk. "I doubt anyone besides myself and Sorrell would try and correct you."

"You certainly do," she grumbled.

They continued down a number of lit hallways and soon came to an area that was clearly restricted. The torches were dark and only the windows above allowed moonlight to guide their path.

They stood across from an elaborately carved door. It ran the length of the wall as well as height, as if made for large groups of people to walk through at one time. Carvings of angels adorned its breadth.

Killian gestured for her to open it. She took the handle and pushed. Nothing happened. She tried again but was denied. Clearly whatever was behind this door was not for them to see.

"It's locked," she whispered, stepping away.

Killian rolled his eyes and went to the door. As soon as he took the handle, she heard a small click and the door cracked open.

"Are you breaking in?"

"The door is not broken," Killian answered. "It simply opened for me and not for you." He extended his hand to her.

She stepped away, "I don't think I want to go in. Killian, I don't exactly trust you..."

She expected him to be upset but he just smiled. Quick as a flash, he snatched out and grabbed her wrist. He pulled her through the door and it clicked shut behind them.

"What do you think you're doing!" she said, pulling away from him with anger.

"Sorrell said you wanted to see the glass ballroom."

Eloria's heart skipped a beat as she turned. He had brought them to the glass dome on the other side of the castle. All around them was starlight. The glass was seamless as it went from the floor and extended over their heads. She could see the ocean spreading endlessly, its waves hardly audible from their distance above. The water reflected the light of the stars and moon back up to the sky. Killian walked quietly towards the center of the room and she followed without conscious thought. The floor below them looked as if it were covered in starlight, yet she thought she could see water below them. She stepped back for a moment, scared that the floor was also glass and that it could break.

"It is completely safe," he said quietly. "You are standing on castle rock but it was built with the help of Mages. They created the floor to reflect the sky from above and sea from below. Even now our Masters cannot recreate it. No one knows how it was done."

She nodded again, hardly able to take in the beauty she saw around her. She continued to walk and gaze at its magnificence. She imagined lovely people with wings flying in and out of the room, smiling in the sun and singing the most wondrous songs.

"It's so…," she turned and to her surprise, Killian stood close behind her. She shook her head, not able to put words to what she felt. He reached up and wiped a tear from her cheek. Her eyes shot to him in bewilderment. His green eyed gaze was already on her.

She quickly turned away, blushing and confused. It was that look again. It was the odd way that he stared at her when no one else was with them. She began to walk away, but he caught her hand and gently pulled her to him. A tingling sensation ran from her hand through her arm. He placed his other hand on the small of her back. She shivered again from his touch. He gently pressed his hand against hers and her body moved as he led their dance.

Killian noticed her discomfort.

"Think of it as a form of training," he said.

He moved more slowly than what she and the Prince had rehearsed. It was as if one couldn't speak too loudly or move too quickly in the glass room. The giant dome seemed to watch and listen like a sleeping beast. Killian stepped softly as they danced. Circling them around the room.

"I apologize for earlier today," he said. "Sorrell spoke to me about it, and I realize that I should not have pushed you so hard. I had my own agenda in mind and did not consider your well being. I am truly sorry for that."

Eloria was dumfounded, "Thank you."

They continued in silence.

"Why are you so mean?" Eloria blurted.

Killian looked amused by her question. "There are a few reasons. For one, you were not what I expected."

"What do you mean?"

He cocked his head to the side, considering his answer, "I suppose that from growing up with the Prince, I thought I knew what Eloria would be like when we finally met her. I imagined a woman who fought better than anyone, controlled magic, and knew our world better than we did ourselves. She was supposed to be this great deliverance from the Evil Ones."

"But instead you got me."

"No, Eloria," he whispered, sending that strange sensation down her spine. "You are a gift to us. The prophecy was always a story that we played at as kids. When you arrived, there was hope. You see things differently than we do, Sorrell has told me. Your eyes," he lifted her chin. "Your eyes notice things that we never have."

"What are your other reasons?" she asked, embarrassed by his words and the attention he was giving her.

"Reason number two," he said with a smile, "is that I'm Guard to the Prince. It's not my place to speak up or share much. My duty is to protect him in every way possible and no matter the cost. Over the years, this has caused me to become a bit blunt and straightforward."

"I suppose those are good reasons."

"The third reason is that my past is complicated. I've seen great pain and great joy. It has never been easy for me to trust others. The Prince, Sorrell, and myself were closer than any other group in the queen's service. When you arrived, that all changed."

"Is it difficult to always be so unhappy?"

"I'm quite happy," he said with a crooked smile. "Trust me, the Prince could tell you a tale or two."

They continued their slow dance, and Eloria was ever aware of his hand on the bare skin of her back. His other hand held hers confidently in the air, his silver ring glinting in the moonlight as he led. He was being polite in the way he held her but something about him was different than it had been before.

"Are you happy here?" Killian asked as he slowly twirled her away then drew her back to him.

"Of course I am. Some things have been difficult to adapt to, but you already know that."

"Our food and my training?"

"Yes," she smiled.

"What about you and the Prince? After seeing everything... seeing this place," he looked at the room around them. "Have you changed your mind? If you could have tonight as your life every day, would you be with him?"

Eloria thought about his words. She had considered that same question and wondered at the idea of that sort of future. She looked at Killian and saw something akin to worry in his eyes but couldn't fathom why.

"I thought about it."

His muscles tensed as he moved them in a circle, still dancing across the room.

"However, there is so much more to this, isn't there? Even if I married the Prince and we lived in an amazing palace, there would still be Evil Ones out there. We would have responsibilities to the people and this, tonight, wouldn't be our life. This would be the rare night that we would fight for each day."

His muscles relaxed, "When did you become so wise?"

"Have you met my reflection?" she joked.

He slowed their dance further until they simply swayed in the middle of the room. Their feet looked as if they stood on waves. Eloria gazed up at the starlight surrounding them. Killian's dimly lit face watched her and he smiled a little. Her eyes were filled with such wonder and light.

"At home, in my world, I told someone once that I felt like a bystander. Later I started to feel like a victim as well." Eloria watched the stars as she was spun on the floor in their dance. "I don't want to be a victim in my own life anymore. You've taught me not to fear pain and I want to be a part of the adventures, not just watch them go by. This prophecy… well it makes things sound bigger than me and I like that. I would rather my story be about saving a world instead of…well…"

He stopped their dance. She let her eyes fall to his. Killian could see that she was apprehensive. He didn't blame her for feeling that way. His hand reached forward, cupping her face in his palm. He ran his thumb gently across her cheek. Butterflies filled her stomach. Her breath caught in her chest. She leaned away without intending to, but his other hand was still on her back, pulling her close.

"Please forgive me for how I've treated you," he whispered. "It is my hope that I can play a role in the story with you. Let me start by treating you better. I'd like to be a hero in your story, not to be seen as the villain which I'm sure is how you view me now."

She nodded, not able to take her eyes away from him. It was as if she were being pulled into their green depths. Her whole body tingled from his touch. She felt his hand slowly pulling her closer. She didn't want to move away. She didn't want to look away. He stopped with his forehead pressed against hers. Eloria watched his chest rise and fall as he breathed. Suddenly, he withdrew from her and removed his hand from her back. She gasped as the warmth disappeared from her skin. Killian glanced towards the door.

"The Prince needs to speak with us," he said.

Eloria was still overwhelmed, "How do you know?"

"Come with me," he gently took her hand and led her out of the glass dome.

She looked back as they walked, trying to engrave a picture of the room into her mind.

"Eloria," he whispered. A small shiver ran through her. "We have to go."

She nodded but couldn't tear her eyes away from the starlit room.

"I promise, you can come back again one day."

Killian softly tugged on her hand and she turned away, following him into the dark hallway. He shut the door behind them with another soft click. He quickly made his way back through the dark hallways and Eloria did her best to keep up. As they turned a corner, she saw the Prince, Sorrell and Fauna waiting for them. The sounds of the music and celebration could be heard echoing through the corridors and Eloria guessed that they weren't too far away from the main room. To her surprise, the Prince and Sorrell stood holding hands.

"Killian," the Prince said with a nod. "Fauna has received news from the beasts."

"A dragon has spoken to us," she spoke in a hushed tone. "It was Emerald from her place on the East Mountains. Her cliff faces the Barren Desert and she sent a message through the beasts to warn us."

"What is it?" Killian squared his shoulders.

"There is movement in the wastelands. A dark cloud is at the border, beginning to cross the desert. Her eyes have seen creatures deformed and…" Fauna paused and looked to the Prince.

"Tell them," he instructed.

She continued, "Emerald said that she has heard of Eloria's coming. The few other dragons that remain awake have tasted a change in the air. She said that if this cloud is of the Evil Ones, and Eloria has truly arrived, she will wake them." Fauna's voice grew excited, "She will wake the dragons and they will fight with us."

Killian stood silently as he processed her words.

184

"They haven't woken in generations," Fauna pointed out. "Some of them have slept for centuries. Even if they learn Eloria is here, many of them may not ally with us.

"The prophecy came from *the* dragon. They will respect the words of their elder. If he wakes, he will lead them."

"Dragons have no leaders. They are independent to themselves. If you travel through the mountains, you risk death to yourselves and Eloria. Everyone knows the High Landing is dangerous, and yet it would be the only way to see the cloud from this end of the mountains. It would be best if you go straight to the king and tell him of this news," Fauna defended her position.

"We must go to the mountains immediately and speak with Emerald," the Prince said confidently.

"But Eloria has not yet finished her training," Sorrell argued. "She's suppose to start her lessons with the House of Beasts tomorrow!"

"Perhaps we can take one day to give her some basics. Her companions can continue her training as you travel," Fauna suggested.

"A days time could be the difference between dragons waking and dragons sleeping. We don't want to miss our chance," the Prince interjected.

Eloria watched them debate back and forth. They had more experience in this matter but it sounded to her like going into the mountains would be more dangerous than she ever realized. For the first time, she understood why Killian had pushed her so hard. She stepped back a little and waited next to him. The Guard remained still, his eyes scanning the floor beneath him as if there was an invisible chart he was reading. When their argument rose he snapped out of his daze.

"We will wait," he said boldly. The others quieted and looked to him. "We need at least a day to gather supplies and information before heading into the mountains. I think it would be safer to gather all of the knowledge from the beasts that we can and have them scout ahead for us, if they are willing. This will allow us time to prepare and for her," he nodded to Eloria, "to get a days worth of training."

The Prince agreed, "This plan is sound. Besides, we do not want the king to leave Kien Illae unless it is absolutely necessary."

"My Prince," Killian said formally, "I believe this is the best way for me to protect you and our company. If we can wait one day, it will be enough. I doubt the dragon will leave her mountain before then."

The Prince stood quietly and thought it over. "Very well. We will wait one day only, unless our information changes. It would be wise for us to rejoin the celebration and remain here for the rest of tonight. The Healers have rooms prepared for us. In the morning, Killian and I will talk with the Houses and send our messages as needed. Sorrell and Eloria will train."

"I would like to spend the day at the House of the Beasts," Killian said quickly. "It would be wise for me to be near if the beasts send more knowledge of the situation. Besides, Sorrell is a better writer when it comes to messages for the queen, it is her House after all."

The Prince looked at him curiously but nodded his consent. They made their way back to the feast. Eloria tried her best to wrap her mind around all the last hour's events. She pushed away her thoughts of Killian and the glass ballroom, not wanting Sorrell to overhear her. She would have to figure that out when she was alone.

They rejoined their table and the Prince had resumed his usual smile. Sorrell also looked as if nothing had happened, but Killian disappeared entirely. Eloria did her best to eat a bit more but in the end gave up on food. A few House Masters asked to dance and she obliged, thankful for something to take her mind off of the coming journey. The words of the prophecy circulated through her head. Another two hours went by but no one seemed to leave the great castle. Eventually, Eloria relayed her exhaustion to Sorrell, hoping she would be allowed to leave the celebration. Sorrell obliged, helping to find Fauna to take Eloria to her room.

Sorrell and the Prince stayed behind while Eloria was escorted away. She was led through a series of halls to an uppermost floor with its own chambers.

"These were the rooms of our Eloria before you. I hope you find them to be comfortable. There will be clothes for you inside. When morning comes, someone will meet you here and bring you to our House. Can you swim?"

"Er, yes?" Eloria answered, not understanding its relevance.

"Very good," Fauna commented. "I will see you tomorrow. Rest well."

Eloria went through the door and found herself in a large sitting room. There were tapestries covering each wall with a large fireplace and mantel to her left. Chairs of gold with large cushions were grouped together along with glass tables where flowers had been placed. The outer wall was made of windows and she saw a balcony outside. There were doors to her left and right and she could only imagine what it must've been like for the Queen Eloria to have lived here.

She went to a door furthest from her and was relieved to see a large canopy bed and wardrobe. She pulled out something simple from the wardrobe and quickly changed, careful not to ruin the dress in any way. She hung it in the wardrobe and donned a simple cotton tunic. With the dress put away, the magical night seemed to come to a brief conclusion. Eloria was happy to be able to stay in Kailani for the night so that she could see more of its beauty before morning. She quickly explored the other rooms finding a washroom, a smaller sitting room, a smaller bedroom, and an empty room with a long table. She assumed it was meant to be for meetings and assemblies.

Not wanting to go to bed yet, Eloria slipped out to the balcony. The cool breeze blew her hair behind her as she hurried to the balcony's ledge. The ocean waves crashed upon the rocks below, spraying their mist into the night sky. She was high above in a tower overlooking the ocean. To her left, she could see the glass dome glinting in the star's light. She could hardly believe her experience within that round ballroom. Eloria closed her eyes and inhaled the sea air, remembering Killian's green eyes staring at her and the way he stood so close.

What is happening? she thought. *Killian, of all people.*

She remembered how her heart had raced as he pulled her close, holding her face with his hand. She quickly shook her head and looked out to the sea.

"Don't get carried away," she said aloud. "It was a party. Everyone has been in a strange mood. Let's see how he acts tomorrow."

CHAPTER 15

As dawn approached, Killian paced nervously in front of Eloria's door. He had hardly slept and laid in bed anxiously waiting for the sun to rise. He had rushed through his morning training and already met with the Prince, Sorrell and the House Masters. When he left their table, he had practically sprinted through the corridors to Eloria's chambers.

"Calm down, Killian," he muttered to himself. "No need to overwhelm her. You're only... destroying people's hopes and dreams."

He shook his head. He hadn't felt this nervous since his own Choosing Ceremony. Stepping forward, he went to knock but the door swung open before his fist made contact.

"Oh! Hi," Eloria said, surprised to see him there.

"Good morning."

They stood is silence and Eloria could see that he looked rather uncomfortable.

Maybe being nice to me is a physical struggle for him, she thought.

"This is for you," he thrust a small box towards her.

"Uh... thank you."

She took it and carefully lifted the lid, curious to what Killian would be giving her. Inside was a folded piece of fabric. Lifting it from the box, she studied the strange item. It was clearly an outfit of some sort, and the fabric felt rubbery in her hands. It reminded her of a bathing suit although it had straps that seemed to wrap around the body in odd patterns.

"Fauna said you needed it for training today," he pointed out when he saw her quizzical expression.

"Oh, that makes sense... I suppose."

Killian was growing impatient, "You need to put it on... before we leave."

"Right, of course. Come in," Eloria said, stepping back into the large sitting room. She quickly went to change and Killian leaned against the door, waiting. He had made a special arrangement with Fauna for today's training and he was interested to see how Eloria would react when she found out about it.

The outfit was indeed a swimsuit and she, like always, felt uncomfortable being around anyone with so much of her skin showing. At home she had always tried to wear the tank top style that would cover her. She was so embarrassed by her body before. This time, she noticed how toned she had become and how much unhealthy 'pudge' had disappeared due to her new diet and training. The straps on this suit were strange and it was a few minutes until she emerged in the strange suit. Killian looked over at her as she reentered the room and immediately threw his eyes to the ceiling.

"Oh... sorry I thought maybe Sorrell had explained. You are supposed to still wear pants...."

Eloria's cheeks flushed a bright red and she ran back into the room, throwing on a pair of grey cotton pants and a shirt. She immediately felt more comfortable in her own skin but was almost too embarrassed to look at Killian again. She hesitantly walked back into the sitting room and Killian dropped his eyes from the ceiling.

"I didn't know," she explained. "In my world we wear just the suit... nothing over it."

He nodded, somewhat confused and walked out the door. She quickly followed and they made their way through a mess of corridors and out from the castle. As they left the castle and walked down the rocky peninsula, Eloria looked back and wondered if she would ever see the magnificence of Kailani again. Its glass dome and shining towers were the beacon of the Ocean Region.

"We need to hurry," Killian motioned ahead of her. "We only have one day and there is much for you to learn."

With one last look, she turned away from the palace and followed after him. When they reached the sandy beach, Killian led them away from the House of Healers. She could make out a large group of huts further down with small boats tied up to a dock that extended on stilts into the sea. It was a twenty minute walk down the beach until they got to the huts. To her surprise, Killian walked right past them to the dock. At the very end, Fauna was waiting for them.

"That was quick," she noted as Killian and Eloria approached.

"I don't want to waste any time," he replied looking out to the sea.

"Welcome, Eloria," Fauna said with a slight tilt of her chin. "Are you ready to open your mind?"

Eloria nodded excitedly, "I can't wait to speak with the animals!"

Fauna's mouth twitched with annoyance, "They are beasts, child. Please remember. The first thing you must know is that beasts think as you and I. They have intelligence and each has their own unique personality just as any man or woman. When our Creator first formed them, He did not intend for them to speak with their mouths the way that we do. That is why we use our minds."

Eloria nodded with understanding. She had seen Sorrell staring at a small doe in the woods during their journey. They both stood perfectly still and looked at one another as if they were having a conversation.

"Beasts speak not only with words but emotions and visions. They will communicate their feelings with you and pictures from their memories will flash in front of your eyes. This is their way of explaining. In order to hear them and speak in return, you must empty your mind of everything. It will take time and you may not hear their words today, but it will be a start."

Fauna nodded matter-of-factly and walked to a paddle boat tied to the dock. She hopped in with ease and Killian extended a hand to Eloria. She ignored his gesture and clambered in after Fauna, not quite as gracefully as she hoped. The boat was rocking back and forth as she hurried to sit. To her surprise, Killian got in after her.

"Aren't you gathering information from the beasts?" Eloria asked with dismay. "Last night you said you had… tactical things to work out."

He gave his usual shrug that told her he didn't care, "No new information has come in. They'll come to Fauna first so it's better that I stay with her."

Eloria rolled her eyes and Killian took a seat by a set of oars. Fauna loosed the ropes on the docks and Killian began rowing them out to sea. Despite Eloria's confusion of his actions ranging from last night to this morning, she couldn't help but be excited about being in the ocean. She assumed today would simply be a day of meditation where no one could distract them. Killian spent the next hour rowing them further into the ocean's expanse. She didn't understand why they had to go so far out for her to clear her mind but she sat quietly and tried her best anyway, using the rhythm of the oars to help. She tried listening for thoughts of the fish below but anything that came to her mind she made up herself.

"This is deep enough Killian," Fauna told him.

"They're almost here. It seems they haven't surfaced for a while," he replied to her.

"Who hasn't surfaced?" Eloria inquired.

"The first beasts to be blessed by the Creator were the whales," Fauna explained. "Therefore, whales have always been the easiest to communicate with and the best way to train all who come to apprentice. There is a pod that lives near here who have offered their services."

Eloria's heart beat wildly. She was going to see whales! She was going to speak with whales! She twitched eagerly in her seat, looking out to the horizon to find them.

"Beneath us," Killian smiled.

She glanced down and saw a large black shadow underneath their boat. Without thinking, she stood in shock. The boat began rocking back and forth. Killian pulled her quickly back to her seat. She peered over the side and saw many more shapes, clearly whales, passing further beneath them and around them. Finally, they began to surface, spraying the boat with water as air passed through their blow holes.

Orcas! Eloria could hardly contain her excitement.

"They're ready for us," Killian said to Fauna.

"Take off your tunic," Fauna nodded to Eloria.

"Excuse me?" she gasped.

"You have the suit on underneath? I asked you last night if you could swim."

All the dots suddenly connected for Eloria. She pulled her shirt off, not giving a second thought to being in her new swimsuit. Killian also stood and pulled his tunic over his head. For a moment, Eloria's eyes left the whales and turned to him. His skin was perfectly tan and abs rippled. She wasn't sure why she was surprised by his perfect body, everyone here had one. He saw her glance and she quickly turned away, looking back at the whales.

"Eloria, you are going to swim to the large one straight out in front of you. That is Noelani. He will help you learn to listen and speak today. Physical contact is very important for beginners so you will ride with him," Fauna said.

"I will be with Muir, the one right by him. We will ride along with you to translate until you can hear him yourself," Killian said. They both stood and when Eloria didn't move, Killian became worried. "Do not be afraid," he said gently.

"I could never be afraid of this," she grinned.

Eloria half jumped and half fell into the ocean in excitement. She came up laughing and began to swim towards Noelani. Killian smiled as he watched her. Once she had reach Noelani, he dove into the water.

Eloria couldn't contain her excitement. All her life she had dreamt of seeing a whale and she felt like she must be in a dream even now. A small calf swam beneath her and another swam by her, looking through the water at the small human as it went by. Eloria could see its eye and immediately noticed the intelligence with which it looked at her. In animals back home, the eyes were blank and she had to look at their body language to guess what they were thinking. When she looked into this whales' eye she could see that it knew and thought as she did. She approached the large orca that Fauna had pointed her to and it blew from its air hole, spraying water all around them.

"You can go to him," Killian said, swimming up next to her. "He welcomes you and is happy that you wish to learn," he translated. "You may ride on his back and hold his dorsal fin, but be careful not to dig your heels into him like a horse." Killian smiled as his eyes stared off to the distance.

"What?" Eloria asked. "What is he saying?"

"He is showing me a memory. An apprentice once came from the Plains and tried riding Noelani as if he were a horse. It didn't go so well for the boy."

Eloria slowly swam closer to the whale. She looked him in the eye and nodded respectfully. She was not afraid of the enormous beast, but had a healthy respect for his power and size. She had heard enough horror stories from her world to know that these whales were not to be taken lightly. The orca, Noelani, nodded his head up and down, as if saying yes. The whale sunk down, into the water and glided gently beneath her. When he rose back up, she was on his back, gripping tightly with her thighs so that she would not fall off. Killian was already on his whale, Muir. He was soaked from head to toe and laughing with the beast. Eloria had never seen him acting so... naturally. Killian looked at Eloria and winked.

Muir and Killian disappeared beneath the blue waves. She looked around for them and a few seconds later, they popped up again with Killian's feet on Muir's nose, propelling through the water like a jet. They circled the boat where Fauna sat frowning at them.

Killian dove back under and they became a blur. Eloria shook her head, convinced that he was simply showing off. Without warning, Noelani's back fin propelled them forward with a great force. He moved through the water quickly until they were a few yards from their original position. He stopped and turned, facing the blur that was Killian and Muir. Eloria became worried at how long he had been under water.

Quick as a flash, the blur began moving upwards, towards the surface. Water cascaded around them as Killian burst through. Muir shot him straight up to the sky, his large body gleamed black and white in the sunlight and almost fully out of the ocean as he leapt. Right before Muir began to fall back to the water, Killian pushed off from him and floated in the air.

For a moment, Eloria wondered if he was gliding on the wind. He hung suspended then arched his body, diving into the water with ease and grace. Noelani and the other whales around them began speaking. They whistled and clicked, as if laughing at Muir's spectacle. Eloria could feel the whale vibrating beneath her as he hummed. She leaned forward and rested her head against his fin, closing her eyes with happiness.

Images flashed through her mind. She saw a whale calf catching his first fish, the pod breaching far out in the ocean. She laughed as more images flooded her mind. The world around her remained, but the memories played over her vision. She heard a faint song, a happy song of the whales.

"Is he showing you?" Killian asked, now alongside them.

"Yes," she gasped. The images disappeared and she focused on the ocean again. She lifted her head from Noelani. "I saw images of the sea and I heard their song."

Killian nodded, "With time you will learn to speak back to them, to hear words as well as images. Even in battle, you will be able to fight while seeing their perspective."

"What do you mean?"

"The Prince and I once fought the Deformed with Adette, a mountain cat from the west. While in battle, our minds remained linked and I could fight while also seeing her perspective of the battle. It gave us a great advantage."

Eloria thought back to the deformed bear that they had met in the forest. "When we were attacked before arriving here, you said that the Deformed spoke to you. I remember seeing it now. What was it like being in its head?"

Killian was silent for a moment as he stared out at the sea. "It is hard, opening your mind to the Deformed. They are filled with hate and pain. The torture they endured turning into what they are becomes them. They will do anything to hurt and destroy in return. They don't just speak to you, they seek to control you and find things that you wish to remain hidden. They can force your mind to break so that you cannot control what they do and do not see. That is why you must not only learn to open your mind but how to close it as well. Never attempt to speak to Deformed unless you have mastered the skill. Even then, it is risky."

"But you did it," Eloria pointed out.

"Yes. I have experience. I've fought these creatures many times before although we try to stay away from their minds. In the forest, I needed to know how it had gotten so far from the mountains and for what purpose. I ran the risk of it being able to break me but it was important that we find out the information it had. I have secrets that could destroy us, and even I must remember that when speaking to any beast."

Eloria nodded and looked out to the sea. "What now?" she asked.

"Now," Fauna shouted to them, "I will teach you to listen."

The next few hours involved Eloria watching memories from the whale and interpreting what she saw to Fauna. The woman explained how to listen, how to speak, how to clear her mind, and ultimately how to communicate with the beasts. By the afternoon, she was able to relay her emotions and some memories to the whale in return.

"Time for something new," Killian said after a while, "We ride the sea. The whales will keep us close but they do not wish to stay in this spot all day. We will ride with them and you can practice reaching out to others. Try not to think, just listen. Under the water, you may find it easier."

The whales began moving further out to sea, and after a short while, they dove under. Eloria took a deep breath when she felt Noelani begin to descend. The water filled her ears and all was silent. He rose consistently with when she needed to breathe although she wasn't sure how he knew. Eventually, they hit a pattern of rising and falling, breathing and listening. This went on the rest of the afternoon.

She heard the whales' song as they swam. Long notes that reverberated through the water. She was able to see Neolani's memories more easily and began to extend her mind to the other whales around them. It was difficult and she still didn't hear words, but towards the end of the day she was able to touch Muir's mind. He relayed to her the rush of jumping through waves near the beach, breaching with his pod. He even sent her a glimpse of what it was like jumping into the air and tossing Killian off his nose. She felt Muir's joy and wondered if he was a younger whale than the rest of them or simply more spirited.

When the sun was setting, the whales made their way back towards the shallows. They stayed at the surface and Eloria was happy for the easiness of breath. Killian's hair was already drying from the breeze and it looked wild around his face. Fauna and the boat were gone but he wasn't worried.

"Muir is smaller than most of his pod, he can take us further in and closer to the Healer's House. We will have to swim the rest of the way. Do you think you can?"

Eloria nodded to him. Her muscles were weak but she was still elated from her day. She pressed her forehead to Noelani's rubbery fin and thought about her day. She remembered her joy at seeing the whales, the excitement when Noelani lifted her onto his back, and the beauty they had showed her. She tried to thank him as best as she knew how. He began to click happily.

"He hears you," Killian said with a smile.

Eloria laughed and kissed his fin. She slid off his back into the cool water. He clicked again then leaned away, diving into the ocean below. Eloria swam to Killian and he extending his hand. This time she took it. He pulled her onto Muir along with him. She sat behind his dorsal fin and Killian perched himself on Muir's head. They heard a chirping come from Muir and Killian pointed out to the sea. Eloria watched as Noelani jumped from the ocean, twisting and landing on his side with a great splash. The rest of the pod began to join in, playing. Muir chirped happily then moved his large tail, propelling them towards shore. After the sun had dipped to the horizon, Killian slipped down from the whale and motioned for Eloria to do the same.

"If he goes any further he'll risk being beached. We swim from here."

She nodded and hopped into the water. "Can you thank him for me?"

"I already have," Killian said with a kind smile. "They called you a whale singer today, because you listened to their stories with appreciation."

"That is an amazing thing to be called," she mused. "What do they call you?"

Killian laughed proudly, "They have too many names for me."

He began swimming towards shore and Eloria followed. "But... what names?"

"Well my favorite is "the one who swims through air." Whenever I'm with them, we play a lot. Muir loves to throw me in the air and watch me dive back into the water. It's fun," he shrugged. "The Prince could never do it because he's so much larger than I."

"Huh," Eloria thought. "I like 'Whale Singer' much better."

When they reached shore, the Prince and Sorrell were waiting for them. Eloria was soaked but couldn't wait to tell Sorrell everything about the day. The memories were flashing through her head as she ran up the beach to them.

"Whoa!" Sorrel exclaimed, throwing up her hands. "Slow down Eloria! Killian, what in the world did you teach her today?"

"We finally found something she's brave at," Killian mused. "She was able to listen almost immediately with touch. Towards the end of the day she was starting to hear others. Senses, no words, but it was good for her first time."

"We received word from a group of Airedales an hour ago," the Prince said to Killian. "There is definitely some sort of dark cloud making its way over the Barren Desert. They came from a village in the mountains that had been attacked. The pack could sense the Deformed before they came and the people were able to get to safety before the village was destroyed."

"What are Airedales?" Eloria asked.

"They are a breed of dog," Sorrell quickly explained. "They live mostly in the forest and plains. Highly intelligent and curious beasts, they always pop up when danger comes near."

"They wish to travel back with us," the Prince told them. "They are seven strong and would join us until the forests' edge."

Killian nodded, his good mood diminishing. His mind started planning and calculating. Eloria could see the Guard taking over again. She wondered if this meant no more happy Killian.

CHAPTER 16

Morning came too quickly for all of them. Sorrell woke Eloria an hour or so before sunrise with traveling clothes and her pack. Eloria noticed that Sorrell was elated as they packed their bags. When she was about to ask, there was a knock on her door. Killian popped his head in.

"Time for training. We have to hurry if we are going to be ready in time to meet the Airedales."

Eloria sighed and let her aching body stalk after him. At the training ring, he tossed her a sword. She immediately used it to guard herself, waiting for Killian to attack without warning.

"I promised you things would be different," he said. "Today let's practice a succession of only three moves."

He named the moves and Sorrell adjusted Eloria's form as she struck the pose. Once she could hit each of them correctly on her own, Killian had her use the moves in combination, over and over until they were ingrained into her muscles. Finally, he joined her and struck his sword against hers, attacking and defending with each of the three moves she had just learned. When the sun was beginning to peak over the horizon, the Prince joined them and it was time to move out. They each grabbed a bit of fruit then donned their packs, ready for a long trail ahead.

Sorrell's elated mood didn't diminish all day, and the Prince seemed strangely happy as well. They chatted with one another about old stories and fun facts about the different regions. Their conversations seemed irrelevant yet they couldn't keep their eyes off each other. Killian didn't seem to notice the two as they trudged through the compact sand and palm trees, making their way to the forest. Contrary to Eloria's thoughts the day before, Killian remained kind and more open to her all day. His annoyed attitude had disappeared and he even walked beside her most of the way. He didn't attempt to make any sort of conversation but remained quietly at her side.

The ocean seriously changes people, Eloria thought as she glanced to her companions. She shook her head as Sorrell giggled, hearing her thoughts. Suddenly her foot caught on a large stone in front of her. Killian's hand shot out and caught her before she even had time to take in a breath. A warm sensation ran through her skin as he pulled her back onto her feet.

"Be careful," he said shortly, pulling his hand away.

She nodded with a small smile. *There it is! He's still annoyed by my clumsiness.*

"Must you think so loudly?" Sorrell laughed back to her. "Use those loud thoughts of yours and practice speaking to the beasts. The Airedales are up ahead."

Eloria looked excitedly ahead of them but saw nothing. She glanced at Killian who was giving her a curious expression.

"What?" she asked.

He looked away without reply.

It was another half mile before she saw movement ahead of them. Brown and black shapes were dashing through the trees. The Prince and Sorrell smiled and their eyes glazed over. Eloria knew they were in conversation with the beasts ahead of them. Even Killian's guarded expression became more cheerful as he shared thoughts with one of the Airedales. They approached a pack of seven dogs who pranced over to the company.

The Prince and what looked like the leader of the pack stood silently and stared at one another. Eloria looked to all the dogs with excitement. She had always thought of herself as a dog person but her family never owned any. These beasts were tall and agile. They stood a bit taller than retrievers but what they lacked in bulk muscle they had in swift movement. Some had long curly hair and others were shaved and looked very regal. Their hair was all brown except for a large black saddle on their backs that spread from their necks and to the tops of their tails. Some had reddish-brown fur while others were tan like beach sand.

Eloria noticed one dog in particular that looked a bit different than the rest. His fur was more black than the others and only his legs and tail had turned brown. His mangy hair didn't hold a curl. When he moved, he seemed to bounce with each motion.

"He is still a pup," Killian noticed her gaze. "They are born all black and their color changes. You can see in the way that he moves that he is still younger than the rest. This is probably his first journey away from the den. Try and speak with him."

"He's too far away," she mumbled.

Killian shrugged and stepped away from her, addressing a curly, muscled Airedale a short ways ahead of them.

"The Airedales are beautiful, aren't they?" Sorrell asked with a smile. "They are the best companions we could hope for. They have great senses and more energy than any other beast. The speed and distance we will need to travel won't tire them whatsoever."

Eloria shrugged, "Wouldn't it be safer to have lions or tigers?"

"The Airedales may not have large teeth or claws but they are swift and have the highest pain tolerance of any breed. They are extremely independent and their minds are tough to break. They will hold their own against the Deformed better than any other beasts in the forest I think."

The Prince turned away from the pack's leader and to his companions, "The Airedales will go with us until we reach the mountain trail. They would like to send two of their dogs ahead as scouts and the rest stay with us for protection and to guide us to the path that we need."

"Apparently the bear we met on our way to the ocean isn't the only Deformed to have crossed over the mountain," Killian informed them. "They have found creatures wandering the woods on their own. Other packs have seen the same and they are working to rid the forest of them."

The Prince nodded and turned back to their leader. He stood silently for a moment then, as one, the pack turned and began trotting away from them. Two dogs sprinted ahead and out of sight. Two more circled around and flanked them on either side about twenty yards or so from the rest of the group. They began walking once again. The leader of the pack stayed by the Prince along with another dog.

The young one that Eloria had been watching pranced his way to Killian and jumped excitedly at his hands. Killian smiled, speaking with the young Airedale. As they walked, he picked up a stick from the ground and threw it far ahead of them. The Airedale growled and barked, racing after it. He disappeared from sight then returned with the stick happily between his teeth. Instead of giving it up, he danced around Killian, daring him to try and take it.

They spent the rest of the day walking on the packed sand and through the palm trees and brush. Killian and the dog continued playing and his smile hardly faded. They reached the edge of the forest at night fall and made camp among the trees. Eloria felt more at home in the woods. The birds sounded familiar once again and the smell of the trees brought her comfort. They made camp in their usual formation. Eloria's legs remembered the familiar sore feeling after walking all day.

Under the moonlight, she could faintly see two airedales circling their camp, keeping watch in their own way. The other dogs spun in circles and curled up on the ground between their two legged companions. Killian took watch, like usual, and the puppy stayed at his side.

Eloria closed her eyes and listened to the sounds of the forest. The crickets chirped and the leaves blew gently in the wind. She felt herself start to doze when something furry rubbed against her. She jerked her head up and was surprised to see the large puppy curling up next to her to sleep. He wrapped himself in a tight ball and rested his chin on her shoulder. Images began blurring past her vision. She saw him chasing a stick, his muscles coiling and stretching as he ran with all his might. The puppy showed her the joy of keeping the stick away from Killian and nipping at his hands in play.

Eloria smiled and glanced up at Killian. He was sitting against a large tree, watching her. When their eyes met he winked at her. She felt her cheeks flush and she quickly turned away. Putting her hand on the dog's head, she showed it her memories of seeing him for the first time and watching him run and play. The young dog groaned in sleepy joy.

Zane, she heard it say to her.

Eloria, she replied with her mind, excited to hear words for the first time.

I will protect you tonight, he said happily, with a naiveness to his voice.

She glanced up at Killian again but he was now standing, drawing his sword to begin his nightly routine. She watched as he began his imaginary fight. His style was different this time. He fought more openly and more forward, as if someone unseen was defending his back. Zane noticed her watching Killian and gave a small bark, drawing her attention back to himself.

He moves fast as the wind and he is hard to catch, he thought to her.

Yes, he is very quick, she thought fondly.

Zane turned onto his back and stretched his paws to the sky with a lazy groan. When stretched out, he was over half as long as she was.

He sure doesn't look like a puppy, she thought to herself. He closed his eyes and fell asleep within seconds, his paws twitching slightly in the air as he dreamed. Eloria smiled and peered at Killian while he did his new routine, watching his arms flex with strength at every attack and his feet move silently as he defended against the invisible enemy.

She guessed that he knew she was watching but he never looked her way. His movements were grand and rhythmic, like how he had fought the Deformed in the forest. She fell asleep watching him whisper in conversation with his Creator as he fought his invisible enemy.

***

The Prince felt a wet tongue on his face. Images of owls flying through the trees entered his mind. He slowly opened his eyes to see an Airedale drooling over him. He sighed and rolled out of his furs.

Next watch? he thought to the dog beside him.

The dog wagged his tail and pranced over to where Killian sat against a tree. The Prince jammed his boots onto his feet and glanced over at Sorrell, asleep in her blankets. She looked beautiful with the moonlight shining down on her. He felt that he could watch her sleep all night and never grow tired of it. With a big grin, he made his way to Killian.

"You told him to lick my face?" he thumped to the ground next to his comrade.

"Someone had to wipe that ridiculous smile off," Killian replied.

"Thanks a lot," the Prince chuckled. "With all respect though… thank you, Killian. I appreciate your help the other night in distracting Eloria while I spoke with Sorrell. I know it must have been such a sacrifice for you to spend time alone with her," he joked.

"Well I had a few things I needed to say as well before we started traveling again. You gave me a good reason to pull her aside. Besides, we have a plan to keep in motion."

The Prince nodded and they sat in silence. The Airedales sat alert and poised. Watching, listening, and smelling for any danger that may be headed their way.

"What do you make of this dark cloud?" Killian asked the Prince.

"I'm not sure what to think. The Evil Ones have always been stuck behind the mountains. It's been an unspoken agreement that it is their territory. The Barren Desert is no man's land. Evil hasn't made advances until our generation. Creation of the Deformed told us they were up to something new. I think this dark cloud that Emerald saw is just the beginning of more disgusting Mage tricks." The Prince traced shapes in the dirt beside him. "Is there any chance it could be black smoke that lingers? Perhaps from their territory that floated our way?"

Killian's eyebrows pushed together, "It moves against the wind. Smoke would have blown away. Besides, Emerald has eyes of a dragon. She would know the difference."

"I think we need to seek her out directly, not travel to the Landing to look upon this cloud."

"We need to see it for ourselves. There's no other way to know what sort of danger it carries. We also need to know how fast it moves and how far it is. We need information to report to the king, not rumors. If the dragon is as eager to meet Eloria as it sounded, she'll find us."

207

The Prince nodded, "I suppose you're right. I feel more protective of Sorrell now that..."

"I understand," Killian quickly replied.

"The sooner we put the High Landing behind us to face Kien Illae, the better off we'll be. I think we are all missing home."

Killian looked to the women sleeping soundly in their blankets and furs. "Not all of us. I'm happy for you and Sorrell, by the way. I don't think I've told you that yet, but I truly am."

The Prince nodded, "Thank you. How are you doing with... all of this?"

Killian's gaze faded away into the forest.

"There's no good way to explain it."

"Are you still angry?"

The Prince saw tears in his eyes.

"I miss her," Killian said. "It's been years since we..."

"I know," the Prince put a reassuring hand on his friend's shoulder.

"Despite how long it has been, there's still an ache. As if an entire part of my life has been ripped away."

"With the way we were raised, it's no surprise. Always having the prophecy crammed down our throats didn't help, but it's time for you to accept the reality before you."

Killian breathed deeply, "I know it sounds ridiculous but Elior... she's become part of us. Her connection with Sorrell is stronger than we realized. You and she seem to have a friendship. But I...."

"You need to deal with the fact that she's here. The prophecy is happening. No more doom and gloom from you."

"'She will love Seraphim wings or doom she will bring,'" Killian recited.

The Prince waived aimlessly, "Words. Meaningless words. My feelings for Sorrell are immovable. The world will learn the truth soon enough."

"Or, if she doesn't fall in love with the Seraphim Prince we have everything to worry about," Killian mumbled.

"It's all up to interpretation. You do your part and our plan will buy us time from the Evil Ones."

Killian nodded, "Sleep helps all worries right?"

"Duty first. Then sleep."

The Prince watched as his companion walked noiselessly to the circle of beds. He lingered next to Eloria for a moment, and the Prince saw a brief look of pain in his eyes.

Brothers, he thought to himself. *I know him better than he knows himself, despite his constant brooding.* The Prince turned away. With a shake of his head he turned his thoughts back to Sorrell.

Killian knelt next to Eloria and lightly touched her face. Her eyes flew open and her body tensed. She immediately reached for a weapon but Killian caught her hand mid air.

"Come with me," he grunted.

Eloria rubbed the sleep from her eyes, "It's the middle of the night."

"Be quiet," he scolded. "Zane is sleeping."

"Sure, let the dog sleep." Eloria stumbled to her feet. "Where are we going?"

Killian pressed a finger to his lips. To Eloria's surprise, he took her hand and led them away from camp. They made their way through the trees until they arrived at a trickling brook. It slithered over tree roots and boulders as it wound its way through the forest.

"The stream will cover our voices," Killian explained.

"What are we doing?"

"Training."

"Are you kidding me?"

"We've worked on your body and mind. It's time to work on your soul."

Eloria was taken aback, "Is this something to do with you being 'the church' or whatever? Sorrell told me what your name meant but I didn't think it would mean a full blown conversion speech."

"Magic. It means magic. Your soul is the gateway to accessing it, so to speak. There are rules to magic as there are rules to using your mind to speak to the creatures around you. Magic is everywhere in our world. The only known place it is absent is the Barren Desert. These tiny balls of light that float around us are bits of magic, waiting to be harnessed."

Eloria looked around at the tiny, glowing objects. After so long in this world, she hardly noticed their presence anymore. They twinkled and floated absently through the trees like oversized lightening bugs.

"Sorrell told me they were harmless. We walk right by them everyday and nothing happens."

"As they are now may seem insignificant, but once they are bound to a physical object they are the magic that make up this world. Builders hammer it into their lumber and into our steel. Healers bind the magic to their remedies and ointments. Mages use it for potions and discovery. It can also be used through one's own body."

"I've never seen any of you use magic before."

"Magic is unstable if not bound to a physical object. It can be temperamental and misused if not done properly."

"Why are you teaching me?"

"The others wouldn't agree, but I think you need to learn."

Killian took Eloria's hand once again and a warm sensation ran through her body.

"Is that magic?" she asked.

"What?"

"The feeling when…"

Killian's brow rose. Eloria's cheeks burned with embarrassment and she was thankful for the cover of darkness.

"Never mind. What do I need to do?"

"This will be your one and only lesson. Magic is something you need to find for yourself, I can only point you on the right path."

"Spoken like a true warrior."

"Don't make fun."

"Sorry."

He held her hand up to eye level. With her palm spread, he rested it beneath a small ball of light as it floated between them. He cradled his hands around hers and the glowing orbs around them stopped their aimless paths. The lights stilled for a moment then floated in their direction.

"Now we are going to merge them into one."

Each small orb floated to her palm, merging as they did. Within seconds, a large ball of light hovered in her hand, pulsing to its own beat. Through the light, she saw Killian wink at her. In that moment, the light burst apart. Settling back into individual orbs, they resumed a lazy pattern through the air.

"To access the magic within yourself, you must find a place of joy and peace. It is a spot between your mind and heart."

"Think happy thoughts? That's it?"

Killian shook his head, "Have you ever had a single emotion completely consume you? But then you found yourself choosing to feel another way or act against that emotion? For me it was failure. There was a moment in my life that I felt so ashamed…but in that moment I found clarity and chose to dismiss my failure. Instead I replaced it with hope. It was both a mental and emotional choice."

"Like flipping a switch?"

"What is a switch?"

Eloria shook her head, "Never mind. I think I understand what you're saying."

"You try it now."

He lifted her hands once again. They sat in silence as Eloria tried to bring the magical orbs to her palms.

"I don't think it's working," she whispered.

"Be quiet."

She inhaled deeply and waited. Killian's hands remained beneath hers, holding them in place. She noticed the silver band on his finger as it gleamed in the moonlight.

"I like your ring," she said.

He narrowed his eyes at her.

Eloria shifted uncomfortably. The lazy bits of magic floated by them.

"The silver kind of glows," she whispered.

"Focus," he scolded.

Eloria sighed. The lights floated by. Small streams of light followed the balls around like little tails. Eloria shifted again, trying to think about moving the magic towards her.

"You've noticed my ring?" Killian asked.

"You do wear it every day."

"Most people don't see it."

"I used to secretly hope it would fall off during training."

The corner of his mouth twitched.

"That way we would have to stop and look for it in the sand. Less bruises for me."

He tried to hide his smile, "Focus on the magic, Eloria."

She shivered at the sound of her name. His voice was like honey every time he said it. Her heartbeat thumped in her ears. The minutes felt long as they waited. Eloria tried to do as Killian had instructed but her mind was preoccupied. Killian closed his eyes, his hands holding hers steadily in the air. As time passed, she wondered if he had fallen asleep.

"Killian?" she whispered.

His thumb stroked the side of her hand, "Focus, Eloria."

His silky voice made her smile at the sound of her name.

"I don't know why it's not working," she confessed.

"There's not much more I can teach you. Take time to ponder it. Practice finding that place inside of yourself. Once you do, it can be a powerful tool."

Killian silently led them back to camp. The Airedales let them pass by. The Prince never turned their way. It was silent as she climbed into her makeshift bed.

"Hey," she whispered across to Killian. "Thank you for teaching me. I understand why no one else wants me to learn magic."

"Why is that?" he asked.

"I could destroy the world. It makes sense that no one would want me to know magic while that is still an option. I'm not falling in love with 'Seraphim wings' right? If I learn magic and turn evil, apparently I could blow this whole place up."

She heard Killian shift under his blankets, "Go to sleep."

CHAPTER 17

Flashes of dawn danced through her head. Images of birds chirping in the trees pulled her out of her dreamy state.

Wake up. It is time to play! Zane thought to her.

"Wake up. It's time to train," Killian said from above her.

Eloria opened her eyes and saw Zane's front paws pressing against her. His tale wagged excitedly. He was already panting.

"Hi," she said sleepily.

"Hi," Killian replied.

He stepped away and nudged the Prince awake. Sorrell was already up from taking last watch. She was doing her own sword and bow practice a little ways away. Like the day before, she had a large smile on her face that Eloria didn't understand. The sun had not yet risen but its light was filling the sky with warm colors. Zane ran around Killian, jumping up and snapping at him in play.

Eloria quickly did her stretches, clearing her mind and meditating with each move the way she had been taught. When she was finished, she joined Killian and Sorrell. She learned five new moves that morning and picked them up very quickly. She sparred against Sorrell first, combining what she already knew with her new moves and using repetition to ingrain the new elements into her muscle memory. She did fairly well against Sorrell then Killian took her place.

"Why do I have to fight both of you?" she asked.

Sorrell replied, "I am fairly good at the sword but Killian is faster than all of us. When you move on to bow training, I'll be the one to teach you. For now, you need to learn to fight me, an average fighter, and Killian, who will keep you on your toes and teach your reflexes to move faster than your mind can tell them."

Killian shrugged, "I can't help that I'm the best."

"You could only dream that it were true," the Prince said, walking up to Sorrell with a smile plastered on his face.

Killian rolled his eyes and advanced on Eloria. They sparred fairly well that morning but Sorrell was right, Killian was too quick. Eloria had trouble keeping up with him and she guessed that he was even trying to go easy on her. Sorrell shouted out instructions on form as they went but Eloria hardly had time to correct it.

The Prince had started playing with the Airedales while they all waited for her training to end. The dogs jumped and snapped at him while he tried to dodge their vicious teeth. One Airedale latched onto his arm, hanging on it while the Prince swung his arm in a circle to shake it off.

Although she knew they were playing, Eloria couldn't help but wonder how they could be so rough on one another. The Prince would tackle and roll with a dog as it bit and clawed at him to be released. By the time he came up from the ground, there were long red and white scratch marks down his arm that began to swell.

Sorrell rolled her eyes. When Killian announced they were finished for the morning, they filled their packs and began their journey once again. Zane sprinted back and forth among the group, clearly having more energy than the rest of his family. He and Killian played with a stick during the morning. For the afternoon he pranced proudly next to Eloria, his front paws lifting unusually high like a show pony.

She practiced listening and speaking with him as they walked together. She could feel her mind growing stronger. As a beast, he understood the world differently. Smells and sounds evoked a different response than a human's. He identified her companions according to how they smelled to him. Killian smelled like the wind. Sorrell smelled like a mountain flower.

Each day became routine once again. Killian woke her and they trained. Sorrell helped teach her how to identify and speak to the beasts. They made camp and Eloria would fall asleep with Zane next to her, watching Killian. She found herself growing fond of Killian despite his silence. She struggled not to blush whenever he chose to speak to her. He had kept his word and things were different. Though he still seemed annoyed with her at times, he was kind and patient. Her skill with the sword grew much more quickly along with her hand-to-hand combat abilities. She remembered things more easily and her body stopped aching each morning when she woke. She felt less helpless around the others and took on more responsibilities when she saw the opportunities arise.

The mountains grew larger as they walked each day and the forest more dense from the tree trunks growing around them. As they progressed, the ground began to rise and fall, slowly climbing them up the mountain. They ate dried meat from their packs along with other leaves and berries from the forest. The Airedales continued with them all the while, keeping watch and providing company to their small troupe.

Eloria and Sorrell began to feel more like sisters than strangers with the same face. She shared stories about her life traveling with Killian and the Prince. Eloria learned that Sorrell's main role with the queen was as scholar and ambassador for the royal family. When she was at Kien Illae, she spent most of her time in the libraries, learning everything she could get her hands on.

"I want to be a part of the queen's court when I'm older. It's my dream to become an advisor," she explained to Eloria. "Whether it be on battle or everyday trade among the regions, I want to have all the knowledge that I can obtain and use it to help others. I love all books and parchments. Their smells remind me of home and the libraries at Kien Illae…" she sighed with a smile, "It is the most beautiful place and holds all of the knowledge of this world. I want to read every book!"

"If you are an ambassador, how will you ever have time?" Eloria wondered.

"Oh, I only travel with the Prince and Killian to assist them when needed," she said casually. "What do you want to be when you are older?"

Eloria was taken by surprise at her question. It was how people in her world had asked about her post-graduation plans.

"Well I wanted to do marine biology when I was a little girl, but I was never good at math or science. I don't have an artistic bone in my body either so… I don't really know." Eloria didn't like thinking back to her world. It felt messy and scattered. "I've never had a dream job…I suppose the only thing I've felt passionate about is staying here. There's nothing for me back in my world."

They walked in silence for a while as Eloria contemplated Sorrell's question.

"Why doesn't anyone ask about my world?"

Sorrell glanced at her with a cautious eye, "Do you remember the story of creation that we sang for you? Do you remember how the Evil Ones came to be?"

Eloria nodded, "Yes, I remember. They tampered with other worlds, but asking questions about me and my life… that's not tampering."

"It is forbidden among us. Learning about worlds besides ours has led people to delve deeper into the possibility of contacting those other worlds. What I did is inexcusable and I was prepared to be imprisoned for the rest of my life because of it."

"How was the prophecy of Eloria to ever be fulfilled if no one tampered with another world?"

Sorrell grinned, "That is exactly what I thought."

Eloria was bursting with questions, "So how did you know how to do it and where to find a reflection? You don't have mirrors here. How did you know that I would be Eloria?"

She shrugged, "I cannot share my secrets."

"If this is some sort of parallel world, why haven't I seen anyone that I recognize?" Eloria thought out loud. "Shouldn't I have run into someone that looks familiar from my world? What about our parents? Are they the same people or do you somehow have different parents?"

Sorrell laughed and quickly walked ahead, ignoring her questions. Eloria rolled her eyes and they continued their long walk through the forest.

***

Eloria woke to a warm sensation flowing through her skin. She felt it spread and opened her eyes, wondering if she was having a strange dream. Killian was beside her, the back of his hand gently sliding down her cheek to her neck.

He held a finger to his lips, telling her to stay silent. She sat up slowly and looked around them. The Prince and Sorrell slept peacefully in their blankets. All but one of the Airedales had disappeared.

"Come with me," Killian whispered to her.

She crept slowly from her covers and reached for her boots.

"You don't need those," he said, extending his hand out to her.

Eloria looked at him carefully, not understanding what he was asking of her. He was in the same mood as the night of the feast.

"I want to show you something," he explained with a spark in his eye.

Eloria took his hand, feeling that warm tingle run down her arm and spine. He pulled her up and gently led her away from the others, not letting go of her hand as they crept through the forest. The Airedale silently watched them as they skipped away from camp.

She followed as he pulled her along. His tunic was almost translucent in the moonlight and she guessed that it was hours since she had fallen asleep watching him train. The cool earth felt good between her toes as they leapt over the mossy tree roots.

They approached a small lake. Killian led her to a mound of boulders that stood four heads high. The lake sparkled under the stars. Eloria saw the Airedales a little further down, all sitting or laying on the ground and staring up at the sky. Even Zane sat still and erect as he gazed to the heavens.

"What are they doing?" Eloria asked in a whisper.

"This way," was all he said as he led her to the formation of rock.

He began to climb, reaching down to help her as she followed. Eloria could see that the top boulder was smooth and mostly flat. When she about reached it, Killian wrapped his arm around her waist and pulled her up to the top. Her heart beat widely at his touch. He didn't pull his arm away as he set her down but instead looked deeply into her eyes.

"Watch the sky," he whispered.

She glanced up but only saw the stars. "Killian this is…"

"Keep watching," he whispered, his arm holding her tightly around the waist.

She stared at the stars and their many points of light. Though her eyes looked upward, her mind was all too aware of Killian's fingers tightening against her. He stared at her instead of the stars above. Eloria was keenly aware of his unwavering gaze.

A black shadow snapped her attention back to the sky. Her eyes tried to catch it but the shadow moved swiftly, blocking out the stars' light for only a brief moment. She gazed harder at the sky, trying to find where the shadow had gone. The trees began to rustle and she felt a strong breeze coming towards them from the forest. There was a low rumble in the air.

Without warning, a beast larger than she had ever seen flew over them. Killian's arm held her steadily as Eloria jumped with surprise. The wind blew around them in a fury as the dragon flew past and back into the night.

"Meet Emerald," Killian whispered against her ear. "Green dragon of the East Mountains."

As he spoke, the dragon circled back towards them and glided over the lake. The Airedales remained motionless as they, too, watched the magnificent creature. Emerald flapped her wings, creating a great gust as she landed a short distance away from the boulders. Killian held Eloria tightly as the wind from her wings pushed against them. Despite its force, Killian had no trouble holding his ground and keeping Eloria from blowing away. The dragon folded her wings behind her and walked on four legs to the rocky formation they stood on.

Killian withdrew his arm from Eloria and she almost begged for him to not let her go, unsure if she should scream or run from the massive dragon. Emerald was as large as Eloria's house and her entire being radiated heat as she approached. Her green scales glimmered in the moonlight. She held herself proudly as she stopped before them, craning her neck down to look at them properly. Her eyes were emerald jewels and they gazed at her with an intelligence beyond that of any beast Eloria had yet encountered.

"Open your mind to her," Killian whispered again, backing away from Eloria.

"It….," Eloria mumbled, not able to do anything but stare at the giant beast before her.

Welcome to the mountains, Eloria, a sweet voice rippled through her mind.

Without having a chance to reply, Eloria began seeing memories flash through her head. To her surprise, they were not from the dragon but Eloria's own memories. She watched visions of her companions walking through the forest together, training on the ocean shores, dancing with Killian in the glass ballroom. The green dragon was searching her mind, watching her memories and drawing out emotions from each one. For some reason, the dragon lingered on the ballroom, pulling the emotions to the forefront of Eloria's mind. She felt her palms begin to sweat and butterflies raced in her stomach.

The dragon released her mind and stared at her curiously. Eloria panted from the shock of having the dragon control her thoughts.

It seems I am the first on my kind for you to meet, Emerald turned her head to the side, as if in laughter. *Do not be afraid. We can see your mind and feel your thoughts without your consent if we wish to. Remember that for the next time we meet. It is what we dragons crave. We have waited long for you to come to this world. It was my kin who spoke of your coming and my kin that will protect you as long as you are here with us.*

Eloria stood staring, unable to speak with her tongue or her mind. The dragon looked at her curiously then turned her attention towards Killian. They stood silently in conversation. Eloria couldn't tell what they spoke of but at one point Emerald let out a short growl and snapped her jaws at him. Not a moment later a deep chuckle rumbled deep in her throat.

Your friend is entertaining, she said to Eloria. *We dragons like to be flattered and he does it better than any other. He tells me you travel with the Prince and your reflection-self.*

Eloria nodded, still unable to speak.

It is good that you are so silent. Emerald hummed, *Words are dangerous things used to both create and destroy. Perhaps, one day, you will say great things and stir the hearts of dragons. Your words may also be our destruction. We have a part to play before all of this is over, and I hope to be at your side in battle.* Emerald shook her head uncomfortably. *I tire of the ground, my wings are meant for flight. Goodbye Eloria, and may your wings grow soon so that you may feel the sky beneath you and the wind at your command.*

Eloria bowed, not knowing what to say to the magnificent dragon. Killian shared a few thoughts with her and she took to the sky, beating them against the wind as she ascended. Eloria struggled to keep her footing and Killian reached out to keep her from falling. Emerald circled above them, gaining altitude and flying back and forth across the stars.

"I know it may not be my place but I thought you would like to meet her," Killian said quietly, not wanting to disturb the night around them.

"She is so beautiful," Eloria awed.

"I doubt we will see her again. It was by chance that she chose this spot for hunting tonight, but I had a feeling she may be looking for us."

"She could see my memories, without me letting her. She made me feel things..."

"Yes," Killian smiled. "Dragons are selfish that way. They humor themselves by bringing up memories that contain heightened emotions. They excel at breaking the mind yet they can block theirs beyond measure. I hope she didn't make you uncomfortable."

"No, it was just unexpected." Eloria watched the large dragon as she continued circling the expanse of sky above them.

"We can go back now," Killian said, beginning to leave the rock.

"No!" Eloria whispered quickly. "I mean… I would like to stay for a little while. If that's alright?"

He smiled, "Of course it is."

They sat side by side on the large boulder. Eloria watched the silent world around her. Zane was leaping around the grassy knoll, trying to catch lightening bugs as they flew lazily by the water. The remaining Airedales noiselessly trod back to the camp.

"Would you like to hear a song?" Killian asked.

"You sing?"

"You know that I do."

"Yes, but I didn't realize you sang alone. Unless there's a lesson involved?"

Killian's lips twitched up in a smile, "There's always something to learn."

"By all means then."

He laid against the rock and began.

"We grow, we train, we choose our House
My mind will be ever keen
On finding the one they told to me
The one to whom I cling."

The notes were deep and Killian's voice was sweeter than Eloria remembered.

"Through the dance I look and search
Smiling faces that do sing
But none so fair as the one I dare
To find and give my ring

There I found you dancing near
I'll hold my breath and wait
for the one they call… my darling

223

She will be my fate

Oh woman so fair and kind
I made my pact with you
The one to which I tie my fate
The one to which I flew.

Through battle I will find you
In the darkest of midnights
For you... my dearest a battle cry
It is for you that I do fight."

"That was beautiful."

"I miss it," he murmured.

Eloria glanced at him, "Miss what?"

"This. These moments in the silence each night. When you can be truly alone and not have to worry about anything around you, just... be."

"But you're not alone. I'm here."

"I feel like myself with you," he whispered, still gazing at the stars.

"What do you mean?"

Her skin began to tingle as she felt Killian's hands wrap around her arms. Eloria watched Zane play with the bugs, splashing in the lake and sending long ripples across the water.

"Killian..."

"Shhh," he pulled her back so that she was lying on the rock next to him. "Watch."

She gazed up at the twinkling stars. Once in a while she could still make out the dark figure of Emerald, high above them. A shooting star blazed through her line of sight. Watching as it slowly burned across the sky, she studied the star with its long, shimmering tale and bright center. When it faded, another took its place not too far away.

"They move so slowly," she awed, watching them travel until they faded too far to see.

"How else would they move?"

"In my world they travel so quickly you can hardly see them. People think it's a sign of good luck and they make wishes," she explained. "There are songs about it."

"That is an interesting idea. That star there," he nodded to a slow burning star moving across the sky. "What would you wish on that star?"

She smiled, "I would wish to stay here forever, in this world and never have to return home."

He studied her face as she watched the sky. The star slowly blazed away and another began shooting across the black emptiness around it.

"Sorrell said you were in danger back in your world. In the nightmare that you shared with her, all those nights ago, she said a man was trying to hurt you."

"In my world people aren't as good. Not like here. I don't have bad parents, they simply forget about me sometimes. My mom likes to be out with friends and when my dad is angry... I don't think he realizes what he's doing."

"How do they forget you? You're their daughter."

"Sometimes I couldn't get lunch at school because they didn't remember to leave me money. When I had practice or concerts for show choir, they forgot to pick me up. I usually have to go to bed without dinner because... My sister is the outspoken one. She stands up to them, but we both got punished because of it. My dad can't think straight sometimes, that's all. You know what I mean?"

"I don't recognize all of your words, but I think I understand what you are saying. That's why you're scared to fight? It's no wonder anger didn't work with you," Killian sighed. "You've changed though. What do you like about your home?"

Eloria told him about the small patch of trees behind her house where she used to play make-believe. She told him about the bike rides she took when she was young and the adventures she had dreamed up while in class.

"That one," Eloria pointed to a star, "What would you wish?"

He remained silent for a while and before the star was out of sight, he slid his hand over hers. She felt that warm shiver run down her spine and her heart raced. Eloria prayed that he wouldn't hear it. He began tracing lines on the inside of her palm with his fingers.

"You're not the same since we left the ocean," Eloria muttered.

"I promised I would be different."

"You've been more than that."

Killian's fingers continued their pattern against her palm.

"I was carrying a burden that I no longer needed."

"Was it your grudge against me?" Eloria joked.

"Truthfully, it was the prophecy. It effects my entire country and the people I'm sworn to protect. I felt dragged down by destiny. That night in Kailani, I decided my fate was my own."

She shall love Seraphim wings or doom she will bring.

The words from the scroll echoed through her mind. Eloria felt no attraction to the Prince. She knew, without a doubt, that they would not end up together. Despite that, she had decided the only way to save the world from doom was to not fall in love with anyone.

"What if I mess up?" she whispered. "What if I bring ruin to everything?"

"I won't let that happen," he said.

"It could. I'm not a strong person, Killian. I could destroy everything."

"Trust me to protect you. I know more about this than you could imagine. Prophecies can be misinterpreted, after all."

Killian's fingers slipped between hers, entwining their hands together as they watched the stars. She felt his ring, the sensation of his touch, running from her fingers to her toes. Eloria tried not to shiver again. They lay together and watched the stars until she eventually drifted to sleep.

She woke again to a tingling in her cheek and felt Killian's hand brush her hair from her face.

"Eloria," he whispered in her ear. Warmth and adrenaline rushed through her like a powerful wave. He backed away as she opened her eyes. "We have to go back," he said softly.

"That's okay. I'll stay here," she closed her eyes again.

"Eloria," he sighed. "I'm sorry but we have to go. Sorrell won't be happy if she finds us out here. It would be a little awkward to explain don't you think?"

He helped her climb back down the boulders. He wrapped his hands around her waist as they reached the bottom, lifting her with ease and returning her gently to the ground. Eloria was keenly aware that his fingers lingered longer than necessary before one hand slid to her arm. His touch tingled as his fingers trailed to hers, entwining together. When she didn't pull away, Killian led her back into the forest, following an invisible path to their campsite.

When they arrived, the Prince was sitting up against a tree keeping watch. Eloria immediately released Killian's hand and fell back a few paces. Killian noticed but didn't comment. The Prince gave Killian a curious look. Instead of offering an explanation, Killian went to his pile of blankets. Eloria climbed into her own makeshift bed. The heart pounding in her chest was a not so subtle message that she wouldn't be falling asleep anytime soon.

CHAPTER 18

When morning came, Killian shook her gently to wake her as usual for training. The sun was about to rise and Zane stood panting next to him.

"I tried to let you sleep longer," he whispered apologetically.

The day continued on like any other. Sorrell and the Prince smiled goofily at one another while Killian remained silent. He played with Zane as he did everyday but snuck glances at Eloria as they trekked. When the sun began to set, they reached a steep incline in the mountain and a small path led towards its invisible peak.

"This is as far as the Airedales will go," said the Prince, pausing to look at the pack leader. The dog gave a small bark and bowed its head. The other Airedales began walking back the way they had come.

Thank you for protecting me each night, Eloria thought to Zane.

He wagged his tail and pranced around her, images of squirrels and rabbits racing past her vision. *I will become faster and stronger than any Airedale, and I will tear apart the dark creatures that walk this forest.*

The pack leader barked in his direction and Zane ran in a quick circle around Killian before sprinting off to rejoin his family. The four of them stared after the Airedales, suddenly feeling vulnerable without their furry companions.

"Let's keep moving," the Prince grumbled. "It'll be a few days until we can make it to the High Landing. It's a miracle that we haven't run into any Deformed so far."

As they hiked up the mountain, Eloria knew her legs would be sore from this new terrain. She quickly ran out of breath and struggled to keep up with the others as they climbed the rickety trail that wound through trees and boulders.

"What, exactly, is the High Landing?" she panted up to them.

"In the Battle of the Ashes, the Evil Ones used magic that severed the mountain. Half of the mountain disappeared and the top was flattened, like a knife cutting through butter. You can stand at the edge and see straight down."

"What happened to the other half of the mountain?"

"No one knows," Sorrell answered. "Some believe that the Evil Ones found a way to transport it to another world. Others say that it turned to ash and drifted away in the wind. That was the last battle that all of the dragons fought with our people. Many of their kind disappeared with the mountain. They have slept ever since. Only a few remain awake and willing to help the Seraphim."

"Consequently it is now the only place to see across to the Barren Desert without going over the mountain," the Prince chortled.

Who comes up with the names around here? Eloria sighed.

No imagination, a voice replied.

Eloria stopped in her tracks. She had heard someone's thoughts in her mind.

Sorrell?

"Yes?"

What was that?

Sorrell turned around quickly, surveying their surroundings and looking for danger. Someone's memories began passing through Eloria's mind. She saw a village of dead bodies and memories of pain and fear entered her mind. The terrible forms of Deformed blurred past. The memory also showed her two men. They were covered in mud and rain. She could make out younger versions of the Prince and Killian.

"Sorrell!" Eloria shouted.

"What is it?" the Prince looked frantically about them.

"I heard you! I heard you!"

Sorrell looked to Eloria in confusion. *What does she mean 'heard me?'*

"I can hear your thoughts!" Eloria explained. "I saw images of a village and felt your memories just now. I heard words!"

Her eyes grew wide as she looked at Eloria. "You've never heard my thoughts," she said quietly.

"I know!" Eloria laughed, excited by her accomplishment.

Sorrell laughed. Stopped. Tried to process what was happening. Then laughed again.

This is amazing! Eloria thought to her.

I can't believe it… it's so strange. You can hear me?

Yes! Isn't it unbelievable? I thought your mind was blocked. Why did you open it to me?

I didn't, Sorrell thought, looking confused again. *I was just thinking about…*

Images of her and the Prince covered Eloria's sight. They were dancing on a beach and she felt Sorrell's joy, greater than anything of this world. Eloria felt Sorrell's love for the Prince.

"*Whoa!*" Eloria thought and spoke out loud.

"No! You weren't supposed to see that. You weren't supposed to feel that!" Sorrell said quickly, looking embarrassed. *I don't know what's going on. My mind should still be blocked,* she thought frantically. *Eloria I have secrets that are not meant for anyone, not even you. Please, I can't give them up by accident. I'm a member of the Queen's House.*

Eloria nodded, *I understand and I'll do my best not to pry. I can hear you, though. That means I'm understanding, doesn't it? That*

230

means I am getting to know this world better. The queen may let me stay after all. Thank you, Sorrell.

Now you know what it has been like for me, she thought with a smirk.

The Prince congratulated Eloria with a strong pat on the back. She glanced up to Killian who was looking at her with curiosity. Without saying anything, he turned and continued up the mountain, not waiting for them to follow.

Sorrell and Eloria continued to speak with their minds as their small company hiked the trail. She shared memories of the years she had spent traveling with the Prince and Killian. Visions of their time in apprenticeship flew through Eloria's head, and she felt as if she was learning and understanding so much more about this world than she had before. Sorrell's link to her mind was not only a way to communicate but a way for Sorrell to teach her as they traveled.

The next day, as the mountain's path grew steeper, Sorrell thought of a new idea for Eloria.

Combat is what we've worked on the most, but you've been slow to pick it up. What if I could put the knowledge in your mind and influence your body?

Eloria didn't understand her concept.

With my memories of fighting running through your mind, your body should pick it up as if they were your own. It might sink in as muscle memory. If nothing else, you will be able to recall the memories.

Eloria wasn't sure if what Sorrell proposed would truly work. Sorrell relayed her idea aloud to the Prince and Killian. They both agreed it was worth a try, even if it didn't pan out to excel her combat skills.

Sorrell spent the rest of that day pouring memory after memory into Eloria's mind. To Eloria's surprise, as she spent time watching Sorrell recall old battles and training, her arm would twitch in a certain action or she would start to duck a sword before realizing it was only in her head. Sorrell's theory was working. Eloria could feel her muscles flex and move as she embodied the memories.

By the time she went to bed that night, her body was not only sore from hiking up the steep mountain trail but also from the combat strategies that she had passing through her mind all day. She fell to sleep the moment her head hit the rough ground beneath her, her body against a skinny tree to keep her from rolling away during the night.

The next morning, everyone was excited to test her skill and see if Sorrell's idea would fully translate to Eloria. Naturally, Sorrell went first. Eloria was apprehensive as they both drew their swords. Killian sat and watched them nonchalantly, expecting it to end up like any other training session. As Sorrell moved forward to attack, Eloria read her thoughts and was easily able to defend and attack in return. Unfortunately, Eloria quickly found that Sorrell had the same advantage and would read her mind and defend as quickly as Eloria had. They fought for almost an hour until they both withdrew, realizing that, for that first time, Eloria could match her skill.

The Prince applauded them with a large grin. Eloria gave a little bow.

"Thank you!" she mimicked an announcer from her world. "None of this would have been possible without the hard work of my partner Sorrell!" She gave a grand gesture to her reflection-self who laughed and curtsied. Eloria beamed at her accomplishment and looked to Killian for approval. To her surprise, he sat against the tree with an unhappy expression, as if the sparring session was worse than ever before.

He stood gracefully and drew his sword. It gleamed in the bright morning sunlight. Eloria's smile vanished. He turned his head to the side, neck cracking, and his muscles flexed quite obviously under his tunic.

Oh no. Eloria's mouth went dry.

Sorrell stared nervously at Killian, wondering if he was about to revert to his harsh lesson plans.

It's alright, he won't hurt you... too badly.

"Sorrell, was I in any of the memories you shared with her?" Killian asked with a monotone voice.

"A few," she answered carefully.

"Good," he smirked, "Don't interfere."

Sorrell quickly jumped away as Killian lunged at Eloria. She saw his right leg lead and his arms pulling his blade straight back. Immediately she recalled a memory of Sorrell training with him at the House of the Guard a few years back. He had lunged at her the same way then as he did now. He came down on Eloria, bringing his sword around to strike. She quickly sidestepped the attack and tried catching him in the side with the hilt of her weapon.

He was faster than what he had been in Sorrell's memory. He was able to dodge the blow and swing his sword in his hand, bringing its blunt end behind her back before she had time to move away.

"Very good," he whispered in her ear, too close for anyone else to hear. His face grew serious once more as he paced around her. "Again."

He advanced on her differently this time, almost sliding into her as he spun smoothly with his weapon to strike. No memory came to her but her body moved on its own. She blocked his attack and side stepped a backhanded push, moving away before going in for an attack herself. Killian moved faster than anyone in Sorrell's memories and Eloria didn't know how her body was keeping up. She wondered if the adrenaline pumping through her veins was giving her an extra edge.

After a half hour, he withdrew, grinning slightly at her last attempt to thwart him. They were certainly not an even match but Eloria kept up with him better than she ever had. He seemed proud although he didn't say it. Sorrell and the Prince stood side by side, gawking at her.

What? Eloria thought.

"That was more than I expected," Sorrell huffed, looking almost as out of breath as Eloria. "I mean, I knew it worked when we sparred but… I never thought…"

"She didn't think you would be fast enough," Killian finished her sentence, sheathing his sword. "You drew upon her memories more quickly than we expected and used them despite the actions of your foe. You made Sorrell's combat knowledge work to your advantage without the same scenarios being implemented. You improvised with the knowledge in your head and your muscle moved without hesitation."

"Wait," Eloria panted. "Are you saying that I'm actually good at something?"

Killian shrugged, "You could hold your own against a small Deformed at this point."

"I've never been good at anything!"

The Prince tossed each of them their packs, "You were decent, but no one can call themselves *good* until they've put a mark on Killian." He sauntered to her and handed her the sheath for her blade. "I would say, however, that you don't need our protection so much at this point. You are one of us now," he winked.

"But I have put a mark on him!" she said excitedly. "I punched him, remember?"

The Prince laughed from deep in his chest, "I think we've all punched Killian at one time or another."

"Let's get moving," the Guard grunted.

Sorrell spent the rest of that day pouring combat moves, battle strategies, and weapon knowledge into Eloria's mind as they continued their hike to the mountain's peak.

That evening they stopped earlier than normal to make camp. The Prince told her that they would reach the Landing by the next afternoon so they needn't hurry. Eloria took a turn sparring with each of them and they stayed up late telling stories of old battles and their time as apprentices.

"What of your world?" Sorrell asked. "What are the battles like there?"

"You clearly don't fight with swords or fists!" the Prince chuckled.

Eloria tried to force a smile but the thought of home made her uneasy. They sat silently in the growing dark as they waited for her to respond. She pulled her knees to her chest, looking across the expanse of forest beneath them.

"It's not a very happy place," she said. "Most people are not kind to others and think only of themselves. Not many are trained to fight but they use their fists to hurt one another when they are mad. Most people follow the same path in life: get through school, get married, have kids, hate the job. To escape the routine and the world around them, they watch shows…" Eloria paused, seeing the confused looks of those around her. "They watch stories that other people write and act out. The stories that people like the most always have to include bloody violence and sex for people to even be interested."

The Prince looked shocked and slightly upset. "Violence is not something to be made an idol of. It is gruesome and unspeakable to take a life. And sex… that is a private affair between a man and his wife. Those who are united make jokes among themselves but it is never displayed."

"I understand that," Eloria said quietly. "The people in my world simply seek something more, an adventure. Lust becomes a part of that shortly after violence. People do not believe in your Creator as they do here."

"There is much Evil," Sorrell said, seeing the memories from Eloria's mind.

"Yes."

"Where do you find happiness in your world?" Killian asked from the shadows.

Eloria shrugged, "Some people are kind and try to improve the lives of those around them. I always found happiness in my books. The books that took me to other worlds and set up adventures. That is where I found the most joy."

"You have been to other worlds?" the Prince gawked.

"It's an expression," Sorrell said lightly. "It is like the books in the queen's library that feel like they take you to another time and place. Reading them is like a sort of magic that no Mage could ever create."

The Prince put his hands behind his head, leaning against a tree. "In that way, you and Sorrell are plenty alike. She never takes her nose away from those dusty parchments."

"You should write about your time here," Sorrell mused. "We can put it in the library as 'The History of the Second Eloria.'"

"That's a terrible title," the Prince laughed.

Killian grunted, "You all should get sleep. It may be a quick journey down the mountain if that cloud is something to fear."

The Prince climbed under his furs. Sorrell and Eloria did the same, quietly giggling to one another. Killian stationed himself against a large tree as he kept watch for the camp. He listened as the two girls shared their favorite stories to one another from their beds.

"...He was a dragon rider," Sorrell was saying. "The only one in this world as dragons are quite prideful. They refuse to be ridden like a common animal. In the end, he left his dragon because he fell in love. Their bond was so strong, that his dragon chose to sleep for the rest of eternity rather than fly without him. It is said that if he ever wakes, he would fly once again with the heir of his original rider."

"I've read dragon books like that, too. Except mine weren't real. One of my favorite books doesn't have a lot of action or adventure, but it's considered a classic. There's a man who is very rich and prideful, like a dragon, but he falls in love with a poor common girl. She always spoke her mind and stood up for herself. I think that's why I liked her so much. I wanted to be like her, even though she was prideful herself."

"What happens?"

"The best part is when he confesses his feelings for her. He gives a big speech about how they shouldn't be together and lists all the reasons. Then he says, 'I love you. Most ardently.' The girl refuses him for a while because he was so prejudice against her upbringing. In the end, he does all these things to help her family, out of love for her. She ends up falling in love with him."

"How romantic!"

Killian rolled his eyes and tried to block out the sound of their giggling.

CHAPTER 19

"It is a bit further," the Prince shouted to them.

The path had grown so steep that Eloria was having trouble keeping up. Their trail had turned into an uphill climb. Her hand slipped from its hold on the rock jutting out of the mountain. Killian quickly snatched her arm before she fell from the wall face.

"Sorrell! Get out of her head before she tumbles off the cliffside," Killian growled.

Eloria ignored the warm rush of adrenaline from his touch and tried to focus on finding a handhold again.

"I'm sorry, Killian, but I thought we wanted her to keep learning!" Sorrell said angrily.

She had been pushing more memories to Eloria since they woke up that morning. Unfortunately, it had been difficult for Eloria to climb when other images kept flashing in front of her field of vision.

Killian didn't reply but the images disappeared from Eloria's mind. He stayed close, ready to catch her again if she started to fall.

"I think your world's gravity is different than mine. It must be why I'm so much slower than you guys. Why don't you put in handrails or rope?" Eloria huffed as she took another step up the mountain, carefully leaning her body forward so she didn't topple down the way they had come.

"Stop talking," Killian instructed. "Stay right behind me and follow my movements exactly."

"You're not exactly the easiest person to imitate when it comes to physical activity."

They continued to climb most of the morning and Eloria did her best to step exactly where he stepped. Finally, the mountain became less of a climb and more of a slope. Sorrell and the Prince disappeared ahead of them. Eloria stopped to take a long draught from her water skin.

"You're being awfully slow today, don't you think?" Killian grumbled.

"You're being awfully rude today," she snapped back at him. "I thought you were going to be nice to me, remember?"

"Doing my best."

"Too bad your mood swings aren't as quick as your sword play."

"At least I have sword play."

"At least I have... a prophecy," she fumbled.

"That's what you have? Really, Eloria?"

A warm shiver ran through her body, "Shut up, Killian."

"Whatever you say 'oh Prophesied one.'"

He mockingly bowed as Eloria pushed past him. A small set of stairs carved into the stone marked their final ascent to the High Landing. As they reached the top, the world opened up before them.

"It's as you described it to be," Eloria awed.

The Prince was kneeling on the ground ahead of her.

"Full of trees and stars and birds that sing
The mountain held its place.
Through rain and sun and snowy gales
'Till man beheld its grace.

The mountain held more life than most

239

Until the Evil came.
There it was devoured in two.
'Twas magic to be blamed.

Then war climbed up its mighty face.
The dragon host all slain.
Forever more ashamed and barren,
The mountain's lost domain."

The mountain's top was a large, flat platform. The sky around them was an ocean of blue with the sun high above marking afternoon. Eloria felt that she could reach up and run her fingers through the colors above them. The opposite side of the mountainous rock had been sheered away, exactly as her companions had described.

Eloria carefully walked across the expanse of rock and stood at the edge. She could see straight down to bits of forest below. The world stretched out before them. Extending out from the mountain, dead clusters of trees were scattered as if sprinkled from the sky above. The Barren Desert was not a desert at all but a burnt wasteland. In place of sand, there was ash and charred stones. Eloria quickly realized what she thought were trees weren't that at all, but unnatural dark shadows spotting the territory.

"There," Sorrell pointed to the sky beyond.

"The dark cloud," the Prince whispered. "Killian…"

"I see it," he soberly replied, joining the others at the cliff's edge.

A black and grey cloud stretched across the horizon. Eloria could see it twist and roll as if storms were brewing inside of itself. There was no lightening inside, only darkness. They heard a distant rumble, very much like thunder, and Eloria wondered how one could invent a cloud that produced storms and thunder but no lightening.

240

"How is this possible?" Sorrell gaped. "There are no clouds. The Royal family is the only way but they... you're..."

"I know," the Prince looked to her with concern. "We will figure it out. Now that we know what Emerald said is true, we must go to the king and queen. They will descend from Kien Illae and join the dragons."

"No, we must go to the great dragon," Killian countered. "There has to be more to it than what we know."

"But we don't know anything," Sorrell peeled her eyes away from the cloud. "Surely it must be a product of the Evil Ones but how, and for what purpose? What use would they have for a cloud?"

"After we encountered the Deformed, the king predicted the Evil Ones must be experimenting with potions and magic in ways that were never intended by the Creator."

"That's the point," Eloria joined. "Isn't their whole purpose to do exactly what your Creator hates? Don't they want to turn everything evil and against His will? That cloud... it's only the beginning of something else."

They fell silent and stared over the ashen desert. The cloud was clearly moving in their direction but they had no way of telling how quickly or exactly how far away it really was. Eloria could hear her heart beating as she gazed at the dark stretch of sky against the beautiful afternoon sun. Such polar opposites that clashed in the heavens above.

It's quiet, she thought.

Sorrell glanced around, *Much too quiet.*

"What happened to the birds?" Eloria whispered.

Killian glanced at the Prince and they silently drew their swords. Their packs were noiselessly placed on the mountain's rocky surface. Sorrell pulled her bow from around her back and notched an arrow. Eloria took off her pack as well so it wouldn't hinder her from battle, but she didn't move her eyes from the trees. A foul smell filled her nose.

The Prince moved back towards the path. Sorrell backed away from the forest and to the edge of the cliff, standing a few yards from Killian and the rest of the group so that she had room to shoot. Her eyes scanned the trees, looking for the slightest hint of movement.

"Eloria," Killian pulled her close.

Her heart raced. At the sound of her name, she visibly trembled. A feeling like sunlight filling her veins caused her to meet his eyes.

"Stay close to me," he whispered. "Keep your mind shut, do you understand? They will try to force their way in." His green eyes were wild with worry. "Keep your mind closed and do not leave my side. If they take over your mind you'll be paralyzed."

"Movement!" the Prince shouted from the path. He kept his back to his companions and his sword between himself and the forest, pulling another knife from his belt. Killian quickly positioned himself in front of Eloria, blocking her from whatever was approaching from the forest. Instinctively, Eloria drew her sword, not bothering to keep it silent as it slid from the sheath.

They stood still as statues, waiting for the enemy to reveal themselves. In the corner of her eye, Eloria saw something move. She peered at the ground beneath Sorrell's boots and saw pebbles slipping down to the cliff behind them, but Sorrell's feet stood motionless.

They've climbed up the mountain!

Sorrell eyes flicked to Eloria with horror. She turned as quickly as she could but it was too late. A large, three fingered hand reached up from mountain's severed half and swiped Sorrell's feet out from under her. She loosed her arrow but it flew aimlessly to the sky as she fell. The Deformed pulled itself up the severed edge. It was unlike anything Eloria had seen as it stood over seven feet tall and had pale grey flesh that seemed to peel from its bones as it moved. It stood over Sorrell on two legs with feet identical to its hands - three long and bony extremities used to destroy.

A knife flew into its side and Sorrell quickly rolled away, loosing another arrow as she rose a few yards from the creature. Killian pulled Eloria away from the edge and swung himself around her. Three more beasts leapt from the side of the mountain onto the flat expanse. They heard terrible screams and roars behind them. Eloria glanced back to the Prince and saw numerous Deformed emerging from the trees. They were surrounded.

Killian didn't wait. At his word the four of them attacked, Killian and Eloria took the beasts on the cliff and the Prince took out the Deformed one by one as they climbed up the path. Sorrell began shooting arrows in either direction, helping where she saw need.

Eloria sliced and cut through the creatures in front of her, careful not to let the acidic blood splatter on her skin. They came tumbling from the path and were climbing over each other to get onto the Landing from the cliffside.

They moved faster than Eloria expected, but she had trained with Killian. There was no one quicker than he. She ducked a swing from a creature's arm and thrust her sword upwards. It caught flesh and she felt the blade dig deeply into its bone. From the corner of her eye, she saw Killian fell another opponent with a grand sweep of his sword.

The creature screamed as Eloria's blade sunk deeper into its bone. The screams tore into her mind. She was overcome with fear and despair. It rushed through her body like a wave. The feeling was uncontrollable. Eloria gasped and released her weapon, watching as it hung on the monster's arm. The scream was not only in her ears but in her mind as well. She understood now why Killian had been frightened for her.

She shook her head, trying to get the horrific feeling to stop. The monster realized that he had gotten in. Her head seared with pain and she backed away, clutching her temple. Her body froze as she stood on the mountain, terrible images flashing in front of her eyes.

Sorrell! she cried out with her mind.

"Eloria!" she heard Killian yell but she could not see him.

Memories of her father with his hands around Justine's neck, his hand coming down on her, the blood running down her arms and no one noticing flashed across her vision. She saw Sorrell's memories of the first time they had met the Deformed, and the pain she felt at seeing the death all around her that night.

She heard Sorrell screaming as well and realized she was experiencing everything that Eloria was. Eloria had opened her mind to Sorrell for help. In doing so, she connected them together and had let the creature into both their thoughts.

New images flashed in front of her, but they were no longer her memories. She saw bones snapping out of place and skin melting to the ground. It was memories of the Deformed.

See what I have seen, the creature spoke with its mind. *See what we will bring from across the mountain.*

She watched in horror as visions of Sorrell's dead body flashed before her, then the Prince's, then Killian lay dead at the bottom of a cliff.

"Killian!" she screamed across the mountain top.

"Eloria!" Killian was hacking away at the Deformed as more continued to climb the mountain. A knife found its target in the creature torturing Eloria, but the Deformed held her mind tightly in its grasp.

A village drenched in rain appeared before her. The sky was black with roiling clouds, and the usual wisp of magical lights that floated through the air were no where to be seen. She saw the bodies of people and beasts laying in mud. A few steps away, a green dragon lay amongst the rubble of collapsed buildings. At her feet, Eloria saw white feathers, floating in a pool of blood.

Death to all, the Deformed laughed in its mind, a sound like grating metal. *Death to Seraphim.*

A warm tingle spread through Eloria's hand. The cold that had overtaken her body from the Deformed started to melt away and the agony of its grip began to diminish. The warmth spread like sunlight, flowing up her arm and into her chest. The weight of fear lifted and the visions before her blurred, mixing with reality.

Something stirred within her and she remembered Killian's words about magic. Focusing on the Deformed, she searched for that spot in her mind. The visions and memories blocked her every effort to find the magic within. Then out of the darkness, she felt it open like a door. The vision of death ceased. The cold and fear disintegrated.

Eloria felt the source of the warm light. Someone's hand was in her own, rescuing her from the Deformed's mind. She tightened her grip around the hand, anchoring herself to the energy that flowed from it.

Acting on instinct, she thrust her palm into the air. Wind rushed around her as she locked her gaze with the Deformed creature. Swords clanged around them and arrows flew as if in slow motion.

The Prince began shouting something but Eloria couldn't hear him over the wind. The Deformed beast gnashed its teeth in hatred. The wind grew stronger, circling around Eloria like a tornado.

A death to come that will change all things, the creature said into her mind.

Images of the prophecy flashed in front of her eyes. She saw the prophecy's script but it was not the one she had seen in Kailani. This was written on a stone wall, framed by firelight.

A death to come that will change all things.

Visions of white wings and an angel appeared before her eyes. In her mind she saw a creature covered in a brilliant light wearing robes and six wings wrapped around himself. Somewhere deep inside, Eloria felt a joy beyond anything she had ever experienced. The deformed creature in front of her began laughing as it shared her vision.

A death to come that will change all things, it quoted again, baring its teeth at her.

Not by your hand, Eloria replied.

It has already come to pass, it laughed.

All grew silent as the wind ceased. Eloria's hand held steadily above her head, waiting for the right moment. The Deformed snarled and lunged, its sharp fingers reaching for her.

In one smooth motion, Eloria lowered her arm to stop the beast. The gathered wind followed her command, sending a forceful torrent of air across the mountain's flat landing. It hit her Deformed square in the chest, hurtling it off the cliff's edge along with any others who had made it onto the landing.

The pain inside of her immediately ceased. She gasped in relief. The magic was gone, but so was the Deformed's dark hold. She quickly looked around for danger but the Deformed were all slain or blown from the mountain. Killian stood with his hand in hers, a dozen Deformed dead at their feet.

"Killian?" Eloria teetered where she stood.

"Breathe." He cradled her face in his hands. "Don't try to move. Focus on breathing."

Eloria did as she was told, focusing on the warm tingle that ran through her skin. Her limbs quickly returned to her and she felt like herself again.

"I'm sorry," she mumbled.

"Keep breathing."

She inhaled deeply until she felt fully in control of her body once more.

"I didn't mean to let it in, or use the magic."

Killian stepped away from her. "Do you realized what you've done? You completely exposed yourself to the Deformed. Now they know exactly who you are and what you're capable of."

"Sorrell wasn't in our minds by the time..." Eloria paused, realizing that Sorrell's mind hadn't been linked to hers in the final moments with the Deformed. Eloria turned to her partner and froze.

Blood trickled from Sorrell's mouth.

"Sorrell!" the Prince screamed.

They watched as a crooked, black knife fell from her hand. Her knees hit the ground and she fell backwards. The Prince caught her head before it hit the rocks.

"Sorrell, look at me," he commanded, brushing the hair from her eyes. "Sorrell it's going to be fine, it barely scratched you."

"It was buried to the hilt, you liar," she smiled up at him.

Killian hurried to assess the wound. He stripped fabric from his tunic and pressed it into her.

"I didn't even notice it," Sorrell laughed. "I looked down and it was there, but they never carry weapons."

"It's alright, we'll get you to a Healer. The blade didn't hit any vital organs. We've been through a lot worse," the Prince smiled but tears fell down his cheeks.

"They've poisoned it," Killian whispered soberly. A black liquid oozed from the gash.

"I knew what I was doing," Sorrell choked, looking at Killian and the Prince. "When we got back from the outer lands, I lied to you both. I didn't return to the Queen's House. The gold dragon called me so I went to the North Mountain. He taught me how... and I brought her here. I knew what I was doing when I brought Eloria."

Eloria took a step towards them but her mind was quickly overcome by Sorrell's memories. A large, golden dragon flashed

247

before her eyes. She saw a cave filled with mirrors of different sizes. Sorrell picked up a small hand mirror and hid it in a satchel. The memory blurred and changed to a vision of Sorrell running through the forest. The excitement and fear of bringing Eloria to this world. She felt as if she couldn't breathe.

"I'm so sorry. I should have told you the truth, but the dragon told me it had to remain hidden. No one was to know how I brought her. There was so much pain in her world. I had to save her. You must go to him! You must go to the North Mountain and he will wake for her. He will wake all of the dragons for Eloria."

Sorrell's hand shook as she reached out for the Prince. He took her hand into his.

"We will," the Prince said. "You need to rest for a moment then we'll all go to the mountain. We can all...," his voice faltered.

Sorrell felt something soft and wet land on her cheek. She glanced up to see large white patches falling from the cloudless sky above her. Each speck had a tiny pattern within.

"Snow," she smiled. "Remember that time you convinced the woodland sprites you would conjure a blizzard? They threw berries at us and we were blue for a week." Her laugh turned to a cough as she spit up blood. The Prince held her as she struggled to catch her breath.

"We three were always getting into trouble. Thank you for letting me be a part of it," she said. "I have never met anyone so strong and so brave as you my prince. Thank you for letting me love you. No matter what happens, remember me how I was, all those years together."

"I will," he choked back more tears. The snow became a heavy curtain of white, covering the mountain despite the bright sun shining down.

Eloria watched as Sorrell sent her more memories. There was Killian and the Prince, laughing at the ocean when they were younger. A large library showed Sorrell reading many books and

248

the secrets that they held. She saw Sorrell too excited to sleep in the Healer's manor, because she knew she would see the Prince the next morning. They danced together on the beach of Kailani as the Prince whispered something in Sorrell's ear.

Eloria stood frozen by the cliff's edge, listening and watching the memory.

"Killian, will you read us our vows?" the Prince asked.

At his words, Sorrell blocked her mind from Eloria's.

"It would be my honor," Killian bowed his head.

The Prince laid his sword aside and held Sorrell's face in his hands. The snow continued to fall around them, and Eloria trembled as she watched her three companions.

"'In the beginning, the Creator made man from the earth,'" Killian's voice rang clear. "'Man was not to walk the world alone, thus a woman was created for him. The love between them is meant to reflect the love that our Creator has for us. It is to be chosen. It is to be fought for. It is to be forever. They are to be joined until they ascend to the heavens.'"

Tears streamed from the Prince's eyes but he did not look away from his beloved.

"Sorrell," Killian continued, "If you accept this man, take his strong hand, his sword hand."

With trembling fingers, she grasped the Prince's hand in her own.

"Tavin," Killian said, "This woman has chosen you until the end of her days. Will you accept her?"

"I will," the Prince cried.

"So shall it be until the end of your days. As is our custom, you will enter Community as one. Tavin of the Guard and Sorrell of the Queen's House, united for no man, beast, or angel to break."

The Prince gently kissed Sorrell.

"Tavin? That's a nice name," she smiled up at him.

"When did you learn the truth?" the Prince asked.

For a moment, Sorrell could not speak. Blood trickled from her nose and mouth. The Prince held her tightly, trying to comfort her.

"Eloria saw things that I never noticed," her voice quivered. "I knew for sure at the feast in Kailani." She smiled as she remembered, "I knew when Killian took her to the glass ballroom. The stars had never shone so brightly."

Killian nodded, "Thank you for bringing her here."

Sorrell smiled to him, "You will do great things with her by your side. Thank you for letting me stay with you all this time."

"I wouldn't have it any other way," Killian replied. "I couldn't keep him away from you if I tried."

"I'm not...," Sorrell's voice faltered as she choked back blood. "I didn't mean to..." But she couldn't finish.

Eloria took a step closer to them but her body was shaking uncontrollably. Sorrell lay on the ground covered in blood and snow. The black liquid spilled from her wound like a dark snake. The two men sat at her side, comforting her the best they could. Rocks skittered at the cliff's edge. Eloria felt something wrap around her leg. She looked down and saw three large, grey fingers.

Deformed.

Sorrell heard Eloria's thoughts.

"Killian!" Sorrell gasped. "Killian, she needs you!"

He quickly looked up to see Eloria standing at the cliff's precipice. A Deformed was hanging on the edge of the mountain, one hand wrapped around her leg.

"No!" Killian bellowed.

The beast chortled and thrust his body from the mountain, launching Eloria off the cliffside with it.

"Tavin, meet me in the mountains," Killian said to the Prince as he stood. "The beasts will know where to find us."

"I will," said the Prince.

"Killian...wait!" Sorrell gasped.

"Eloria shall always have my protection, dear sister, but you already know that. Rest safely with my kin."

He raced across the mountain's platform and threw himself off the edge. They watched the place where he disappeared until they heard Killian cry out in pain. Sorrell shivered at the sound.

"It's alright," the Prince cooed.

"It feels so odd not being next to her," Sorrell's voice was weak. "How quickly our lives have changed."

"I would have made you my wife within the year. Prophecy or no. Why didn't you wait for me?" the Prince asked.

"It wasn't my decision of when she came. I only knew she had to, and it was my responsibility to bring her."

"You're my wife now. Surely you no longer need to speak in riddles."

"I like to keep you guessing."

The Prince ignored her humor.

"I've loved you since the day I saw you in the mountains," he said. "You have followed me ever since that day, and I'll follow you anywhere from this day. You're the fairest of all, Sorrell."

"You were raised with angels. It's no wonder you are such a romantic."

"Have you ever seen an angel? Were you there when they came to the palace?" the Prince asked softly.

"No," her voice quivered. "Tavin, I'm afraid."

He held her tightly, "You have nothing to fear. Theirs are the voices that carry the heavenly songs. You've never heard anything like it, Sorrell. When you meet them, all your fear and pain will disappear. That's nothing compared to when we'll meet the Creator one day. Peace will overwhelm you until it becomes the most inexplicable joy. The angel's wings carry them over mountains and to the stars. They have six wings, did you know? Pure white, as the snow, and more powerful than any dragon's. They will keep you safe until I'm by your side again."

"My angel has no wings," she whispered.

Her hand fell from his.

"Sorrell?"

There was no reply.

His chest heaved with sorrow, "Wait for me, my love. Wait for me with the angels. You will not have to wait long."

CHAPTER 20

Eloria couldn't scream. She couldn't breath. The wind rushed past her so quickly that it stole the air from her lungs. She was falling. Dropping faster and faster. As she struggled for air, everything around her went black.

Killian took four long strides then kicked off of the mountain's edge. He welcomed the adrenaline rushing through his veins as his body left the firm ground below. The wind blew past him like a torrent as the familiar feeling of free fall overcame him. He could hardly remember the last time he had leapt from such a height.

With a deep breath, he tapped into the magic within himself. The skin on his back ripped open and his bones began to brake. With a cry of pain, his wings burst free, spreading to their full span. His bones reshaped themselves to accommodate his true form, and his skin stitched itself back together. He caught a glimpse of his shredded tunic flapping towards the ground below.

Folding his wings behind him, he dove towards the helpless Eloria. Her body whipped about in the wind as if in a current of water. As he neared, he measured the distance between himself and the desert below, knowing he wouldn't have much time before the unnatural shadows of the desert converged on them.

He reached for Eloria's hand, pushing himself to her. He grasped her wrist and wrapped his arms around her. With a mighty rush, his wings stretched to their full span, sending them into a horizontal glide across the barren landscape below them. He held the girl tightly as he circled back to the mountain. His wings beat against the air, furiously fighting to rise higher.

In minutes, he had regained the distance that they had fallen. He glided in a wide circle that sent them rising above the mountain, his wings cupping the wind to propel them upwards. They passed over Tavin where he sat with Sorrell's body.

Killian's chest ached with sorrow as he glided over the boarder. He flew along the mountain's ridge, silently through the sheet of snow. Finally, he circled a dense area of forest and slowly began to descend. When his wings were too large for the trees' canopy, he wrapped them around himself and used the wind to guide them to the mossy ground. Lightly touching the earth, he released the air back to the skies.

As gently as he could, he placed Eloria on the ground. After a quick assessment that she had not been physically wounded, he drew away from her.

"Wake up," he said.

The girl remained motionless.

"Hey!" he said as loudly as he dared. Knowing that Deformed could still be in the forest, he didn't want to draw unwanted attention. "You're going to make me say it aren't you?" He crouched next to her. "Eloria," he whispered.

Her body twitched. She gave a slight moan as if dreaming. A twig snapped behind them and Killian quickly turned, his wings stretching to their full span.

Emrys Killian, a large mountain cat thought to him. It stood a few yards away, white from the snow.

The beasts always knew his true identity although they played along with the ruse. The green dragon had been particularly difficult to convince to keep his secret.

May I seek your help? Killian thought to it.

The cat lowered its head respectfully, *We serve the line of Seraphim.*

There is a man on the mountain's landing. We have lost someone dear to us... Grief kept him from forming the words. The snow was already spreading from the mountain's landing to the forests and he knew he didn't have the power to suppress it. He sent images to the mountain cat, hoping not to overwhelm it with his emotions.

The beast saw memories of the Deformed attacking the Seraphim and three others. A female bled on the mountain and a strong one with hair like the sun held her in his arms. The mountain cat could feel the grief and anger inside of the winged man's mind.

I understand, Emrys. The cat's tail twitched with agitation.

He travels in my name, Killian thought. *He will need protection through the mountains until he is finished mourning, but he must leave the landing with all haste.*

It will be done. Others of mine are beyond, at the stream. We shall do as you ask.

Killian bowed to the beast, *Thank you.*

The female is cold, it said. *There is a den not far. It will keep you dry and safe until the sky is itself again.*

The mountain cat silently disappeared back among the trees. Snow fell in large flakes around them and Killian did his best to keep a storm from rising. Clouds now covered the sun, and he quickly knelt at Eloria's side. Her hands trembled though she did not wake. Killian did not feel the cold.

He carefully lifted Eloria from the ground, waiting for his touch to wake her. To his surprise, she remained unconscious. He hurried forward, his feet noiselessly gliding over the branches and roots. It was not long until he found the cavern that the mountain cat spoke of. He ducked beneath the rocky overhang and lay Eloria on the ground.

"Please, wake up," he whispered. "I don't even know what's wrong with you."

He waited but she did not move.

"You weren't supposed to have that power yet," he sighed. "I've been careful. Tavin thought the sooner it happened the safer you'd be. I thought we still had weeks before…"

"Stop talking," Eloria mumbled.

He was silent as his green eyes watched her.

"Where's Sorrell and the Prince?" she asked.

"On the mountain," he replied.

"Where are we?"

"A cave, a few leagues away."

Eloria squinted up at him. "Stop looking at me like that," she scoffed. "I know I messed up by doing magic, but you don't have to look so upset about it." Her face grew pale, "Why do I feel so dizzy?"

"A Deformed pulled you off the mountain. You were falling to your death."

Eloria pressed a hand to her head as if checking for a fever, "You should leave the jokes to the Prince."

"Elor…," he stopped himself. "I'm not joking. A Deformed threw you from the mountain and I saved you. You're welcome."

He leaned in closer. She quickly put a hand on his chest, pushing him away. Her fingers retracted quickly when she recognized the sensation of his bare skin.

"Where's your shirt?"

"Open your eyes."

"My head is spinning. I think I might be sick."

"Open your eyes, Eloria."

She did as she was told. Killian's piercing green gaze was unwavering. She was immediately embarrassed by how intimate it felt. Eloria glanced away from his eyes to the large wings behind him. Her body shot up from the ground.

"You have wings!"

"Yes."

"No, you have actual wings!"

"Yes."

"I was falling then...," Eloria stammered, remembering. "You... you fell! I heard you scream in pain and then... are you alright? Did they hurt you?"

"I'm fine," he said calmly.

"But you were in pain...," she said in confusion.

"Pain is temporary."

"Where is your shirt?" she cried. "Why do you have wings?"

"I'm the Seraphim Prince," Killian said bluntly.

"But the Prince," she breathed heavily. "I mean, we call him 'the Prince' for goodness sake! Are you brothers or like an... illegitimate child or something?"

"No," Killian watched her closely. "I am the only child of the king and queen. When we spend our years among the people, we use a decoy in order to experience the real lives of our people. Tavin's parents died when he was very young. He was brought to Kien Illae and raised by my parents. When we came of age, he agreed to go with me into Community and be my decoy. That was his Choice."

"But...," Eloria was dizzy again as she tried to make sense of it. "Where is your shirt?"

"What else do you remember besides my clothes?"

"Sorrell was talking about... Before she...," Eloria's heart quickened. "Where is she? Where's Sorrell?"

Killian's heart sank, "She's gone."

"But the Prince was going to heal her. It was only a small knife and she was going to live." Eloria's body began to tremble. "You have magic and Healers and dragons and wings! She can't die!"

"The knife was poisoned. She knew it was over before we did."

257

Eloria thought back to the battle. The Deformed were dead around their feet, the wind had blown them from the rock face. Then the crooked, black knife...

Eloria crumpled to the ground, sobbing at the realization of what had happened. Thunder rumbled through the sky and the snow turned to sleet outside the cavern mouth. Killian reached for her but quickly thought better of it.

"I'm sorry," he whispered.

Eloria looked at the man before her. Large, white wings filled the cave with a pale glow. His shirtless torso moved slowly with his breathing, wings shifting as he did. Small wisps of magic floated through the air around him, oblivious to the world.

"If you're a Seraphim, why didn't you save her?"

"It doesn't work that way."

"Then what good are you?" Eloria's tearful gaze met his. His green eyes were piercing as he looked back at her.

Her anger faded and was replaced with a pain unlike anything she knew. It filled her chest and lungs. She struggled to breathe as tears poured down her cheeks. For the first time, she hardly noticed Killian's touch. She didn't feel his wings as their feathers brushed against her skin. She didn't feel a shiver or sensation when his arms wrapped around her. Only sorrow, grief, and emptiness ripped through her core.

She couldn't tell how long she stayed engulfed in Killian's arms. Eloria sobbed until she finally fell asleep from exhaustion and an aching desire to escape this new reality. She dreamt of Sorrell's face and the horrible images the Deformed had put into her mind. Many times she woke with a start, jumping from the horrors of her dreams or the feeling of falling, only to feel Killian's tight arms safely anchoring her to him. Her body would slide back to sleep in Killian's embrace, seeing nothing but his wings as she drifted away. The silent snowfall became a welcome guest in their cavern.

When Eloria's dreams faded, she woke to the sound of trees creaking from the weight of snow. Her eyes opened to see a wall of white feathers before her. She was laying against Killian's chest. His wings were stretched out around them, covering them in a protective ball. She glanced up to see that Killian slept peacefully.

Eloria rose, being careful not to wake him. Her muscles ached from sitting and she wondered if it had been days or hours of being in the cave. Gazing at the giant wings before her, she stared with wonder. Her hand brushed against the feathers. They were surprisingly soft and felt more like fur than feathers of a bird. They shone with a white brilliance that seemed to give off its own light. When Killian breathed, they moved ever so slightly. Eloria gently pushed the wing away. She walked to the cavern's mouth, gazing out at the white forest. She shivered, realizing Killian's wings had been protecting her from the cold while she slept.

There was a rustling behind her and she turned to see Killian standing, folding his wings behind him. They looked at each other in silence, his green eyes boring into her as if trying to read her mind. She thought she would feel embarrassed for crying in front of him and for waking up in his embrace, but she could see the same pain in his eyes, if not more. There was nothing embarrassing about the loss of a loved one. It was clear he understood that as well.

He stepped next to her and put a gentle hand on her arm. A warm shiver ran through her body when their skin made contact. The cold seeped away and her body relaxed under his touch. When her shivering stopped, he dropped his hand away and ducked out of the cavern. She wanted to ask where he was going but she knew he was not ready to speak.

He walked into the forest, snow falling down the bare skin of his back. When Killian disappeared among the trees, Eloria turned back into the cavern and did the stretches she had been taught. Her muscles released their tension by the time she finished.

She carefully removed her boots and used the snow to wash as best she could. Despite her best efforts, her clothes ended up quite wet and she sat freezing cold against the rock wall as she waited for Killian to return. Time stood still in the cavern and she couldn't tell if it was night or day due to the dark clouds above them. She did her best to keep Sorrell from her mind, but the pain in her chest was a constant reminder.

After what seemed like hours, she saw Killian's winged figure walking back through trees. He had a strange bundle under one arm and something large slung over his shoulder. When he reached the mouth of their shelter, he tossed his items onto the floor and shook his head and wings. Snow flew off his hair and feathers, reminding Eloria of how a dog would shake after swimming in a lake.

She watched as he unwrapped a giant leaf and revealed a pile of dry twigs and sticks. The other large item on the ground was a felled turkey. Eloria immediately felt indebted to Killian. Despite his own anguish, he was looking out for his companions as always. She immediately took the sticks and began laying them out for a fire the way she had learned at the House of Healers. Killian dragged the turkey back into the snow to clean and carve.

Eloria enjoyed having something to focus on besides the pain inside her chest. She imagined Killian felt the same. When the fire was hot and ash lay beneath the sticks, he brought strips of meat to it and they cooked their meal. After they had silently eaten their fill, he returned to the forest to bury the animal carcass and came back with his hands full of berries.

Eloria couldn't help but smile. No matter their circumstance, there were always berries to eat in Loraillvon. She gratefully accepted them and took up a spot against the wall across from

Killian. She was still cold and her clothes were damp despite the small fire at the mouth of the cave.

When Eloria finished her berries she folded her arms around her, shivering from the cold. She gazed out at the heavy snow. Though Killian wasn't crying, the snow seemed endless. Eloria supposed that they wouldn't be leaving their rocky cavern until his pain had lessened. Until he was able to stop the snow outside.

Eloria stared out to the forest for uncountable minutes until she slowly drifted asleep once again. She shivered from the cold and went in and out of her sleeping state until she felt a hand slip behind her back. Killian was sliding his wing and arm around her once again.

She turned into him as his wings surrounded them and covered her from the cold draft. Eloria drifted into a dreamless sleep, happy that she wasn't alone with her sorrow.

Killian shifted slightly and Eloria's eyes flew open, fearing danger or the Deformed. Her body tensed and she quickly took stock of her surroundings.

"I'm sorry I woke you," Killian said softly.

She glanced up and saw that he had been crying.

"In our world, when we lose a loved one, it is custom that everyone remains silent and mourns with the family. No one speaks until a family member does. It is a sign that they are over their initial mourning."

Eloria nodded.

"Were you waiting for me to speak? Or shall I wait for you?"

"You knew her the longest," Eloria whispered, her voice raspy from not being used.

"Yes, but you shared her mind."

Eloria shrugged, "I suppose, at this point, we've both spoken anyhow..."

Killian smiled down at her, "I suppose that is true. I did not want to alarm you by remaining silent for your sake. It seemed best if I explained."

He walked to the cavern's opening, the tips of his wings dragging on the ground behind him. Eloria watched as he took a deep breath, his bare chest rising and falling. The rain outside turned back to a peaceful snow.

"I'm afraid that's the best I can do for now, and it will follow us as we travel until…," he paused, "Well, until more time has passed."

"As long as you can promise the sun will shine again, then I won't mind the snow."

Killian turned back to her, "You do not like the snow?"

Eloria glanced at the large white flakes, "In my world it snows too much. It seems clear that in this world snow is not necessarily a positive thing either. I always prefer sunshine."

"The sun will shine again, I promise you." He sat down against the wall across from her, letting his wings fall lax to either side of him. "Do you mind?" he asked.

She looked at him curiously.

"My wings," he explained. "Do you mind them?"

"Not at all. I think they're beautiful."

"It can be uncomfortable when they are hidden. I haven't been able to use them in a long time."

"I don't mind," she said with a quick glance.

"I'm sure you have some questions about what has happened. Things you've done and things that you heard Sorrell say."

Eloria looked down with embarrassment, "I honestly haven't thought about much besides…"

"I understand," he said quietly. "We cannot leave until the ground has had time to dry. It would be too difficult for you to travel. Take your time and ask whatever may come to you."

He folded his arms across his chest and leaned his head back against the stony interior of their room.

"Why can't you fly us back to the Prince?" she blurted out.

"That didn't take long, did it?" he sighed. "His name is Tavin, you don't have to call him the Prince anymore. If we tried to fly back, you would freeze from the snow and it is a long way. It would be uncomfortable for both of us if I had to carry you."

"Don't you have super strength from being an angel?"

"I'm a Seraphim, not an angel. While I am stronger and faster than most, I have my limits."

"How long will it take us to get back to them?"

"Tavin needed time alone," Killian's eyes glazed over as he thought about his comrade. "He will travel to us when he is ready. You've slept for a number of days already, so he could arrive anytime. We will then travel to the heart of the Forest Region. That will be the opportune place to work with your new powers."

"What powers?"

"The wind that you summoned on the mountain was Seraphim magic. Your Transformation has begun."

"My Transformation?" Eloria's mind swirled.

"The prophecy, remember? You are the new Eloria, to become the second Queen Transformed. 'From a world of reflection, Eloria returns,'" he recited, "'When Evil rises and the world be burned. She shall love Seraphim wings or doom she will bring. A death to come that will change all things.'"

"Stop it! Don't quote the stupid prophecy to me. Explain it!" Eloria felt panicked. "Explain everything to me! Why do I have powers? Why am I being transformed? Who are you if the Prince isn't the prince? Is your name even Killian?"

His wings shifted as he leaned forward, "My name is Emrys Killian Samuel von Gabriel, son of Forfax and Gloribel, of the line of Seraphim. The royal family chooses one of their middles names to be known as during their time with the people. It's sort of a family joke. Other families don't have middle names. At our name day, only our first name is announced. The people know that the Seraphim prince's name is Emrys, so I chose to go by Killian when I came of age.

"Tavin has been acting as prince for years. When you arrived at the Choosing Ceremony with Sorrell, I could see that you were from another realm. It is one of the Seraphim powers so that we will know if someone has been tampering with worlds. Somehow, Sorrell managed to hide it from me. We were together only a few days before you arrived. Still, I should have been able to sense her tampering before she had a chance to bring you through."

"What other powers do you have?"

"We have wings, obviously. The weather reflects our emotions as well." He nodded to the snow outside the cave, "Snow is sorrow, storms are anger, and rain is sadness. Do you remember when the Deformed attacked us near the ocean?"

Eloria thought back to her first encounter with the Deformed. "You created the lightening?"

"I can manipulate it to my will. My anger caused the storm, but I am able to use the lightening as a weapon, like I did that day with the Deformed."

"You missed," Eloria spat, remembering how the monster had almost killed her.

"I'm out of practice," Killian huffed. "As we grow in our power, we can control more aspects of it. Though I am filled with loss and sorrow, I have not caused a blizzard. When your training was atrocious, I held back the storms. Understand?"

"How kind of you," she snapped.

"I can also fly without my wings because I can manipulate the wind. It follows our bidding no matter where we are. That's what you did on the mountain. You tapped into the Seraphim power and summoned the wind to your command."

"I don't get it. How do I have that power? Why am I being Transformed?"

Killian shifted uncomfortably, "It's because of me. While we were at the ocean, Sorrell gave me a rough scolding about how I had been treating you during training. When you and I were in Kailani, it became obvious how wrong I was. You were doing your best and I wasn't adapting to what you needed. So I changed."

"I have powers because you were finally nice to me?"

"It was more than that," he replied. "Take my hand."

He reached out for her but she pulled away.

"Please, I need to show you."

"Don't touch me," she mumbled.

He pulled his hand back with a hard look in his eyes. "Fine. We'll do it another way."

She slunk against the wall, afraid of what he had planned.

"Eloria," he whispered.

The warm shiver ran through her body and she visibly trembled.

"That feeling is the Transformation flowing through you," he explained. "I noticed it the first time I said your name at the Choosing Ceremony. The more intimate we become emotionally and physically, the stronger the Transformation becomes. Every time I say your name it changes you. Every time I touch you, it transforms you. I distanced myself from you at first because I didn't think you had what it took to save us. At Kailani, everything changed."

Eloria's mind raced, "So every time you've said my name or taken my hand, it was to enact the Transformation?"

"Perhaps not entirely for that reason."

Eloria blushed.

"You told me once that the prince used to make you recite the prophecy, because he wanted to know everything about it. That was really you. You and Tavin, reciting the prophecy and growing up waiting for me to arrive."

"I spent my whole life waiting for you," he said quietly. "As boys, Eloria was our imaginary friend that fought great battles with us. She was real to me before you ever came to this world. As we grew older, I left that imaginary friend behind, but I felt like everything I did was a step closer to meeting her. The real Eloria. When you finally came, it wasn't how I thought it would be. You were different than we had imagined. I felt as if the real Eloria was still waiting for me out there."

"I wasn't good enough, you mean?"

"Yes," he grunted. "I didn't think you could survive in this world let alone save it."

"Sorry that I've been such a disappointment."

Killian shook his head, "You've proven me wrong in many ways. Every day you've become more and more the Eloria that was meant for this world, not the illusion of a young boy's fantasy. You are transforming even without my help."

"It scares me, I suppose. To think that something is happening to me without realizing it."

"Nothing about it should be painful."

Eloria blushed, "Sorry for panicking. As I said, it was scary to hear… that's all."

They sat in an uncomfortable silence. Eloria racked her brain for a question that would make sense to ask. There was so much she didn't understand.

"Will you tell me about Sorrell and the Prin… Tavin?"

"It's not my place."

Eloria nodded, "I understand, but there's so much I didn't know about her. And I don't know anything about Tavin besides that he was the Prince which is clearly not true."

Killian smiled, "Very well. The Prince and I were a ways out from our Choosing Ceremony. We were with a diplomatic envoy to a large Mountain Region. It was a village of Mages and Builders. They live in trees much like the Ceremonial Woods, but much better engineered and the forests in the mountains are quite dense.

"Tavin challenged me to a race, to see who could reach the top of the head Mage's tree house without using magic or ladder. I fell twelve feet up the tree and broke my arm. Sorrell was the first to see us. She helped us to a Healer then chided Tavin for not using his Seraphim powers to save me. I'm sure it's not hard for you to imagine.

"We spent the rest of our time with her. When we discovered that she was starting her year of training soon like us, we invited her to join us. It wasn't long until she felt like a sister. Tavin loved her instantly. But being my decoy, he wasn't allowed to tell her the truth about us. As close as we became, she never suspected that Tavin wasn't a Seraphim. We went through training together, made our Choice, then spent the last few years touring and serving our Houses alongside one another. There were times when our work split us up, but we were never apart for long.

"Tavin was planning to propose to Sorrell at the end of the harvest. That's when he would have been released from my side and I would leave Community to take up my responsibilities with the royal family. When you came, everything changed. He asked my permission and he proposed the night of the ball at Kailani."

"I saw Sorrell's memory of it," Eloria said. "She was so happy."

"He still hadn't told her the truth about who we were, but she had started to suspect anyway. Apparently you saw things about me that she had never noticed. In the end, she discovered the truth for herself."

"I guess that's what Tavin meant when he said I was his type."

"You are more like her now then when you first came here. You have her strength and sharp tongue."

267

Eloria couldn't help but smile, "When it came to you, Killian, I always had a sharp tongue."

He returned her smile. "If you don't mind, I would like to remain close to you. I understand if you are upset with Tavin and I for lying to you about my true identity, but our moments together were important to me. I can't really explain it, but I know that I need to continue protecting you. I will help you learn to control your new powers and they'll continue growing."

"What do we do now?" she asked. "Am I still supposed to train with each house when the Deformed are attacking? Who are we without Sorrell?"

"You are the prophesied, and I am your protector. We'll have a bumbling, blonde brute join us along the way," he smiled.

"Killian?"

"Yes, Eloria?"

She felt the tingle flow through her. Adrenaline pumped into her body as she worked up the courage to speak, "The part about the prophecy, about loving Seraphim wings…"

"Killian!" a voice shouted from the forest.

He bolted up.

"Eloria!" the voice echoed through the trees.

"It's Tavin," Killian said. "Wait here."

CHAPTER 21

He didn't have to go far before Tavin's large silhouette came into view.

"I'm back, brother," Tavin quickly embraced him.

"I'm glad you found us."

"They took her body," Tavin said. "Not even hours after... I couldn't fight them off. I had no choice. They took her body."

"The girls looked identical. Perhaps the enemy thought they had the prophesied instead."

"It doesn't matter now," Tavin wiped away a tear. "We need to get to the forest. We've lingered in these mountains long enough."

"Come on, it'll help her to see you."

As the men approached the small cave, Eloria stepped forward hesitantly. She remembered how much she looked like Sorrell and wondered if her presence would only cause him more pain. Tears filled her eyes unwillingly.

"Oh, Eloria," Tavin said.

He wrapped his bearlike arms around her in a strong embrace.

"I'm so sorry," she whispered.

"There was nothing we could do," he said gently. "We've spent our lives preparing for things like this, though we ask the Creator that we'll never lose someone. We never taught you how to be ready for death. I suppose you can't truly be ready, but you were Sorrell's reflection-self which makes you her family. Because of

269

that, I will do everything in my power to protect her family. It is what she would have wanted."

"Thank you," Eloria replied.

"Killian, it's time to stop the snow. There's been enough sadness. We must continue on despite it."

Killian closed his eyes. His chest rose and fell in a deep rhythm until the snow ceased its descent.

"If we're lucky, no one from the villages would have seen me flying."

"Either way, we can't risk you being spotted like that," Tavin eyed his wings.

"Eloria, don't be afraid," Killian sighed.

"Afraid of what?" she asked.

His wings rose up to the cavern's ceiling. Killian's face twisted with pain. Both wings snapped, as if breaking, and fell loosely to his side. He grunted as they snapped again. With a short cry, Killian's body shook and his muscles flexed. Blue veins popped under his skin like snakes along his arms. His wings hung limply at his side then they retracted into his back, disappearing altogether. He gasped and fell to his knees.

"Killian!" Eloria ran to him, checking his back for scars. The skin was smooth and perfect.

"And that…," he huffed, "is how my wings disappear."

"That's terrible."

"It's not so bad," Tavin grunted.

"Says the decoy," Killian joked.

Tavin looked about the small cave then noticed the ashes from their little fire. He nudged a burnt twig with his boot.

"Honestly, Killian?" he huffed. "This is it? She'll freeze like this!"

"What?" Killian stood baffled.

"Did you think the rock was going to keep her warm?" Tavin scolded. "She's not a Seraphim. How do you expect her to survive if you won't even light her a proper fire? I'm gone for a few days and this is what happens."

Killian threw up his hands in disbelief, "She had me! We didn't need a stupid fire."

Eloria blushed.

"Ha!" Tavin grinned. "I just wanted you to admit it."

"Idiot," Killian smiled back.

It was Eloria's turn to be baffled.

"Don't be embarrassed," Tavin said, "The mood was a bit grim, so I thought I would cheer things up. Killian has always considered himself to be too good for a warm fire anyway."

"Let's get moving," Killian interjected.

Eloria laced up her boots and they set off through the forest. As they walked in silence, Eloria was keenly aware of the pain inside her chest again. Snow began to fall but Tavin said nothing. The inches that already covered the ground made it difficult for Eloria to travel. She stumbled over hidden roots and stones.

Tavin struggled almost as much. At one point, he stepped in a ditch and fell into a mound of snow four feet deep. Upon pulling himself out, he was covered from head to toe. His cheeks had turned rosy from the cold and snow hung on his eyelashes.

Killian continued on while they stumbled after him. For three days they traveled this way. At night they found shelter in rock formations or tree overhang. During the day, they trudged through the snow, ever moving upwards along the mountains. On the fourth day, Eloria woke to sunshine. The snow had melted around them and the grass and flowers were still in full bloom.

"Hi," Killian said to her as she rose.

"How did the snow melt so quickly?"

He glanced at the forest around them. "Since we're in the mountains, the ground soaks up the water more quickly and directs it to the streams. We won't have to worry about puddles

271

the rest of the way. We continue uphill," he pointed. "The mountain ends a few leagues further, then it's true Forest Region."

The sky was painted in pink and orange as the sun began to rise. Light poured over the mountain around them and streams gurgled happily. It was only a few short hours until they left the trees behind them. The large hills were covered in tall grass and flowers. They were at such a height that they had a clear view of the foot hills that stretched to the forests below.

"I thought we were near the ocean?" Eloria asked.

"That's the way we came. Since leaving the Landing, we've been headed Northwest, towards Kien Illae. This is all mountain territory until the forests below. The heart of the Forest Region is actually part of the foothills to the west."

The sun shone all day which lifted their spirits. They spoke often of Sorrell. Sharing in dark and painful moments then helping to lift each other out of them again. They didn't stop until late into the nights and they woke before the sun's light was anywhere near the mountain tops.

To her relief, the grassy knolls were not steep or much harder to walk than their hiking path up the mountains. The sky stretched out before them and the mountains looked more distant each day. As they climbed up a fielded hill, Eloria could see smoke rising in the distance and a large wall.

"Community," Tavin said. "If anyone asks, we are traveling for the Queen's House. No one needs to know who we are for now."

"You can get in a little bit of training while we're in the forest. We'll stop to see the Mages then we can return home to Kien Illae to wake the dragon," Killian said.

"You'll take me to your home... which is a castle," Eloria mused.

"Yes. Is that a problem?"

"I will have to meet your parents and try to explain how I'm turning into a Seraphim?" she glanced up to Killian.

"We could keep things simple and not say anything. That would save us both an awkward conversation with my father."

"Ugh, don't even say it," Eloria whined.

"What?"

"The thought of a king giving me a Seraphim transformation talk," she scoffed.

"Trust me," Tavin chimed in, "It's worse when the only examples are their own ancestors."

Killian cringed and quickly led them to the village ahead. The gate was carved elegantly to reflect the landscape around them. The doors stood open with a cobbled stone road and thick hydrangeas along its path. They soon approached little buildings both of logs and stones, each a small cottage with a bit of smoke rising from the chimneys. Everything was silent as they made their way through the village. No no was in sight and little noise came from the houses.

"It's a shame that you've not spent more time in Community," Killian said.

"We were at the ocean for quite a while," she pointed out.

"The area by Kailani is mostly used for training and setting up those who are coming of age. That sort of lifestyle is quite different from normal Community. We were so busy teaching you about the Houses that we forgot to introduce you to daily life."

Eloria had not considered the day to day activities of the people in this world. "Everything Sorrell taught me was combat training and of her time working for the queen. I never thought to ask about what others did."

Killian paused as they crested a small hill. "Those are trade shops," he pointed. "See the signs above the doors? The symbols on them signify their House and trade. It's universal throughout each territory. That way travelers always know where to go."

Eloria saw small engravings on a swinging wooden sign. They were symbols of the talismans that had been at the Choosing

Ceremony. There was a small bottle representing Mages, a lace pattern for Healers, and another sign for the Farmers.

"I'll get you some weapons," Tavin said. "Killian, please barter for a shirt. You're making us look conspicuous."

Killian and Eloria made their way to the Healers shop and knocked on the main door. They heard mumbling and some clay pots banging together. A second later, a small window next to the door swung open.

"The sun has not yet risen, how early do you think I.... Oh! Well you are not Slenan at all!" An elderly woman peered through the window to the two strangers. Her wispy hair floated around her head as she surveyed them curiously. Seeing Killian's bare torso, her eyes narrowed.

"Excuse me, kind Healer," Killian spoke with a voice sweet as honey. "My friend and I are on business for the Queen's House and ran into trouble. We need to resupply before continuing our journey. Would you be so kind as to help us? I do apologize for the hour if we woke you."

She grumbled something incoherent. The window slammed shut and Eloria began to feel uneasy. The village was eerily quiet and she noticed all of the doors and windows were closed tight. Despite the early hour, she expected that they would run into someone along the path. They had seen no one.

"Does it feel odd to you?" she asked Killian.

"The people in the mountains are more cautious than others. They've been dealing with the Deformed and attacks from the Evil Ones for years. We may not find the warmest of welcomes here." He cast a weary glance at the buildings around them.

The window shutters flew open and slapped against the building's stone. The noise echoed throughout the village.

"You are from the Guard?" the woman asked, eyeing Killian's toned figure.

He nodded.

"What about you, Sorrell? Do you need different clothing this time as well?"

Eloria stood dumbfounded, unable to answer the woman. The pain that had slowly diminished inside of her chest the last few days came full force once again. Aching and emptiness filled her body. A bitter wind blew through the vacant street.

"Do you know Sorrell?" Killian asked hurriedly, stepping in front of Eloria.

"Of course. She comes through these parts twice a year. I've been holding her things for her. Did you want them?" she asked, ducking her head to see around Killian.

"That would be so kind of you, thank you," Killian smiled.

The old woman gave him a grunt and tossed a bundle of clothes at him. She shuffled away to fetch Sorrell's things. Killian quickly unrolled the bundle and donned a sleeveless grey tunic, leather vest, and a wool shrug that wrapped around one shoulder.

"Why did she call me that?" Eloria whispered.

"Whatever you do, don't speak," he said quietly. "You may look like Sorrell but your accent will give you away. Everywhere we've traveled the people knew that Eloria had come to this world. They expected to see two girls that looked alike. Without Sorrell, you look like one of us... like her."

"But we were so different," Eloria shook her head.

"You've been here for a while now, remember? You have changed. The last few weeks, there were times that even Tavin and I had trouble telling you apart. Remember that Seraphim were the ones gifted with the Sight, to see things from other worlds. I am the only one who can tell there is something different about you."

The woman appeared at the window again and held out a satchel and clothing. Eloria tentatively took it from her and stepped back behind Killian.

"Food and weapons?" Killian inquired.

The woman lifted her chin towards the shops to their left. "You'll need the Farmers and Builders for that."

"Thank you again for your help, and sorry for the early hour," Killian smiled sweetly.

"If this man gives you trouble, Sorrell, get rid of him," she cackled. "Queen's business or not, you don't seem yourself, and I've never seen you travel with companions before."

Eloria nodded but kept her mouth shut. Killian placed a gentle hand on Eloria's back and guided her away.

"Thank you again!" he said with a wave.

The woman swung her shutters shut with a loud *snap*!

"When was Sorrell here?" Eloria asked.

"I'm not sure. There were times that she had business with the Queen's House and had to leave us. The few months before you arrived she was away quite often. Even if she was going to see the dragon, I don't know why she would come this far into the mountains."

The second shop keeper was a skinny man with a more pleasant attitude.

"Sorry about the old woman," he said with a lazy smile. "She's been bitter since the Deformed started crossing our borders. Not much trust in new people these days. For a Healer, she's got a short fuse."

Killian's smile was a work of art, "She was lovely. It is simply our bad timing that caught her off guard. We arrived earlier than we realized and should have waited for the town to wake before intruding."

"No need for a fuss," the man yawned. "We've grown complacent here in the mountains. Not many wake until the sun is over the hill. If you stick around, you can join us for a meal."

Eloria's mouth watered at the thought of good food. The berries and foul they had hunted were hardly an adequate meal the past few days.

"We appreciate the offer," Killian smiled. "We must continue on our path, nonetheless. The queen's business waits for no one! Whatever traveling food you have will be more than adequate."

Eloria changed into her new clothes in the shop's back room. She tied her hair behind her with a leather strap and wished, once again, that she had a mirror. She wondered if she would recognize herself or only see Sorrell staring back in her reflection. When she rejoined Killian, the shop keeper had disappeared.

"I was beginning to think you were the only grump in this world," Eloria grinned. "Apparently everyone's cheery nature only goes so far."

"At least we keep you guessing. Here," he handed her Sorrell's satchel, "You hold on to this."

Eloria weighed it in her hands, trying to judge its contents. The leather was worn and bleached from sunlight. There were no symbols or designs along its strap or edges. She wondered what sort of belongings Sorrell would leave behind with an old Healer.

"Should we open it?"

"It's up to you. As I've said before, you shared her mind. That makes you closer to her than anyone."

"But you united Tavin and Sorrell before she died, didn't you? That means he is her family."

Killian looked at the satchel curiously, "Sorrell often spoke in riddles."

"Before she died, I saw a memory of her putting a mirror in a satchel like this one. I don't know what else she would have hid."

"The choice is yours."

Eloria contemplated the bag for a moment.

"If you don't mind, I think I'll hold on to it. It seems right to give it to Tavin, but I don't want to cause him more pain. Would it be alright if I waited?"

"If that is your wish," Killian complied.

They met up with Tavin who had procured new weapons for each of them. After a few minutes of strapping everything on, they departed from the village.

"Do you see that large tree?" Killian pointed towards the forest. "It stands higher than the rest and its leaves are a shade darker?"

Eloria followed his gaze, "Is that where we're going?"

"The heart of the forest," Killian smiled. "Where Mages abide and magic is bound. If ever you were to be affected by our world, that will be the place most potent."

"There's no telling how you'll react in the forest," Tavin spoke gravely. "It may be that nothing will happen as you've been in our world for quite a while. It may be that you remember nothing by the time we leave its trees."

"Don't scare her."

"Those trees are said to be the first ones created when Loraillvon came to be. They produce the strongest magic known to us. Her time there may be the key to us defeating the Evil once and for all."

Tavin shrugged up his pack and walked on. Eloria squinted to see the tree more clearly. Her hands shook after what Tavin had said. Suddenly a familiar tingle of warmth overtook her. Killian's fingers ran down her arm as he gently took her hand. Her body pulsed with excitement at his touch.

"No need to be afraid," he smiled. "The prophesied and her protector, remember?"

CHAPTER 22

"This is preposterous! I am the Prince. I demand entry for me and my fellow companions," Tavin fumed.

"Do what it says," Killian sighed.

"I still don't understand. Why can't we keep going?" Eloria asked.

The trees around them were as large as houses. They stood taller than skyscrapers with leaves that nearly blotted out the sky. Despite the coverage, the ground below was still filled with red hues from the setting sun.

"The heart of the forest is a sacred place. With threats rising throughout Loraillvon, they must have heightened their defenses."

"To translate for the Guard," Tavin interjected, "They put up a magical barrier by binding potions to the trees. I've read about this kind. It only allows entry to those who speak their true name."

Eloria looked around but saw no sign of magic.

"Better we get to the other side of the border than stand around waiting for nightfall," Killian said.

Tavin turned on him, "You're usually the cautious one. If we speak our true names, someone may know who you are. The arrival of Eloria will be announced throughout the entire Forest Region. I thought you were trying to avoid that kind of attention."

Killian lowered his voice, "It's better we get through the boundary line than wait for nightfall. While keeping her a secret is preferable, I'd rather the whole forest discovers the truth than us tarry outside the border. As for you and I, they will hear our names but not to whom it belongs. At this point, it's only for my parent's sake that we are still playing at this ruse. Most magical defenses go unmanned. They may not even be listening."

"Very well."

Tavin looked about the forest airily then raised his chin.

"Tavin of the Guard."

A silver shimmer ran through the air before him. He stepped through.

"Your turn," Killian gave Eloria a small nudge.

"Eloria of... uh..." she glanced back to Killian. He nodded encouragingly. "Uh... Eloria."

The air shimmered again and she stepped through the silver curtain. Tavin clapped her on the shoulder and they looked to Killian.

"This could take a while," Tavin snorted.

"Why?"

"Have you heard how long his name is?"

Killian approached the invisible border. He knelt down and placed a hand in the air before him.

In a whisper, he said, "Emrys Killian Samuel von Gabriel, son of Forfax and Gloribel, of the line of Seraphim."

The air before him burst into explosions of light, as if light bulbs were surging throughout the forest. Floating balls of magic spiraled into the air and disappeared within the tree canopy. Killian stepped through the barrier.

"Show off."

"Sorry, my prince!" Killian smiled as he hopped over a large tree root. "No one can resist a member of the Seraphim family arriving to their region."

"Let's go. They'll have a royal welcome prepared by the time we get there."

Over the next hour they weaved in and out of thick tree trunks. The hilly terrain continued to deter Eloria's ability to keep up with the men. When the trees' bases began to merge together, they crested the final hill. At the top, Killian waited for Eloria to join them.

They stood at the outskirts of a great crater. A large waterfall descended from between the trees and formed a small lake below. Around the lake were homes and shops crafted out of smaller trees that more resembled the normality that Eloria was used to. Forming the crater itself were the bases of trees larger than Eloria had yet seen. Their roots were stairways from the lake village up to more homes and shops within the trunks of the monstrous structures around them.

A fanfare of flutes and stringed instruments played from below. Tavin waved politely and made his way down the carved staircase before them.

"What do you think?" Killian asked.

"Of the Forest," she said in wonder. "Eloria of the Forest. I don't even care what House I end up in. I want to live here."

"Let's not make any decision until you've seen my castle."

"It's like a Swiss Family Robinson kingdom! That's it. This whole time I've been in Disneyland."

"Come with me, Prophesied."

They descended to the valley below as hundreds of people gathered. They cheered for the prince and his companions. Tavin smiled kindly as they worked their way through the crowd. So many gathered that Eloria had trouble following his tall blond head.

"Prince!" she hollered, but her words were drowned out with the cheers of everyone else.

"Killian!" she looked about but he was no where to be seen either. She allowed herself to be pushed through the crowd, hoping they were all headed towards Tavin as well. A large man's elbow was thrust into her chest.

"Whoa," Killian's arm caught her from falling. "Watch yourself. It's manic when the prince makes an appearance."

Eloria quickly regained her footing.

"Come this way. We don't need to stick around for this."

Killian's hand slid to her hip as he guided her through the throngs of people. When they were almost out of the crowd, they heard Tavin's voice rise up.

"Good people of the forest! Thank you for your warm welcome."

The cheers rang out louder as Tavin greeted them.

"Many of you have heard the rumors, but for those that have not - I come to share great news with you! News that we have waited centuries to hear."

"What is he doing?" Killian gaped.

"We have travelled far, fought great evil, and lost loved ones. But I'm here to tell you that my company and I have brought you news of the prophecy."

Killian's eyes grew wide, "Let us leave this crowd."

He hurried them out of the throng of people, but it was too late.

"The time of Eloria... is here!" The Prince's voice rang out. "Eloria, please join me."

All eyes turned to them. Killian's hand disappeared to the small of her back. Eloria smiled shyly to the people around them, unsure of what to do while Killian muttered silent insults at Tavin under his breath.

"I'm going to kill him... This was not the plan... Such an idiot..."

"What do we do?" Eloria whispered.

"Play along," he said. "Remember our time at the ocean? It'll be a celebration of Eloria and the prince for a while again."

The people parted as Killian and Eloria made their way to Tavin. He stood on another carved stairway. As Tavin reached down towards Eloria, Killian's hands slid away. Tavin took her hand in his and held them up for the crowd to see. They exploded in celebration once again.

"'From a world of reflection, Eloria returns,'" he recited. "'When Evil rises and the world be burned.'"

The crowd joined in.

"'She shall love Seraphim wings or doom will she bring. A death to come that will change all things.'"

Eloria looked to Tavin and saw tears in his eyes. But he did not falter. He did not stop.

"'On winds they fly to the desolate place. Where a Queen Transformed finds Evil's true face. On black wings they die and fall. When he follows her to Qwells Vraugh. Where feathers and scales reign down. Love of another face will be found.'"

Killian shivered.

"'The people will be with fear when the time of Eloria draws near.'"

The assembly grew silent. Solemn.

"We have been with fear," Tavin shouted loudly. "We have watched as Evil has risen and burned our homes, our villages, and our land. A death has come..."

Tavin's voice broke. His lip quivered as he looked at the people before him.

"A death has come. It has wrought a weight and a change on our hearts that I cannot put into words. We have flown on the wind to escape the evil that plagues our borders. I've seen our people overcome by fear. But I tell you this..."

Tavin glanced to Killian. Without words, they both knew the anger the other felt over Sorrell's murder. Killian knew that Tavin wanted justice. They both knew Eloria was the way to get it.

"From a world of reflection," Tavin roared, "Eloria has returned!"

The great crater of people erupted. Their cheers shook the trees around them.

"We will find the place called Qwells Vraugh! We will destroy the Deformed! We will defeat the Evil Ones once and for all!"

Killian's hand appeared on Eloria's back once more. He pulled her away from Tavin and up the stairs. Tavin continued speaking as they climbed higher above the crowd. The steps wound back and forth beside the great waterfall until they were walking on stairs carved into tree trunks. Balconies for shops and homes began passing them by, but Killian passed each them as they continued to climb.

When they were stories high over the gathered throng, Tavin reappeared behind them. At the same time, Killian veered to a side path and stopped at one of the many balconies. Before them was a large double door that had been carved into the tree.

"Nice speech," Killian grunted.

"This is the home of the Head Mage," Tavin said to Eloria, ignoring the comment. "He will be a part of your training while we are here."

"I thought we were going to seek out the great dragon? How long will we be staying in the forest?"

The door before them opened. A couple old enough to be Eloria's parents stepped forward to greet them. The man looked basic from what Eloria could tell. He wore simple, green tunics and looked as if his years were beginning to show. The woman, however, was younger than her husband, with a long dress of shimmering silk. She had long, strawberry-blonde hair much like the queen's. Her smile was gentle yet she had a dangerous spark in her eye.

"Welcome, Prince Emrys and Eloria," she said. "What a rousing speech you've given us."

Tavin bowed politely, "We seek your hospitality. Eloria has come to train with the Head Mage and learn to bind magic."

The man stepped forward, "It would be an honor to take part in Eloria's training. You must be weary from your journey. We have plenty of houses for you to stay in. Please, my wife will show you to your beds. You must excuse me but, with your arrival, we need to bind more magical defenses to our borders. Protocol and such. I'm sure you understand."

"Thank you for your protection," Tavin smiled. "It is not often my family arrives without prior notice. I cannot express how grateful I am for your hospitality."

"Never would we turn you aside," his wife smiled. "This way."

She led them further up the stairs towards the tree tops. The steps were now carved into the trunk of the tree in lieu of its roots. They approached a grandly carved archway that led to a private balcony.

"Our royal houses," the woman smiled. "Eloria will stay here."

"We'll be staying together," Killian said.

"Young Guard, that is not permitted here," she replied. "The boarders are quite safe as you have seen. No one may enter without proclaiming their true name, and not all names are allowed entry."

"While we trust your security," Tavin said, "We have been on the road together for months now. It would be strange leaving one another alone after all this time."

"Eloria will be quite safe, I assure you."

"We will be staying together," Killian argued.

The woman thought patiently to herself.

"Very well. You may sleep on the balcony if you wish. Otherwise, your house is four branches higher on the right. Enjoy your stay, dear ones."

The woman walked confidently down the steps and back to her own home.

285

"Really, Killian, it's not a problem. I'll be fine. It's not like I'm afraid of the dark."

He raised a quizzical brow, "Why would the dark scare you?"

"Oh. Is that not a thing… here? Never mind. I'll be fine. Really. See you in the morning then?"

Eloria made her way into the designated tree house. Despite the excitement, she had no energy to explore the rooms. There were multiple doors and stories within the tree but she fell onto the oversized cushions on the main floor. As she unstrapped her weapons, the loneliness surrounded her. Tavin was right, it had been a long time since she had been alone. Even at the ocean she knew Sorrell was near enough to hear her thoughts.

Tears spilled down her cheeks as she remembered her reflection-self. She felt the dark hole in her chest grow. Her thoughts turned to her old therapy sessions. Dr. Donna had once asked her to fill in a heart with color. It seemed like a lifetime ago. Right now, that heart would be covered in black. She struggled to breathe as her mind replayed Sorrell's death. A cold wind blew through the house.

"Eloria," Killian said from outside the door.

Warmth ran through her and the darkness faded a little.

"Yes?"

"Are you alright?" his voice was muffled through the wood.

"I'm fine," she choked. "Thanks for checking in."

It was silent as she listened for him. The darkness slowly began to creep back into her mind. The deformed's images flashed in front of her. She remembered Sorrell laying on the ground covered in blood and snow. The strange black poison that spilled from her body.

Eloria sobbed uncontrollably. She didn't feel the anger that Tavin had. She only wanted her friend back. She wanted the suffering and the fear to end. She fell asleep amid her sobs only to dream of the deformed attacking the forest. She dreamt of angels and dragons falling out of the sky into puddles of black poison. The sky was black with lightening that struck from no where. Distorted faces rose from the ground and came for her.

She woke with a start. From fear and the cold, she shivered uncontrollably. She went to the balcony and breathed in deeply to clear her mind. Snow was falling through the trees. It twinkled in the torchlight from the balconies, as if it was fairy dust.

"It can be beautiful, despite the sorrow."

Eloria turned to see Killian sitting next to the door. He had changed his clothes to a simple tunic and his sword lay by his side.

"They said we were safe inside the forest. You didn't have to stay."

"It's my duty to protect you. Even if the enemy doesn't take a physical form."

"You heard me dreaming?" Eloria sat next to him.

"Sorrell's absence is still with all of us. As is the fear that the Deformed put in your head. One slip and everything they show you comes flooding back."

"Does that happen to you? I thought you could defeat them with your mind."

Killian inhaled deeply. "Winning a battle doesn't mean you're not harmed in the process. The Deformed that I have faced still revealed things to me that I never wished to imagine. The battles within the mind are often the hardest."

Eloria's tears welled up again, "It scares me."

"I know." Killian brushed her hair away from her face.

"I wish she was here. She was supposed to show me what to do."

The snow fell steadier. A breeze blew through the trees. Eloria leaned into Killian and felt his warmth run over her body. The fear subsided but the sadness remained.

"Why does it have to be so cold?"

Killian wrapped his arm around her. "It's a reflection of our loss. How cold our hearts feel without them."

"I'm sorry you're still mourning her," Eloria said.

"It's supposed to be raining right now, but rain would flood the valley and wash away peoples' homes. I am turning the rain into snow."

"How do you do that?"

"I'm saddened that Sorrell is not here, but I no longer feel such sorrow. Seeing Tavin be in so much pain is hard for me. But knowing that you are afraid and alone... I mourn for you."

"Oh," Eloria was lost for words. "Please don't put yourself through that because of me."

Killian smiled, "I'm keeping a village from flooding, remember?"

He began humming a haunting melody. Eloria recognized it as a lullaby from one of Sorrell's memories. She rested her head against him. They watched the snow shimmer by. She imagined each snow flake being one of Killian's tears. His honeyed voice played in and out of the notes and lulled her towards sleep.

"I wish you had your wings," she mumbled as her eyes closed.

"Sleep," he whispered.

Eloria drifted away feeling his hand gently stroke hers as his song continued.

CHAPTER 23

"What powers do you have thus far?" the Head Mage asked.

"Well...," Eloria glanced at the small audience around the room. It was mid morning and she had already been through a series of physical trials to assess her combat skills. They were now in a large tree deliberating where to begin her Mage training.

"They're going to determine how far along in the Transformation you are," Killian had told her.

"Doesn't that mean figuring out how close you and I are?"

"Don't worry about it. We've got this taken care of," Tavin had shrugged.

Now the room full of Mages were waiting rather impatiently for her response. Eloria sat on her hands.

"She connected her mind with that of her reflection-self. She has summoned the wind, but only under extreme duress," Tavin answered by her side.

"The Deformed attacked us," Eloria clarified.

"Is that all? No signs of having the Sight? Control of the weather? Flight?"

Tavin tapped his foot impatiently, "We've had no circumstances to know if she has the Sight. Flight is determined by her control of the wind and no, she has not progressed that far."

"She has influence over the weather," Killian spoke from a back corner of the room. "It's subconscious, but it bends to her."

Eloria looked at him with surprise.

"Ah, yes, thank you," Tavin coughed. "My Guard, Killian, has been in my confidence since we were young. He's been traveling with us all the while."

"His highness mentioned it a few weeks ago, I apologize for interrupting," Killian bowed to the Mages.

"Very well," the Mage Master scribbled something on his parchment. "Would you speak her name for us?"

Killian tensed. He and Tavin had discussed Eloria's Transformation in depth. They knew the king and queen would want them to continue to keep Killian's identity a secret, so Tavin had to successfully portray the Seraphim prince. This was a test they had not thought of. Although Killian was already in the shadows, he ducked his head and held his hand over his mouth.

"Yes, very good," Tavin turned confidently to Eloria.

She looked up at him from her chair.

"Eloria," Tavin proclaimed.

"Eloria," Killian whispered.

She shivered as her body tingled with excitement. It took all her strength not to glance in Killian's direction.

Tavin smiled, "Anything else?"

As the Mages spoke, Killian smirked in victory. A shimmer of silver drew his attention from across the room. The Mage's wife was watching him. She nodded to him discretely before making her way out of the room.

"We will reconvene tomorrow with a confirmed training schedule. Please take the day to yourselves, my prince, to enjoy the forest and perhaps greet the people. They've been eager to see you both again. Needless to say, the site of our Seraphim prince and his Eloria together is certainly a boost in confidence. Information on the golden dragon is still being gathered for you. We'll let you know when it's ready."

Killian quickly left the room. Across a small rope bridge stood the Mage Master's wife. Her long hair blew gently in the breeze as she turned to acknowledge Killian.

"That was a discreet trick," she smiled.

"You saw?"

"Don't worry. No one else in that room knows."

"We would prefer it stay that way, Tesra."

The woman, Tesra, laughed, "I'm good at keeping secrets, young Guard. Your prince and I have that in common."

"Your discretion is welcomed."

The other Mages began exiting the tree house. They spoke excitedly of Eloria and the prince as they passed by Killian. The woman watched him cautiously as they passed.

"Something is not right about Eloria's power."

"She's fine," Killian snorted.

"This is not the first Transformation that I've witnessed. There's a gap, or perhaps a break. Something between you that is incomplete."

Anger rose in his chest, "What would you know of it? She is Eloir... she's different. Nothing is going to happen the way it's supposed to. This will not be a normal Transformation."

The woman shook her head, "No. A prophecy does not change what the Creator Himself put into place. There is something missing."

Killian turned away.

"Your friends come," Tesra smiled. "Bring the girl to me. I will seek out the problem."

"It is not your place," Killian spat.

"That is my exact place, young Guard. Since the day of your birth that has been my place. Bring the girl to me in the evening. I'll make sure we are alone. Your friends come for you now."

She disappeared amid the crowd of Mages. He didn't wait long until Eloria and Tavin were at his side.

"That was close," Tavin whispered.

"Wasn't sure if it would work," Killian replied.

"I feel like a dissected frog," Eloria complained.

"Frogs have nothing to do with this. At least they didn't give us the Transformation talk," Tavin winked.

Eloria's cheeks burned a bright red.

"Cut it out! She's been through enough today."

"I need to go anyway. I have to write the queen now that Sorrell... Well, one of us has to let them know what we're up to. Give me a little while then we'll make our public appearance."

Tavin skipped off to the other side of the valley. Eloria stretched her limbs, happy to be out of the spotlight.

"Feel like exploring?" Killian asked.

"Can we do that? Aren't I supposed to only train or travel in my spare time?"

Killian shrugged, "I'm your instructor, remember? Anything we do counts as training if I say so. Besides, spending time amongst the people is a cherished Seraphim tradition. It's about time you did that."

"Alright, I'll go. But please don't make me try any new foods."

"Even better," Killian pulled a loaf of bread from behind his back.

"Are you kidding me?" Eloria squealed with excitement. "Wait, where were you hiding that?"

"Come with me, Prophesied. They have grapes here too."

Eloria rushed after him. The valley below had large shops and taverns. They spent the rest of the morning visiting the different emporiums and the sights of the forest valley. Beautifully made dresses hung on branches for the women of the village to buy. Elaborate leather belts and vests lay on tables to entice the men. Many blacksmiths worked in their shops to create weapons and tools. At one particular smithy, Eloria was enamored with the craftsmanship of the knives they had forged.

"They are forged with binding magic," Killian explained. "They use the magic to make the weapons lighter, faster, sharper, and anything else you can think of. As long as the Builders know how to use the magic correctly, they can bend and bind it to the desired object in their forge."

"It's beautiful," Eloria awed. "Sorrell would have loved these. I wish I could buy one."

"Buy?"

"Don't tell me you simply take what you want," she smirked. "That would be snobbish of you."

Killian ran his finger over the silver blades, "We trade what we can, but everything here is for you to take. There is no price for taking what you need. If you have a good to leave in its place, then the Community is better for it."

Eloria watched the market around her and saw exactly that. The members of Community took what they liked. If they had something to leave in its place, they did. If not, the stall keepers had no quarrel when the person walked away with their wares.

"There's one more thing I want to show you," Killian smiled. He led her through the valley and towards a small hut beside the lake.

"Is anyone looking?"

"I don't think so," Eloria glanced around.

He pulled her behind the hut and thrust his body against the wood that formed the walls of the valley. A small cavern opened before them.

"What is that?"

"Tavin and I found this place when we were younger. The tree is bound with magic in this exact spot. Few people know it exists. This path leads up the tree and behind the falls."

He led her through the tunnel. When the magical door closed behind them they were pitched into darkness. Eloria followed the sound of Killian's footsteps as they wound their way up the tree.

Her hand caressed the smooth, wood wall until their path became narrow.

"Sorry," Eloria mumbled as she bumped into Killian.

"There's a knot in the wood that opens the next door. Help me find it."

Eloria ran her hands along the tree's walls. With no light to see, she hoped she wasn't working her way backwards. The smooth grain was soft against her fingers. She followed as it curved to the left.

Killian's body suddenly pressed against hers. She felt his breath on her neck. Eloria tried to move aside, but she seemed boxed in. When she opened her mouth to explain, she felt a finger touch her lips.

"Wait," he whispered.

Eloria waited, though her heart pounded in her chest. She hoped her couldn't hear it, or feel it for that matter. An orb of light floated through the wall beside her. It bobbed in a whimsical manner before coming to a stop above Killian's palm. The little ball of magic only lit a small space around them, but it was enough to see how close Killian's face was to hers.

"It's behind you."

"What?"

"The knot," he explained.

Eloria noticed an uncomfortable lump pressing into her back. She tried to turn to face it, but couldn't move. Killian released the ball of light from his palm.

"Stop moving."

One of his hands slid around her waist then pulled her closer against him. The other reached out and twisted the knot in a clockwise fashion. The door slid open. Light spilled over them as Killian released her.

"After you," he gestured.

Eloria followed a tight corner that twisted up and into a wide cavern. A gaping hole beheld the waterfall from behind. Reflections of the water bounced off the mossy walls around them.

"This is one of my favorite spots in all of Loraillvon."

"It's beautiful."

Every few seconds Eloria could see the village below through the falling water.

"What do you do up here?"

"Train mostly. It was the only time I really got to be alone. Other than when I flew, of course."

"Of course," Eloria smiled.

"Once we went into Community I didn't get to do it much. I cherished coming to the Forest so that I could be here. My parents would search for hours. Tavin always covered for me."

"Nothing has changed then," Eloria grinned.

"Tavin has," Killian kicked a chuck of moss into the falls. "He covers his pain with jokes, but he's not the same without Sorrell. The light is gone from his eyes."

"I didn't know that. Why is he trying to put on a good face?"

"He doesn't want you to worry."

They were silent as the sound of water echoed through the cavern.

"It's captivating, isn't it?" Eloria said. "Like staring into a fire. You'd think it would be boring but for some reason you don't want to look away."

"I have something for you."

Killian pulled a small silver ring from his pocket. It gleamed in his hand as he extended it towards her. As Eloria took it from him, she saw that the band was made up of silver leaves. Gold lettering was inscribed inside the leaves in a language that looked unfamiliar.

"It's wonderful," she whispered. "Did you get it from one of the smithies?"

"No," Killian smiled. "It's from Kien Illae. Actually, it's from heaven. I brought it with me from Kien Illae though."

Eloria's mouth fell open.

"It's not that big of a deal."

"You handed me an object from heaven. That's a big deal."

"We all have one," Killian shrugged.

"You're the only person I've seen wear jewelry in this world."

"All of the royal family has their own," he said. "They are forged by an angel in the white flames. It's designed with an irreplaceable magic."

"I can't accept this," but Eloria couldn't seem to offer the ring back to him.

"The ring will help you tap into the magic inside of you," Killian explained. "Think of it as a training tool. There is magic within the silver that tampers with the eyes of anyone who may gaze upon it. They will look right past it unless it is specifically pointed out to them."

"But I saw yours the first night we met."

"You are different."

She slipped the ring onto her finger. It was a perfect fit.

"There is a legend that says the angels find us by our rings," Killian smiled to her. "I know you aren't Seraphim but I wanted you to have it."

"What does the inscription say?"

"Each ring is different. When you're ready, you'll be able to read it."

"That's quite ominous."

"Would you care to practice?" Killian asked with a grin.

"Magic? Again?"

"How about control of over the wind? You did it on the landing. Want to learn more?"

"I suppose so."

"Having great power does not mean you must use it in large quantities," Killian said. "We use our control of the winds and the weather in both battle and everyday life. To do this properly, you must be able to control it in the smallest of ways. Let me show you."

Killian pointed to a small flower growing in the moss near the cavern's edge. With a flick of his fingers, the petals blew off the flower.

"You did that? Without touching anything but the flower?"

He nodded, "When you have full control of your power you can use it in everything you do. Have you ever noticed how silently I walk through the forest or snow? That is because I lift myself off the ground. I can hover slightly above the earth without effecting the leaves and twigs below me. It also gives me the advantage of not leaving any tracks."

Eloria watched as he demonstrated. His feet hovered ever so slightly above the earth but was hardly noticeable unless one was looking for it. He then explained how to access the magic more quickly by using the ring's power. When it was her turn to try, she could feel the band hum against her finger. She chose an object in the cave and motioned towards it. A strong gust of wind blew through the waterfall, splashing Killian.

"Oh!" Eloria exclaimed. "I'm so sorry!"

He shook out his hair, "Try again."

They went on for hours until Eloria could direct the wind to follow her most detailed command.

"Well done!" Killian applauded as a wisp of moss floated gently to the ground. "Learning to use powerful amounts of wind as a weapon will be even more entertaining."

Eloria smiled with pride, "This was a perfect place to practice. No distractions."

"Want to hear my favorite thing about this little hideout?"

Eloria nodded.

"Stand against that wall," he pointed. Killian stood on the opposite wall from her and began to sing.

> "We grow, we train, we choose our House
> My mind will be ever keen
> On finding the one they told to me
> The one to whom I cling."

He took a step to the side. The sound changed and his voice echoed differently off the walls. Sweetly as ever, he continued.

> "Through the dance I look and search
> Smiling faces that do sing
> But none so fair as the one I dare
> To find and give my ring."

He took another step and his voice multiplied ten times over, as if a choir sang with him.

> "There I found you dancing near
> I'll hold my breath and wait
> for the one they call Eloria
> She will be my fate."

She shivered at her name and suddenly remembered the song. It was the same one Killian had sung when he first snuck her away from camp. The night they had met the dragon.

"My name wasn't in the song before," she whispered.

> "Oh woman so fair and kind
> I made my pact with you
> The one to which I tie my fate
> The one to which I flew."

Another step closer.

> "Through battle I will find you
> In the darkest of midnights
> For you, Eloria, a battle cry
> It is for you that I do fight."

He took another step and stood over her, pressing her back against the stone wall. His green eyes bore into hers.

> "For you I will protect or die
> It is for you that I will cry
> Your heart is my awakening
> For you are my prophesied."

He leaned in closer, cradling her chin in his hand. Eloria's heart raced. The familiar, warm tingle made her tremble. Lifting her chin up to him, Killian bent towards her. His lips brushed over her cheek, moving towards her mouth.

"Killian!" Tavin's voice echoed through the cavern.

Eloria's breathe caught in her throat. Killian froze.

"Killian? Eloria? Are you up here?"

Eloria looked into Killian's eyes. He tucked her hair behind her ear and pulled away. Tavin rounded the corner.

"I figured you would come here," Tavin sighed. "Killian could never stand all the attention. Always going to your hiding spot."

"Sorry for not meeting you," Killian said casually. "I forgot how long it took to get up here."

"Yeah it's been a few years. Either that passage got more narrow or I've grown since last time." Tavin looked about the cavern. "Either way, no more hiding from our responsibilities. It's time to let the people have a look at us. Ready, Eloria?"

CHAPTER 24

Eloria's cheeks ached from smiling. They had been walking for hours through the interchanging staircases to visit each home in the valley. Tavin seemed to be unbothered by the exchange of pleasantries with each person, but Eloria grew weary. Killian had disappeared the moment they left the caverns.

"Final house," Tavin said. "Ready?"

Eloria shook out her arms and hopped in place, "Let's do it."

The older couple that resided in the small tree nook offered them baked goods. They expressed their excitement at meeting Eloria and told her stories of how they dreamed of her arriving. After a short time, Tavin kindly excused them from the home.

"I'll walk you back to your guest house," he offered.

"Thanks. I don't know how I will make it up those stairs. My legs are jello and my cheeks feel like bricks. How do you do it?"

"Years of practice," Tavin laughed. "You better get used to it, future Queen Transformed. This will be your life soon enough."

Eloria stopped in her tracks, "Future queen?"

"Don't tell me you haven't thought about it."

"I really haven't," Eloria gawked.

"How are you doing with that?" Tavin asked. "We haven't had a chance to talk, but you're my family now. Does the prophecy still worry you?"

Eloria wasn't sure what to say. "It's kind of embarrassing to talk about. Killian and I are… friends, I guess. He's not mean to me anymore. It was confusing after Sorrell… We haven't talked about how we feel about…you know?"

Tavin nodded, "How do you feel?"

Eloria couldn't hold back a sheepish grin.

"I see," he laughed.

"Let's say I'm not worried about destroying the world anymore."

"If you ever need someone to talk to about it, I'm here."

"You are Killian's brother. I can't have girl talk with you."

"You are my family now too."

They arrived at Eloria's guest house. Sitting by her door was a plate of bread, cheese, and grapes.

"Looks like someone was waiting for you," Tavin said. "Get some sleep. Training will start early in the morning."

And it did.

For the next three days Eloria sat through lectures to learn the basic principles of binding magic to objects. They started early in the morning and went until sundown. She hardly saw Killian and Tavin but there were always signs that Killian had been keeping watch each night. Whether it was a plate of food or new supplies at her door, he made it known that he was nearby.

On her fourth day of training, Killian was at her door by first light.

"How would you like to leave the books behind for a day?" he asked.

"I can't do that. My training is the reason we're here."

"We also came to gather information on the gold dragon. However, your combat training is lacking. It's been quite a while since you've sparred. I can't have all my hard work slipping away. It took me too long to get you to this point."

Eloria rolled her eyes, "Your hard work? I'm pretty sure I'm the one with scars and bruises to prove otherwise."

Killian took her hand, "Come with me. One day with the sword. That's all I ask."

A warm sensation ran the length of her arm. It never lessened or disappeared.

"One day. But we blame you if I get into any trouble."

"When will you learn that these people listen to *you*?" he asked with a smirk.

Killian led them to the valley floor to a large grassy knoll. There were tables of weapons available and dozens of people training across the grounds. They started with hand to hand combat then slowly progressed through the different weapons. Killian was as fast as ever, but Eloria was able to hold her own. The pair were covered in sweat and grass when they finally broke at mid-day.

"You haven't lost a step," Killian said.

"I think you've gotten faster," Eloria huffed.

Killian tossed her a flask of water, "Probably."

"Who are they?" Eloria nodded to a small band of men headed towards them.

Killian squinted in the sun to get a better look. "Admirers of yours?"

"Very funny." She could already feel her cheeks start to ache.

A large man stepped out from the throng. He sized Killian up in a quick glanced and laughed.

"Can we help you, sir?" Killian's voice was pleasant.

"You are the Guard that travels with our prince?"

Killian glanced at the men behind him, "I am."

"What gives you the right to train the great Eloria?"

Killian smiled, "Our Queen Gloribel gives me the right. She tasked me with her training the night she arrived in the Ceremonial Woods."

The men snickered to one another. They were built heavily, like Tavin, but of a shorter nature. Their singed arms and leather tunics indicated that they were Builders.

"My name is Tyre," their leader said. "I was there the night Eloria arrived. It was my Choosing as well."

Killian bowed his head, "Congratulations on making the Choice, young Tyre. It was a great night for us all. My own Choosing was years ago. Not quite as memorable as yours, I'm sure."

"What is going on?" Eloria whispered.

"Builders and their egos," Killian mumbled.

"We saw you sparring and thought we may join you," Tyre stretched out his hands. "Perhaps our honored Eloria could keep tally?"

"Me against all of you?" Killian asked.

"It would only be fair. After all, you are Guard to Prince Emrys."

"Eloria, would you mind? All you have to do is sit back and decide who wins."

"Seriously? You are going to fight them?"

Killian shrugged, "It's only sparring."

"But they are huge! And there are...," she tried counting the men, "Almost seven of them."

Killian gently pushed her towards a large boulder, away from the sparring ground.

"I'm fast, remember?"

Eloria stood against the rock and watched as the men took their stance. Killian looked small compared to the large Builders around him. Without a word, the battle began. Killian purposefully moved slower than he normally would. He wove in and out of the men but never advanced on them. He held a defensive position as they continuously took turns going at him.

Tavin approached Eloria with a shake of his head.

"This happens every time we come to the forest," he sighed. "Builders and their egos."

Eloria snickered.

"They see a scrawny Guard and have to make a scene."

"Killian isn't scrawny."

"Have you seen *me*?" Tavin flexed a large bicep at her. "That boy is a twig compared to these oak trunks."

Eloria's apprehension took the better of her, "He won't get hurt, will he?"

"Trust me when I say that the hardest part of this fight will be for Killian to deny his Seraphim instincts. Don't worry, he's had plenty of practice with that."

They watched as the large Builders advanced on Killian as a team. He continued to move at a slow pace, until one of the swords caught him under the eye. Killian quickly drew away from the throng. Tyre put up a hand as he allowed Killian to regain his composure. He carefully reached up to the cut and looked at the blood on his fingers. One of the Builders laughed aloud.

A low rumble echoed through the sky.

"Uh oh," Tavin said.

Killian tossed his sword to the ground.

"What is he doing?"

Killian charged his opponents, dodging blades and fists. He disarmed one man and sent him stumbling backwards. The second man he laid to the ground with a powerful fist to the chest.

Tavin stepped toward the brawl, "Killian! That's enough."

But Killian didn't stop. He moved faster between the rest of them, knocking swords out of hands and sending men sprawling across the green. One man's axe was lodged hilt deep into the ground.

"Killian, that is enough!" Tavin roared.

The sky darkened and rumbled again. The men on the ground looked up in fear.

But Killian continued. He took out the remaining men until Tyre was the only one left. In one swift motion, he put the bulking, mass of a man on the ground. He held a sword to the Builder's throat.

"Killian!" Eloria cried.

His body shivered. Green eyes immediately found hers.

"You're done," Tavin commanded, now at his side.

Killian looked at the trembling man beneath the sword. Tyre's eyes were wide as he waited for the blade to make its final move. Killian stepped away and tossed the weapon to the ground.

Tavin walked towards him, "We need to..."

"No. We don't."

Killian stormed from the sparring grounds and disappeared towards the village.

"Healing potion, for your troubles," Tavin tossed a small bottle to one of the men. "You should be honored that he was so patient sparring with you. He became a Master in every aspect of the Guard a year after his Choice. The only reason that man is not Head Master of his House is because he swore his life to protecting Loraillvon and the Seraphim. Do not challenge him again."

Thunder shook the ground beneath them.

"Yes, Prince Emrys," they mumbled in unison.

Eloria rushed to join Tavin. They hurried back to the village, looking for Killian.

"The thunder..."

"I know," Tavin's eyes scanned the crowd around them.

"We were only training. He acted like sparring with them would be fun."

"Do you know your way back to your lessons?"

"Yes, but..."

"Please go, Eloria. I need to speak with Killian alone."

Tavin worked his way through the crowd, leaving Eloria alone in the village market.

"Hello, dear Eloria," a voice said from behind her.

She spun around to see the Head Mage's wife. Her long, silver dress shimmered from the light around them.

"My name is Tesra. We haven't met, but I was hoping to get an opportunity to speak with you. There are aspects of your training that are vital we discuss."

"I was actually going to look for Killian and the prince."

"Very good. We'll need the Seraphim present for this as well."

"Oh, alright then. He headed that direction," Eloria pointed.

The woman's eyes twinkled, "You and I both know that Tavin is not the one we seek. Where is Emrys Killian?"

***

Tavin hurried through the village and into the small forest inside the crater. Knowing his comrade, the trees were his first refuge if he couldn't be in the sky.

"There you are! I've been all over this valley looking for you," Tavin huffed.

"I'm in no mood to be chided," Killian sat lazily against a tree stump.

"I can tell. You completely lost control back there."

"I did not."

Tavin balled his fists, "Eloria wasn't angry, and we all know I don't have that kind of power."

"I messed up," Killian shrugged. "They all thought it was you anyway."

"You got upset and that is where you messed up. You have *never* lost control like that. Ever. In all of the time that we've been together. It was only fortunate circumstances that led me to find you at the sparring grounds. What would have happened if I wasn't there? You couldn't stop either. You were about to take that Builder's head off."

"They needed a lesson in humility."

"When did that become your job to give?"

They were both silent. The valley floor seemed shrouded in nightfall from the clouds above.

"I apologize for coming on so strongly," Tavin sighed. "Believe me, I tried showing off for Sorrell a time or two. I really got into trouble doing it. I was jealous a few times, too."

Killian looked at him with disbelief, "You think I was showing off for *her*?"

"Every man does it," Tavin shrugged. "It's hard to get a blade to the face when your girl is watching."

"She is *not* my girl," Killian fumed. "We're not children, Tavin. I've been following the plan ever since Kailani. The plan that *you* put into motion before the enemy advanced. All this time I've been playing along. Jealous? Showing off? Do you truly think I'm daft enough to have feelings for that girl?"

"You mean… all this time?" Tavin was taken aback. "I thought your feelings had changed."

"I've been following the plan. Why would you think anything had changed?"

A twig snapped. Both men turned to see Eloria and Tesra watching them. Killian glared at the tall woman that had interrupted.

"Eloria!" Tavin stood in surprise, "I'm so sorry. We didn't think…"

"What plan?" Eloria asked.

There were few times in her life when Eloria had felt truly brave. Once, when she had stood up to her mother, once when she had fought the Deformed, and now. Though the thought of fleeing crossed her mind, more than that she felt brave.

"What plan, Tavin?"

"Eloria, we didn't…"

"What are you doing here?" Killian interrupted.

"I knew something was amiss with her Transformation. It was unbalanced. Incomplete in some way," Tesra replied. "Now I know why."

"She knows who you are Killian," Eloria said.

"Of course she does," Killian continued to glare, "She's my godmother."

"Eloria, this is Tesra," Tavin explained. "She was sworn protector and decoy for Queen Gloribel when they were young."

"The girl asked you a question," Tesra turned her eyes to Killian. "What plan?"

He folded his arms.

Tavin shifted uncomfortably. "At the ocean, it was clear that your training wasn't improving. We received word that the Evil Ones were turning their focus on us, following the rumors about the new Eloria arriving to our world. We needed more time to train until you could defend yourself. Killian and I had a plan, a way to help the enemy believe that things were turning in their favor. We believed that if the enemy saw us losing the war, they would slow their advances."

"What was the plan?" Eloria repeated.

Killian turned to her, "It was clear the people weren't seeing a connection between you and Tavin. The Kailani ball was a last effort to put on a good face. Don't you see? Everyone believes that Tavin is the Seraphim prince. 'She shall love Seraphim wings or doom she will bring,'" he quoted. "To let the enemy think they had the advantage, I stepped in."

"I don't understand, Killian. What did you and Tavin do?"

"The ballroom at Kailani, taking you to see the dragon, all those times we snuck away from Sorrell and Tavin at night. That was all a ruse. We knew the enemy was watching somehow. We had to make it look like your were falling for someone else, someone who wasn't a Seraphim."

Eloria thought back to the moments they had spent in the forest. The way he took her hand. How he whispered her name. She remembered how closely he held her while they danced under the glass dome of Kailani. The delightful sensation that spread through her entire body at his touch.

"The enemy would see you falling in love with a non-Seraphim when all the while you were falling for the true Seraphim. They would stop their advances, thinking they had the upper hand while we secretly grew your power."

Eloria's mind raced, "Do you…"

"Do I love you?"

Her eyes grew wide with apprehension.

"No." Killian looked at her without guilt or shame. His face was hard.

"Every moment we had together was a game to you? Another form of training?"

Lightening flashed through the sky. Killian glanced at the light then back to Eloria. Thunder shook the tree canopy above them. A larger *boom* shook the ground beneath them.

"You said you would do anything to stay here; to save this world," Killian shrugged. "Unrequited love isn't the worst thing to happen."

"Says the unrequited!"

"I'm trying to be honest with you!" he yelled in return. "The prophecy did not lie. Sorrell's death has changed everything. We didn't want to deceive you, but I have to save my people. You are the key to that. By spending that time with you, we deceived our enemies and gave you powers that otherwise would have waited until you learned the truth about me."

"Killian, what have you done?" Tesra whispered.

"I'm not going to let a prophecy dictate my life," he defended. "I will not fall in love because of old words from a dragon."

"We brought you to the forest so that you and Killian would have more time with one another," Tavin confessed. "The real training was for you to grow in your power. For the Transformation to continue before we sought out the dragon."

"At what point would your grand plan be successful?" Eloria fumed. "Once we shared a magical kiss and I sprouted wings?"

Killian looked away.

"You're kidding me!" she exclaimed.

"Powers will slowly be available to you through physical touch and use of your name," Tesra explained. "A kiss from a Seraphim gives you access to all of their power. Everything except the wings. Those are given by an angel at the uniting ceremony."

"Sorrell told me a little about your world," Tavin interjected. "In Loraillvon, we don't take physical touch as lightly as your people. If you truly wish to be with someone, that is how you show them. The night I proposed to Sorrell we shared our first kiss. The day that Forfax and Gloribel first shared a kiss, he gained use of his full Seraphim powers. He had full control for a year before they married. At their ceremony, the angel in attendance gave the couple the Creator's blessing. He touched Forfax's back and thus he had wings. According to the Seraphim family traditions, that is how the Transformation is completed."

"Your plan was to bring her here, and give her full use of the Seraphim powers?" Tesra was bewildered.

Tavin glanced sidelong at his comrade, "The Mages would have helped teach her to use them properly."

Lightening clapped above as they stood in silence. Killian closed his eyes and leaned against a tree. Eloria watched him in disbelief.

"Will you please calm down?" he sighed. "A storm is only going to draw attention to us."

"I'm not doing anything!" Eloria defended.

"Do I look angry to you?" he asked. "You are radiating fury. Control yourself. You're clearly in pain."

"Don't worry. I remember my lessons," her lip quivered. "Pain is temporary, right?"

"Eloria…"

"Don't you dare say my name!" she spat.

"We can't stop the Transformation simply because we feel differently for each other. You fell in love with me as the prophecy foretold."

"You tricked me! I'm not about to be anywhere near you now that I know what you've done. Unrequited, remember? If you so much as look at me as if I'm a weapon for you to wield, trust me when I say that I will take every last bit of your training and teach *you* something new about pain. I will show you how exceedingly long and unforgiving it can be."

"He will no longer change you," Tesra stated. "Killian?"

"Doom our people because of her embarrassment?" he scoffed.

Tesra's lips pressed into a thin line. Her eyes grew wide as she looked to the young Seraphim prince.

"Fine," Killian said. "I will not touch you. Nor will I use your name without your permission."

The air shook around them as thunder rumbled once more.

"The day grows late," Tesra held her chin high. "Come with me, Eloria. It would not be wise for me to leave you with these…boys."

Tesra wrapped her arm around the young woman as she led Eloria away.

"Be thankful if I don't write to your mother about this," Tesra shouted back to Killian.

He rolled his eyes as the women disappeared. Tavin dug his boot into the ground, drawing aimless patterns.

"What now?" Killian was exasperated.

"So you don't love her?"

"You know that I don't."

311

"I thought things had changed."

They stood silently as flashes of light ran across the sky.

"She's quite angry," Tavin noted. "Unless that's you?"

"It's not," Killian glanced at the clouds.

"Well, our first plan has failed. Is it time for the second one?"

"That was the second one," Killian sighed. "There is no third. Let's get back to the house. I'll need to temper this storm before she lets it get out of control."

They trudged back to the valley and made their ascent to the guest house. Killian lingered on the balcony as Tavin headed inside.

"Are you coming?" he asked.

"It's better I do it from here," Killian replied. "The clouds have grown darker."

"Have you ever met a Seraphim with a broken heart?" Tavin asked.

"No, why?"

"Well if she's anything like Sorrell, you're going to have a late night trying to calm that storm."

Tavin disappeared into the house. Killian swung his legs over the railing of the balcony and watched the people below. They looked as small as bugs from the height of his tree. He felt the familiar urge to jump. His back itched to let his wings be free.

Instead, he closed his eyes and focused on the storms above. Breathing slowly, he calmed his mind. He imagined warm days as a child. The simplicity of spending his time exploring his palace. Learning to spar with Tavin.

Thunder rumbled above him.

"Come on, Eloria," he mumbled to himself. "You're not that strong."

He focused harder, picturing the angel messenger that was sent to his family. He remembered the joy and warmth at being in its presence.

Light flashed across the sky and lit the valley below through the canopy of the trees. Killian jumped at the flash.

"That's not possible," he whispered.

He looked to Eloria's balcony a short distance below him. To his surprise, she stood outside the house garbed in her traveling clothes. Her weapons were strapped about her person. A pack was belted to her back and there was a satchel across her chest.

"Tavin," Killian called. "Come look at this."

"I thought you were going to fix the storm," Tavin said as he joined him. "What are we looking at?"

"There," Killian nodded. "What do you think she's doing?"

Tavin peered in Eloria's direction. "How long has she been standing there?"

"I don't know."

The two men watched her closely, waiting for movement.

"I thought she was angry," Tavin said. "She looks rather calm to me."

They watched as Eloria wrapped a shawl about her.

"She's running away," Killian realized.

A loud *pop!* sounded in the distance. They both looked to the forest in surprise. Another loud *pop!* sounded from behind them.

"Is that the smithies?" Tavin looked around.

An explosion of booms shook the massive trees. A frazzled red shimmer lit up the forest beyond. It formed a wall of sparks up to the tree tops then dissolved away. The small balls of light that floated aimlessly through the air froze in place. They began to tremble and buzz with excitement.

"The boundary," Tavin gasped. "Someone has come through!"

A woman's scream echoed through the trees. A hideous shriek rose from the valley below. People were hurrying to their balconies to see what the commotion was. They leaned over the rails, looking for what had caused the popping. From the corner of his eye, Killian saw black shapes moving up trunks. A wave of cold and fear overcame him.

"Deformed!" Tavin shouted.

"They've climbed the trees! Deformed!" Killian yelled to the people around them. "Get out of the trees!"

The people around them looked in terror but did not move.

"Killian, you have to…"

"We have to get everyone out of the trees!" Killian cut him off. "I'll climb higher and guide them, you get everyone further down. If we create a barrier on the valley floor, we might stand a chance."

Large, dark shapes slithered and climbed their way around the trunks.

"Killian!" Tavin grabbed his tunic. "You have to get her out of here. You have to get Eloria out! Everything is lost if they take her."

Killian remembered the girl on the balcony below. Without thinking, he launched himself down the staircase. He could see bear-like Deformed crawling across the trunk in her direction. Eloria stood over her balcony like all the others, looking at the chaos below.

"Eloria, run!" Killian shouted. "Run!"

But it was too late. A monstrous Deformed thudded onto her balcony. Killian's mind raced. The valley below would be flooding with Deformed in minutes. The trees were no longer safe. He leapt from the staircase to her balcony and charged. The Deformed stepped towards Eloria with its teeth barred. Killian dropped to his knees and slid under its massive form. In the blink of an eye he was on his feet. He wrapped his arms around Eloria and vaulted from the balcony.

CHAPTER 25

Eloria quickly recognized the feeling of free fall. She grasped at Killian as she felt herself slipping. He cried out as his wings burst from between his shoulders. There was a sudden jolt as the air caught beneath them.

Eloria was wrenched from his arms. She felt her body whip against the wind. Killian dove towards her. The valley below was mess of Deformed and people running about in panic.

Killian caught Eloria's wrist and pulled himself to her. She wrapped her arms around his neck as he scooped up her legs.

"Hold me tightly," he commanded.

He put his feet beneath him and stretched his wings to the sky. Tavin, who was hurrying to the valley floor, watched as Killian plummeted to the ground. With a loud thud, a torrent of wind blew everyone off their feet. The grass rippled like water from the blast. Small trees snapped in two. In the center of the blast, Killian knelt with Eloria safely tucked against his chest.

"Show off," Tavin smiled.

He ran to join them.

Killian gently set Eloria on the ground.

"Are you alright?" he asked.

Her body trembled.

"Rise, Loraillvon!" Killian shouted to the people around them. They looked at him in wonder. "Stand and defeat this evil! Rise!"

315

A large, young Builder, Tyre, stood from the ground with sword and hammer in hand. He thrust his blade through the Deformed beside him.

"To Prince Emrys!" Tyre bellowed.

Both Deformed and villagers rose from the ground. Tyre and the people gathered behind Killian and Eloria.

"Form a rank!" Tyre commanded them. "Anyone without a weapon get to the back. What are your orders, Lord Emrys?"

"Get the elders and children to safety," Killian spoke without hesitation. "Block the Deformed from your mind at all cost. My comrade is on his way. Follow him until it is over."

"As you command. Don't hold out on us this time," Tyre smiled.

Killian pulled the shredded tunic from his body. His skin tore apart between his shoulders. With a grunt of pain, his wings folded into himself and disappeared. Tyre removed a layer of his own tunic and handed it to Killian. He nodded his thanks as he donned the oversized garment.

"Stay with me," Killian said to Eloria. "I'm getting you out of here."

They drew their swords. With a roar, Killian charged the nearest Deformed, slicing his blade through its tough hide. Eloria kept her mind shut to the noise around her. She charged after him with her own blade swinging. Killian dodged and weaved between Deformed, working his way through the valley.

When there were more than they could handle, a torrent of air knocked the monsters off their feet. Tyre and the other villages did not hesitate to kill the creatures as Killian continued forward.

The ground became wet with acid blood. Drops of it burned their way through Eloria's clothes and her skin sizzled. As they made their way forward, Killian fought their way to a set of stairs leading out from the crater. When they were near, he broke away from the group with Eloria close in tow.

They ascended the stairs two at a time, running into the forest and away from the village. Eloria ran as fast as her legs would allow, trying her best to keep up with Seraphim ahead of her. The thrumming of her heart raced in her ears, blotting out all sounds of the battle behind them. She still held her sword, but her arms were numb with exhaustion.

The trees spun in front of her. A root snaked around her boot, dragging her to the ground.

"We have to keep moving," Killian's voice commanded. "Get up."

"I can't," she gasped.

Run Eloria, she heard in her mind.

Images of trees whizzing by appeared before her. The joy of stretching muscles. The excitement of feet pounding against the earth.

"Someone's in my head," she cried.

"Deformed. Get up, Eloria!"

His voice rang like bells and the sound of her name sent a torrent of adrenaline through her limbs. It was the jolt she needed. Her hands tingled as blood pumped vigorously through her. She rose to her feet and ran. From behind them, she heard the soft thumping of paws. More images of trees and sticks passed through her mind.

Zane?

Foul smelling monsters came for you, he thought to her. *My cousin beasts have come to the forest to save you. We followed the dark cloud. I'm here to take you to the mountain. The monsters cannot climb to the dragon's den. You will be safe there.*

The Airedale sprinted to the front and led the way. Eloria and Killian both felt the fear from the Deformed on the fringe of their minds. They were being followed.

After hours of running and stumbling through the trees, they had finally travelled enough leagues to be clear of the forest's heart. Eloria was barely conscious as she fumbled through the grass to keep up with Killian. The mountain loomed overhead and Killian knew the Deformed were almost upon them.

They had stopped for only a few minutes during the night in order to rest. Killian kept watch while his companions dozed, but it was short lived. Despite their steady speed and continuing to walk all through the day, the Deformed had caught up to them. The sun was almost fully over the mountains when Killian knew it was time to change tactics. Fear lingered on the border of his thoughts, but he knew it was not his own.

They're close, he thought to Zane.

Yes, the dog seemed to pant even in his mind. *The wind is carrying their scent to us. They gained ground during the morning.*

I cannot carry both of you up the mountain, Killian's heart broke to say it to the young Airedale.

My feet belong on the earth, the pup thought back to him. *I am fast as the wind from the ground. I will run to your den and find your pack. They will fight the creatures with their claws of silver.*

Killian's muscles ached as they continued up another hill. *The Guard will see you coming. Reach out to them and they will aid you. Let them know that Emrys has sent you. Try to keep my secret, but if it means your life, share your memories with them. Show them my wings and they will fight with you.*

The line of Seraphim is true. Its people good. They will aid me without question, Zane thought proudly.

Thank you for protecting her.

Zane lifted his nose in the air. A growl rumbled through his chest.

They are here.

Eloria's head snapped up at hearing the dog. She looked around them, as if waking from a dream. Killian removed his oversized shirt.

Run Airedale, he thought to him. *Be fast as the wind and I will see you at the palace. Call on the Guard.*

The dog shook his body as if to dry off and stretched his paws, yawning with a loud moan. He glanced to the girl then sprinted away, disappearing over the hill. Killian rolled his shoulders as his back itched with anticipation.

"What is he doing?" Eloria asked. "We can't split up! They'll find him."

"The House of the Guard is close and they will aid him," Killian spoke quickly as he handed Eloria his shirt. "We must go up the mountain, but I cannot carry both of you."

They heard growling from the way they had come and Killian knew the Deformed would crest the hill in seconds. He took a deep breath and bent forward, preparing for the pain that would come. His muscles shook as he tried to remind himself that the pain was momentary, just as he had taught Eloria.

With a cry of agony, the skin between his shoulders ripped apart. He felt his bones breaking then resetting as his wings stretched to their full span. His back itched in anguish as the skin restitched itself together around his wings. He breathed quickly, trying to hide the pain from Eloria as he moved his wings, stretching and rolling his shoulders to help the discomfort fade.

She watched him with concern.

"It's not that bad."

"It sounds like you're dying," she argued.

"The price for fitting in," he shrugged.

With an angry growl, a Deformed came bounding into view from behind Eloria. Its skin hung loosely from the bones, and the beast seemed to be a mountain cat that had been turned. It had the same pale grey fur as the others of its kind. Killian could see its red eyes as it charged them. He quickly threw his hand towards the creature, sending a torrent of wind that knocked it to the ground. Without a moments pause, it rolled to its feet and gave a vicious snarl, glaring at the winged man.

"Killian, behind you!" Eloria screamed.

He turned quickly to see two more Deformed charging in their direction.

"They were waiting for this," he said quickly, putting his arm around Eloria's waist. Immediately he felt her shiver. Every fiber of his body ached to be closer to her, to change her. He pushed away the feeling as best he could and lifted her legs with his other arm.

"We are going to move fast. Hold tightly to me."

He looked quickly at the Deformed that had surrounded them. There were nine in total, all racing at him and attacking with their minds.

"I'm not afraid," she said as she wrapped her arms around his neck.

He closed his eyes and tapped into his power, feeling a euphoric joy that had been inside of him for as long as he could remember. Not taking the time to be discreet, he bent his knees and gathered the winds to him. In any other instance, he would slowly rise and not make a show of it. In this case, he wasn't waiting a moment to get off the ground. He pushed off the earth and wind shot around them, thrusting them into the sky. He lifted his wings above his head then pushed them towards the ground, sending them higher. He felt a current of air and quickly angled to it, letting it lift them up the mountain's side.

The Deformed turned into specks below them. He watched as they ran in the direction of Kien Illae, following Zane's scent. He looked for the Airedale but could no longer see a trail. He continued to take them higher, each flap of his wings pushing them upwards.

"There," Killian said, looking up at the mountain. "Do you see it?"

Eloria saw a large, dark opening in the mountain's side.

320

"Where are you taking us?" Eloria shouted over the wind.

"To the golden dragon. The one who spoke the prophecy."

He had only seen it once before in his life but he had been much further away. His father had told him never to disrupt the dragon's home unless it was of the greatest urgency. He was told that the mountain and the fields were the mighty beast's palace, just as Kien Illae was his.

It took the better part of an hour until they approached the mouth of the cave. Killian glided in, almost the size of a bird in comparison to the width of the opening. He carefully set his feet on the ground and let go of Eloria. She stood in awe at the size of the cavern. It was as if the entire mountain had been carved away to house the dragon. She could walk for miles and still not reach the other side. Against each side of the wall, Eloria saw frames of all sizes, propped against the stone.

"Are those…?" her heart jumped at the thought.

"Reflections," Killian said quietly.

Eloria took a step forward but hesitated. "No one has mirrors in this world because that is how you see into other worlds. Why does the dragon have them?"

"Dragons are not originally from this world. They were brought here by the Evil Ones' tampering. They collect the glass because it reminds them of home. They hoard it within their caves. No one on our side of the mountains knows how to view other worlds except for the dragons. That is how Sorrell learned. Not only did this dragon speak the prophecy, it also showed Sorrell how to bring you here."

Eloria carefully walked towards a large mirror propped up against the rock's wall. Killian had said that she changed over the past few months but she hadn't really believed him. Now, as she stepped forward and stared at her reflection, she saw what he meant. It was as if she were looking at Sorrell. Her skin had tanned and the blemishes had disappeared. Her hair was a shiny strawberry-blonde, and her body had become lean and fit. The only things that remained were her scars and slightly un-proportioned features.

"I'm not the same person anymore."

"You aren't, not really," Killian said. "After the Choosing, people go through a process of becoming someone new. While their past is still a part of them, they set their old ways behind. They become someone different. Not just in name, but in practice as well. The elders call it self-conclusion. A process of dying to one's old self. I think you have changed more than anyone thought possible."

"I don't feel like the same person that first came to this world." Eloria ingrained the image of her new reflection into her mind. "Have you ever seen your reflection?"

Killian nodded solemnly, "When we were young, my parents took Tavin and I to a mirror so that we would know what it was. While our people do not know how to harness the magic within the reflections, the mirrors are a danger, nonetheless. It was the strangest thing, to see myself looking back at me."

"But you can see your reflection in water, can't you? Anything with a smooth surface would show a reflection," she thought.

"Yes, but a pure reflection, like a mirror, is the only way. Water would work, but have you noticed the water here is never still? The lake where we met Emerald is one of the few, and only at times. The dragons were brought through by lake," Killian said, nodding towards the inside of the cave. "The Evil Ones enchanted the water to stand still and that's how they arrived in this world. The gold dragon was brought here before the Creator walked among us."

"How big is this dragon?" she asked, realizing that Emerald may be a baby in comparison to the beast that called this mountain home.

"You would know," Killian said quietly, narrowing his eyes toward the dark cavern, "if he were here."

"But…," Eloria glanced at him. "I thought he didn't leave the mountain."

"He doesn't," Killian said wearily.

His demeanor changed and he motioned for Eloria to wait as he walked towards the deep interior, stepping quietly in case he may be wrong about the dragon. He heard something echo from within and he stopped, peering towards the noise. A light began to grow from the darkness and he heard footsteps coming towards them. Immediately he knew.

"Eloria," he returned to her side. "There's nothing for us here. The dragon is gone. We're going to go to Kien Illae. It will be the safest place for you now."

"What's going on?"

He cleared his throat and gave his wings a quick shake, lifting them off the ground as he squared his shoulders. He watched as the torchlight grew closer. Light refracted off the flames and bounced around the cave from the many mirrors. It was like starlight filled the cavern.

"I would like for you to meet my father," Killian said.

A tall man in gold and white armor approached them. He was twice the size of Killian with a thick, muscled figure and large hands and shoulders. From his back protruded wings as large as he was. They glowed against the darkness behind him and his dark hair ruffled as a breeze blew into the mountain. Killian watched as the man dropped the torch to his side.

"King Forfax," Killian bowed respectfully.

The man's smile was beaming as he sized up his son. With a deep laugh, he threw his arms around him. Killian smiled and hugged him in return.

"My son!" the man said, holding Killian at arm's length while he looked at him properly. "It has been far too long since you've come home to us."

323

Killian saw tears in his father's eyes and wondered how long he had been waiting in the dragon's cave for them to arrive.

"Father, may I present…"

"Eloria!" the king beamed. "Welcome to our world. You look much more like Sorrell than how the queen described. From everyone in Kien Illae, we are so sorry for the loss you have faced. She was a member of our House and we, too, spent time in mourning. The emptiness that still lingers in our libraries is a remembrance of the girl who filled it with joy."

"Thank you, sire," Eloria whispered, quickly looking at the ground as she spoke.

"Have you heard the news?" Killian asked eagerly.

The king nodded, "The dark cloud over the forest. We saw it but had no way of warning you in time. It formed so quickly."

"There were Deformed below. They are coming in droves over the mountain to find her," he said, nodding towards Eloria. "We need to speak to the dragon with all haste."

"The dragon will not return until tomorrow." Forfax put a hand on his son's shoulder, "You have had a long journey. Come home and rest. We will speak of everything in the morning. Besides, your mother is worried sick about you and the girl."

"It has been a long journey. I fear there is more to come before any of us may truly rest."

"You are home now," Forfax said proudly. "Let us focus on that blessing and celebrate it, even if only for a few hours." He lifted his large wings and looked at Eloria. "Let me take your bags and lighten your load. Kien Illae is not far to fly but neither of you need the extra weight."

Eloria carefully handed the large man her packs. She felt strange to let a king carry her bags. She guessed the alternative was for him to carry her but she felt more comfortable in Killian's arms. He smiled at them both then put a strong hand on Killian's shoulder.

"Let us go home," he said with a smile.

Killian and Eloria watched as he stretched out his wings and dove from the cave's ledge. He dropped for a few seconds before catching a current of air and gliding off in the direction of Kien Illae.

To her surprise, she could see the ocean and forests from where they stood. By the ocean's shore, something glinted in the sunlight. She could make out turrets and stone structures rising high above the ground.

"May I?" Killian asked, extending his hand towards Eloria.

"I suppose it's the only way off the mountain."

"I apologize for pushing you off that balcony. If it's between my promise and your life, I'll choose the latter every time."

"The prophesied and protector, right?"

"If I hadn't then we would be dead."

"It's not your choice to make, Killian."

He shivered slightly. "I may not feel the same for you, but I take my responsibilities to protect you most seriously. Let me rephrase my intentions. I promise, that if there's no immediate danger, I shall not enact the Transformation."

"You won't use my name?" she clarified. "You won't even bump me by accident?"

"I shan't."

"Very well then," she sighed. "You may fly me off the mountain."

"How very kind of you," he remarked.

He wrapped his arm around her waist. His eyes caught hers and he stopped. He felt torn as he tightened his grip around her.

"Killian," she said softly. "I have to get off the mountain somehow."

"Sorry. It's just that..." He gave her that look again then quickly shook his head. "Hold on tight."

He scooped her up and, instead of dropping off the side of the mountain like his father, he simply stepped away. The wind and his wings sent them gliding gently away from the cave. They floated high above the grassy hills and followed the king to the palace of Kien Illae.

CHAPTER 26

The sun was low in the sky when they approached the palace.
Eloria could barely comprehend the size of the castle as they came
upon it. It was more than a simple mansion or palace like the ones
from her world, but was large enough to house entire cities. Along
with numerous turrets and domes, balconies had been built all
around the castle. Large windows graced every tower. Bridges with
archways connected different areas of the castle together.

The fortress truly was as beautiful as Killian had eluded it to be.
Its four sides looked upon the four different regions of the
kingdom. Large statues of kings and queens had been built in
various areas surrounding the palace and Eloria could see
numerous courtyards with fountains and gardens spread inside the
citadel walls.

The king began to descend onto a large balcony among a
cluster of turrets. Killian did the same. The queen stood regally as
she watched her husband and son lightly land on the balcony's
cool stone. Her wings were spanned out behind her, as if she may
take flight as well. Killian set Eloria gently on her feet. He walked
to his mother and she smiled, happy to see her son again. She
extended her hand and he bowed slightly.

"Welcome home, Emrys," she said in the way that only a
mother can. Her eyes were filled with compassion as she quickly

looked him over, pausing on his wings. "You are so tired! Your wings are trembling. Come in and rest."

"I'm fine. The Prophesied, however, could use a soft bed."

"We meet again, Eloria," she said with a smile. "I am Gloribel, and this," she motioned back to the king, "is Forfax. You have experienced far more of our world than I ever intended, but I rejoice that you and my son have returned safely. We welcome you to the city of Kien Illae. We hope that this place will be a home to you and that you find peace and rest while you are here."

"Thank you, Queen Gloribel." Eloria attempted a clumsy curtsy.

"The gold dragon will be returning in the morning and we will speak to him then. In the meantime, let's get you both some food and a change of clothes. You can rest safely tonight."

The queen extended her hand towards a large wooden door that led into the castle. Eloria followed Gloribel, excited to see the palace, but noticed that Killian and Forfax remained behind. She paused. His father whispered into his ear and Killian hunched his shoulders. Eloria immediately recognized the posture and watched as his wings seemed to break then disappear. He didn't cry out this time but silently stood as his body shook with pain and exhaustion. His father handed him a tunic and Killian slipped it over his head, barely able to lift his arms.

"As much as we can, we must keep up the appearance that Tavin is still the prince," Killian said as they rejoined the women. "Those who live in the castle do not know the truth and we need to keep it that way."

"I don't understand," Eloria sighed. "How do people not know? You live here."

"We took the boy in when he was a baby," the king replied. "They are the same age and looked alike as children. We treated them equally to the point that people forgot who was the prince and who was the orphan. As they grew older, Killian's hair darkened and so he hid his wings while outside of his own corridors. We began the ruse of Tavin being the prince and no one thought otherwise."

"Let's go inside," Killian urged.

Eloria fought to keep her eyes open despite her exhaustion. She didn't want to miss a thing despite her body aching for sleep.

"This is the prince's private area of the palace," the queen explained. "Killian and Tavin have shared it all their lives. There are many rooms and no one enters unless they are requested. It is that way for all the private living areas. You will not need to worry about running into anyone that you do not know while you are in this part of the castle."

Eloria gazed at the finely adorned sitting room that they stood in. Lavish furniture, flowers, vases, sculptures, and a tall chandelier filled the space with light. They walked silently out of the room and into a hall that had a ceiling made of windows. Large frames hung on the walls with scenic pictures of kings and queens, dragons, and angels. As they passed an oversized silver frame, Eloria stopped and stared with wonder.

"Is that the prophecy?" she asked.

Forfax nodded, "A scribe copied the original text generations ago and it was hung in this area so that the royal family would always have a reminder of its words."

Gloribel led them further down the corridor before stopping at another thick oak door.

"This will be your room," she said kindly, opening it for her. "Killian will be nearby if you need anything. Please rest as long as you need. There is already food and drink inside for you as well as clothes that we thought would fit you."

"Thank you for your hospitality," Eloria said, trying her best curtsey, once again.

"In the morning, we will dine together then go to meet the dragon. There is much work to be done now that you are here."

The king and queen silently left the hall, leaving Killian and Eloria alone once more.

"It may be strange to be alone for a while, but the feeling will pass. If you need anything, I'm only a few doors away," he pointed to a door down the corridor. "Please rest. I'll be here when you wake."

"Do you think Tavin is alright?" she asked.

"He will be. It was always the plan that if something were to happen we would meet back at the palace. I'm sure he'll arrive in a few days."

She slipped into the room as he closed the door behind her. There was a large bed with an open wash room. Too tired to think, she unlaced her boots for the first time in days and fell into the fluffy mattress. She fell asleep almost immediately.

The sun was a little over the horizon when Eloria finally woke. She had slept deeply all night and felt extremely rested. It was a surprise to find that she had slept past sunrise after weeks of waking up at dawn. She took her time to wash and changed into a simple cotton dress that had been provided for her. It was strange to not wear the tight pants and laced up boots. For a moment, she wondered if it was safe to be in a dress in case of attack before remembering she was in Kien Illae, the most secure place in all the kingdom.

She picked at some of the food in her room then did her routine stretches, clearing her mind and enjoying the sun that shone through the windows. When she finished, she carefully opened the door and peered into the long hallway. Killian stood a little ways down, wearing gleaming silver and gold armor. She was surprised to see him in anything besides his leather tunic. Yes, she couldn't help but admire his dashing new look. Killian had his sword in a gem covered scabbard at his side and she could see knife hilts protruding from his tall boots.

"You look... special," Eloria giggled.

"Yes, hello and good morning," Killian sighed. "Let's go."

He stomped off down the hall. Eloria followed him through a series of corridors, all as richly decorated as the last. Crossing a stone bridge that had windows as its walls and ceiling, she caught a glimpse of the ocean as well as a large expanse of fields stretched out as far as the eye could see. After weaving through more hallways, they exited the castle completely.

"Where are we going?"

"The dragon arrived a little while ago. He is too big to land anywhere in the castle or its balconies so we must go to him."

Eloria's heart fluttered with excitement, "The gold dragon that spoke the prophecy! We can ask him what it means and what I am supposed to do?"

"I don't think it will be that easy," Killian grunted. "You must be prepared. Dragons have a certain ability and magic within themselves, unlike any other beasts from our world. Once you are introduced to him, he will most likely… greet you," Killian cringed as he said it.

"How do you mean 'greet me?'"

"Dragons can break through your mind without any effort. He can bring up any memory and emotion that he wishes by looking at you. Because you are Eloria, we think he will try to know all of you. Every memory you've ever had. It shouldn't hurt you physically, but mentally it can be quite discomforting. You may experience things that have been buried deep within. He is large and moody, but he is loyal to the Seraphim."

Eloria took a deep breath. From all of her training, she had learned to be brave and not fear pain. Despite this, a feeling like tightening knots turned in her stomach. Killian lifted his hand to comfort her but quickly decided against it. They made their way across a groomed courtyard towards another part of the castle. Eloria gasped as a golden wall began to move. She realized it was not a wall at all but scales larger than she was.

"This is Errapel," Killian said quietly. "Healer of the Mountains and first dragon of Loraillvon."

It was difficult to tell which part of the dragon she was looking at. Its long neck rose high above them and seemed to ignore the small company below. Eloria guessed that the beast was larger than the glass dome of Kailani. Killian led them around the massive creature, keeping a safe distance from the heat that radiated from its body.

"There's one other thing," Killian smirked.

"Good morning, Eloria," Queen Gloribel said kindly, turning to them as they approached. "Forfax you have already met but please allow me to introduce you to my parents."

Eloria's jaw dropped as a man and woman turned away from the dragon to look at her. Both looked hardly older than Forfax and Gloribel. They had large wings that protruded out behind them. The man wore a fine silk tunic with dark trousers and his wife matched with a silk dress as beautiful as the queen's. They had shining blond hair and light green eyes.

"My grandfather and grandmother," Killian said.

"It is a pleasure to meet you."

The woman stepped forward, "We are happy to have you at Kien Illae and blessed that you have been safe in your travels. Gloribel and Forfax have told us much about you."

The woman gave her hand a quick squeeze before turning away. She noticed that his grandmother also wore a silver ring similar to Killian's. The man gave her a nod but returned his attention to the dragon.

"You didn't tell me you had grandparents," she whispered to Killian.

"I have parents don't I? Why not grandparents? You're now surrounded by the Seraphim family." Killian turned to his father. "Would you introduce her please. She does not wish for me to use her name."

With a nod, the king spoke out with both his mind and voice, "Errapel, it is my honor to present to you the one of whom you prophesied. Our second queen transformed. Eloria."

The dragon's neck coiled down from above. His head lowered to the ground. He turned his face so that one eye gazed upon her. His iris burned with golden flames and immediately her mind felt as if it were being ripped apart.

Memories of her entire life flashed before her eyes and waves of emotions crashed down on her. Visions of her parents and their house, easter egg hunts as a little girl, and Justine building snow forts during winter. Memories of school and Christmas' flew past her vision. She remembered the joy of holiday vacations and the dread of going to school each morning. Every moment of her life flashed before her so quickly that she couldn't keep up in identifying them. The emotions brought forth from each instant felt like a brick to her chest. It continued as she saw the forests, Tavin and Sorrel, Killian flying down the mountain, and their journey together.

Then something shifted. Eloria began to see things that didn't look familiar. A vision of hundreds of men and women clad in armor. Dragons flying together through a clouded sky. With the vision, a voice reverberated through her body as the dragon spoke.

From a world of reflection Eloria returns. When Evil rises and the world be burned. She shall love Seraphim wings or doom will she bring. A death to come that will change all things.

Visions of Sorrell laying on the mountain in Tavin's arms flashed through her head. To her surprise it wasn't her memories but those of Tavin and Killian as they looked down upon Sorrell's bleeding form. The vision changed and she saw Killian jumping from the castle walls in the dead of night, his wings emerging from his back. She felt the pain that he felt when his wings burst from his skin. Beside her, she noticed Killian cringe as he saw and felt the memories that the dragon shared as well.

On winds they will fly to the desolate place where a Queen Transformed finds Evil's true face. On black wings they die and fall when he follows her to Qwells Vraugh.

The vision in her mind changed from the castle to a city made of black glass. Tavin stood before her, hooded on a dark city street. The next moment, she stood in the ashen desert. Wings made of pitch black feathers rose around her. They were covered in the acidic blood of the Deformed. Pain and guilt flooded over her from whosoever memories she watched.

Feathers and scales reign down. Love of another face will be found. The people will be with fear…

White and black feathers fell from a dark sky. Eloria watched in horror as she saw dragons falling through the sky above them. One by one they dropped into oblivion. The vision before her shifted again, a battle ground covered in blood as Deformed and men fought against each other. Then they were in a forest. Two men led a charge, one of black wings and another of white. The two men moved the same and Eloria tried to identify them but they didn't look like any of the Seraphim that stood in the courtyard with her now. Eloria and Killian felt the anger, fear, and longing. The emotions were so overpowering that Eloria felt as if her chest would explode.

The visions and memories disappeared. A gold eye from the dragon moved closer to the small group before him.

The time of Eloria draws near, he thought with a deep voice.

It sent a shiver through each of them. They stood in silence as they tried to comprehend what they had seen. Killian's body trembled uncontrollably.

The dragon turned his attention to Eloria alone. *Welcome to Loraillvon, land of the Seraphim,* he thought to her. *We are both from other worlds, you and I, and can remember a home far different than where we find ourselves now. I envy the vividness of your memories. My old home seems like nothing more than a dream after all these centuries. It was a world larger than this where even I could nest comfortably despite my expanse. The mountains were alive with fire and their peaks reached above the clouds. Our wings could take us to the sun and the stars. Here we dragons are pulled to the earth to return when we are tired. I pity those born of this world who know no other way of living.*

Eloria remembered Emerald saying that dragons liked to be flattered. *Your wings may yet take you as high as the sun for your magnificence surpasses it already.*

The gold dragon lifted its head and his body shook as if he were laughing. Everyone but Killian seemed to relax as they watched Errapel's response to her.

You flatter me well child, he turned his head to better see the small gathering of people. *Speak aloud for all to hear. My mind may speak to whomever I wish, but they cannot hear yours.*

She nodded, "Thank you, Errapel. I'm here because it would seem you spoke a prophecy about my coming to this world. Many things that you have spoken have already come to pass."

Indeed they have, the dragon thought. *The other child from this world has passed. I have seen the false prince's memories, as I shared them with you.*

Killian stepped forward, "What you have shown us…is that the future?"

The dragon's chest rumbled and the air around them shook. *I shared memories of past and future with only those that needed to see them. And none of you saw the same. They are memories that I saw long ago. The magic inside me gives me the ability of foresight. There is nothing more I will tell you.*

"What of battle?" the king asked. "We do not wish to take a life whether it be our people or theirs. Is there any way to avoid bloodshed?"

Although I have slept for many generations, my ears have heard this world during my slumber. The beasts speak highly of you, Forfax,

335

and the line of Seraphim that began when I first arrived in this land. Your family has served Loraillvon with respect and kindness. I am not its king, however, therefore I cannot tell you how to lead. Bloodshed will happen, it has been prophesied. All you can do, king, is choose how it comes to pass.

"So we do nothing," Killian bit his words. "We let people die simply because you will not explain your visions to us?"

The dragon's thoughts were harsh and quick, Do not reprimand me young prince. My wings took flight before your line began and my wings will carry me long after it has ended. The dragon's body moved like a golden mountain swaying in the wind. The evil that exists in this world is by the choices made of each individual. When the Creator entered this world as man and was killed, He took the true evil of this world with Him. It is every person's freedom now, whether they are born on this side of the mountain or the other, to choose which side they are on.

Killian did not reply but was agitated by the dragon's words. Errapel's throat emitted a purr.

Do not be afraid, young Seraphim, he thought with a gentle voice. The future I shared is not due to your actions alone. Many have a part to play in the battle of this world. You are the Immortal Church. As such, remember that the war has already been won. In that, you should find comfort.

The dragon lifted its mighty head from the ground and stretched his wings, extending them across the entire field in which they stood. Now that Eloria has arrived in this world, we dragons will wake once more. We will help you in this affair whether it be with tooth and claw or by our magic. My kin are waking all throughout the mountains and my time here is ill spent.

"We understand," the king spoke quickly. "Thank you, Errapel, for coming to us first."

The massive dragon rose to his hind legs and lifted his membraned wings. They thrust down and created a torrent of wind that ripped the ground apart below. With another quick succession, he slowly rose from the courtyard and high above them.

From the castle above, Eloria heard people shouting and cheering as the dragon flew away. She looked up and saw hundreds of people lining the balconies and bridges along the palace's edge.

"We could clear the courtyard but not much else," Killian grunted as he saw the crowds that had gathered. "Everyone wants to catch a glimpse of the golden dragon."

"We need to discuss what the dragon told you," Gloribel said fervently. "Any clues that he might have given us will be crucial in helping us for a defense against the Evil Ones."

"He shared his vision with all of us."

Gloribel nodded and turned to the elder two Seraphim, "Let us go to a more private place to discuss this. We need to hear all the parts that the dragon shared before the House Masters arrive."

The group made their way back to the castle but Forfax and Killian lingered behind.

"Eloria," Forfax said to her. "May we speak with you for a moment?"

She stood nervously before the king.

"It is my duty as a king transformed to teach you how to use your new abilities," Forfax smiled. "Although you are not yet fully transformed, I wondered if you would mind spending some time with me to train a bit more."

"She would love to learn, Father," Killian grunted. "She doesn't fear much these days. Be weary of what you allow her to do."

"She will be fine," Forfax said. "Join the others, my son. They will need to know what you have seen."

Killian sauntered off to join the others. When they disappeared, Forfax rustled his wings.

"Killian tells us you haven't learned to fly."

"No," Eloria confessed. "I can mostly… point the wind."

Forfax nodded, "That is the first, and most pertinent step, in harnessing its true power. But let me teach you how to use it to its full potential."

CHAPTER 27

It was late into the night when Eloria finally returned to the castle. Forfax had spent the better part of the afternoon having her direct the wind one way or another. By evening, she still wasn't able to lift herself off the ground.

As she approached her room, she was surprised to find Killian waiting at her door.

"We've known this prophecy for ages," his voice was solemn. "We hoped after speaking with the dragon we would be able to do more, but these visions have been useless."

Eloria didn't know how to respond.

"The Masters of each House have arrived to deliberate. No one knows how the black cloud formed over the forest or why it disappeared shortly after. Tavin is back as well."

"Is he alright?"

"He's fine," Killian said. "Angry mostly."

"I'm sorry," Eloria looked at the ground.

"My father tells me you didn't fly today?"

"I couldn't quite figure that out."

"Would you like me to help you?"

"No," she huffed. "Thanks for the offer, but we agreed you wouldn't be doing that anymore."

Killian stepped close to her, "Are you afraid of the height?"

"No," she laughed nervously.

"I would never let you fall."

Reaching up, he moved her hair away from her face, carful not to brush his fingers against her skin.

Her heart skipped a beat. "Killian, stop."

"It would be a simple touch. Just for a moment," his voice was like honey; sweet and inviting. Eloria felt his fingers slide over the fabric of her gown. They touched her hips then slid up toward her waist. "I'll put my arm around you, and next thing you know we'll be floating."

His green eyes bore into hers, as if begging for the chance to be closer to her. Eloria's expression hardened as she met his gaze.

"Unrequited, remember?"

She pushed him away and slammed the door shut behind her. Killian stared at the door in disbelief.

"Ooof!" Tavin exclaimed from down the hall. "That couldn't have been easy!"

"Shut up. You big oaf," Killian trudged over to him.

"Even I, the great prince, haven't been turned down that badly. We all know I am a man desired by all."

Killian clenched his fists in frustration as they walked to their rooms. They came to an ornately decorated door and made their way inside. A large, informal suite spread out before them with a balcony and tall chandelier. There was a short, wooden table between two sofas. Sloppy carvings of the prophecy defaced the table from when they were young boys. It had a vase of flowers on it now with trays of fruit and bread.

Weapons hung on the walls with knick knacks that they had kept from their childhood. To either side were separate bedrooms that they had had since they were toddlers. Despite the years, neither had wanted to move to a different part of the castle or to a new room. They had always felt more at home knowing the other was near.

"We have something for you," Killian said as Tavin sank into a large arm chair.

He fetched a small traveling bag from his room and set it on the table before Tavin.

"It was Sorrell's," Killian explained. "A woman from the mountains mistakingly gave it to Eloria, not realizing that she looked upon a different face. Eloria had it with her when we fled the forest."

"When was Sorrell in the mountains?" Tavin replied.

"The woman said she had been through twice a year for some time now. It seems she always traveled the area alone." Killian looked to his friend with pain in his heart, "She had many secrets Tavin. Somehow she met with the gold dragon without anyone knowing it. She called Eloria here. Who knows what else she was hiding."

"Why are you giving this to me now?" Tavin asked.

"Eloria wanted to wait a while."

"You are mad at her. That's why you're giving this to me?"

Killian rolled his eyes, "She wanted you to have it eventually. I'm not going to let it sit around until she decides when. Open it."

Tavin reached for the bag. "Books most likely. Maybe ink and some parchment. A few knives. I doubt we will find anything to tell us more about her."

"You married a girl with plenty of mystery," Killian sighed. "We didn't look inside or tamper with anything. Eloria decided it belonged to you."

Tavin opened the flap.

"Books," he smiled.

He pulled two from the bag and placed them on the table. The first was *A History of the Seraphim Bloodline*. The other was *Loraillvon's Greatest Wars - Volumes 1 & 2*. Next he pulled out a small fragment of glass, about the size of his palm.

"A reflection," Killian awed. "I suppose that makes sense. If the dragon was teaching her, she must've gotten it from his cave."

"It's hard to believe," Tavin sighed as he placed it, reflective side down, onto the books. He peered into the bag quizzically then tipped it upside down over the table. "There's something else, but it's stuck."

He jiggled the bag. With another hard shake an object clattered onto the wooden table.

"Get back!"

Killian immediately jumped away when he saw it. Adrenaline shot through his body. His sword was in his hand without thinking. He stood a few feet from the table, staring cautiously. His mind raced for answers. Tavin had leapt away as well.

"Tavin, don't touch it," Killian instructed.

His eyebrows furrowed, "How did she…"

Killian lowered his sword and took a step closer to study the object. It laid so innocently on the wooden table. Killian struggled to comprehend its meaning.

Why would Sorrell have it? he thought frantically. *How would she know about it?*

Realization hit him like a brick. Quickly sheathing his sword, he found a piece of fabric and covered the object. He wrapped it in the cloth, careful not to touch it himself.

"We need to see father. Now!" he shouted.

Killian's his feet carried him to the door. Tavin's eyes grew wide as he came to the same understanding as Killian.

"I need to know you are with me," Killian said.

Everything grew still as he waited for his brother's reply. Tavin's eyes met Killian's and he saw there was no doubt inside him.

"I am with you, my prince."

CHAPTER 28

Eloria heard movement around her. She moaned and sat up on her elbows, trying to open her eyes. She had been sleeping peacefully and dreaming of a sunlit forest covered in flowers. Her eyes had to blink a few times before she noticed a young woman standing next to her bed. Three others were in the room as well, taking food bowls away and putting clothes in their place.

"I'm so sorry to wake you, but the prince requests to see you," the woman next to her said kindly.

"Oh, it's no trouble. I thought you were here to tell me I slept in too long," Eloria yawned, happily remembering her dream. "Sorry, I should have woken when you knocked."

The woman smiled, "You must have been very tired."

The window across the room was open, letting in a cool breeze. Eloria breathed in the night air as she slowly crawled out of bed. She changed into the clothes set out for her while the others gave her privacy. To her relief, she put on pants, tunic, a light shouldered cloak, and her tall boots. As comfortable as her dress had been the previous day, she felt more secure in her regular traveling clothes.

"I'm ready," Eloria said once her boots were laced up. "Is Prince Emrys in his rooms?"

"He is meeting with a few others in a different area of the palace," the same woman spoke. "We will guide you there. It is a large castle and we would hate for you to get lost."

Eloria followed them into the corridor. Her heart beat wildly as to what was so important to wake her in the middle of the night. She hoped they had deciphered a piece of the dragon's vision. Forfax had promised to tell her right away if they discovered anything new.

They walked through endless corridors and turned so many corners that Eloria certainly felt lost. The silence among the small group grew awkward. Eloria suddenly realized she might appear unkind by not speaking to them. She had only been in the palace a short time, but she wanted to make a good impression with the people there. After all, she was a legend.

"Are you a Healer?" she asked politely.

"No, Lady Eloria. I am of the Queen's House," she glanced at her companions.

Eloria caught the exchange. "I apologize. I haven't been in Community much so I'm still learning."

"It's alright," she smiled again. "Myself and Akan are both of the Queen's House. She is a Guard," the girl said, nodding to a dark haired woman, "and she is a Healer."

Eloria looked back at the man, Akan, and smiled kindly. His dark, slanted eyes made her uncomfortable. She noticed that he had a thick leather vest and knives strapped about him. As she glanced around the small ensemble, she saw that they all wore weapons on their person, even the Healer.

"You stay armed?" she inquired. "I've only seen members of the Guard carrying weapons in the castle."

"For your safety," the woman said.

Eloria tried to push it from her mind. Whatever Tavin and Killian had to tell her was going to need her full attention. The corridor opened into a large atrium made of gold pillars and

344

marble floors. A chandelier cast a dim light through the round space. Long windows around the room let in the pale moonlight. Eloria saw a grand staircase that her escorts quickly directed her towards.

As they came around a pillar, she saw Killian and Tavin. They stood in front of the stairs in waiting. Eloria noticed that Killian wore his armor once again. His jeweled blade had been replaced with a more practical sword.

Her companions halted at the sight of the two men. The woman grasped Eloria's arm to hold her back. She rolled her eyes at the reaction.

"I know it may be uncustomary, but I don't bow every time I see the prince. It would waste quite a bit of time for me, don't you think?" she joked.

"Eloria," Killian said.

A warm rush consumed her.

"Would you come with me, please?" his voice was stern.

Don't say my name, she thought angrily.

The ring on her finger suddenly began to hum against her skin.

He promised he wouldn't say... my name! She looked to him again.

Killian was afraid.

"I'm sorry," the man, Akan, stepped forward. "We have specific instructions to take her to the queen."

"The queen?" Eloria asked, "You said the prince needed to see me, and there he is."

She tried to pull her arm from the woman's grasp but her fingers were like talons.

"Please, don't hurt her," Killian said. "As you know, she is very precious to me, and you wouldn't want to make me angry."

The moonlight faded from the room and a bright flash of light filled the space. In that same moment, thunder shook the air around them. The crystals on the chandelier trembled. Its tinkling echoed through the atrium.

"You really don't want to make him angry," Tavin's voice was grave as he squared his shoulders.

"It is brave of you, Emrys, Seraphim Prince, to give up your identity," Akan's voice dripped with sarcasm. "It is only fair I return the favor. I am Akan," he bowed, "and I see now that you know our truth. Tell me, how long did it take you to discover?"

Killian's eyes narrowed on the tall, dark man before him.

"Akan?"

The man was silent.

"Tell me, Akan, do your people know the meaning of their names or are they freely given? Your name alone gives you away, if nothing else."

Killian moved towards them.

"Akan: the one who troubles."

Lightening flashed through the atrium with his step.

"Akan: the one who deceives."

Another flash of lightning.

"Akan: the one who steals forbidden things."

Killian stopped only a few feet away from them.

"You see Akan, Eloria is a forbidden thing. But you will not steal her away. I won't allow it."

Eloria did not understand what was happening. She tried pulling away once again, but the woman dug her nails into Eloria's skin. She looked at her in protest when something glinted from the woman's belt. There, subtly hidden within her clothing, was a crooked, black knife. Images of Sorrell flashed through her mind and Eloria gasped with understanding.

"You're the Evil Ones," she whispered in shock. "But you look like us?"

"Yes," Tavin's voice was heavy with pain. "Not all Evil comes in the shape of the Deformed. The Evil Ones that we have fought all these years look like us. They are like us in every way. The only difference is their decision to denounce their king and turn away from their Creator. They destroy and tamper with worlds when they have no right."

"That winged rat is not my king," the man spat. "We have no king to wield their power over us. We control our own power. We bring both life and death as we please."

Lightening flashed dangerously close. Thunder shook the floor beneath their feet. Killian's eyes were filled with disgust.

"Only the Creator breathes life into this world. Do not fool yourself into thinking otherwise. I am the Immortal Church," his voice rang with power, "and as such, I will give you another chance to turn away from evil. Leave the girl and we will find a safe place for you in Loraillvon."

The people around Eloria laughed. Each drew their weapons. Killian pulled his sword as well. Tavin reached to his back and took out his two blades. He bent knees, preparing to attack.

"Eloria can only fulfill your prophecy if she lives," Akan hissed. "We have our own ways, Seraphim. She does not need to be stolen for us to succeed here tonight."

Without waiting for a reply, Eloria reached for the black knife. She twisted it back against the woman, thrusting its blade between her ribs. There was a cry of surprise. Eloria launched herself free of the captor.

Tavin and Killian reacted quickly.

Killian's sword moved faster than any other, but somehow the dark haired woman he fought held her own. They danced between the tall gold pillars. Tavin's blades were locked with Akan's and the fourth woman's. From across the room, the wounded girl raced towards Eloria with a crooked knife in each hand. Black liquid oozed from her side but it did not slow her.

Weaponless and undefended, Eloria lifted her hand to use the wind. She closed her eyes and tapped into that place of magic like

Killian had taught her. She found it almost immediately and a euphoric joy filled her mind. Eloria felt as if light ran through her veins. The silver ring on her finger pulsed as she gathered the air to her command.

As she lowered her hand to release the torrent, she felt a sharp sting in her side. Her arm went numb and the wind she had gathered dispersed carelessly around them. Warm liquid dripped down her stomach. Eloria looked down to see a crooked, black knife buried in her abdomen.

Her hands shook as she unconsciously reached for the blade. It slid out of her body with ease. As it clattered to the ground, a burning fire shot through the sliced skin. Bile filled her throat. A thick, dark substance oozed from the wound.

"Killian," she whispered.

The woman across the room laughed bitterly. Eloria looked at the blood running down her clothes. Her vision blurred. She could feel her chest heave with shallow breaths.

Forfax and Gloribel arrived with dozens of armored men. They descended upon the battle before them.

"Killian," Eloria struggled through her haze to find him.

A monstrous shriek filled the air. Her senses immediately snapped back as adrenaline took over. She pressed her hand against the wound to stop the bleeding and hurried towards the others.

I have to find him, she thought desperately. *I can't die. I can't go back.*

The ground below her shook. The shriek grew louder, deafening everyone who heard it. From above, the chandelier broke from its hold and fell to ground. Crystal skittered across the marble floor. The windows exploded inward as a terrifying beast thrust its head through the wall.

Eloria froze in shock. It was a dragon turned Deformed. Its jaws snapped angrily as it fought to get into the atrium. Fiery heat from the monster's maw filled the room. The beautiful scales that once covered its face had turned into snake-like skin that sagged around its eyes and jaw line. Acid blood spilled from between its teeth. To her horror, its crimson red eyes narrowed in on her.

Eloria's adrenaline faded and the room began to spin once more.

Killian, she thought, *I have to find him. I can't go back!*

There, around the next pillar, she saw him fighting. Her feet stumbled forward without prompting. The woman he faced was thrown to the ground by his sword. One of the other Guards descended upon her.

Killian! Eloria cried.

The room around her spun. She felt her body fall. Before she hit the cold marble, warm arms wrapped around her. A head full of dark hair turned towards her. Bright, green eyes surveyed her body.

"Save me," Eloria begged.

A sword was rushing towards Killian's head. Before she could warn him, Eloria felt her body fall to the ground. Killian was on his feet again, countering the attack and pushing the foe away. She watched the fight as the room continued to tilt around her.

Someone took Eloria by the arm. They dragged her across the floor towards the monstrous Deformed. She struggled to get away, but the black poison inside her body kept her from fighting back.

"Come along, precious Eloria," Akan laughed as he pulled her to the creature. Blood dripped from the side of his mouth. A deep cut had split his face in two. "There is someone who wants to meet you."

Eloria's vision began to fade. There were shouts of anger and screaming, but her mind couldn't make out their words. She crumpled to the ground as she lost all control of her body. Akan hoisted her over his shoulder and marched to the deformed dragon.

She stared at the marble floor, unable to make sense of the world around her. Blood flowed like water across the smooth surface. Floating atop the red river were white feathers.

CHAPTER 29

A chirping echoed through her head and Eloria grew impatient.
What is that bird so happy about? It is only sunrise…

If she could stir up a small breeze in its direction, maybe it
would fly away and perch on a different tree, leaving her in peace.
She tried to lift her arm but nothing happened. Her finger
twitched slightly, but it was heavy as a rock.

I'm more tired than I realized, she thought groggily. *Maybe we
trained too hard yesterday?*

The chirping continued, steady and rhythmic. Not wanting to
open her eyes, she tried lifting her other arm but it, too, denied
her request. Giving up, she decided the bird wasn't worth her
energy. She waited for the colors of the sun to play across her
eyelids but only a bright, pale light shone on her.

That's odd. Weren't we in the forest when…

Memories of battle flashed through her head. The king was in
his grand armor with the queen. Killian had been dancing with his
blade through marble pillars. She was trying to find him. They had
been separated somehow.

The chirping grew louder, its high pitch hurting her ears. The
pale light was giving her a headache. A smell filled her nostrils. It
reminded her of…

She stretched out her hands to feel the furs around her. Instead
of soft hide and course hair, she felt rough cotton between her

fingers. The chirping grew louder. Eloria wondered if the bird had flown to the ground next to her.

Not a bird, she realized. *A machine.*

She put all the strength she could find into lifting her eyelids. They raised ever so slowly. The bright, strange lights blinded her. She blinked heavily, trying to adjust, focusing on the sights and scents around her. The smells felt unnatural, strange. The touch of the rough fabric was foreign to her. Her eyes cleared and she stared in horror.

The beeping continued, steady and constant, telling her that her worst nightmare had come true. She lay covered in papery sheets and a thin cotton blanket. Pale florescent lights filled the room. There was a window to her left but the curtains were closed tightly.

Her mind was thick and sluggish. The beeping of the heart monitor next to her started to pick up speed. Her veins felt as if fire pumped through them When she tried to move, a searing pain cut lines into her skin. She glanced down and saw bandages covering her arms. There was an IV in one vein and she realized oxygen was being forced up her nose from a tube strung around her face.

"Killian?" she whispered.

Her voice shook with fear. She looked around the small room. She was alone.

With trembling hands she pulled the oxygen from her face. There was a bandage on her neck and head as well. Her arms stung as she moved. Killian's lessons on tolerating pain were now second nature. She pulled the IV out of her arm and the monitors from her chest. The beeping immediately turned to one long, high pitched note.

With a grunt, she pulled the blankets away and swung her legs over the side of the bed. Immediately, they burned with pain and she saw that they were bandaged as well. She carefully lowered herself to the floor. The tile was cold on her bare feet. She made her way into the bathroom next to her bed.

"It's okay," she croaked. "This world is… It has mirrors. Every room. Find a reflection."

She slowly turned in the small washroom and saw that above the sink hung a large, smooth piece of reflective glass.

I have to get back, she thought. *I have to fight with them. The dragons are waking for me. I can't let it burn. I have to save them.*

Breathing deeply, Eloria stepped in front of the mirror.

"No!" she cried.

She had seen herself in the mirror fragments in the dragon's cave and she remembered how she had changed. She had looked more like Sorrell than she ever imagined possible. Her skin had grown tan from the sun, her body lean and strong from fighting, and her skin and hair had grown healthy and fair.

The person staring back at her now was the opposite. Her eyes were red and puffy, framed by pale skin. Her lips had a purple hue. The hair she wore was mangy and lackluster. Inflamed bumps of acne stood out like a sore thumb. The weight that she had lost from training and travel has reappeared. Her face was more round than she ever remembered seeing it. She stared at the stranger in the mirror, hardly recognizing herself.

"No," she whispered, her throat sore. "I have to get back. I need…"

Tears filled her eyes as she remembered.

I need Sorrell. I need my reflection-self to return.

Emptiness consumed her. Sorrell was dead, which meant there was no way back. There would be no one to look at her from the other side and bring her through. Anger gripped her and she waited to feel the wind blow up around her. For thunder to roar through the sky. But nothing happened.

"It's over," she said to herself, staring at the person across from her. A stranger looking back in the glass. "It's done. I can't go back."

She stared at the pale, ugly version of herself. Her heart thumped wildly and her limbs felt sliced by a knife. Her mind was racing, trying to understand what was happening but all she knew was that there was no going back. She was done.

With a rage unlike anything she had ever felt, she screamed at her reflection and threw her fist at the girl across from her. The glass cracked beneath her knuckles. She hit it again. The glass splintered and broke around the impact. Blood covered the glass. With another scream, she began beating her fists into the mirror. Rage and loss overwhelmed her and each glimpse at the person in the mirror reminded her that she couldn't return to the man she loved. To the world she loved.

In the distance she heard people yelling. Someone grabbed her arms, trying to pull her away. She ignored them and threw another punch to the loathsome pale face that stared at her from the wall. The mirror came tumbling from its mount above the sink. The people in the room quickly backed away. Eloria stood motionless as the mirror fell and shattered around her. Everything fell silent.

A man and woman in white nurses gowns stared in surprise. At the bathroom door stood her mother, Beverly. Her eyes were watery, as if she'd been crying. She looked truly terrified of her daughter.

The man reached cautiously out to Eloria, "Let's get you back to bed and take a look at those hands."

Eloria glanced down and saw shards of glass protruding from her knuckles. Blood was dripping onto the tile floor. She nodded and took a step towards the door. Her mother quickly backed away.

Eloria hardly noticed as she walked over the glass and tiny shards cut into the bottom of her feet. She sat on the bed and waited. The man nudged the other nurse and they slowly approached Eloria. Gently lifting her hands, they started speaking in medical jargon that Eloria didn't understand. She waited patiently as they collected supplies to remove the glass.

"I'm Eloria," she said to the woman across from her.

"I am Veronica. I'm glad to see that you are awake, honey," the woman eyed her cautiously.

"You look familiar," Eloria thought out loud, noticing the woman's face. "Have we met before?"

"I've been your nurse since you arrived. Perhaps you remember the sound of my voice."

Eloria studied the woman's face and immediately remembered her time at the ocean. There was a girl that she had met there. A Healer had helped her with her training and showed them to their rooms their first night at the guest house.

"Vineeta?" Eloria whispered, realizing with surprise who the woman was.

"It's Veronica, sweetheart." The nurse hooked the monitors back up to Eloria. The loud beeping immediately resumed as it rang out her heart rhythm. The man began tweezing glass shards from her hands and cleaning up the cuts.

Beverly slowly moved to the chair across from Eloria's bed. She stared at her daughter as if she were looking upon a corpse. Eloria wondered if the blood was upsetting her. The nurses finished their work.

"Honey, we need to discuss what happened to you," Veronica pulled a stool to Eloria's bedside. "Beverly, would you like to join us?"

Her mother swallowed, scooting her chair closer to the bed but not to her daughter's side. Eloria no longer felt apprehensive around this woman but almost pitied her. Her mother looked petrified. She felt the urge to take her hand and comfort her.

"What is the last thing that you remember?" Veronica asked as she pressed a small button on the wall.

"From here?" Eloria wasn't sure which last memory the woman was referring to. There were two worlds colliding inside of her head. She couldn't focus on which was most important at the moment.

"What is the last thing you remember from home?"

Flashes of Kien Illae raced through Eloria's mind. She saw the gold pillars and the sunlight shining through the windows. She heard Killian's accented voice and the smell of flowers on the wind. An image of the glass room of Kailani faded in and out of her mind.

"Home," she tried to focus. "You mean my parent's house."

"Of course," the nurse nodded.

"I remember… a fight," she tried to see through the hazy memories. "My sister and father were arguing and there was some aggression."

Eloria knew her mother was weary of people knowing the truth. Beverly didn't want anyone to know what had happened, but Eloria was no longer afraid. She wouldn't hide in fear anymore.

"I ran away from the fighting because I was afraid," Eloria spoke confidently. "Seeing my sister get hurt was painful for me, and she hurt my parents in return. I was afraid back then of being a part of it."

"Back then?" Veronica asked.

"Yes, it happened quite some time ago. I left the kitchen and went to my bedroom. I panicked. I remember packing a bag, thinking that I had to escape before I got hurt as well. I used to be afraid of pain."

"You used to be?"

"I can write it out if that'll be easier," Eloria smiled.

"I'm sorry. Please continue."

"I packed a bag but didn't know how to leave. I wasn't thinking clearly because of the yelling. That's when I remembered my mirror. I had been... communicating with someone inside of it. Her name was Sorrell and she's from another world. I know it sounds crazy but that's why I've been away. That night, I went through the mirror. I've been in that world ever since."

"Oh my word! Kaylin!" her mother sobbed.

"Eloria," she corrected without thinking.

"Kaylin, you've been here. You've been in the hospital," the nurse said to her.

"What do you mean?"

"You went missing for a few days but someone found you," the nurse said quietly. "The man found you covered with cuts on your arms and legs. The loss of blood rendered you unconscious, and you were immediately brought to the hospital. You've been here for a few day now."

"No," Eloria shook her head, not believing what she was hearing. "No, I was in another world. I can't make this up, it really happened! Time must run differently there or something, because it's been months. I was there for months!"

"Kaylin, you tried to kill yourself," her mother cried. "They call it 'cutting' or a gothic term like that. They say that you were trying to be in control, to divert your pain so you hurt yourself. You almost died! Now, don't play games. We won't ignore the real situation that's happening."

"Mom, I didn't try to kill myself." Her voice rose. "I have to get out of here. They need me and they will be trying to find a way to get me back."

"Kaylin," the nurse laid a gentle hand on her arm. "You're shaking quite badly. We need you to wait while…"

The door opened and Dr. Donna entered the room. She walked proudly to the nurse and whispered something in her ear. Eloria watched as the nurse nodded and whispered back to her. She caught the words 'other world' and 'Sorrell.' When she finished, the nurse stepped away to stand beside her mother. Dr. Donna took her place on the stool. She smiled kindly to Eloria. There was a strange excitement in her eye.

"Hello Kaylin. I heard you had quite the scare when you woke up. Can you tell me about it?"

"My name is Eloria," she whispered in agitation.

"I know it's difficult, Kaylin, but try to focus," Dr. Donna cooed.

The male nurse reentered the room and started fiddling with the IV bags behind her.

"I was upset," Eloria said. "I didn't recognize myself in the mirror."

"Because of the other person, is that right? You said you had been seeing someone else in the mirror. A girl that was the perfect version of yourself?"

Eloria nodded.

"Kaylin, you have been suffering from several different physiological conditions. The official diagnosis is that you have multi-personality disorder, schizophrenia, and you struggle with severe depression. You created a perfect version of yourself, but when things got bad at home it was too much for you to handle. Your system overloaded and there was an influx of chemicals to your brain. It created an imbalance. Instead of coping like the rest of us, you created a safe world for yourself. You made a place where you had friends, peace, and you could hide away from your problems. In your mind, you became someone new. You created a version of yourself that was strong and brave and fearless. While it is all very admirable, it is not reality."

"I'm not making it up!" Eloria pleaded.

"Kaylin, do you remember when you and this Sorrell girl first spoke?"

"Yes. It was… months ago now. Maybe almost a year ago."

"According to my notes from our sessions, you never made contact with the girl in your reflection. You never tried speaking to her or communicating in any way."

"I didn't tell you everything," Eloria's arm felt cold from the IV's injection. Her mind grew hazy. The room tilted ever so slightly.

Is the black poison still in my system?

"Kaylin, did you choose your new name or was it given to you? The word, Eloria."

"I… I chose it."

Dr. Donna nodded. "Was it one of the first things you did when entering this new world of yours?"

Eloria shook her head, trying to clear away the confusion.

"It was the first night I was there, but what does that have to do with anything?"

"Within your reflection, you created a friend who was the perfect version of you. She helped you deal with pain and fear. When she wasn't enough, when she couldn't save you, you exploited the opportunity to become her yourself. "

"That's ridiculous."

"I'm guessing that somehow this friend ended up no longer being part of the picture? Did she leave somehow? Move away, transfer jobs, did you get in a fight?"

Eloria's body was no longer trembling. She didn't feel as interested in the conversion as she was a minute ago.

"Sorrell died."

Dr. Donna nodded, "In order to become, what you considered, the better version of yourself; the friend that you created had to be removed from the equation. Most patients who see imaginary friends can't recall when they met. As much as I want to believe in this new world that you discovered, you can understand how silly

359

it all sounds. So, can you tell us when you first met this girl in the mirror?"

Eloria opened her mouth to reply but couldn't. Her mind felt like sludge, but worst of all, she didn't have an answer for the therapist. Sorrell had always been there, she couldn't recall for how long or when it all started.

"It is ok if you can't remember," Dr. Donna cooed. "You see this girl has never been real. It's been your imagination all this time."

"But she died... Sorrell died," Eloria tried to explain but couldn't find the words. Her body felt numb. It was as if she were on the border between waking and sleeping.

"She was always dead, Kaylin. She never existed. Was their a man in your new world too? Tall with dark hair and an accent?"

Eloria stared at her wide eyed.

"That's the man who found you. He brought you here to the hospital and has been visiting. You see, you've been taking your experiences in this world and morphing it to a situation that your mind would accept. A scenario that you could cope with."

"She thought she recognized me, too," the nurse said.

Eloria waited for the fear to set in. For her heart to race. But nothing happened. The subtle, bleak reality sank in and she stared at the blankets, only confused on how this could have happened. How had her mind created such fantasies without her realizing the truth?

"We've put you on some medications to help," the man said, stepping out from behind the dripping IV bags. "Tell me how you feel."

Her tongue was thick and her mouth felt dry as she searched for words. "I feel fine. I mean... I don't feel anything."

Dr. Donna smiled at Beverly, "Good. That means the medicine is working."

Eloria nodded, still trying to understand what had happened. Sorrell wasn't real. None of it had been real. Dr. Donna patted her hand. Eloria glanced at the spot, feeling something strange against her fingers.

"I'll leave you alone for a little while. I'm sure this is a lot to process," she said. Beverly followed her out the door. The nurses flitted around checking monitors and writing things on their clipboards. Eloria stared at her hand.

"Excuse me?"

"Yes, honey?" the nurse, Veronica, replied.

Eloria fought the grogginess that was overtaking her.

"Why didn't you take all my stuff?" Eloria asked. "My clothes and jewelry? Why didn't you take them?"

The nurses glanced at one another.

"We did sweetheart," Veronica replied. "Your clothes, shoes, and jewelry. They interfere with our machines, but your parents have them."

Eloria couldn't pull her eyes away from the silver ring around her finger. The band gleamed as if newly polished.

"Sweetie," Veronica followed Eloria's gaze to her hand. "Is there something you need?"

Eloria's fingers wiggled off the ring. She pinched it between her thumb and index. Inscribed along the inside, almost too small to notice, were gold letters. Her eyes followed the letters as they swirled in front of her. She remembered being given the ring. At the time, the letters had been foreign to her. Unreadable. Now, she slowly began making out the words along the band.

"Kaylin, what are you looking at?"

"Nothing. It's only my imagination."

Acknowledgments

This book, and the entire series, would never have been possible without two people. Firstly, my husband. Samuel - you put up with my constant mumbling, my exclamations of shock at my own revelations, and have given me the space to safely write. You've made sacrifices so that I can hone my craft and do what I love. Thank you.

Secondly - Sharla Ball. If you hadn't read Self-Conclusion and geeked out with me, the Loraillvon Series wouldn't even exist. Your constant patience to listen to me hash out plots and dream up characters is what I've always needed. It's your openness to always talk books that has kept me going.

To my beta reading team: Cheryl, Vicky, Natalie, and Matt. Your feedback and typo catches make my work quality. No novel is perfect, but you get me closer to that line each time. The story is better because you read it. Thank you.

To my readers. Being a writer is hard. Having people read my work makes it all worth it. I implore you to support authors. Buy their books. Encourage others to read them. Leave reviews. Reach out to share your thoughts on the story. These books don't continue without your involvement.

I appreciate everyone for venturing into Loraillvon. For giving it a chance and finding it worthy. This place that I love more and more with each book, and a place I wish everyone would visit with me.

Thank you.

ABOUT THE AUTHOR

T.K. Johnson's imagination and love of fairy tales nurtured the writing of fantasy stories from a young age. The Johnson family strives to find a life of simplicity and purpose within each day, committed to a relationship to know their Creator fully.

Johnson writes fictional novels featuring a bit of action, intrigue, and riveting plot twists. With a strong preference for relatable characters, Johnson authors potent relationship dynamics that speak to the realistic hardships of love and camaraderie.

Outside of writing, Johnson lives a minimal lifestyle. This includes restoring a 100-year-old tiny house. She finds the best time to write is with her family relaxing around the fire on a chilly autumn day.

Keep up with her work by visiting www.tkjohnsonbooks.com or via social media @tkjohnson_author.

ALTER
SNEAK PEEK

"You're killing her," the man sitting on the street laughed. "Don't go in there!"

The tall, dark haired lad that he spoke to paused. In his arms lay a young woman. Her red-stained clothes were sticky against his skin. Fresh blood still ran down her arms. A rush of adrenaline filled his veins. He shifted the woman's weight, breathing deeply to ease the pain pulling at his chest.

"They're a bunch of madmen inside. Don't trust 'em!"

The young man shook his head, ignoring the words of the vagabond on the street. He hurried through the automatic doors.

"I need help!" he shouted. "Can someone help?"

Immediately he saw two emergency room nurses hurry to him.

"Can you tell us what happened?" one nurse asked.

"Follow me," another quickly led him through an inner set of doors.

"I found her," he was ushered into a curtained room. He laid the girl on a hospital bed. "She's bleeding from her arms, and I think her legs too."

He held the young woman's hand as they hooked her up to various machines. They beeped and chimed harsh tones that made his ears ache. Through the flurry of activity, he tried to understand what the machines were communicating. As the doctors worked, he turned his attention back to the girl. He waited for her chest to rise and fall, for her eyes to flutter open, for her fingers to move.

"Sir!" A nurse yelled behind him. "Sir, can you answer any of these questions?"

"Uhh," he turned. "I'm sorry. I didn't hear you."

"How do you know her?"

"I... uh," the young man struggled to focus.

364

The girl's lips moved. He leaned forward. Her eyes opened and she stared dreamily around the room.

"It's alright," he said. "You're going to be safe."

Her eyes turned to him, "What's happening?"

Memories of a mirror flashed through his mind. The rush of wind. The smell of leaves. He remembered finding her on the ground, covered in blood.

"These people are going to help you."

"Killian," she said, "Don't leave me."

Her eyes rolled back. One of the machines rang out a long, piercing note.

"Sir? Sir! I need you to come with me."

Strong arms pulled him away from her side. He felt a hand against his back which steered him out of the room. The door clicked gently behind him as rushed voices slipped through the cracks.

"Sir? I need you to focus. Can you tell me her name?"

"Is she going to be alright? I need to stay with her."

"Sir!"

Fingers snapped in front of his face, snatching his attention away from the closed door to the woman before him.

"Sir. Take a deep breath. I need you to tell me her name."

"It's...ah...her name?"

"Yes. What is her name?"

"It's...," he looked down at his blood soaked clothes. "We were in the woods..."

"The woods?" The nurse asked as she scribbled on her notepad. "You can tell me how you found her in a moment, but did she tell you her name?"

"She said it right before..."

"It's very important we know her name, sir."

"Kaylin," he remembered. "She said her name was Kaylin."

Made in the USA
Monee, IL
30 September 2021